#5 OPERATION HIGH DRAGON
WARBOTS
G. HARRY STINE

I0666452

Imholt Press

Originally published by Pinnacle Books

Copyright © 1988 by G. Harry Stine

Currently Published by Imholt Press, LLC

ISBN: **978-1-7337983-4-1**

For more information contact **tim@timothyimholt.com**

WITHIN SECONDS THE AFT HATCHES POPPED OPEN.

By the time Major Curt Carson clambered down from the flight deck, the Jeeps had already debouched. He unslung his *Novia* assault rifle and with First Sergeant Edie Sampson close behind, led the Sierra Charlies out of the hatch. They moved quickly to the cover of the thick woods. Carson knelt in the underbrush and keyed his helmet tacomm. "Alpha, report!"

"On the ground and moving toward objective!" came Kitsy Clinton's reply.

"Bravo, report!"

"Right behind Alpha!" Jerry Allen replied.

"Incoming! Incoming!" came a sudden call from Kitsy Clinton.

"What the hell?" Jerry Allen yelled. "Nobody was supposed to be here!"

And as Carson looked up he saw that a bright red spot had suddenly appeared on the white fur front of Edie Sampson's parka.

TO:

Colonel Harry Clement Stubbs, USAFR

"If wise, a commander is able to recognize changing circumstances and to act expediently. If sincere, his men will have no doubt of the certainty of rewards and punishments. If human, he loves mankind, sympathizes with others, and appreciates their industry and toil. If courageous, he gains victory by seizing opportunity without hesitation. If strict, his troops are disciplined because they are in awe of him..."

-Tu Mu, Chinese tactician 803-852A.D.

Forward

In this fifth installment of Warbots, G. Harry Stine takes us from his awesome introduction into his vision to the world of robotic warfare into one where the Warbots are ready to fight whatever little hotspot that needs military attention all over the globe. It isn't that far off from what we see today. At the time this was written no one would have considered it possible, but today we take some of what he showed us for granted.

The mark of a great fiction writer, especially science fiction, is that he makes us think. In this book he takes us into that same battlefield, with some upgraded Warbots sporting some new Artificial Intelligence, but he brings in a new topic for us to think about. Women on the battlefield.

In Warbots book 1 we were transported into a world where robots to the fighting through telekinetic links, and a new enemy shows us that these robots are not up to the task of fighting all enemies. As a result, humans must fight side by side with their warbots. That meant that over time women in combat units had become the norm. Robot operators are safe, they are way back behind the lines, well not anymore. Now they are side by side with the bots, including the women.

He shows us that the women can be as tough as the men, and in his fictional world they fight side by side and, yes, there is some concern, but the women have more than a few things to say about potentially being removed from these roles.

In this book we are transported into a world of robotic warfare trying to protect us from cyber threats from the Eastern Block nations of the world. Sound like something that might actually be a problem that happens in our lifetime? The world being attacked by a cyber threat that could render the very smart electronic devices we depend on useless?

I hope you enjoy this installment into Warbots, I give you Warbots Book 5: Operation High Dragon.

Timothy Imholt PhD

Chapter One

Chahssohvoy Krasneey Dvahdtsat Dvah - also known to the United States Aerospace Force as "Red Sentry 22" and logged in the UN registry as "Kosmos 3818" - plunged through near-Earth orbital space on its polar orbit. It was a Soviet surveillance satellite.

Its high-resolution sensors were so good that they could read a chessboard from its orbital vantage point some 200 kilometers in space. Its on-board computer recorded these sequential images of the Earth below in a range from the infrared to the ultraviolet. The on-board artificial-intelli-gence circuits had evaluated the data it had recorded and made notes of images it believed its human masters might find especially interesting.

Now it waited patiently for the proper signal from the ground that would cause it to transmit the digital-pulse data downward, where it would be recorded, processed, and eventually displayed on huge wall screens deep beneath the ground at a place called *Zahvohd*, or "the Factory," tunneled deep into the Ural Mountains west of Magnetegorsk.

And, because of SMART-III -the Strategic Military Arms Reduction Treaty Number Three - its secret codes for triggering a data dump were also known to the United States, in the same manner that the United States satellites such as Poker Hand 11 could dump their data to *Zahvohd* on Soviet command. Thus, Red Sentry's data could be downloaded and displayed at another place, deep beneath the Blue Ridge Mountains, known only by the code name Tiffany.

And, of course, since a secret known to two parties is really no secret, other had the necessary information to access Red Sentry's data.

Red Sentry was certainly no secret to the United States Aerospace Force. Once the Soviets had provided the access protocols and procedures, American experts quickly identified the nanochips, neural networks, and artificial-intelligence banks being used by the Soviets. These were either direct copies or actual surplus equipment the Aerospace Force had sold as scrap five years before. An American expert on Soviet technology had pointed out many years before that the best Soviet design bureau was the American aerospace industry. Technology knows no country, and the KGB and GRU had managed by devious means to steal or buy whatever they wanted.

However, if Red Sentry's artificial-intelligence circuits had been capable of registering emotion, the satellite would have been surprised by the detection of a series of radio signals emanating from the surface below as it swung southward over the expanse of the Indian Ocean.

Chahssohvoy Krasneey recognized the signals as an interrogation. So, it automatically responded with a burst of digital pulses signifying it was ready to download its data. Although the satellite didn't expect the interrogation signal for nearly another hour, when it would sweep northward over North America, it wasn't capable of evaluating the unusual circumstances that might have caused the interrogation signal to come early. Often, it was interrogated by American or Soviet intelligence-gathering ships in strange locations, so it was ready at all times to download if requested.

In a transmission burst of several seconds, it downloaded the photographs it had taken on its current trajectory over the Chinese provinces of Zdungaria and Sinkiang, where the People's Republic of China and the Union of Soviet Socialist Republics shared a common border.

Then it paused and waited for the receipt of any instructions.

When the reply came from the group below, the bit stream was shunted to the main satellite computer.

The reply contained instructions plus something else.

By the time Red Sentry swung northward over the United States and Tiffany commanded a routine download data dump, the satellite was sick.

Captain Matt Crowell was on duty, monitoring several surveillance satellite outputs deep within Tiffany. He was tired. He'd been on watch for seven hours now. As usual, nothing unusual was happening. Space around the Earth out to lunar orbit was as busy as usual with satellites, space stations, space factories, space transports, cargo ships, incoming cargoes from the planetoid belt, and the usual military vehicles. All were identified. All were transmitting radar beacon codes in accordance with international law. All manned vessels were under the control of one of the space traffic control centers. With all the high-tech weapons deployed out there, space was far more peaceful than the Earth below because of the sophisticated robotic and AI tracking and control equipment covering everything out to the orbit of the moon.

"Captain Crowell, this is Tiff," the artificial voice of the master Tiffany Space Control Center computer said to him. "Red Sentry Twenty-two seems to have a problem, and I should therefore bring it to your attention."

Matt Crowell sat up, then leaned forward over his console. "This is Captain Crowell. What's the problem, Tiff?"

"Red Sentry Twenty-two appears to have something wrong with it," the computer replied in its flat, uninflected voice.

"Wrong?" Matt echoed. "Tiff, project the orbital elements and the last orbit's ground track of Red Sentry Twenty-two."

A Mercator projection of the world suddenly appeared on the big screen in front of Crowell. Then the bright light of an orbital track appeared. The flashing point of light bearing an alphanumeric designator data block "Kosmos 3818" on the trajectory display identified the present position of Red Sentry 22. The satellite was coming northward over Tiffany.

Working back along the ground track, Crowell saw that Red Sentry 22 had performed as expected, passing over the troubled Sino-Soviet border areas.

"What's the problem with Red Sentry Twenty-Two?" he asked the computer.

"All data from the last orbit is missing," the computer reported. "This is highly unusual."

"What is unusual about it, Tiff? Did the GPU turn it off?" Crowell probed for more information.

"One question at a time," Tiffs Mod Ten AI circuitry told the human operator, signaling that the double question had temporarily confused it. "The GPU did not turn it off. That is one factor that is unusual about it. Except when it is over regions where the GPU wishes to gather high-resolution imagery or its own AI circuitry tells it that ground target might be of interest, the Red Sentry self-programs into surveillance mode. That satellite type is never turned off."

"What is the other usual factor, Tiff?" Crowell continued to press.

"Red Sentry transmitted more than a series of null-signal pixels. It also transmitted a mixro olgaric restorive, blur wecor muneratize..." After spurting these nonsense syllables, Tiff's computer voice suddenly stopped. The little loudspeaker on the control panel then began to chirp and warble and rasp in the sounds of reduced baud-rate digital signals dropped from their gigahertz computational frequencies down to low-kilohertz voice-reporting frequencies.

"What the fuck is going on here?" Crowell blurted out.

As if in partial answer to the watch officer's question, the big orbital display screen projections suddenly wiped over and were replaced by surrealistic projections of colorful, flowing shapes.

Data disappeared from the console displays in front of him and scrolling screens full of computer garbage took their place.

The air conditioning fans suddenly changed their sounds. Some sped up. Others slowed. A blast of hot air roared out of the ceiling duct over Matt Crowell's head.

Crowell hit the Tiffany internal communication system button and tried to call the colonel. But whatever had happened was also affecting the computer-controlled voice telephone system of the complex.

Seventeen other men and women in the room were also having their own problems with the computer system that controlled all their displays, their telephones, and the environmental control system of the underground Tiffany complex.

Captain Matt Crowell knew that the whole Tiffany computer system had crashed. It wasn't supposed to do that. It had *beaucoup* redundancy built into it to keep it from crashing. But it had indeed crashed, and in spectacular fashion.

Crowell had to get it off-line as quickly as possible lest it send incorrect data and commands to other facilities and computers of the National Computer Command Network. If the sick Tiffany computer somehow took all or a major part of NCCN down with it, the United States would be nearly naked to a preemptive strike.

When a big, powerful, artificially intelligent computer such as Tiffany starts to go insane - which is what Matt Crowell guessed had happened, although he didn't know the reason - the thing to do is kill it.

Although he'd been trained to do it, he'd never carried out a kill before. Computers *never* went down anymore! They had too much redundancy built into them, and they were programmed to report glitches and error signals. But there was always a first time, and Matt Crowell figured that this was it. He knew he had to kill Tiffany J.I.C. - Just In Case. "All hands!" he shouted. "Emergency power down! Pull the plug! *Now!*"

His first move was almost instinctual. He whirled in his chair, reached up, smashed the thin plastic cover, and pulled the big Red Handle Number One on the wall behind his watch console post.

That cut Tiffany's main power.

The emergency lights and fans came on, powered by a totally separate power system with its own internal facility generators.

Matt Crowell hesitated before taking the next step. Killing the main power would only "stun" Tiffany and essentially knock it unconscious. The final step would be to dump the memory units and AI blocks by disconnecting them from their maintenance

15

electrical supply, a built-in battery system that prevented the computer from losing all its memory in the event of a power failure.

He didn't break the cover and pull Red Handle Number Two.

That was both the big mistake and the final salvation.

"Lieutenant Marlo!" he snapped to the young woman on the console level below his station. "Inform National Security Command! Report that I am on the hot line to Kaliningrad." Then he said to himself as he reached for the red telephone that was not connected in any way to the Tiffany computer complex, "Goddammit, I hope Vladimir is still on watch!"

The hot line was a direct link to his counterpart in the main Soviet Space Defense Complex underneath Kaliningrad northeast of Moskva. There were other hot lines, including direct computer link and teletypes and even holographic teleconference nets. But the audio-only telephone link was fast, secure, and reliable. It went directly via fiber optic cable across the Atlantic direct to Kaliningrad. It was redundant and operated via several parallel circuits and cables. A major disaster would have to occur before the telephone hot line went inop.

Captain Matt Crowell was indeed in luck. Captain Vladimir Semenkov of the GRU was on watch.

When the two of them talked, they spoke what they termed "Russlish," a strange combination and amalgamation of Russian and English. Each spoke the other's language fluently, but they usually talked Russlish to ensure that idioms and shaded meanings were correctly transmitted. Because few people would understand Russlish, their conversation is reported here in English. Some terms have been converted into colloquial ones.

"Vladimir, I've got a piss pot full of problems here," Crowell admitted candidly to his Soviet counterpart.

"Well, we both have to down-zip our pants to get it out, Matt. Is it serious enough for me to push the big button, or can we talk it out as usual?"

"I think we can talk it out. I downloaded the data from Red Sentry

Twenty-Two - uh Kosmos Thirty-eight-eighteen - and it had none. Blank Then Tiffany went ape-shit," Crowell explained. "What the hell are you socialist faggots doing over there? Trying to screw us again?"

The strong ideological humor was not only a means of identifying one another, but also a way to cut through the suspicion that often cloaked official communications between the two nations. The two men had never met. But they'd grown to know one another better by telling jokes over the hot line during test periods. They had soon learned that their senses of humor, while different, were similar enough for them to share a laugh; thus they were able to maintain some perspective on the situations they had to confront. And those situations could have been serious enough to have threatened either country.

Crowell's superiors didn't care. Semenkov's superiors were the new technical elite of the Soviet Union, the ultimate product of *perestroika* and the resulting *uskorenie* or "acceleration." They were far more lenient than other Soviet officers of an earlier time.

"If I didn't know you better, Yankee imperialist dog, I'd suspect that you and your apple-pie-eating capitalists had managed to fuck up our heroic socialist surveillance satellite with your inferior equipment," Vladimir's voice replied. "It hasn't come back over our horizon yet, so I don't know what's going on. Contact in seventeen minutes, then I can look at it. Matt, what's your version of what happened?"

"It was empty and it might have done something to take out Tiffany...and that's serious hardball, Vladimir. Real serious," Matt reminded him. "If something like this had happened fifty years ago, our grandparents would have played leading roles in radiation sensors...and you and I wouldn't be around today. Now, I know what you've got in Red Sentry Twenty-two. We probably sold some of the critical AI stuff to you, or you wouldn't have been able to launch it. So, come clean with me, Vladimir!"

"Believe me, *tovarisch*, Kosmos Thirty-eight-eighteen is only a peaceful earth-looking resources satellite to balance the face you've got Poker Hand Eleven in orbit," his Soviet counterpart told him. "Nothing offensive about it at all. "Nothing offensive about it at all. And, by the way, you don't have to be paranoid to know someone is really out to get you! You invaded the Motherland once; we haven't gotten around to reciprocating yet. We shouldn't have sold Alaska to you."

"That was a bargain," Matt admitted. "By the way, want to sell Siberia? If the price is right, you can get your hands on some hard currency. And you won't have to worry about fighting the Chinese someday."

"No, the Zionists in Israel have already submitted a bid to fight the Chinese for us at cost plus ten percent...in gold, I might add. Matt, you know China is the reason we've got Red Sentry up there. You imperialists are rotten at the core and therefore too soft to fight us. And why should we fight you when you'll collapse anyway? But the Chinese have a common border with the Motherland. And they've come visiting too many times in the past," Vladimir explained.

It might have sounded like black humor and totally unrealistic under the circumstances. But both men were high-tech warriors who would never fight face-to-face in personal combat. It was their job to sit helpless in deep holes in the ground, play with the toys, and try to keep each other's organizations from going ape at the slightest glitch in the surveillance and tracking systems. They were subtly different from line troops. It was their mission to stand guard, to figure out what the hell was going on if something went wrong, to talk with the adversary and keep mistakes from happening, to resolve little tech glitches if possible without making a National Security Council agenda item out of them, and to pass along the warning to the high brass only if their personal judgment told them the other side was indeed sending up the Big Balloon.

As a result, they spoke to one another in a personal code, and they had transmitted an enormous amount of information back and forth in the conversation thus far. Like any two warriors anywhere, they had developed a contract. Their superiors might not have understood. But the two men knew that when they were on the hot line and the situation was grim, it was their job to keep from blowing the other guy all to hell without getting creamed themselves.

If either one had *ever* gotten officially serious on the hot line, it would have indicated that the situation was indeed very bad, and the consequences were beyond their control.

The only bitch between them at the moment was that the United States had downloaded a Soviet surveillance satellite, gotten nothing, and had one of its defense computer complexes crash as a result. Matt wasn't accusing Vladimir of anything. He was warning his soviet counter-part that trouble might be brewing. And Matt had learned in an off-the-wall way that the Soviets had had nothing to do with it. Otherwise, Vladimir would have been guarded, defensive, and suspicious. He wasn't; he'd replied in the familiar manner they'd worked out between themselves.

Everything was copacetic in Kaliningrad.

"Check it out when you can eyeball it, Vladimir," Matt requested. "Let me know if you get the same zilch download."

"If Red Sentry is broken, we will send you a bill for fixing it," Vladimir told him.

"Not to worry. I'll check with the factory here, but it's probably still under warranty."

"If you broke it and will not pay for fixing it, we will probably come over to kill, loot, and rape your women."

"You've got it backwards, comrade. But if something is indeed wrong with your bird, it would sure help if we knew about it, too."

"I will tell you in twenty minutes if a problem really exists. Trust me."

"*Nyet, comrade.* I trust you only when we've cut the cards. But not to worry. I haven't punched the alert yet. What I do thirty minutes from now remains to be seen." Captain Matt Crowell paused, then added, "Vladimir, I'll be in a heap of trouble if you're shitting me. And we're both in deep slime if we can't figure out who or what is doing this."

Chapter Two

Major Curt Carson wasn't having problems with his first sergeant, but she was up to her armpits in a heap of trouble of her own.

"Major," First Sergeant Edie Sampson complained to her company commander, "good old Henry Kester really had our company records screwed up! He must have used his own data base program! This is a real sheep screw!"

Curt was looking over her shoulder as she sat at the terminal in her cubicle off the day room of Carson's Companions. What he saw on her terminal screen didn't look at all unusual. "Edie, I've been working with this data base system of Henry's ever since I took command of the Companions," he told her. "He had a workable system going."

"But it's not regulation," Sampson pointed out.

"Hell, of course it isn't!" he told her impatiently, then tried to slip back into the role of an officer and leader. "Henry had to adapt the Army's basic Robot Infantry data base program because it wasn't applicable to our operational function as Sierra Charlies. As you damned well know, we had to write the goddamned book for the Sierra Charlies...and Henry had to rewrite the data base to accommodate what we were learning as we went along. Edie, you'll get it eventually. I don't expect you to be up to speed as my first sergeant immediately. Keep a cool stool and a hot pot; do it your way and lean on me if you have to."

Curt knew it would be many months before First Sergeant Edie Sampson was able to fill the shoes of her predecessor. Master Sergeant First Class Henry Kester had recently been kicked upstairs to become Regimental Sergeant Major of the 3rd RI Regiment, the Washington Greys, upon the retirement of Regimental Sergeant Major Thomas Jesup. Henry hadn't taken the promotion gracefully, although he knew it was a step forward. The old sergeant had been a combat trooper for about thirty years, and he didn't relish the fact that he'd be doing more terminal keying than fighting in the field. On the other hand, Kester had confided to Curt during his promotion party at the Club that maybe he was getting a little bit too old to crawl around in the mud on his belly while being shot at.

Actually, Curt knew all too well that no one would ever be able to fill Henry Kester's shoes in Carson's Companions. Kester had been with the company when Curt had joined it as a raw brown-bar fresh-caught out of West Point. The old sergeant had taught Curt most of what he knew. Without Kester, Curt couldn't have turned Carson's Companions into the best company in the Washington Greys and the 17th Iron Fist Division. And without Henry Kester – who'd been an old "eleven alpha" infantryman, had converted to an "eleven delta" warbot brainy, then changed partway back to an "eleven echo" Sierra Charlie or Special Combat soldier - Curt would never have been able to make the Companions the first unit in the Army of the United States to operate with the new special-forces human-warbot Sierra Charlie doctrine.

"Can I call Henry and ask him what the hell he did here?" Edie wanted to know.

Curt shook his head. "Negatory! Regimental Sergeant Major Henry Kester has his own hands full trying to learn how to be boss noncom to a whole damned regiment rather than a company. Tom Jesup didn't hand him a bed of roses, either."

Edie Sampson looked like she was pouting, but she finally straightened her back and threw up her hands, trying hard to control her redhead's temper. Thus far, she'd done an outstanding job of keeping her emotions under control, especially in combat, where she'd saved Lieutenant Jerry Allen's buns more than once, and even in situations where the whole company had been up an evil-smelling tributary with no visible means of locomotion and no previous knowledge of aquatics, as the saying went. She cursed the absent sergeant anyway. "Henry Kester, damn your ornery hide, one of these days I'll figger out a way to get even with you for this!"

"Henry's thinking the same thing about Tom Jesup," Curt pointed out. "He's having to drain his own swamp."

"But he's got our whole training schedule fucked up," Edie pointed out to her company commander. "Nowhere do I find a sked for working with the Mod B Hairy Foxes and Mod C Mary Anns. If the balloon goes up on us - and it's had a definite history of doing such a thing – we're sure as hell going to be bravo delta. The whole thing could turn into an even bigger sheep screw." She obviously didn't want to be the top kick if a Zulu Mission came along and revealed Carson's Companions to be a "broken dick" or not working.

"Sergeant," Curt told her firmly, "stop sniveling. FIDO."

Edie Sampson sighed. In response to her company commander's order to "fuck it; drive on," she replied in exasperation, "Yes, Major." She paused, then went on in a tentative manner, "Major, Lieutenant Allen is an officer, and I know that even as first sergeant of Carson's Companions I don't have any authority over him. But I was just wondering if you had any plans on how to handle him."

Curt sighed. Lieutenant Jerry Allen was an outstanding platoon leader and had proven himself under the test of fire. But since Lieutenant Adonica Sweet, fresh out of OCS, had joined Frazier's Ferrets in the Greys to replace Lieutenant Phyllis Kirkpatrick - who'd been wounded in Mexico and thereafter elected to transfer to a less hazardous full-warbot outfit - Jerry Allen had been in a rut.

His company commander could understand it. Adonica Sweet had been their guide in Trinidad, and she was a pretty, perky, and competent young woman. At OCS, she'd also taken advantage of Army medicine; remedial orthodontics had removed the large gap between her front teeth, the only imperfect factor in her otherwise natural beauty. Allen had fallen for Adonica on Trinidad, and they'd maintained a torrid relationship ever since. She'd applied for and received a posting to the Greys because her father had served in the regiment. And since she'd arrived, Jerry Allen had been more than a little distracted.

"Lieutenant Allen is scrupulously observing Rule Ten, Sergeant," Curt reminded her.

"Hell, he acts like he's letting his gonads program his cerebrum," Sampson muttered.

"Probably. It happens to all of us at one time or another."

"Especially when we were younger," the new first sergeant observed. "Ah, youth! It's much too good for the kids!"

"I'll chat with Captain Frazier about the situation," Curt promised. Actually, he already had done so and had short circuited Frazier's immediate reaction, which had been to clamp a restriction on Lieutenant Sweet. That, of course, would only have made it worse, and Curt was able to convince Frazier of this. Both admitted there was little that could be done unless Rule Ten was busted or the level of performance of either or both young lovers showed deterioration. Thus far it hadn't, but Curt knew the situation was a ticking time bomb.

This was just another bit of heartburn resulting from the gender-integrated Army. But Curt had to admit that these problems were a whole hell of a lot less serious than they might be in a segregated outfit.

And that was also one of his problems at the moment. With Sampson and Dillon moving up, he had a vacancy for a squad leader in Jerry Allen's Bravo platoon. Thus far, Major Pappy Gratton, the regimental adjutant, had presented Curt with a list of people to fill that slot; they were all male. No female NCOs had been assigned to the Greys since the whole regiment had gone Sierra Charlie after Trinidad. Curt didn't think the new women NCOs joining the Army were getting a fair shake. He had no special preference for women, but he did want a fair choice, and he didn't know what he could do about it. Having women in combat assignments was still a very sticky situation, and the Army was now wondering how they'd let it happen. Curt knew; it was the inevitable consequence of shifting away from all-warbot operations, where women were as safe as men warbot brainies running warbots from the rear area. With the Sierra Charlie concept, these same people were put in the field with their warbots. When the Army woke up to the fact that this had happened, it was too late to stop it.

But the high brass didn't seem to be encouraging it.

Curt heard someone come into the day room. It couldn't be Kitsy Clinton and Jerry Allen; they were down in the warbot shop with their platoons in a training session learning how to field strip and carry out Level One repairs on the new Hairy Foxes and Mary Anns with their improved AI and selectable ammo feeds. The new warbots were more complex than the primitive lash-ups they'd been living and fighting with since Trinidad, and Curt wasn't at all certain that the tech-weenies had really improved on the old warbot mods. He knew he should be down there with his troops but breaking in a new first sergeant had chained him to the terminals instead.

Because he wasn't expecting anyone, he straightened up and went out to see who his visitors were.

And was both surprised and delighted.

Lieutenant Colonel William Bellamack, the regimental commander, was accompanied by two people Curt hadn't seen in a long time.

Chapter Three

Curt saluted.

Brigadier General Belinda J. Hettrick returned Curt's salute with a smile. She'd lost a lot of weight and had a strange gray pallor to her skin, but her sunken eyes above her gaunt face were full of life and sparkle, telling Curt that although she might have gone through a very rough time, she was still Belinda Hettrick behind those eyes.

"Colonel Hettrick…uh, sorry, *General* Hettrick!" Curt said with a grin. "Damn, it's good to see you again!"

The former commanding officer of the Washington Greys replied with a wan smile, "And good to see you again, *Major!* My, the make sheets have been good to both of us, haven't they?"

"And Walter Reed was obviously good to you, General. You look a hell of a lot better than you did when I saw you being stuffed into an evac aerodyne at Strijdom!" Curt recalled.

"Well, I damned near *did* go permanently AWOL, but I decided to hell with it. If they wanted me, they were going to have to come and take me after one hell of a scrap. Toughest fight of my life, however," Hettrick remarked with a conviction in her tone that told Curt the woman was even tougher than before, even though she'd spent long months in Walter Reed Army Hospital after being hit by a poisoned Bushman arrow in Namibia.

Curt turned to the other woman who'd accompanied Hettrick. "Colonel Lovell! It's been even longer!"

The woman who'd undergone her own battle with hell as a Jehorkhim hostage in Zahedan was nowhere near as frail as Hettrick. Colonel Willa Lovell, an M.D. and a neuroelectronic researcher at the Army's Fort McCarthy Proving Ground, had the bloom of health on her cheeks. Curt remembered her well from long days in Charlotte Amalie before the Trinidad operation, when they were working out the rough-hewn early Sierra Charlie warbot techniques. She'd always been a stunning woman, and today was no exception. Even the sameness of Army Class-A Greens couldn't hide the fact that Willa Lovell was not only attractive but knew how to project sensuality. Instead of returning Curt's salute, she merely extended her hand in a gesture of informal familiarity. She certainly had the right to do that as a result of both Zahedan and Charlotte Amalie. And it was her nature as a military scientist to be less formal and traditional than a combat officer. "That it has, Major, and we're going to see if we can't do something about that…"

"Major," Bill Bellamack broke in, "can we sit down somewhere? These ladies want to talk with you."

Curt indicated the chairs arranged around the Companions' day room. "Be my guest. Lots of room out here, and the company isn't due back for several hours yet. Or we can go into my cubicle, which isn't nearly as roomy."

Lovell looked around. "Anyone else here?"

"Another old comrade you may remember," Curt told her, then called out, "Sergeant Sampson, front and center!"

Edie came to the door of her cubicle and broke into a grin. "Well, strap me into a harness and plug me into a wall socket! Colonel…no, General Hettrick! And Colonel Lovell!" She stepped up to them and saluted.

There was a warmth in the greetings between the three women that was different from that with Curt, but it was more formal, nonetheless.

Hettrick noticed Sampson's stripes and rockers. "Kicked you upstairs, I see."

"Yes, ma'am! First sergeant of the Companions now!" Edie told her proudly.

"Well, Henry Kester's still bitching about having to turn over the Companions to you," Hettrick told her. "That old banty rooster would have spent his whole life down in a combat unit without getting to enjoy the perks of a regimental sergeant major."

"Yes, General, but I'm willing to bet that nothing can keep Sergeant Kester in the regimental OCV if a furball gets going outside," Sampson responded.

"General, I have no heartburn if Sampson stays," Lovell told Hettrick. "She and I have blown away a few people together. And she's shot them off my back on occasions."

"Good!" Curt noticed that Bellamack was somehow feeling a little left out of the camaraderie. But the regimental commander had taken over the Greys after Namibia, and he couldn't be expected to share the closeness of these four, who'd seen combat together. "Shall we sit down, then?"

"Yes, please," Hettrick remarked. "I still get a bit tired, but I can snap and pop if I have to."

Once they were seated around a table, Bellmack began, "The general and the colonel are here to conduct a special experiment. Major, I think you'll be happy to know that the general has been assigned to a new office in the Pentagon that will deal strictly with Sierra Charlie matters."

"Sounds good, General," Curt put in as Bellamack paused. "It'll be a relief to have someone up there who treats us as something more than an experimental new idea…"

Hettrick tossed her head. "Don't think you're home free just because an old Sierra Charlie happens to be holding down a desk at Playland on the Potomac. The warbot generals are still running the Army. The Sierra Charlies are allowed to exist only because the Greys proved the concept worked and saved the warbot brainies' butts four times in a row. By the way, nice job down in Mexico, Curt."

"Thank you, General." Curt was having a little trouble handling the fact that his former regimental commander and close friend was a one-star now. He was having even more difficulty getting used to Hettrick's frail appearance. Curt knew the old Belinda Hettrick was behind the gaunt mask and that it would take some time yet before the self-admitted "battle ax" was back to being and looking her old self again.

"I was rather surprised at Captain Morgan's highly critical personal report," Hettrick added.

"Captain Morgan let her brass get a little green," Curt remarked, using West Point slang for an officer's exhibited jealousy. "She'll get over it...I hope."

"Oh, knowing Alexis, I'm sure she will...once she gets the hang of company command," Hettrick added. "But, back to business."

"Curt, remember Doctor Rhosha Taisha?" Willa Lovell asked.

"Remember her? She's one woman who's hard to forget!" Curt exclaimed, recalling the beautiful but vicious Eurasian neurolectronics expert who'd tried to work him over when he was a Jehorkhim captive in Zahedan.

"I thought so, too, but probably for different reasons than yours," Lovell remarked. "Her experiments got me thinking, especially after we put humans back on the battlefield with the Sierra Charlie doctrine."

"Don't tell me you've worked out a way to computer-control us like a warbot, Colonel," Edie Sampson muttered darkly. "The Sierra Charlies won't buy that..."

"No, no, not at all, Sergeant!" Lovell suddenly put in. "Taisha was trying to control human warriors with computers, but she failed because she had no data on how a soldier thinks in battle."

"Well, we don't think very much when we're in combat, Colonel," Curt admitted. "Although we're not warbots, we have to respond without question to orders - which is why we're disciplined - and we have to react almost instinctively to combat situations -which is why we undergo such rigorous training."

"That's what you say," Lovell told him. "But what actually happens? We don't know! Except for a lot of debriefs and interrogations done after the fact, no one knows exactly how a soldier acts or thinks in combat. The literature is all very subjective..."

"As an offshoot of neuroelectronic warbot technology," General Hettrick put in, "Colonel Lovell now has a way to get real-time physiological and psychological data from a human being engaged in any activity. And the Sierra Charlies are the first field soldiers available as data sources since we got that technology. So, the Army has authorized a new research program that I'm supervising from the Pentagon and Colonel Lovell is conducting from McCarthy."

"With slightly modified linkage harnesses and a new channel added to the tacomm units, we can get right inside the head of a combat soldier for the first time in history." There was excitement in Willa Lovell's voice. Curt thought he'd heard that sort of excitement in another woman's voice once, and that had been Dr. Rhosha Taisha.

Curt thought he could see what was coming, so he held up his hand. "Whoa there, Colonel! Are you thinking about wiring up the Sierra Charlies?"

"Matter of fact, yes, exactly!" Willa Lovell told him. "We've done some preliminary work at McCarthy, and we have baseline data on several hundred officers and NCOs. But they were engaged in normal, everyday activities, not combat. So General Hettrick and I are here at Fort Huachuca to work with volunteers from the Sierra Charlies. We want to get a handle on how and what a combat soldier does under battle stress."

"Curt, I thought about you and the Companions first," Hettrick admitted. "You and your company are the best combat troopers I know. You've all undergone the mental discipline and training required to operate neuroelectronic warbots, so all of you have your brains in gear. You've also participated in three operations as Sierra Charlies. We'd like to instrument you so we can get data on how a soldier thinks in combat. Now, I can't order you to become a guinea pig for this sort of thing. So, I've got to ask if you'll volunteer."

"I can't speak for my company. I'll let you ask them yourself," Curt said after a brief pause. "But I have one question: Are you looking for a way to make us more efficient and more warbotlike in combat? Are you trying to find a way to factor out the human variables in the battle equation so you can run more predictable war games? I guess I'm trying to find out why you're doing this. Why do you need this information?"

"So that we can finally learn why people fight," Colonel Willa Lovell replied simply.

"Hell, Colonel, I can tell you that! We fight because…because…well, because we have to, I guess," Curt said lamely. He thought he knew why he fought. Now he wasn't so sure.

"Exactly! For a couple of centuries now, theoreticians have tried to answer that question," Lovell explained. "One group of researchers claims we fight because we're competing for scarce resources, which doesn't make much sense in a world of growing abundance. Another theory says we fight because it's built into our cultural heritage, but that hypothesis breaks down every day in the modern world. Yet another bunch of theoretical types claims we fight for biological and reproductive reasons, sort of as a natural means of selection of the fittest, which again goes to worms because modern war wipes out the best people of a generation but which is reinforced by the sexual high you've all told me you get from combat."

"You've experienced it, too," Curt reminded her.

"I know. I remember the aftermath of Zahedan," the Army scientist said quietly.

"So, what does this mean, Colonel?" First Sergeant Edie Sampson wanted to know. "Are you going to be recording our thoughts with linkage harnesses under our body armor while we run around out there getting shot at? That stinks, ma'am! Some of the things I think about are my own private thoughts, and I don't like the idea of other people snooping…"

"Can you run a warbot, Sergeant?" Lovell asked rhetorically.

"Sure, Colonel! Ran a lot of them before we went Sierra Charlie."

"Then you know how to carry out thought suppression and side-channeling to keep your stream of consciousness thoughts from messing up your warbot linkage, don't you?"

"Damned right! Every warbot brainy learns how to do that, Colonel," Sampson told her unnecessarily. "A warbot's gotta receive only the thought commands you want it to pay attention to. Otherwise, it would be even more erratic than a human soldier under fire."

"So that's why I want to use former warbot brainies with that sort of mental training and discipline," Lovell explained carefully. "I don't want to pick your brains. At first, all I'm looking for is basic physiological responses to combat. This is the sort of baseline data I need to proceed, and I need to get it from a company of volunteers like the Companions."

Curt didn't like the idea, but for reasons he couldn't put his finger on. "Sounds like a modern, high-tech, neurolelectronic update of Masters and Johnson," Curt observed, referring to the highly documented observations of human sexuality conducted in the previous century.

"Not at first," Colonel Lovell admitted, then went on, "Of course, we'd like to get that sort of data eventually in order to determine the real reasons why people fight, but..."

"But I vetoed the acquisition of personal thought patterns, even from volunteers," Hettrick interrupted. "As Colonel Lovell knows, the reason I'm in this loop is to provide an interface between the science types such as herself who always want wall-to-wall data and the Sierra Charlies who have been shot at...like thee and me."

Curt looked at his regimental commander. "Colonel Bellamack, you haven't said very much. What do you think about all this?"

Wild Bill Bellamack had a noncommittal expression on his horselike face. "The general has come to Fort Huachuca with orders from the Army Chief of Staff," he said frankly. "I'll cooperate as long as volunteers are used - as I'm sure they will be - and provided this doesn't screw up our training or affect the regiment's ability to respond and perform."

"Will you try it, Curt?" Hettrick asked.

Curt paused before he answered. Then he said, "Because you and the colonel asked, I'll personally do it as a favor, because we've known one another for a long time as well as under high-stress conditions." After a short pause, he added, "But because I can't and won't volunteer the Companions, and I won't do this without them, I have to give you a tentative maybe. I'd like you to explain this all to the Companions. Maybe the second time through the briefing, I'll get a better feel for it myself."

"What's the problem, Curt?" Willa Lovell wanted to know.

"Right at the moment, I don't like the idea of being a guinea pig," Curt admitted frankly. "But, on the other hand, if you can get information that helps us face combat a little easier or gives us a better chance of surviving a furball or lets us come out the other side a hell of a lot less beat down and sexed up, I guess it's probably worth it." He paused, then went on, "But, General, I'd like to ask you for a favor in return..."

"Name it," Hettrick replied without hesitation. She wasn't keeping score on favors granted or given, and neither was Curt. But, if she could do it at all, she'd gladly grant any favor the man asked.

"With Henry Kester moving upstairs, Sampson taking over as first sergeant, and Dillon assuming the duties of Allen's platoon sergeant, I'm short a squad leader," Curt explained. "Joanne Wilkinson tells me we'll have to take who we get."

Hettrick shook her head. "No way! The Greys have always screened replacements."

"Some new ruling for us Sierra Charlies, I'm told," Curt explained. "You remember when our TO was expanded after Trinidad to allow for squad leaders?"

"Yes, I was still in command."

"Remember that I bitched and sniveled when only men were available for those slots?"

"Yes, I didn't like it either," Hettrick admitted.

"I want the option of being able to select the best man *or* woman for my empty squad leader's slot," Curt explained. "Can anything be done, or are we stuck with chauvinism in charge of the Pentagon?"

Hettrick knew only too well of the ongoing political battle in Washington over the fact that the shift from the existing Robot Infantry doctrine to the Sierra Charlie doctrine had allowed women to serve in combat positions - mainly because they'd been warbot brainies and had thus slipped in the back door, so to speak. It was a little late to stop women fighting alongside men in the Sierra Charlies, but this didn't keep the conservative generals from resisting. "We won't see the end of that sort of discrimination in our career spans, Major. However, I think I may be able to do something. The deputy chief of staff for personnel is approachable. I'll do my best to see you're offered a choice."

Chapter Four

The UN Space Security Commission had convened on neutral territory - as usual - at Laejes in the Azores. They could have met by neurophonic linkage and thus saved themselves a long trip to these isolated mid-Atlantic islands, but some members of the Commission didn't have advanced neuroelectronic technology. And some of them suspected others; they worried that their inner thoughts could be penetrated and recorded somewhere. So, for these highly sensitive meetings conducted between military men using diplomatic procedures, face-to-face meetings were the norm.

The current chairman of the SSC, General Nigel Cleaver of the Australian Space Defense Corps, looked around the room.

The space powers of the world were all represented by generals from their respective space military forces.

And not a one of them held a rank lower than that of a general officer. Even Sweden and Japan, whose space defense forces were quite small, like Australia's, had a general officer sitting on the Commission.

But, because the news media were never informed of these meetings, none of them wore anything but the plainest of their national uniforms. This was a working group, not an ego outfit. The only reason they wore uniforms at all was the fact that, as professionals, they were proud of their status as servants of their states, people who were pledged to place their lives on the line for their countries.

General Cleaver looked around the round table and rapped his knuckles on its surface. "Let us please come to order, gentlemen. This meeting of the United Nations' Space Security Commission has been convened at the specific request of two members, the United States of America and the Union of Soviet Socialist Republics, under the terms and provisions of Article Fourteen of the third Strategic

Military Arms Reduction Treaty and under the protocols of the Treaty of Hiroshima. Will you all please sign in by typing your personal password into your terminal keypads? Thank you. According to the protocols, this meeting will be recorded for the Commission's use, but no member is authorized to release the minutes to other than his own government without a specific unanimous vote to that effect from the Commission." So much for the initial protocols and boilerplate.

Cleaver continued, "In view of the unscheduled nature of this meeting, which was requested outside our normal meeting cycle, we shall dispense with the usual formalities of reading the minutes and other parliamentary protocols. Let's get right to the subject matter of the meeting." He turned to the American on his right and the Soviet on his left. "Gentlemen, you both requested this meeting. Which of you wishes to take the floor first?"

General Michael B. Chaffee of the U.S. Aerospace Force looked at his counterpart from the Soviet Union. "Viktor, it was your satellite."

General Colonel Viktor Gregorevich Shishkov of the *Voyska Kosmonautika Oborony,* or VKO, shrugged. "Michael, it was your computer that was first damaged. Let us talk about this by taking occurrences in the order they happened. Please go ahead. Describe what happened, please."

Chaffee placed his hands upon the table's surface and folded them in front of him. He looked around the faces at the table. "At oh-seven-thirty-four Zulu yesterday, a standard data dump command was transmitted from the Tiffany Space Defense Command Center near Washington through the Cheyenne Mountain complex to the Soviet satellite Kosmos Thirty-eight-eighteen," the American reported flatly. "Within forty seconds of the receipt of the downloaded data, the entire Tiffany computer complex went down. It was not a power failure. The entire computer complex crashed."

A murmur went around the room. Basically, no one believed that a computer crash had any international security ramifications.

"So?" Shishkov interrupted. "Are you claiming that our Kosmos

36

satellite was the cause?"

"No, Viktor, or I would have mentioned it to you beforehand; I have no intention of attempting to embarrass you or any other member before this Commission. That isn't what we're here for," Chaffee replied in tones as blunt as used by Shishkov. "Our experts have found no problems that could possibly be attributed to that. Fortunately, we have a complete history of what occurred because the watch officer didn't kill Tiffany. He rendered it unconscious and had the presence of mind not to dump the memory cores when he pulled Tiffany offline. He's been officially commended for not only following protocols but keeping a cool head in what could have been a critical situation."

"I believe our watch office was equally careful when the two watch officers were on the hot line," Shishkov put in.

"They were," Chaffee agreed. "Viktor, we have no beef with the Soviet Union...for reasons that will become clear when you present your side of the story. In any event, gentlemen, it required about eleven hours for our programmers to discover that Tiffany was sick. Very sick. Because the watch officer didn't kill Tiffany, the memory cores were available for analysis by our programmers. Initially, they were able to determine only that the download from Red Sentry Twenty-two - sorry, that's our designation for Kosmos Thirty-eight-eighteen; I'll try to remember to use the international designation hereafter - our programmers discovered that the download contained about twice the number of megabytes normally associated with a Soviet surveillance satellite data dump."

"Objection!" Shishkov shouted. "Kosmos Thirty-eight-eighteen is a peaceful earth-resources satellite!"

"Objection denied, Viktor," General Nigel Cleaver replied quietly. "No one is here except space warriors. None of us have a need to posture for the news media. You're relatively new on the Commission, Viktor; in a few more months you'll realize that none of us have many secrets from the rest, much as that may pain some members. *Chahssohvoy Krasneey Dvahdtsat Dvah* is what you call it, and it's 'Red Sentry Twenty-two' on our displays, as well. I can even tell you which American and Japanese circuits are inside it, although it may take a few minutes to report the serial numbers of those units. However, it's not required that I reveal how I got that information. Now, Mike, please continue."

"Something other than a normal data dump was transmitted by Red Sentry," Chaffee continued, deliberately using the covert military name for the satellite so that there could be no more insistence by Shiskov of the "peaceful" intentions of the bird. It probably was "peaceful" in Soviet terms, "peace" still being defined by Marxist-Leninist doctrine as that state of affairs when Mother Russia and its Marxist-Leninist government would be dominant over the capitalists everywhere. Anything that led to that condition was, naturally, of "peaceful" intent. "It took a while to discover that it was another program overlying the data dump and actually interleaved between standard dump data strings. It was strange. None of our programmers had ever seen anything like it. One of our Navy's programming pioneers, Rear Admiral Adele Hooper, happened to remember something she'd heard in the late twentieth century and called a retired IBM programmer she knew. Turned out that the strange interleaved program sent down by Red Sentry was something our people are calling a 'path program.' That stands for 'pathological.' It's related to the old 'virus' program of the last century..."

"Ah, so!" breathed General Chiaki Dui Nishida of the Nippon Space Self-Defense Force. "But all modern computers and intelligence amplifiers have built-in protection against accepting or being affected by virus programming!"

Chaffee shook his head. "All of us occasionally become ill, right? Why? Because in spite of modern biotechnology, pathological organisms continue to evolve and mutate. No reason why a path program can't exhibit the same characteristics..."

General Hanandra Singh Chaibber of India's Aerospace Defense Arm shook his head. "Nonsense, Mike! You speak as if a program can evolve! They're not evolutionary organisms. Neither are computers!"

"But they can and do, especially in artificially intelligent units. Not that I think that happened here. On the other hand, computer programmers are human organisms, and they can learn, quickly and sometimes easily if they've been taught how to do it!" interjected General Lars Bengt Bergaust of *Starnavapnet*. "Someone could have developed the modern version of a virus program..."

"Apparently they did," Chaffee observed. "When Admiral Hooper and her people got into the path program, they discovered it was written in such a way that the receiving computer would perceive it as part of the data stream until the data got into memory and the computer began to process it. Then the path program scrambled Tiffany's image processing program and proceeded to make Tiffany sick. We believe that *someone* uploaded that path program into Red Sentry Twenty-two for the explicit purpose of inhibiting the surveillance data. Fortunately, we have back-ups for all Tiffany's programs, so we can kill our master computer, do an arctic boot, reformat, and emplace our programs again. That's my report for the moment, but I'll have something more to add when Viktor finishes."

Cleaver looked at the Soviet general. "Viktor?"

"The *Voyska Kosmonautika Oborony* at Kaliningrad had the same problem when Kosmos Thirty-eight-eighteen passed over the Soviet Union during the remainder of that orbit," Shishkov began. "Unfortunately, the watch supervisor did not believe the report of the watch officer's conversation on the hot line with the Tiffany complex, and our Svetlana computer complex therefore became infected with the path program as well. Fortunately, the watch officer acted on his own volition to protect state property, and the damage to Svetlana was not as extensive as that to Tiffany. I can therefore confirm the existence of a path program in Kosmos Thirty-eight-eighteen. Because our computers were also affected, the Soviet Union cannot be blamed for installing the path program." He did not add that the watch supervisor was even then on a slow train to Tomsk and that the watch officer had received the Order of Lenin and a promotion to major.

There was silence in the room when the Soviet general finished.

"Tampering with a surveillance satellite is a serious offense," Cleaver finally said. Everyone in the room knew from their own space defense tracking systems that nothing had come near Kosmos 3818; whatever or whoever had installed the path program in the satellite had done so by remote means.

"But certainly not contrary to any treaty," was the remark from General Ku Chiehkang of the People's Space Navy of the People's Republic of China.

"No one thought of such a thing when SMART-Three was drawn up and signed," said General Jean-Francois Beaudry of the *Legion d'Espace*.

"It may not be contrary to SMART-Three and the Treaty of Hiroshima," commented General Pedro Castillo Andrada of the *Forca Estrella Brasileira*, "but it is certainly an act that tends to increase international tension. To do what has been done requires an intimate knowledge of the Soviet satellite..."

"Ahem. We all have that sort of knowledge," Cleaver admitted quietly. "Anyone in the room could have done it."

Everyone looked at everyone else. That was true. Silence.

If one of the nine space powers represented in the meeting room was responsible for installing the path program in the Soviet satellite, the nation's representative remained silent and impassive.

"Very well," Cleaver began, breaking the silence. "The Commission is expected to act to relieve military tensions, if possible. Does anyone have a suggested course of action?"

"The United States of America will immediately release the details of the path program," Chaffee volunteered, removing a hard-copy printout plus a memory cube from his briefcase.

General Colonel Viktor Shishkov did so as well. "The Soviet Union will do the same simultaneously." It was patently obvious that the USSR didn't want to be considered the black hat in this incident.

Chaffee knew that the Soviets hadn't installed the path program, but he didn't know who might have or from where the signal might have been uploaded.

"We've checked and tested our American Poker Hand satellites," Chaffee went on, "and we've ascertained that none of them have at this time been infected with a path program."

"The Soviet Union is still in the process of remotely inspecting its satellites for the same purpose," Shishkov added. "We cannot tell you at this time that all Soviet satellites are not infected. We are replacing Kosmos Thirty-eight-eighteen today and will send a crew to recover it for inspection purposes."

"I therefore recommend," Chaffee said, "that our first step is to quietly warn all nations with ground station capability that there's a possibility a path program may be in any satellite and may, in fact, even be proliferating. In short, this may be the start of an epidemic. As soon as we've worked out an immunization program - we should have that within twenty-four hours now that we know what the path program amounts to – we'll gladly share it with everyone."

"The Soviet Union is also working on the same thing," Shishkov insisted. "We are well known for the ability of our mathematicians, and we shall release an immunization program in a short time."

"If I sound like a biotechnician," Chaffee remarked with a slight smile, "it's because we're faced here with something highly analogous to an organic disease. The first step is to stop the spread of the disease. So, don't interrogate satellites that you suspect might be contaminated until we have an immunization program ready to go. Or, if you must interrogate, do so with care, because your ground computers may become infected. If they are, power down and wait for our computerized flu shot. In the meantime, we should act to locate the source of the disease."

"The Soviet Union will launch a special *Ekron* satellite very soon for the purpose of watching for the transmission of signals to our Kosmos satellites," Shishkov offered.

Chaffee said nothing. He didn't want to reveal that the search had already started, using BLINT satellites. It was senseless to let everyone know what was going on. He didn't totally trust some of the other space powers, although he had grown to know and trust their representatives on the Commission. If one of the space powers was indeed behind this, it would be downright stupid to let their Commission representative know and thereby risk the possibility of a slip. So, Chaffee was playing the American cards close to the chest. Let the Soviets have the honor and glory of announcing their launches; everyone would know what those Soviet satellites were and where they were, so anyone could cease path program uploads while those birds were looking. The United States was looking already.

But they hadn't found anything yet.

"It appears," Chairman Cleaver observed, "that the only thing the Commission can do at this point in time is to warn others of the possibility of infection of their space-fed computers by a pathological program. I want to thank the representatives of both the United States and the Soviet Union for sharing with us the details of the incidents and their data concerning the path program. The next step is to develop an immunization program, something both the United States and the Soviet Union are doing..."

"With the data about the path program," General Beaudry interrupted, "France will also begin the development of an immunization program..."

"May I suggest," said General Chaibber, "that we establish a hot line between the programmers each of us will assign to the job? If we work together on this, we may be able to develop the immunization program much quicker."

"Japan would be honored to establish and coordinate such a network," General Nishida put in quickly.

"Sweden wishes to become involved in that as well," General Bergaust volunteered.

Cleaver sighed. It was his job as chairman of the Commission to head off any possible conflicts such as the honor of being top dog for the cooperative programming network. It was a difficult thing to get generals from different countries to meet in the first place, there still being some distrust in various governments. The generals themselves had few problems once they were together, because they were all military professionals, and, as military leaders, they would be the first ones involved - and perhaps killed - in any conflict that broke out. Besides, the assignment of being a representative on the Commission carried many military and political perks. But there were times..."Chaibber, please work with Bergaust as co-chairman of the programming network subcommittee. Inform us of the details of the network so we can all log on and begin work on this."

Chaibber nodded toward Bergaust. "An honor, sir. Shall we meet to discuss initial details immediately after adjournment here?"

"Of course."

"Any further discussion? And further business that should come before the Commission at this meeting? Anyone wish to say anything?" Cleaver prodded the members, making sure everyone had the full opportunity to say anything, add anything, or bring up any point that might have been missed.

"Very well! We shall convene again once we have further information to discuss. In the meantime, we shall maintain communications on our discreet Commission communications network...unless that becomes infected as well, God forbid! This emergency meeting of the UN Space Security Commission is hereby adjourned *sine die.*"

Chapter Five

"Colonel, I hate to snivel, but we've got some real heartburn." Major Curt Carson was ragged, tired, and chafed. He'd spent the entire day out in the field on a live-ammo training exercise with the Companions. Although Curt was fit, hard as nails, and accustomed to the field combat environment, he hadn't had a pleasant day.

Bellamack turned from his terminal. It hadn't been a good day for the regimental commander, either. Bellamack was, like Curt, a field combat officer. Although he'd been a warbot brainy who'd been introduced to the Sierra Charlie concept upon taking command of the Greys, he was basically a man of action rather than a desk officer. And he'd been a desk officer all day today. Bellamack hadn't grown accustomed to the increased administrative load of regimental command. In spite of computers, intelligence amplifiers, and other high-tech devices to help handle data, no substitution had yet been found for human judgment. That meant that the tough decisions were always left to Bellamack. And it appeared to him that Curt had one of those tough calls, the sort of thing that the commanding officer had to handle because it was the commanding officer's job. "Goddammit, Curt, who the hell doesn't? You look like you had a tough day, too. So, take the load off your boots and have a seat. What's the bitch?"

Curt slid the office door closed and slipped into a chair alongside the terminal desk. He got right to the point. "Colonel, it's damned uncomfortable to wear Colonel Lovell's pickup harnesses under body armor. The harnesses bind the slipping movement of the armor's inner lining; that makes the armor catch up on the harness and pull it away from the skin, which in turn leaves a welt where the sensors separate. Once the sensors separate, the whole harness rubs back and forth with body movement, and this just chafes the living shit out of the wearer's skin."

"So?" Bellamack asked as Curt paused.

"So, I've got four of my Companions out of action with badly chafed backs and shoulders," Curt reported. "The rest of us are only hurting bad."

"Why come to me? Have you told this to the R-and-D types from Colonel Lovell's lab?"

"Yes, sir," Curt replied formally.

"And?"

"Those tech-weenies are far more interested in their equipment than in us," Curt told him bitterly. "They make us strip, and they reattach the sensor harnesses. Then we go out and go through it all again. I was told by one bone-dome lieutenant that it was the sort of thing we had to expect out of experimental equipment."

"Well, it is R-and-D stuff, Curt," Bellamack tried to console the upset company commander. "Once they get enough data, they can revise the harnesses to be more comfortable..."

"Yes, Colonel, but in the meantime, it's tearing up my troops."

"Can our medical staff do anything?"

"They're as helpful as they can be under the circumstances," Curt explained, "but they've been told by the McCarthy people to keep their hands off the harnesses."

"Have you reported this to Colonel Lovell?"

"No, sir, I haven't."

"Why?"

"She's back at McCarthy Proving Grounds for the rest of this week."

"Okay, now you've clarified why you came to me. You've exhausted all your options," Bellamack decided, rubbing the back of his head, which was now covered by a thatch of graying black hair, the hallmark of a Sierra Charlie soldier. "And, knowing you, you've obviously developed some sort of recommendation for me to consider. At least, you'd damned well better have. What do you want me to do?"

Curt liked the man's direct, no-nonsense approach. The no-bullshit attitude of Colonel Wild Bill Bellamack had gone a long way toward helping a former war bot brainy from the pure neuroelectronic Robot Infantry adapt to the unique new procedures of the human-plus-warbot Special Combat OF Sierra Charlie regiment that the Washington Greys had become. "One of two things, Colonel. Either rescind the standing order about wearing body armor during training exercises or let us shit-can these god-damned sensor harnesses."

Bellamack started to say something, but the intercom on his terminal chimed. The display screen told him he had another visitor. With a single motion, he reached out and touched the "enter" stud. "I think," the regimental commander said, "that another company commander probably has a similar bitch. I might as well handle the whole thing as a conference bitch."

Captain Alexis Morgan walked in, removed her battle helmet, and saluted. She walked as if she hurt all over. She was dirty and grungy and looked tired, too. She shook out her mane of corn-colored curls, now free of the confines of her helmet; she looked somewhat surprised at seeing Curt in the commander's office, but she greeted her commander first: "Colonel."

"Captain?"

She nodded toward Curt. "Major."

"Good afternoon, Captain," Curt replied. His former platoon leader was maturing into a company commander, but she seemed to have lost something in the process. Maybe it was hidden under a certain amount of aloofness that Alexis had developed as a result of trying to show her former company commander that she was as good a company commander as he'd been. The two of them still had an ongoing relationship, but it wasn't quite the same, and it often puzzled Curt.

And Alexis Morgan's attention was devoted to her company right then...and Curt was pleased because he'd tried to teach her that leadership included taking care of those you led, particularly in the highly trained and strongly professional Army of the Robot

Infantry, and especially in the mixed human-robot force of the Sierra Charlies. "Colonel, I've got a real problem that I need to talk to you about."

Bellamack indicated another chair. "Put your rifle and helmet on the sidebar, Captain, and sit down. I suspect you've got the same problem as Major Carson."

Ridding herself of her helmet and *Novia*, Alexis settled herself slowly and carefully in the other chair as if something were chafing her. She replied, "Colonel, I think all four combat companies have the same problem."

"The McCarthy sensor harnesses?" Bellamack ventured.

"Yes, sir. My spine and the back of my neck feel like they're on fire," Alexis admitted. "Five of my company are unfit for duty now because of the chafing. We're all rubbed raw. The McCarthy special troops aren't at all helpful. Our own company biotech saved our butts. But to get to the sources of the trouble and relieve the irritation, you have to strip to the skin - remove cammies, body armor, and harness. And, Colonel, you know how difficult it is to just slip in and out of body armor."

"Yeah, it's tight. It's designed that way," Bellamack said .

Layered polymer armor depended not only on its tensile strength but also on its ability to spread the force of a bullet impact over a wide area of the body. Nothing yet developed could prevent a bullet impact from raising a big welt and leaving a mass of ruptured capillaries around its impact point, and occasionally a high-velocity round would actually break the skin, but the tension of the body armor absorbed most of the kinetic energy of a round and spread it laterally across the body rather than allowing the kinetic energy of the round to jelly the tissue under the impact as earlier armor tended to do.

The necessary high-strength materials had been around for years, but the development of the existing body armor so essential to putting human beings back in the battlefield had depended on what Curt, Colonel Willa Lovell, and others had learned in eastern Iran during the Zahedan hostage affair. There they'd confirmed the effectiveness of ancient Mongol taut-silk body armor, something that would usually stop an arrow or allow it to be pulled out with little damage.

"Yes, sir. I don't mind the tightness," Alexis admitted. "It does double duty because it also provides a lot of support for certain body parts of both sexes."

Another knock came on Bellamack's office door. Someone else had bypassed the computerized secretary with its announcement capability. This time it was Captain Russ Frazier of the Ferrets. He was a short, pugnacious-looking man who really was pugnacious. He'd been trained up by Marty Kelly, who, after being wounded in Namibia, had been promoted and sent over to the 7th Robot Infantry Regiment (Special Combat), the Cottonbalers, to form a new Sierra Charlie company. Since it was general Army policy to keep combat units together as teams, such a transfer had been unusual. But after the chaos caused by Kelly in Namibia, regimental morale had required Curt - then temporary regimental commander - to suggest to General Carlisle at division command that a troublesome outfit, Kelly's Killers, be put under new command. Russ Frazier had stepped up from Kelly's Alpha Company to reorganize the outfit as Frazier's Ferrets, and they'd done well in Mexico. But Frazier was a Texas A&M man, and he'd been strongly influenced by Kelly. He wasn't another Marty Kelly, but he was aggressive in the former company commander's mold.

"Colonel, the Ferrets have a problem, and I'm told you're in the problem-solving mode at the moment," Frazier remarked.

"Come in and sit down...if you can find a place to park it, Russ," Bellamack said sourly, adding, "You might as well join this communal snivel and bitch session."

Frazier complied in smooth movements interrupted only by an occasional slight grimace that told everyone he was chafing, too.

"Don't tell me. Let me guess," Bellamack said before Frazier could speak further. "The McCarthy experimental linkage harnesses are chafing your troops under their body armor, right?"

"Yes, sir. Chafing them raw. How did you know, Colonel? Don't tell me it's *that* obvious in the way I walk!" Frazier replied sharply.

"I would be damned surprised if you had any other sort of a whine right now," the regimental commander said. "All right, allow me to bring you up to speed, Captain. Major Carson has just suggested that I either rescind the order to wear body armor on training exercises or let you quit wearing the sensor harnesses," Bellamack told his company commanders. He looked alternately at each of them. After a short pause, he went on, "I'll do neither."

Chapter Six

"What? Colonel, this is tearing us up…" Curt began.

Bellamack got to his feet and began to pace back and forth behind his terminal desk. He went on testily, "I won't rescind the order to wear body armor! I can't afford to have someone hurt or even killed by live ammo in training. Congress and the news media love the Sierra Charlies as heroes, but they still haven't gotten totally used to the idea that people have to be put at risk and probably killed because of the new doctrine. Remote-controlled neuroelectronic warbots were supposed to eliminate the human hazard of war forever and ever. Well, you're the people who rediscovered the fact that warbots, like tanks, can control ground without occupying it, but that battles and wars are won by human beings called infantry who go in and make the enemy call it quits by violence that scares the living shit out of him."

He paused in midturn, then went on, "Hell, we all know that. You've been through far more personal combat than I have. But I saw it at the Battle of Bisbee for the first time. Be that as it may, until the public gets used to an old idea once more, I can't jeopardize either my troops, my command, or the new Sierra Charlie concept, which, God knows, we need pretty damned bad! So, we will wear body armor. You've got to get used to fighting in it, anyway."

Bellamack stopped behind his desk, held up his hand to squelch any comment from the three officers at this time, then leaned on the terminal and added, "Secondly, although I probably could get away with an order to rescind wearing those sensor harnesses the tech-weenies have foisted on us, I won't do it. It might rebound to the detriment of General Belinda Hettrick."

As he paused there, Curt asked, "Colonel, why is that?"

"That lady has her neck out a mile for us," Bellamack advised them.

"That sounds like Belinda Hettrick," Alexis Morgan remarked, "but why? And in what way?"

"She's not only a warbot brainy who understands the way the warbot generals think, but she's the only actual Sierra Charlie - one who's been shot at – who's now a general officer and knows how important the Sierra Charlies are to the security of this nation and the free world," the colonel pointed out in frank tones. "She's a genuine war hero as a result of Zahedan, Trinidad, and Namibia. With General Carlisle – who's also encouraged the development of the Sierra Charlie concept - she raised enough hell at the general staff level that General Brooke established the new OSCAR desk in the Pentagon."

"OSCAR?" Russ Frazier echoed. "New one on me, Colonel. Will you translate the acronym, please?"

"Office of Special Combat Assault Robotics," Bellamack accommodated him. "It's a semi-temporary-permanent in the Army sort of way, if you know what I mean..."

"Yeah, temporary if the high brass doesn't like it, and permanent if they do so long as it doesn't plow their turf," Curt muttered.

"You're right," Bellamack told him. "OSCAR is new. The warbot generals don't really appreciate the intrusion of an actual combat soldier onto their warbotic turf. This McCarthy Proving Ground experiment recording and analyzing the emotions and physical reactions of people in actual combat is General Hettrick's idea. She dreamed it up at Walter Reed while the medics were working the Bushman poison out of her system."

"I didn't know that," Curt admitted, but he privately wondered why someone like Hettrick, who knew the Sierra Charlies as well as she did, would subject them to such a hassle. He voiced his concern. "But why?"

Bellamark clarified this for Curt. "No one has any solid data on what happens when a person fights. Or why. That includes barroom brawls, alley fights, professional boxing, contact sports, and lethal encounters of all sorts including combat and war. In short, with all the high-tech neuroelectronics, biotechnology, and computer assistance, no one but no one realized that we now have the technology to help answer a very old question: Why do we fight?"

"Yeah, I remember the general talking about that when she popped the experiment on us and asked for our support," Curt recalled.

"General Hettrick is buying us time," Bellamack added.

"Time?" Alexis didn't understand.

"Time, Captain Morgan, time. Time for the Sierra Charlies not only to continue to prove their necessity in modern armed conflict," Bellamack said, "but also time that will soften much of the emotion involved with putting people back on the battlefield. And while she's doing that, the Army's going to get answers to some very basic questions that may have an enormous impact on the armed services. She's got her neck out because she was the one who dreamed this up and then went to Colonel Lovell at McCarthy to design the experiment. Then she went and knocked on doors in the Pentagon, using her war-hero status, to get this through because she knew it would protect the Sierra Charlies. If it goes tits-up because the Washington Greys chicken out or fail to cooperate, this regiment may end up being the only Sierra Charlie outfit in the whole goddamned Army…and General Belinda Hettrick may end up with a ruined career as a result."

"Well, hell, I don't want that to happen," Curt muttered darkly.

"But, dammit, Colonel," Russ Frazier complained, "it's physically painful to wear these goddamned experimental harnesses under our body armor. We've got to do something! My troops told me they're going to ditch either the body armor or the harnesses. The two are incompatible!"

"No, they won't. As I told you, I won't rescind the orders to wear both the body armor and the sensor harness," Bellamack repeated.

Alexis quietly added, "Colonel, you don't have to do either one."

Bellamack did a double take and stared at the attractive young company commander. "What's that?"

"Sir, I didn't have the opportunity to make a recommendation earlier," Alexis said slowly. "But I have a different one. I think it's a solution."

"Well, for God's sake, let's hear it!"

"In the Zahedan hostage rescue mission," Alexis pointed out, referring to operations Squire and Cyclone, when the Greys took their neuroelectronic warbots into the isolated Iranian city in an attempt to rescue 105 hostages, including Colonel Willa Lovell, held by a fanatical Muslim sect, "we wore standard mobile linkage harnesses under our body armor."

"Uncomfortable as hell," Russ Frazier put in.

"But at least it's designed to be worn for hours under body armor," Alexis reminded him. "Maybe you've forgotten, since it's been about two years since we started our conversion to Sierra Charlies."

"Captain Morgan, a full warbot linkage harness is over-kill for the sort of data Colonel Lovell is collecting," Bellamack pointed out, resuming his seat. He had a hunch that Alexis Morgan indeed had something in her suggestion, but he wasn't sure of all the ramifications yet. "Colonel Lovell doesn't require the full feedback capability of a regular neuroelectronic mobile linkage harness. She's only downloading from your nervous systems. All the uplink systems in the harness would be unused. She doesn't intend to feed neuroelectronic data back into your nervous systems."

Alexis shrugged. "So? Those circuits can be dead-ended at the connector."

"Uh, Alexis," Curt ventured, "what you suggest will work...except we're going to have to shave our heads again."

Alexis Morgan looked at him. "Would you do it for Belinda Hettrick?"

"Damned right! So would you!"

She ran her hand through her mop of hair and smiled. "This will grow back in a few months. I don't mind looking like an ordinary warbot brainy for a while if it helps General Hettrick and the Sierra

Charlies. We're pretty damned special, and I like that. Let's find another symbol for the Sierra Charlies."

"Why don't you think about that, Captain?" Bellamack suggested, feeling that assigning such a job to her would hold down the bitching and sniveling that was certain to occur when the Sierra Charlies had to relinquish their unique badge and take on the appearance of warbot brainies again.

"Thank you, Colonel, I'll do that," Alexis promised.

"Okay, Colonel, in the meantime, what do we do about the problems with these goddamned experimental harnesses?" Curt asked. "Damned if I'll ask my troopers to crawl back into those things. As it is, a quarter of my company is on sick list, and the rest are within a fraction."

"Same here, Colonel," Alexis reminded him.

"I'm having some problems with the Ferrets, as 1 said," Frazier reminded them. "The only one who's totally tactical and gung-ho is Lieutenant Sweet."

"Yeah, she's a pistol, isn't she?" Curt recalled with a grin, remembering how Adonica Sweet had fought valiantly alongside the Companions as their "native guide" on Trinidad.

"Yeah, the Princess of the Regiment," Frazier observed.

"Watch it!" Alexis Morgan counseled, "or we'll get together and pick a Regimental Prince...and you'll be in deep shit, Russ." The women of the Washington Greys had an inner beauty all their own because they were combat soldiers who were as good as the men...and often far stronger, less emotional, and with greater staying power. It was an unwritten rule that some were physically more attractive than others - Alexis didn't have to worry on that account - but that no one of them was ever singled out because of it. Adonica Sweet qualified, of course, but the unwritten rule was insurance against jealousy or "letting your brass get green."

Bellamack reached over and keyed his intercom. "Captain Gibbon?" he called for his intelligence/communications officer.

A female voice replied, "Captain Gibbon is in linkage training with the birdbots, Colonel. This is Sergeant Crawford."

The Washington Greys had requested and gotten an additional quota of neuroelectronically operated, remotely piloted reconnaissance craft, bird robots, to carry out battlefield recon and surveillance. They'd been short of these in Namibia and Mexico. Major Fred Benteen had done a little pleading topside and got the regimental TO&E revised to permit additional recon warbots, and Lieutenant Dearborn and Sergeant Sanchez in Supply had managed to get additional warbots for this purpose; Gibbon was therefore involved in training combat company personnel to use them, since the Intelligence Unit was chronically shorthanded in a combat situation. It was taking time to shake out the TO&E of a Sierra Charlie regiment.

"Put me through on voice-only to Colonel Willia Lovell at McCarthy Proving Ground," Bellamack told her. "I don't care where she is or what she's doing. I want to talk to her. Then get someone from Supply standing by on the line, because I want to talk with them when I get through with Colonel Lovell."

"Yes, sir!"

As Bellamack turned to his three company Commanders, Captain Joan Ward of Ward's Warriors appeared in the door to his office. She was dirty, grungy, and looked very tired. She walked in a painful and uncomfortable fashion. Looking at her, Bellamack remarked, "From your appearance and actions, Captain Ward, I think I know exactly why you want to talk to me. Well., Major Carson, Captain Morgan, and Captain Frazier beat you to it."

"Damn! I was farther out in the field than they were!" Joan Ward muttered.

"Makes no never mind," Bellamack told her. "All of you, attention to orders. Get out of those McCarthy sensor harnesses right now. Turn them in to Supply no later than tomorrow before twelve hundred hours. Stand down from field training until further notice. Go to battle sims and video training. Spend a little time with your warbots and personal gear. It may be a few days before we can get enough standard mobile linkage harnesses for everyone and allow the tech-weenies to rewire the connectors. However, in the meantime, shave your heads"

Chapter Seven

The "game" of electronic warfare had been played intensely by every major technical nation in the world for nearly a hundred years.

Everyone has electronically snooped on everyone else since 1939 when early British radar detected the 236-meter German LZ-127 *Graf Zeppelin* that had accidentally strayed well inland over the British Isles while monitoring English radio transmissions; the British didn't communicate with the German dirigible commander to tell him that the ship was off course because this would have revealed that the British radar was tracking it!

To maintain security in a world where everyone was snooping, some transmissions used encryption or buried solid data in continuously transmitted streams of garbage. But everyone knew more or less what the other nations were transmitting or detecting. Strangely, it was a very stable situation.

However, it wasn't an easy job to track down an intermittent transmission that might also include a virus program.

An intermittent is the bane of technicians as well as scientists. The most elusive of all data points is the nonrepeatable one that may occur at any time and in any location. It's something that happens when you least expect it. Then when you go looking for it, it's gone and the system won't give up its secret. Chasing clown an intermittent in an electronic device is pure hell. Trying to get a handle on a nonpredictable and often nonrepeatable event such as a meteor is a similar hell to a scientist who loves the predictable. In fact, science thrives on the predictable and tends to ignore the odd data points that fall "off the curve."

Trying to locate the source of the signal that had disabled Red Sentry 22 wasn't difficult at first. Soviet data indicated - and it was confirmed by United State Space Track - that Kosmos 3818 was operational when it passed over the Soviet ground station near Semipalatinsk. At least, the *Voyska Kosmonautika Oborony* said so. The American ELINT satellite, Peeping Tom 4, stationed in inclined geosynchronous orbit, confirmed that Semipalatinsk and Kosmos 3818 had communicated on the satellite's southbound course before it passed beyond range of the station and over China's Tarim Basin. Something had happened between that point in the orbit and the time when White Sands had picked up Kosmos 3818 coming over North America and transferred the downcoming signal from White Sands to Cheyenne Mountain to Tiffany.

This narrowed the search to a strip running around the Earth 3,200 kilometers wide and 25,500 kilometers long - a mere 82 million square kilometers in which a transmitting station only meters square might be located.

The only way that much area could be scanned, much less searched, within a reasonable time period and therefore at a reasonable cost was from space.

It wouldn't have been difficult had the signal from the ground been a steady or even a repetitive one. But, since it was probably an intermittent signal sent in a burst taking only a few seconds, the task would have been insurmountable.

Except to a robot.

And that's exactly what the United States Aerospace Force had in geosynchronous orbit 36,300 kilometers above the Earth.

In fact, the USAF had more than one robot ELINT monitoring station up there. Nearly a hundred of them swung in inclined geosynchronous orbit, weaving around the Earth like a skein of yarn; viewed from the ground, their ground tracks traced north-south figure eights in the sky over a given position.

According to stories circulated by Rumor Control - and therefore of suspect accuracy - an advanced American robotic ELINT satellite was theoretically capable of picking up the signal from a child's walkie-talkie hand-held transceiver on the Earth's surface below.

Actually, nothing could do that. There was a maelstrom of radio transmissions and other electromagnetic signals created by mankind's civilizations on Earth. Any small signal quickly became part of the overall "noise" background.

But a signal specifically generated and targeted to a satellite could be detected, recorded, and its source located with reasonable accuracy.

It required only that an unsleeping, ever-alert robot in space - an automatic ELINT satellite - watch quietly, passively, and very patiently for another signal from that 81-million-square-kilometer area.

Fortunately, a robot can be very quiet, passive, and patient.

Patience really wasn't required.

But a certain amount of sneakiness was.

Added to a bit of deception.

"Got it, General!" The young Aerospace Force captain had a big grin on her face as she was allowed to log into the neurophonic conference linkage. The young woman was full of enthusiasm that wasn't damped by the over-powering presence on the network of the highest of the high brass: General Edward S. Carrington, the chairman of the joint chiefs of staff; the Army chief of staff, General Otis R. Brooke; the National Intelligence Agency chief, General Albert Murray; and General Michael Chaffee, the U.S. rep to the UN Space Security Commission. Her smile was broad and almost impish. The neurophonic linkage was so good that Chaffee almost believed she was sitting across the table from him.

(Actually, the linkage computers and intelligence amplifiers were sending the proper signals to the linkage harness on his head and along his spine; these signals were recognized by his brain, which projected the image directly on his visual cortex.)

Chaffee didn't attempt to formalize her report. He knew that the Special Team had been working steadily for over 40 hours and the details were available in the database if wanted. The important thing now was to work with the findings and worry about the background details later. "What have you got, Captain?" Chaffee asked her.

"Red Sentry Twenty-four was hit an hour ago. Uh, sorry, it's called Kosmos Thirty-eight-twenty in the UN register. At any rate, Peeping Tom Eight-zero and Niner-seven both detected the signal sent up to Kosmos Thirty-eight-twenty from the ground," the little captain reported.

"Fairly narrow beam," General Carrington noted, calling on his own Aerospace Force operational background.

"Yes, sir! Very narrow. Peeping Tom Niner-zero may have detected it, too, but if so, it was way down in the mud," she replied.

"Location?" NIA Chief Murray wanted to know.

"Still computing, General."

"Since those particular satellites picked up the signal, Kosmos had to be over the Indian Ocean," Carrington observed.

She nodded. "Yes, sir!"

General Otis Brooke muttered, "Who the hell has space data facilities in the Indian Ocean?"

"Damned near everyone in space, Otis," Murray told him. "We do. So do the Soviets, the French, the Australians..."

"And it could have come from a ship," Carrington added.

"Captain, why is the pinpoint calculation taking so long?" Brooke asked her.

"General, it's a phase triangulation problem," she tried to explain. "The math is very complex."

"Been about thirty years since I tangled with trig at West Point," Brooke admitted sotto voce.

The little captain heard him anyway. She had a Ph.D. in math from Cal Tech, but she didn't even try to explain the equations. "The computer has to match the phase of the upgoing signals as received at the two satellites, correct them for atmospheric distortion, then take into account the phase difference in the signals downloaded from our Peeping Toms…and that depends on exactly and precisely where the Peeping Toms were located when they received the signal. Sort of a reiterative kind of a solution, sir. Even the computers have to chew on that one for a few minutes!"

"Please stay on the line, Captain," Chaffee told her, "and let us know as soon as you have a solution."

"Yes, sir!"

Murray looked at his colleagues, who seemed to be in the conference room with him although they were at several places around the United States. "If it's come from a facility in the Indian-Ocean, gentlemen, I think we should go have a look for ourselves."

"You don't think it wise to inform the rest of the UN Space Security Commission?" Chaffee wondered.

Murray shook his head. "No, I don't, Mike."

"Sounds like you don't trust the Commission, Al," Chaffee observed.

"Not completely, and not because I happen to be chief spook," Murray admitted. "I've got some soft gee-two, nothing I want to chat about, but semi-hard. As my pappy used to tell me, it's no damned good unless it's hard. Anyway, it's apparent to me that someone on the Commission is either hiding the fact that their national military or intelligence forces are doing this…or they don't know it's being done by their own people." No one on the net wasted his time asking Murray where he'd gotten this hot skinny.

"This heartburn doesn't have to come from a space-faring nation, Al," Brooke reminded him. "Anyone with a ground station could do it. The technology and the hardware are up for sale almost anywhere around the globe."

"Well, let's think this one through," Chaffee suggested. "First of all, only two Soviet surveillance satellites have been hit to date. No one has tried to play with one of our birds. France, Brazil, Australia, Japan…all their surveillance satellites haven't been touched. And they're in polar orbits just like Red Sentry. But no one except the Russkies have been hassled."

"Coincidence."

"No, Otis. Not coincidence. Not when whoever is doing this knows damned good and well that it's an offense serious enough to come before the UN Commission," Murray reminded him. "It's being done purposefully. Why?"

"Someone wants Sov surveillance satellites blinded," Brooke replied.

"Or wants a Sov surveillance satellite's data wiped before it gets to the Russkies," Carrington added.

"Bingo!" Chaffee exclaimed. "Now, who?"

"Who doesn't like the Russkies?" Carrington put in.

"A whole hell of a lot of people are still scared shitless of the Big Red Tide," Chaffee pointed out.

"Including ourselves," Brooke said.

"Yeah, but this virus seeding isn't being done by us...or I'll have someone's balls on the wall," Carrington promised. "Including yours, Al, if NIA happens to be behind this."

"I'm not. You know damned good and well I'd pass the Quiet Word to you at JCS just to keep you from getting as nervous in the service as you are at the moment," Murray told him quietly.

"Maybe we're not supposed to know," Brooke ventured to suggest.

Murray shook his head. "You're not hassling NIA's turf right now, gentlemen. It's not budget time."

"And we're not taut with the Sovs at the moment, either," Chaffee pointed out. "They're being glasnosty again at the moment. Real easy to live with."

"Believe that, and I'd like to talk to you about some land in the Orinoco River delta that I think might be of interest to you. Mike, don't go soft on the Sovs. Read Soviet military doctrine again," Murray suggested. "The principle of a surprise attack is still the cornerstone of Marxist-Leninist doctrine, especially when such a preemptive strike can be rationalized as a defensive response to an anticipated attack on the Motherland."

"Hell, if that was true, Al, they would have creamed us on any number of occasions during the last seventy-five years," Carrington observed.

"Well, I don't know all of the crew in the Kremlin," Murray admitted, "but I imagine the leaders of Politburo, the KGB, and the Red Army sit down together every morning, look at the situation, and then say to each other, '*Nyet*, comrade, not today.' Better part of valor, and all that…"

Chaffee wasn't convinced by the chief spy's continual and unchanging suspicion of the Soviet Union. It was, of course, a consequence of the job of each man to approach the situation as each had. The UN Space Security Commission representative had worked with his counterpart on the Commission and believed him to be an honorable man by Chaffee's lights. "Al, that scenario falls apart because the Sovs know that we know that one of their surveillance satellites was disabled…and we've got no reason to do that to them and thus provoke a confrontation."

"We'll see, Mike. We'll see," Murray remarked thoughtfully. "In the meantime, I suggest we keep it to ourselves until we find out who's doing it. We might be surprised."

"Probably," Carrington added. "Most probably. Or we'd have a much better grip on the situation than we appear to have."

The little Aerospace Force captain's image coalesced before them. "General Carrington, sir, we've got a fix. Rough first approximation, but good enough to warrant a closer look. Sixty-nine east, forty-nine south."

"The hell and gone from anywhere!" Murray remarked explosively.

"Indian Ocean for sure" was Carrington's input.

"Yes, sir. Specifically, a place called Kerguelen Island."

Chapter Eight

General Belinda Hettrick had somehow managed to pull the right strings or push the right buttons in the office of the deputy chief of staff for personnel.

"Corporal, please tell me why you applied for duty in the Washington Greys," Major Curt Carson asked the image of the soldier on the video screen.

A mere personnel interview didn't rate the use of the wide-band holographic conferencing capability of the Army's communication system. But the face of the young girl's image on the screen showed a broad, round face that was somewhat flat with subdued cheekbones and vaguely Oriental features. She wore her black hair bound up in several long braids on her head. "Major Carson, I'm the eighth generation of my family to serve the United States Army and the first woman in my family to do so. I wish to serve in your unit because the Sierra Charlies of the Seventeenth Iron Fist Division are the only troops in the Army who fight the way my ancestors did."

This took Curt aback and piqued his curiosity at the same time. The Army's 101 personnel files no longer indicated such personal factors as religious or ethnic background. So, Curt asked her, "Corporal, do you mind if I ask you who your ancestors were?"

"Not at all, Major," she replied with swelling pride in her voice. But it wasn't vain pride. "My ancestors never fought against the United States Army. From 1875 onward, they served as valuable allies on the Great Plains with Brigadier General George Crook and fought with units of the Fourth Infantry that were later incorporated into the Third Robot Infantry, the Washington Greys. I'm a direct descendant of White Man Runs Him, a Crow Indian scout who served with the United States cavalry during the Indian Wars. The Crow Indians have served with honor ever since."

Curt raised his eyebrows. "That partially explains your unusual name, Corporal."

Corporal Dyani Motega smiled and replied, "Yes, Major. Although it may seem unusual to some, it's an Amer-indian name. My grandfather translated our family name from English back to its original form, and it's now our legal family name."

"If you don't mind my asking, what does it mean?"

Without hesitation, she replied, "I am 'Deer Arrow.' "

"And you're a full-blooded Crow Indian?"

"I don't know exactly, Major. Mostly, I guess. Some blood from other tribes got mixed in over the years on the reservations and in various Indian schools. My family tried to keep the records accurate, but that's often difficult to do after eight generations. But I consider myself to be a Crow Indian."

"I can tell you're proud of it," Curt remarked.

"Yes, sir! I am." she told him bluntly. She was duly respectful but never obsequious during the entire interview. Curt sensed immediately that this young woman knew who she was and what she wanted from the system.

Her appraisal of the Sierra Charlies tactics as being similar to Indian counterparts fascinated Curt. He'd never considered them in that light. So, he asked, "So you think the Sierra Charlies fight with Indian tactics?"

"Sir, I've studied the reports from your last three operations," she explained in a serious tone, her face impassive. "The Sierra Charlies don't fight actual Indian tactics, but you use the closest modern version. My forefathers were horsemen and then infantrymen and then tankers. My father was a warbot brainy, but only because that was the *only* combat assignment available. If you accept me, I'll be the first of my family in several generations to be a real field combat soldier again."

Curt watched her image intently. "Corporal, we don't fight warbot tactics. In a Sierra Charlie outfit, you can be killed. Really killed. The

Washington Greys have suffered casualties in our last three operations. Are you fully aware of this possibility?"

"Yes, sir. Although I don't intend to be killed or wounded, I know that the possibility exists. I think I'm willing to accept that reality. But I won't know for sure until I have to face the situation in combat. But I'm probably going to be scared as hell, sir! And I'll have to deal with that myself when the time comes." In her quiet, impassive, and controlled way, she was certainly gung-ho and fired-up, Curt decided.

Dyani Motega's 101 File record was sparse, as it is with any new soldier. A mere 19 years old, she'd enlisted as soon as she was old enough to sign up, and she'd just finished Basic at Fort Benning. She hadn't led her class at Benning. The comments on her training evaluation forms indicated that her instructors believed she was dedicated, motivated, capable of learning. When given a direct order, she'd carry it out, but the reason she didn't score at the top of her class was her demonstrated individuality in combat training exercises. She didn't seem to be totally willing to knuckle under to superior officers when she thought a better way to do something was available to her that didn't countermand the orders she'd been given. Hence, she didn't come out of Benning at the top of her class. Otherwise, she'd done exceptionally well.

Curt thought he knew why. It was in her genes.

However, Basic training never made a soldier. Nor is it possible for any superior officer to really tell whether or not a person is a good combat soldier before combat occurs. So Curt was far more interested in the person's background, which, to him, meant a great deal more in the case of Dyani Motega. It indicated a family commitment to military service, plus a consideration for tradition. Curt knew from his own situation that these two things counted quite heavily on the side of a good combat trooper in the twenty-first-century all-volunteer Army, which demanded that its combat soldiers be intelligent as well as physically fit and thoroughly trained. Tradition and unit pride had a lot to do with the fact that the modern Army was, by all standards of past comparison and current performance, an adult, professional military force.

But he knew a potential problem lurked in Carson's Companions. "Corporal, if you're accepted into Carson's Companions of the Washington Greys, you'll be serving under a platoon sergeant from Montana. Do you think that will cause any problems?" Curt would have to run this past Platoon Sergeant Tracy Dillon, too, of course. But he had to learn whether or not this Crow Indian maid might harbor some resentment against the people who took her tribe's land a couple of centuries ago.

Her reply was immediate. "No, sir! Not at all! At least, not in my case," Corporal Dyani Motega stated emphatically. "I've never been to Montana. As my One-oh-one indicates, I was born at Fort Riley, Kansas. But, like any Army brat, sir, I've lived on Army posts all over the world. I hold no grudges handed down from past generations. The world was different then. I've got to live in this world."

Curt had made up his mind. But he had to check the situation with Dillon. "Corporal, thank you for the interview. I must tell you that I'm impressed. Let me run this by some of my subordinates, and you'll hear from me no later than Monday morning."

"Thank you, sir. I hope Sergeant Dillon won't have any heartburn about me," she told him quite frankly. "And it would be an honor, sir, for a Motega to serve again with a Carson."

In response to Curt's startled expression, which came as a result of her revelation that she knew a great deal about Carson's Companions, Corporal Motega added, "Sir, you should know that I've done my homework."

"That you have, Corporal. That you have."

After punching off, Curt noted that it was too late in the day to call Tracy Dillon. It was chow time, but perhaps Curt could find the platoon sergeant at the Club afterward. It was Friday, and Wild Bill Bellamack had called for a Stand-to at 1730. That was becoming a traditional part of Bellamack's style of command, just as it had been with Belinda Hettrick. It was a time for relaxation after a week of hard work, a chance to socialize, an opportunity to let off steam, and a chance to speak unofficially with superiors and subordinates alike.

Furthermore, in the modern Army, the artificial separation between officers and NCOs had disappeared more as a result of social progress than from any effort for democratization. Technology had been the leveling factor. The differences between commissioned and noncommissioned officers not only lay in the different methods of appointment and promotion, but primarily in the areas of education and responsibility. In this regard, the Army had become less like the classical conscript armies of the past, which had to enforce strict discipline by often brutal methods, and more like modern nonmilitary organizations with their distinctions between managers and workers or engineers and technicians. The old military discrimination between officers and NCOs, inherited from Europe, had finally succumbed to the sentiments expressed in the Declaration of Independence.

So, there was only one regimental Club.

If you didn't like it, you didn't have to go there. If a Stand-to was ordered, you had to go but you had to stay only long enough to make your presence known to the CO. But from a practical standpoint, one who didn't participate in the activities of the Club probably was having some personal problem with the situation, which called for a visit from the chaplain and, in the extreme, transfer out. But that rarely happened. The *esprit de corps* and the morale of the Washington Greys were always high because of a proud 250-year tradition exemplified by the array of streamers on the regimental colors.

Curt powered down his terminal and his communications unit, decided he'd better shave before going to the Club, and walked out to go to his quarters. The light turned itself off as he left.

Chapter Nine

Everyone was at the Club because everyone knew the consequences of denying tradition. The most recent example had been the arms scam in the 21st Robot Infantry, the Gimlet regiment, from which Lieutenant Colonel Bellamack had come. The Gimlet regiment had been effectively destroyed; the Army was still trying to rebuild it afresh.

When Curt showed up on schedule at the Club, it was obvious that the Greys were feeling rather rebellious that night. They'd been training intensely but for no specific operation or objective. Somewhere in the melee, a group was singing:

"So come join the Army today.
There's medals, promotions, and pay;
And there's no prohibitions on heroic missions;
I'll give you my place if you'll stay!

See them marching in formation,
See them lining up by grade;
Every day a new vacation;
That's the Army on parade!"

When Curt checked in with the colonel, the regimental commander looked around the Club and observed, "It threatens to be a social furball tonight."

"Yes, sir. Everyone's a bit uptight, partly because of the McCarthy experiments," Curt reckoned.

"More damned trouble there?" Bellamack asked. "I thought we got the harness situation straightened out."

"It's the damned tech-weenies, Colonel," Curt explained as a robot brought him a drink. "They're interested only in their goddamned experiment!"

"I know. You aren't the first company commander who's come sniveling about it today. That's why I asked Colonel Lovell to show tonight," Bellamack told him. "I want her to hear the bitching and take some of the heat."

"She here?"

"Negatory. She may have gone back to McCarthy for the weekend."

Curt was disappointed. Willa Lovell was a highly attractive woman. She was fun to be with at the Club and elsewhere.

He found lieutenants Adonica Sweet and Jerry Allen together as usual and as anticipated. Off duty, the two seemed to be inseparable. This bothered Curt a little bit. As a result of the kind of lethal business they were in, either of them might not come back in one piece from the next actual shooting mission. While this wasn't a problem for warbot brainies, in Curt's opinion it wasn't a good thing for a Sierra Charlie to grow too emotionally attached to another Sierra Charlie.

But he was really searching out Platoon Sergeant Tracy Dillon, whom he found at the bar with Platoon Sergeant Betty Jo Trumble of Morgan's Marauders. "Evening, Major!" Dillon called out as Curt slid in next to them. "Buy you a drink?"

Curt returned the salutation, set his glass on the bar, and said, "Thanks, Tracy, I'm nursing this Scotch and water. I wanted to tell you I've found a new corporal to take over your old squad."

"Orgasmic! Means I won't have to continue wearing two hats!" Dillon replied enthusiastically.

"But I wanted to check with you first to make sure you wouldn't have problems."

"Problems, Major?"

"Corporal Dyani Motega will be the first female squad leader in the Greys," Curt began.

"Got no problem with that, Major!" Dillon told him. "Before I joined the Greys, I didn't believe a woman could put up with all the dirt and fear of combat. Jeez, was I ever wrong! Some of the gals in the Greys could plow my field any time they wanted to. Especially Edie Sampson."

"The gal I've got in mind is also a Crow Indian," Curt pointed out, watching Dillon closely.

Only a slight hesitation marked Dillon's reaction to this news. He quickly asked, "So?"

"So, I wanted to make sure you have no problems because you happened to grow up in Montana."

There was just a slight pause before Dillon replied with a shrug, "I never knew much about the people on the reservation southeast of Billings," he explained. "I'm from the Great Falls area. We never had much contact with the Indians."

"Tracy, I noticed a slight hesitation in your answers," Curt pointed out. "Come clean with me. Do you have any problem being with or working with Indians?"

This time the platoon sergeant's response was instantaneous. "No, sir!" Then he added, "But you've got to remember I'm a Westerner."

"Yeah, I know it. That's why I asked you about Corporal Motega. And please elaborate on your last statement."

"Out where I come from, we're aware of the Indians," Dillon admitted. "And maybe a little worried about some of them. Maybe because of stories. Maybe because some people are still feeling a little guilty about what the white man did to the Indians."

"What do you mean, Tracy?" Sergeant Betty Jo Trumble spoke up. "The guilty types are usually Easterners who came west recently. Hell, I'm an Okie, and I grew up with Indians all around me. We made them rich! They still own most of the state, and they've done real well with all the oil money they've gotten. Took them a while in some cases, but that was a long time ago, and they've learned. What's so different about the Indians up in Montana? I hear they got real rich with the coal they got on their lands."

"I don't have any trouble with anybody anywhere who's good at what they do and who doesn't want to get in my pockets to pay for something I didn't have no part in," Dillon tried to explain. "So, I don't abide the Indians who try to make me feel guilty for what happened back in the nineteenth century. I guess it depends a whole hell of a lot on what kind of a person this new corporal is."

"I know enough about her to want her in the Companions," Curt told him frankly. "She's an eighth-generation Army brat and enlisted the first day she was qualified. She's especially proud of one of her ancestors who was a Crow Indian scout for the cavalry."

"Hey, orgasmic!" Betty Jo Trumble erupted jubilantly. "And she'll be the first female Sierra Charlie squad leader, too! Major, I think you made a great choice!"

"Major," Tracy Dillon admitted, "I got no heartburn if she's the kind of people I think she is from your description."

"Good! I just wanted to make sure, Tracy," Curt told him, somewhat relieved. "You're going to be her immediate superior, and I didn't want to saddle you with a situation you'd have trouble with."

"Sir, if this new corporal is anything like Lieutenant Clinton or Sergeant Sampson. I think she'll be a credit to the outfit," Dillon said.

Curt felt better, but he knew he'd have to stay on his toes with the situation. He told himself that maybe he was worrying unnecessarily, perhaps because of his own background. So he went looking for some more of his Companions, primarily Lieutenant Kitsy Clinton.

Captain Alexis Morgan found him first. She looked like she was having a good time. Company command was obviously a strain on her, and she was just as obviously relieving tension that evening. "Well, hello there! What's this hot skinny I get from Rumor Control that you're getting an Indian scout?"

Curt looked quickly at her and told her sharply, "Alexis, that's the last time l want to hear you use that term in connection with my new squad leader!"

"Oh, boy, aren't you taut tonight!" Alexis observed.

"Corporal Dyani Motega has an outstanding background."

"So, the rumor has it. Pretty name. Unusual. Sorry about that! I didn't think it was a sensitive issue."

"It isn't yet, and I don't want to let it get that way, especially before she arrives. She's going to have a tough enough time integrating into a new outfit right out of Basic. So, apology accepted. Let's sit down before we fall down," Curt suggested, motioning toward a table.

Alexis sat, and it was obvious to Curt that she'd been under pressure.

Curt looked her over. "You, dear lady, have obviously had one hell of a rough Week."

"Does it show that badly?"

"In some places and in some ways, yeah," Curt said, trying to draw her out and get her to talk about her problems. "It would be interesting to find out if your gripes coincide with mine."

"Goddamned McCarthy harnesses," Alexis complained bitterly. "Bad enough that the tech-weenies keep screwing around with our warbots trying to 'improve' them. Now they're wiring us up for computer control. Just a damned good thing we don't have to wear those harnesses when we're off duty or in bed…"

"Yeah, I draw the line at computerized sex, too."

"Kinky. Real kinky," Alexis bubbled. "Someone will do it."

"Probably already have, judging from the porno disks. So, what else is bugging you, Allie?"

Alexis sighed deeply, then growled, "Dammit, sometimes I wish these goddamned training exercises weren't so realistic! They're killing my Marauders! And killing me! Something must be wrong. I find myself wishing that somebody somewhere would do something nasty so we'd get the usual orders telling us to go out and piss on another brushfire."

The whole regiment was apparently feeling that way, not that any of them were real war lovers. But endless high intensity training can wear down an outfit. And they were becoming bored. The Washington Greys were reacting to the situation that evening. The Club Rebellion continued as the chorus of the old ditty was heard throughout the Club:

"Bless 'em all, bless 'em all!
The long and the short and the tall!
Bless all the generals and their bloody buns,
Bless all the colonels, the fat-headed ones!
I'm saying goodbye to them all,
The long and the short and the tall.
Here's to you and your sister,
You can shove it up, mister,
I'm going back home in the fall!"

That's not where the Washington Greys were going, but they didn't know it right then.

Beer mug in hand, Regimental Sergeant Major Henry Kester approached the two of them and asked, "May I join you for a moment?"

It would be a cold day in hell when Curt refused any request from Henry Kester. The fact, that the old warrior had sought them out told Curt that Kester had something he wanted to say to them. "Take the load off your bunions and put it on your buns, Henry. How goes the rat race?"

"The rats are winnin'," was the old sergeant's distracted response. He went on, "I couldn't help noticin' the daggers flyin' between the two of you. It ain't none of my business, of course, but may an old friend say somethin'?"

"Henry, I'll always listen to you," Alexis admitted. "When you were the Companions' first sergeant, you saved my ass more than a couple of times and thank God you're again in a position where protocol allows me to use your shoulder for support."

"The hell with protocol," Kester told her. "I'm available at any time for any reason, ma'am. Now, if you'll pardon a personal observation, I've noticed from two points of view - as the Companion first sergeant and as regimental sergeant major - that commanding separate companies has had a definite effect on the two of you. It ain't been helped, either, by the regiment being in a constant state of overtraining; fighters should be used and allowed a whole hell of a lot of time off when things get dull and boring. It's been a long time - since before the Mexican operation - since the two of you conveniently disappeared at the same time on the same weekend. It don't fool an old soldier."

He held up his hand as Alexis tried to interrupt. "Humor an old comrade for a moment, Captain. Both of you are hot-blooded young war horses, and to you variety is the spice of life. Or it damned well ought to be. No one else except the two of you gave much of a damn about what happened in Trinidad and Namibia and Sonora when ships passed in the night, so to speak. I amend that: A lot of your friends wondered why both of you let your brass get green and tried to get even with each other." Again, he held up his hand to silence what Curt started to say. "You don't need to justify anythin' to me. Or anyone else. Take it from an old soldier: Yield to temptation, because it may not come your way again. And be glad when it does. Do I need to say more than to point out that a long weekend's comin' up with nothin' goin' on here and Tucson not that far away...? Now, I've shot my wad and I'll shut up and let you buy me that beer."

"The colonel..." Curt began.

"The colonel is a good commanding officer," Kester pointed out unnecessarily. "He knows his people. He's a relative newcomer and too much of a gentleman to talk to you the way I just did...but I was never authorized to be a gentleman by act of Congress. He told me to give these to you." He pulled two folded hard-copy printouts from his shirt pocket and handed one to each officer.

It was a three-day special pass for each of them. Curt looked at his former first sergeant. "Damn your ass, Henry, why couldn't you just give these to us and let nature take its course?"

"Because I wasn't sure it would."

Alexis smiled at him. "Henry, you're right. You're getting too old for this sort of stuff. Your judgment is slipping. But thank you for your concern. Major, is there any need for further discussion?"

"I don't believe so, Captain."

"Very well, Major, I'll meet you in the parking lot in fifteen minutes. Be there!"

"How about that?" Regimental Sergeant Major Henry Kester said out loud to himself, because the two young officers appeared to vanish instantaneously. "I must be getting' old and slippin'. I give some friendly advice and get stiffed out of a drink!"

Chapter Ten

The approach to Kerguelen Island was made under deep stealth conditions at low altitude with totally passive surveillance techniques.

Captain Roger Willcox was getting stiff and cramped from sitting in the cockpit for more than twenty hours. The biotechnology computer of the SRO-17 Albatross did its best to make him comfortable, but neuroelectronic stimulation of nerves and muscles was only effective for about this length of time. Willcox had subsisted on a very low residue diet for days before the mission, and his piddle pack had a lot of capacity left. But these very long multiday low-speed missions stressed a human being's body and brain in spite of linkage and artificial intelligence.

It was a long over-water flight south from the main U.S. Aerospace Force base at Bahrain. And there was nothing out there but water and sky and clouds. It would be an even longer flight before the long-range, low observable strategic reconnaissance observation plane finally touched down near Perth, Australia.

The mission objective was simple: Get very high-resolution images of Kerguelen Island without befog detected. Stealth was important. The United States didn't want to tip off whoever was running that satellite-infecting station on Kerguelen. So active space surveillance technologies couldn't be used.

High-resolution surveillance and reconnaissance satellites couldn't do it. Kerguelen Island was cloud-covered at this time of year, April being the start of the winter season in the southern hemisphere. Although infrared sensors and side-looking synthetic-aperture radars could cut through clouds, the resolution on the former wasn't good enough and the active emissions of the latter might give away the fact that the island was being scanned.

Nor could an HS-40 Black Lightning or other high-flying hypersonic recon aircraft or spacecraft do the job. The clouds were low-lying, probably down to a thousand meters or less above the waters of the Indian Ocean. And a hypersonic recon craft could be detected if the satellite infection station on Kerguelen happened to have high-resolution Doppler radar as part of any air defense system. No one knew what the detection and defense capabilities of that facility were.

So, the only way to get the data was to go in low, slow, and silent.

Which meant using an SRO-17 Albatross, a craft highly stealthed against radar and infrared, slow-flying with a low wing loading to minimize the inevitable turbulence caused by anything that flies through the air, silent as a sailplane over target, equipped with side-looking passive sensors responding to illumination of the target by space-borne discrete-frequency ultraviolet lasers, and human controlled because of the extremely long range over which it could operate.

Willcox was also maintaining communications silence. In fact, all emitters and transmitters on board were off. As the island target grew closer, he instructed the aircraft's robot pilot to slowly reduce infrared and turbulence emissions.

According to plan, the SRO-17 was also watching for anyone out there painting the aircraft with radar or lidar.

"Shit," Wilcox thought to himself and wished he could. "Anyone on that rock with any sense at all is inside in this weather. Only the goddamned penguins would be crazy enough to be outside!" As he talked to himself, the SRO- 17 was being bounced around in gusty winds, its hydrophobic surfaces shedding the rime ice that tried to form and adhere as the craft flew through endless snow and ice showers a thousand meters above the churning whitecaps of the Indian Ocean below.

But his mission rules were quite specific: Get in, get the data, and get out without being detected.

That's what the United States Aerospace Force trained him to do and paid him for doing.

Except this was no practice mission over northern Alaska or Greenland or Baffin Island. Or skirting the Soviet Union or the People's Republic of China on an BLINT mission. It was a long, long flight almost to the very limits of the range of the aircraft and the capability of the human pilot.

The SRO-17 was a very "black" and supersecret aircraft. Everyone else was going high and fast. The Albatross was different in its capability to go low and slow. And quietly. Its ancestors were the Quiet Stars and other silent aircraft used in Vietnam in the twentieth century. And it took a special breed of pilots to fly them.

The turbulence of the wind bounced the craft around in the sky. It was almost at the limit of the capability of the camera scan platforms to maintain pointing stability and accuracy. If this kept up or got worse over Kerguelen, it might abort the mission. Willcox didn't want that to happen. He didn't want to have to do this again real soon.

The long, slim wings bent up and down as the wind gusts hit the craft. A casual observer, not knowing that the wing structures were made of highly engineered composite materials designed to flex, might have expected the wings to be twisted off at any moment. But Willcox was the pilot who'd ridden a Kansas thunderstorm up and out the top of the anvil head. So, to him this turbulence was merely irritating, not terrorizing.

The aircraft "told" him that Kerguelen Island was now 45 kilometers ahead and to the east. As it had been instructed, the ship's artificially intelligent command computer began turning on various sensors.

Willcox noted with satisfaction that no radar or lidar was painting the ship.

Maybe he'd pull this one off on the first pass!

He sure as hell didn't want to have to stick around, make another pass, and thus double the chances that he might be detected and attacked.

And he didn't like the idea that he was reconnoitering the total unknown. If he'd gone against the Soviets or Chinese or even the ABC Allianza, he would have been briefed on potential threats ahead of time. But no one knew what the threat might be on Kerguelen Island or who might be doing things there.

He picked up a visual, and it was a bleak sight as the SR0-17 slipped in and out of the clouds at 1000 meters. He wouldn't command the ship to go lower; the summit of Kerguelen's highest mountain, Mount Ross, was still above his altitude at 1721 meters, but he'd stay at this altitude unless the forward visibility went to worms. If the sensors could see in the visual range or if he lost situational awareness, he'd have to turn south to clear the island because he didn't want to climb up into the icing and turbulence of the cloud deck overhead.

The infrared sensors gave him a very low contrast picture. Everything was just goddamned cold out there. He did note with interest several hot spots here and there. Were those coming from his target? He spotted more infrared targets where Port-aux-Francaise was supposed to be.

What the hell were the other i-r targets? There were a piss pot full of them out there on those mountainsides.

No radars or lidars painted the ship as it silently flew along the ragged southern coast of the barren island.

The Albatross popped in and out of the low clouds as it made its pass. Willcox was certain he hadn't been spotted visually. Anyone outdoors down there on a cold, windy, snowy day like this sure as hell wouldn't be looking up for aircraft. They'd be trying to keep from being blown away.

Since he hadn't been detected, should he stretch his luck and swing north of the island, then turn to make another pass farther north of the first pass? His instincts told him to get the hell out of there. But if he didn't get a second pass and provide some super-stereo data on those unknown hot spots, he might be sent back to do the job again. And he didn't like the idea of having to do that.

The U.S. Aerospace Force was supposed to be a professional outfit, he reminded himself. That meant it did the job it was given. So, at a distance of 100 kilometers east of Kerguelen, he added power, turned north, and swung in a huge arc around the island to approach it again from the west.

This time, he had the SRO-17 make a second pass 60 kilometers to the north of the first ground track.

The damned hot spots were still there!

That's enough, he decided. He was responsible only for getting the data, not interpreting it. Survival overwhelmed curiosity. With the wind at his tail, he told the aircraft to settle down on a course direct for Perth.

Hours later, technicians pulled the data pack out of the belly of the SRO-17, and then biotechnicians extracted the weary pilot and took him off to be ministered to by the base biotechnology computer. The data had a Cosmic Priority on it. It was relayed raw by satellite from Perth to Tiffany, and then the data pack was loaded on a special fractional orbital courier that would deliver the actual data recordings to Washington 45 minutes later.

When it was seen by Generals Carrington, Brooke, Murray, and Chaffee, the first pass at data reduction had been done.

"Dammit!" Carrington swore as he studied it. "Nothing but nothing on visual!"

"Did you expect that?" Murray asked.

"I expected to see *something* with this sort of resolution!" the chairman of JCS replied. "And there are so damned many i-r targets that they all can't be the infection station!"

"Hang tight," Murray advised him. "The second pass is coming now. I've asked that the data be correlated with the latest French charts of the island."

This time, the i-r data and the passive ultraviolet readings were overlaid on a three-dimensional wire grid chart of the island itself. Then the computer laid on the French chart data from *l'Institut Geographique National*.

"That's better," Murray remarked as he looked it over.

"Hot spots are still there," Chaffee pointed out.

"True, but notice that some of them correlate with known fumaroles. Kerguelen is a volcanic island," Murray told him.

"Not all of them correspond to volcanic hot spots," Brooke said.

"Well, gentlemen, the French data is eleven years old," Murray admitted, "but it's their latest information. Not a whole hell of a lot changes on that island, so there's no urgent requirement for the French to spend francs to update maps and charts more often than every twenty years or so."

"Who cares, anyway? Who in the hell *lives* in a place like that?" Chaffee asked rhetorically.

"About thirty French oceanographers and meteorologists," Murray told him. "They man the scientific research and communication station at Port-aux-Francaise. They're reprovisioned and rotated by a ship that visits twice a year. Basically, Kerguelen Island has no permanent population."

"Except penguins, I guess," Carrington mused. "Okay, so where's the infection station? Sure as hell can't be French! They wouldn't put it at Port-aux-Francaise anyway. They're the first to be suspect, and that would be the first place anyone would look…"

"No, it's not the French," Chaffee ventured to guess. "Beaudry is far more likely to be on Shishkov's list than ours."

"And France has no problems with the Soviets," Murray added.

"Be that as it may," Carrington remarked, trying to get the meeting back on track, "where the hell is the infection station located?"

"Could be any of those uncorrelated hot spots," Brooke mused.

"What do we have here? One-centimeter-resolution data, I understand. Right?" Chaffee asked.

"Right," Carrington echoed.

"So, we're looking at the big picture on screens with much lower resolution. The data reduction people sure as hell ought to be able to go in there and study each uncorrelated hot spot at high resolution," Chaffee suggested.

"Uh, yup!" Murray agreed, then suggested, "Why not send a direct dub of the raw data over to my people at Langeley? We'll put it on the new gigacomputer for gross screening and use Carlotto image enhancement techniques to spot unusual data so we can then look at suspect spots."

"We can do better than that. Anyone who's established a manned station on Kerguelen will have to supply it," Chaffee pointed out. "That means logistical support by either long-range supersonic transport aerodynes or ships. Even a 'dyne needs a landing pad, especially the big cargo jobs; we can look for the distinctive shape of a pad. If supply is by ship, it would have to get in and out without being seen from Port-aux-Francaise…which means either a site on the western side of the island or the use of a submarine."

"Are we going to need Navy input here?" Carrington wondered.

"Maybe," Murray replied. "But let's not waste time. Ed, you can call in Lew if we need him."

"Okay, Al, can we count on you to supplement the Aerospace Force data reduction on this, which Mike will monitor?" the chairman of the joint chiefs wanted to know as he tried to organize this project. "In the meantime, we've got to select the assault force to send in there once the station is located."

"Can do," Murray remarked. "And I'm ashamed to say that we'll probably have to call on the Army, Brooke. The Marine Corps doesn't have the strength to do it these days." The Army's technological clout with the Robot Infantry and the subsequent decline of the use of manned combat forces had reduced the Marine Corps to providing embassy and naval base guards plus ship-based companies. These days, the Marines were indeed the few and the proud. Actually, the Marines had no one but themselves to blame because they'd stoutly resisted robotization; they didn't want to become warbot-weenies, as they called the Army warbot brainies, and they'd refused again and again to integrate women into any sort of combat position. Maybe the Army's revival of human combat troops in the Sierra Charlie regiments would also revive the Marine Corps of old.

"Otis, it's going to be up to the Army to provide the assault troops to hit the station when we find it," Carrington pointed out to the Army chief of staff. "Again, since we're going to do this on our own because Al doesn't really trust the others on the UN Space Security Commission, it's going to have to be pretty well covered. Got any ideas off the top of your head?"

"Well, Ed, it's probably going to be another Sierra Charlie operation," Otis Brooke admitted.

"What's the matter with the warbot outfits?"

"Nothing, and I'd like to use one of them as well. That would give me the option of flexibility when Al and Mike find the station," Brooke pointed out. "I'll probably use the Dragoons or the Ready Rifles from the Twenty-sixth Division as my warbot outfit. I think I can pull them out of Sakhalin and Thailand without causing too much fuss at the moment; those hot spots are relatively cool. I've got two Sierra Charlie regiments - the Washington Greys and the Cottonbalers from Jake Carlisle's Seventeenth Division. I'll probably use the Greys; they're experienced whereas the Cottonbalers are in the Virgin Islands fine-tuning their transition from a full Robot Infantry unit to Sierra Charlies."

"Otis, we've been sending the Greys in to piss on brushfires a hell of a lot recently," Carrington recalled. "Would your people consider setting up the Sierra Charlies as a separate special action brigade?"

"You mean like the old Special Forces or the Delta Force?" Brooke shrugged. "Maybe. But the problem with outfits like that is keeping them busy. They go to hell in a hurry if they just sit around and try to maintain capability by training. That's why the airborne and special forces rotted away in the past. I'm not sure we know enough yet to keep such special units properly motivated.

"Well, it's a side issue at the moment, Otis, but you might want to put some of your staffers to thinking about it. Maybe it will give that new one-star - Hettrick, I believe her name is - maybe it'll give her something to keep her busy." Carrington had no male chauvinism in him; the Aerospace Force had a lot of women pilots who were pretty damned good. And the flyboys thought they were the first to allow women into combat because they always prided themselves on being far more liberal and less tradition-bound than the Army. On the other hand, the Army could have told them a few things about women in combat going back to the Revolutionary War.

"I'm obviously going to need naval support and transportation," Brooke reminded the CJCS. "And how far can we go before we'll need a presidential order to proceed?"

"The President is aware of the situation," Carrington assured him and looked at Murray as he added, "We keep him advised of the situation at each morning's briefing. When the time comes to put the troops ashore on Kerguelen, you'll have your ass covered with all the necessary paperwork. And it's so goddamned far away from anything that we can probably maintain security even from the news media and then announce it after the fact. That would certainly simplify matters. Worst that can happen is that we disturb a few penguins and French penguin watchers. In the meantime, let's move right along on our assigned tasks. While Mike and Al are pinpointing the objective, Otis can be getting the troops in position. Otis, pick a combined arms commander for the mission, preferably Army since your bodies will be doing most of the nasty work. And let's move right along. God knows we don't want this Kerguelen infection station to knock out any of our space surveillance stuff. That might bring the alligators right up to the door."

Chapter Eleven

It was cool at sunrise on the slopes of Mount Lemmon at 1500 meters altitude. It was high enough that ponderosa pines could grow, even at the latitude of Tucson. No clouds were visible in the dawn sky.

But it was warm and comfortable inside the Xanadu Dome. And the transparent low-reflecting plastic barrier was totally invisible. It was as though the sumptuous and sybaritic dome's interior were somehow outside and yet at the same time inside.

To the two occupants, it was as if they were a thousand kilometers from anyone and especially from civilization. Yet within a few meters, carefully hidden and unobtrusive under the floor on the lower level of the dome, legions of robots waited patiently to provide whatever service the occupants desired.

It was the ultimate retreat from the everyday world, a place where one could really get away from it all.

And it was indeed luxurious.

"I've never experienced a more beautiful dawn," whispered Alexis Morgan, her naked body caressed by the soft, slick satin coverings of the bed.

"It's been a long time, hasn't it?" Curt Carson asked unnecessarily.

"Yes. Too long. Thank you, dear, for splurging on Xanadu. It's just what a tired warrior needed." She moved slightly against him, intensifying the highly sensual feelings of the moment.

"I agree. This has turned a tired warrior into a tiger," he told her, reciprocating with a slight movement on his part.

"Oh, yes!" she breathed. "I wish this could go on forever."

"Then we wouldn't have the next time to look forward to," Curt reminded her as he caressed her cheek.

"Just think. For the first time in I don't know how long, I'm rested and bathed and fed and otherwise totally satiated," she admitted. "I don't hurt anywhere. In fact, I feel good everywhere."

"So do I, and you're very good, Allie. You've always been good medicine for me. You're as tender here as you are ferocious in the field," Curt said, deliberately flattering her because she liked that.

"A woman likes to hear that."

"And you're all woman."

"Which is why I hate to share you with others."

"There's a lot of both of us to share," Curt pointed out. "Dear, move a little this way right here...Orgasmic! You know, when you're rich, it's easy to share because there's so much..."

"You won't be very rich after you pay the tab for this place," Alexis guessed.

"Money is only a way of keeping score," he advised her. "The pay scale be damned! We're both rich in other ways!"

"But it wouldn't be right for a girl not to be jealous..."

Curt didn't reply to that. He was feeling very good, and it was obvious that the feeling was very, very mutual in the way Alexis was acting and responding. He muttered softly in her ear, "You taste good...and feel good...The tech-weenies will never get their answers. *This* is why we fight!"

"How do I compare?" Alexis wanted to know.

"To what or to whom?" ·

"Zeenat Tej. Or Fredrica Herrero."

"You don't. There is no comparison."

"How should I take that, sir?"

"Any way you want to, but don't belittle yourself in the process, Allie."

"Beast!" She did little things to him.

And he responded in kind.

A very, very soft chiming filled the dome. It was a subdued, unobtrusive sound just barely loud enough to be heard. It was almost apologetic in its act of interruption. People came to Xanadu because they wanted to get away from the world. But there were situations where the patrons had to be reached for emergency reasons. It was only with great reluctance that the management permitted any intrusion on its guests.

Which is why Curt knew the request for communication wasn't trivial.

He suppressed a curse. It wouldn't do any good. Besides, he, too, was rested and well-fed and clean and satiated as well. It was hard to get angry when the world had been so goddamned good to him for two days.

"Do you have to respond?" Alexis wondered.

"I should, you know. They don't intrude here unless it's a message from a disembodied voice on high or something of similar clout."

"And you answer to a higher authority, of course."

"Always. Anything with silver oak leaves or higher rank. And if the person interrupting doesn't qualify, I'll continue to be catatonic insofar as the rest of the world is concerned..." Curt disengaged himself, rolled over, and said to the phone, "Audio only! And this damned well better be important!"

"Is your job important, Curt?" It was the unmistakable voice of Major Pappy Gratton, the regimental adjutant.

"Hi, Pappy! Sure as hell is! And it must be damned important for you to call me," Curt replied. He was pissed that the three-day vacation had been interrupted, but he'd gotten rested enough with Alexis to have a better outlook on the world. "What did you do to get through?"

"Told that overprotective sonofabitch who screens incoming communications there that I was calling pursuant to a presidential order."

"Oh, shit! I know what that means! Here we go again!" Curt burst out.

"Right you are. All leaves and passes revoked. Recall, old chap. You and Alexis stop whatever you're doing and shag ass down here ass-app. Oscar meeting at thirteen hundred hours today. Colonel Bellamack says be there!" the adjutant told him.

Curt scrounged around and found liis watch. It was the first time he'd looked at it in two days. It said 0624 Zone 7 time. "Pappy, I'm not sure we can get down off this mountain and over the road to Huachuca in time to be there by thirteen hundred. Any way we can get an aerodyne pickup?"

"Negatory. Hope you've got a vehicle."

"Yeah, I picked up a rental heap in Sierra Vista Friday night."

"So, get moving."

"It's more than a hundred and fifty clicks..."

"So, get moving," Gratton repeated.

"We'll be there," Curt promised and switched off.

"It figures," Alexis muttered. "I've often suspected that the Army implanted some sort of little gadget in me when I went through one of those damned medical tests early on. Any time I start enjoying some of what I'm paid to defend, it sounds an alarm somewhere, and the Army calls and wants me to come back and get tired and dirty and miserable again."

"If I use my influence," Curt kidded her, trying to negate some of the disappointment so obvious in her tone of voice, "I can maybe get you transferred to a nice, cushy staff job somewhere..."

She threw a pillow at him in a release of tension. "And leave the field clear for Kitsy Clinton? Nuts! By the way, if you're unhappy, I understand the Marines are looking for a. few good men...But, come to think of it, you probably won't qualify..."

He tossed the pillow back, whereupon she attacked. The impromptu wrestling match ended when he let her pin him.

"Uncle?"

"Flag of truce," Curt suggested. "Time out. Let's continue this later. If we don't get the hell out of here soon, we'll miss the tick for the Oscar brief."

Alexis sighed and got up. "Back to the real world!"

They made it back to Fort Huachuca just barely in time. "You've got eight minutes to make the Oscar meet," Pappy Gratton told them.

"Would have had more time except for a run-in with the state gendarmes," Curt admitted.

"Let me guess," the adjutant remarked. "Speeding ticket."

"Yeah, and no consideration for those of us who fight to defend the free world," Curt muttered.

"Well, I wouldn't think you were an officer either!" Gratton said as he looked Curt up and down. "Except for the fact that you dress as badly as most officers who aren't used to wearing civvies every day."

"What's wrong with my clothes?" Curt wanted to know. "I paid a wad for this sport coat."

"Some horse is going to get cold tonight," was Gratton's only comment. "I suggest you ditch it and show up in shirtsleeves, since you don't have time to change anyway. And as for you, Alexis, ditch that hat!"

"What's wrong with my hat?" she asked him, adjusting the green beret on her head. "If I stick a regimental badge on it, it could pass as official special unit head-gear."

"I wouldn't try it," Gratton advised. "Only Green Berets are authorized to wear something like that; the Army has no more Green Berets, but they still have the regulation that says you can't wear it. Besides, Wild Bill Bellamack is in a foul mood. This Sunday afternoon Oscar briefing interrupted his golf game...and he was shooting under a hundred, or so he said. And beating Joan Ward for a change."

"Jeez, no wonder he's in a foul mood. Not many people can beat Joan without a sizable handicap," Curt observed, then turned to Alexis. "Let's go, Captain!"

The two of them showed up in the briefing room hungry and road-weary, wearing the civvies they'd hurriedly donned hours before in the Xanadu Dome. Curt took the adjutant's advice and left his sport coat outside with the rest of his gear.

The Companions were present, all of them in fatigues. It was apparent to Curt that some of them had dressed hurriedly for the Oscar briefing. First Sergeant Edwina Sampson was sharp and natty. So was Lieutenant Kitsy Clinton. But Lieutenant Jerry Allen looked like he'd rushed to make the tick.

"Sorry for the civilian attire," Curt apologized to his company. "I've been on the road since oh-seven-hundred. Jerry, you look like you dragged in from Australia."

Allen smiled wanly and replied, "No, sir, not quite that far. Only the Copper Queen in Bisbee. But that was far enough."

Curt didn't inquire what the lieutenant had been doing in Bisbee. That was Allen's own business. However, Curt was sure Jerry had been accompanied by Lieutenant Adonica Sweet. As long as Jerry Allen maintained a high professional performance level on the job, Curt didn't give a damn what went on off-duty. Except that Curt was worried about Jerry developing too intimate an emotional relationship with the new lieutenant.

"Major, our new squad leader reported aboard this morning," Edie Sampson told him. With a wave of her arm, she motioned someone to come over.

They were joined by a small young girl whose face Curt recognized at once.

"Corporal Motega! Welcome aboard!" he greeted her.

She saluted stiffly and replied, "Major Carson!"

Curt returned the salute and put forth his hand. With a moment's hesitation, Corporal Dyani Motega took it in a surprisingly strong grip.

"Don't be put off by a certain amount of informality, Corporal," Curt told her. "Because we have to live and fight together, the Companions are rather like a large family."

"Yes, sir. So I've noticed, sir," Motega replied curtly. "However, as an Army brat, I've seen this in other outfits."

"Good. Are you getting settled in all right?" Curt asked.

"Sir, it's been rather a rush. I came in at oh-nine-hundred, and it's been busy getting my gear stowed and getting to this Oscar meeting."

"Yeah, it's been a busy Sunday," Curt agreed.

"Any indication of what's going on, Major?" Kitsy Clinton asked.

"You've been here today longer than I have," Curt told her. "What does Rumor Control have to offer?"

"Nothing."

"Nothing?" That was unusual.

"Nothing, Major," Edie Sampson confirmed. "Couldn't even get a rumble out of Henry Kester. He doesn't know, either."

The door on the left side of the platform at the bottom of the briefing amphitheater colloquially known as the "snake pit" opened and Major Joanne Wilkinson, regimental chief of staff, stepped onto the stage. "Ladies and gentlemen of the Greys, the regimental commander!"

" 'Ten-HUT!" barked Regimental Sergeant Major Henry Kester in a parade-ground voice that echoed off the walls.

Lieutenant Colonel William Bellamack, attired in combat cammies, walked through the door. "Carry on," the colonel snapped, then added, "Take your seats." It was as much of an invitation as a command.

Bellamack took center stage and faced them, legs apart and hands clasped behind his back. "Thank you for making every effort to get here on a Sunday afternoon. I know most of you were elsewhere and had to return quickly. Others had plans and activities that were interrupted. I'm sorry about that, but this is the Army, and we're supposed to be ready at any time, including Sundays. We have a tendency to forget Pearl Harbor because it happened a long time ago."

He looked around, then went on in a puzzled tone of voice, "I'm not exactly sure why we got the orders we did. They are the goddamndest orders I've ever received, and I can't make any sense out of them. But I'll let the staff members brief you first. Captain Atkinson?" Bellamack looked directly at his Plans and Operations staffer, then sat down.

Captain Hensley Atkinson was an experienced operations officer. She'd done an outstanding job in Namibia and Sonora. She looked at her commander and acknowledged, "Colonel Bellamack." Then she turned to the regiment. "At oh-four-hundred this morning, JCS Execute Order JCS-OP-thirty-three-dash-two was transmitted by the Seventeenth Iron Fist Robot Infantry Division to the Third Regiment, the Washington Greys. The Regiment has been ordered to participate in Exercise Rapid Reformer. This is a training operation and a test of the ability of the Army to redeploy a regiment of Sierra Charlie forces in the shortest period of time to an overseas location. The exercise will be conducted as if it were an actual combat operation. Therefore, the regiment will begin to redeploy from Fort Huachuca for airlift at twenty-hundred hours today from Libby Army Airfield to Rhine-Main Air Base, Germany, and thence to Wiesbaden. Upon arrival in Wiesbaden, the regiment will report to the commander in chief, European Tactical Command, for billeting to await further orders." She turned to Bellamack and nodded, saying, "Sir!"

"Thank you, Captain. Logistics?" Bellamack spoke up. "Major Benteen?"

The chief of S-4 and the commander of the supply and service company took center stage. "The regiment will deploy with a full complement of personnel and equipment as specified in the Table of Organization and Equipment. However, we shall not deploy with logistical supplies. In short, without ammo, food, water, fuel, or spare clothing sets. The JCS Executive Order specified that the regiment is to receive whatever logistical supplies it requires for any follow-on exercise once it reaches Germany, where these supplies have already been stockpiled. In short, the regiment will deploy ready to fight but without the necessary supplies to do so." He turned to Bellamack, nodded, and said, "Sir!"

"Thank you, Major. Adjutant?"

Major Pappy Gratton took the stage. "All leaves and passes are hereby revoked and canceled. All personnel are hereby on Yellow Combat Alert. For this deployment, each person will wear Mark Eleven database dog tags with all information necessary for overseas deployment - medical and shot records, pay records, and equipment capability records. No other documents or personal effects will be carried. Personnel will operate with standard issue personal and combat gear. Sir!"

"Thank you, Major. Communications and Intelligence?"

"Colonel," was the salutation from Captain John Gibbon, the S-2 staffer and the regimental intelligence and communications unit commander. "We have been instructed that this exercise will be conducted under Tactical Security procedures. Personnel will not be allowed to leave the post or to communicate off-post. All communications links have been either cut or are being monitored. Personnel may contact family members and next of kin upon our arrival in Wiesbaden. In short, ladies and gentlemen, we are to proceed as if we were indeed being deployed for actual combat purposes requiring security as to the movements of the regiment until deployment has been completed. Could be worse. Could be like Namibia where we couldn't tell *anyone*. Sir!"

Bellamack got to his feet again. "Because of the exercise nature of this activity, the Service and Supply Company will be deployed first in order that facilities will be ready to receive us. Companies will then deploy by number, and the Headquarters company will deploy last. Any questions?"

Curt squelched an urge to ask several. But this did not keep Captain

Russell Frazier from raising his hand and, when recognized by Bellamack, standing to say, "Colonel, do we take the experimental McCarthy harnesses with us?"

Bellamack thought for a moment before he answered. "I haven't received orders to leave them behind. I'll check with Colonel Lovell as soon as I can reach her. Therefore, until I receive orders to the contrary, take the McCarthy equipment."

This news was greeted by muted moans around the snake pit. It was obvious that the Greys didn't like this additional encumbrance.

"How about the technicians from McCarthy? Do I have to plan for their deployment as part of the regiment?" Captain Atkinson asked.

"Yes," Bellamack replied without hesitation. "We'll work out the administrative details later. But for this exercise, attach the McCarthy personnel temporarily to Major Gydesen's biotech unit."

"Yes, sir."

Captain Alexis Morgan raised her hand and was recognized by the regimental commander. She stood and said in a loud, clear voice, "Colonel, I don't understand this exercise. The Greys don't need training or practice in off-post or overseas deployment. We were on the way to Trinidad and Namibia within forty-eight hours, and within twelve hours we put the whole regiment on the road for the Sonoran operation. Either this is overtraining or someone at JCS level doesn't understand how fast a Sierra Charlie unit can move."

Bellamack nodded. "I know that, Captain. Perhaps this is more of a training exercise for the people in Europe than it is for us." He recognized another questioner. "Sergeant Kester?"

"Colonel, somethin' doesn't make much sense here," the old soldier pointed out. "Joint Chiefs have never exercised the European support elements; they've never needed to because the various rapid deployment exercises were more critical for the units bein' redeployed. The support elements are always prepared to open the warehouse doors. Somethin' else is going on here. Has to be. Is the Big Red Tide getting' ready to come in on us?"

"You know as much about that as I do, Sergeant."

"Yes, sir, and I haven't gotten the usual subtle advance signals that somethin' like that is happenin'. The Russkies haven't even started movin' units around for the usual Eastern European spring war games. In any event, sir, this exercise don't seem like no usual rapid deployment one. Somethin' else is in the wind," Kester guessed.

"I haven't been told," Bellamack replied, then added, "Maybe we'll find out what the hell's going on when we get there...and maybe we won't. In the meantime, we haven't got a hell of a lot of time to generate rumors. Everyone is going to have to shag ass to be ready when the Aerospace Force gets here in a few hours. And the trash haulers are in the air already. Captain Ward?"

"Colonel, exercises of this sort aren't normally conducted under such a tight security lid," Captain Joan Ward pointed out. "Did D-oh-D give any explanation why Rapid Reformer is classified?"

Bellamack looked straight at her and answered her with one word: "No." Then he said to the regiment, "We don't get paid to ask questions; we get paid to go where we're told to go and do what we're told to do. And we've been told to do something. So, let's do it smartly and on the bounce. The regiment will execute Order JCS-OP-thirty-three-dash-two! Dismissed!"

Chapter Twelve

Aerial photo interpretation had come a long way since people sat with watering eyes looking through stereo microscopes and going over each square millimeter of a set of vertical photographs. Computers and robots now did much of the drudgery.

But a human being was still needed in order to make judgment calls.

And that was the job of Major Constance Carlotti, who sat quietly contemplating the scene of Kerguelen Island reduced from the raw data brought back from the recent SRO-17 overflight.

The initial run-through in the computers had eliminated the dropouts and noisy pixels. The second run had enhanced the contrast, and the third had performed yet another contrast stretch.

Connie Carlotti studied the mosaic made up of digitized photos of the western half of Kerguelen.

Nothing unnatural had showed up yet in the data.

Which, as far as she was concerned, was just about the level of competency she expected from a computer. Connie Carlotti didn't really like computers; she was a mathematician, and to her a computer was nothing more than a big, fast adding machine. She didn't like reliance on such machines to make decisions that would affect human lives. She preferred to exercise human judgment. Thus, if something went wrong, it was because of human error and not machine error.

Although it was early in the reduction process, she decided to try creating an artificial image of the island, one generated by a mathematical tool called "fractal geometry," and then superimposing the artificial fractal image over the real image. Statistical fractal geometry had the unique capability of being able to generate images that appeared to be natural.

Her plan was straightforward. When the computer compared the artificial image to the real image, the computer would be able to pick out or "hit" those portions of the real image that did not appear to be natural in comparison to the fractal image.

In spite of the fact that she basically distrusted computers, Major Carlotti didn't mind talking to one; verbal programming and instructions were another tool for her to use when it would have taken her more time to punch a keypad or run a mouse. So she told the computer, Magnum, generate a fractal image of the existing data using a statistical fractal dimension of one-point-three-four."

"I will need additional computing power and memory." The computer told her. "Otherwise, I will require approximately five times ten to the ninth microseconds to complete the computation.

Carlotti didn't have 83 minutes. JSC was riding the Tiffany staff hard for answers to the question: What's on Kerguelen that shouldn't be there, and where is it? So she ordered Magnum, "Invoke Cosmic Strategic Security with Platinum Priority. Get access to Penta-Four, Level Three, and acquire whatever computer power is necessary for this job. Utilize multiple parallel processing. I want a Carroll synthesis based on three independent data reductions. Execute!"

"By your command!"

Within a second, Tiffany had linked with three of the biggest and most powerful megacomputers in the Pentagon. These were immediately put to work to generate three separate quick-look fractal images which would then be displayed for her judgement call. Using the paradigm, "What I tell you three times is true," she would then program Tiffany to make a composite image of the three separately-generated images. IT would be up to her to select the best of three or to combine two or more in order to make a "best guess" synthesis.

In five minutes, she had the first pass of the fractal image.

"Tiffany, here are instructions," Carlotti commanded verbally. "Combine the real image with the indicated fractal one. Look for discrepancies between the fractal and real images. Report the discrepancies as hits and highlight them on the display."

The image on the screen shifted, blurred, then took sharp form again. "I have four hits for you, Major," the computer reported. "I am indicating them at this time." The computer highlighted four parts of the image that didn't have the characteristics of "naturalness"-i.e., they had a combination of straight lines, regular edges, symmetry, reflectivity, and other attributes of the sort of pattern that human beings everywhere, regardless of culture, build into their devices.

"Make another pass," she instructed. "Perform another contrast stretch. Enhance contrasts and the edge effects again. Give me your evaluation of each hit."

One image was highlighted while the computer explained, "This hit appears to be a very unusual block of ice in the Cook Glacier moraine. It is my suggestion that it be discarded."

"Discard it," Carlotti told it after inspecting the image to see for herself. Sometimes artificially intelligent computers couldn't do the sort of random visual pattern searching and recognition that human beings carry out naturally.

A second image was highlighted. "This target may be an honest trick of light and shadow," the computer called Magnum reported. "It exists only in the data from Run One. It has a tendency to disappear when compared against the image taken on the second run of the SRO- 17."

"Tag it as a 'possible' and keep it in storage in case we don't get a positive hit on the others," Connie Carlotti ordered it, and it did so.

"This third image shows an unusual 'tail' of very low contrast parallel lines," Magnum reported as it was highlighted. "I do not know what to make of it, but it appears to be man-made."

"Give me five-times magnification of hit number three," Carlotti ordered and looked at the image. She guessed that it could be parallel vehicle tracks that the ever-present wind had partly filled with snow and ice. "Operate on the premise that this portion of the image may be parallel vehicle tracks," she went on. "The main object of this hit looks like it's also partly snow-covered. Invert the image."

When Magnum turned the image upside-down on the computer screen, it changed its gestalt or apparent image identification. Carlotti knew that she was looking at what was probably a disabled sno-kat vehicle abandoned in a glacial outwash named *Plaine Ampere* at the upper or northern end of a very deep fjord called *Baie de la Table*.

This clue then drew her attention to a very weak contrast image of what looked like a set of dual tracks partly hidden in the soft ground of the glacial outwash plain. It was indistinct. "Magnum, attention to my mouse inputs. I'm tracing what I think may be a road. It's disconnected. Look for the other segments of it. Use virtual image generation and puzzle matching algorithms."

Magnum found additional tracks by using a process of virtual imagery. It constructed virtual or unreal images of a two-track vehicle road. It then began fitting these virtual images into the gaps between the real images. It was "playing" the computer version of the human game of "connect the dots" to draw a complete picture. Magnum fitted the virtual images of "road" into the puzzle of "no-road" to provide a guesstimate image of what a road would look like if all its observed segments were connected.

The road led from the head of the Baie de la Table northward, around the east spur of the mountain called les Trois Menestrels, and then to the northwest up the Cook Glacier to a 750-meter-high ridge called la Mortadelle.

"Follow that road," Carlotti told it. "Where does it go? Does it terminate at another target?"

"Affirmative. It does. A fourth hit exists on this ridge at the termination of the road."

This time, the target was bigger than a sno-kat.

And it had what appeared to be some regular grids associated with it.

But Connie Carlotti couldn't identify the fourth target. It was too indistinct on the stereo image the computer was working with.

Fortunately, the pilot of the SRO-17 had instructed the ship to make a series of sequential images on two separate passes with different viewing aspects.

"Magnum, retrieve the other images of this site from other mission data stored in your memory. How many different views of this site are available?"

"I have four different aspects available."

"Combine the available data from these frames with the existing vertical plan view and give me an enhancement and further stretch. I want a dilate/erode ratio of three," the mathematician ordered and added almost as an after-thought, "Then I want your best guess concerning the vertical extent of the suspected targets."

The results blinked onto the display screen.

What she was looking at was again a shadowless low contrast image enhancement. "Assume a sun angle as a function of time and date of acquisition. Construct and display shadows."

The computer built up an internal three-dimensional image of the Mortadelle ridge for Major Constance Carlotti.

"Take the vantage point down to three thousand meters' altitude and rotate the image in the horizontal plane."

The display picture began to slowly turn as if she were viewing it from an aerodyne slowly flying around the ridge.

When she saw it, there was no question in her mind what it was.

She was looking at what was obviously and unmistakably a human-built manned station with carefully camouflaged and stealthed dwellings and a huge hidden antenna pointed skyward.

Although she was excited about her discovery, she wanted to confirm it. "Magnum, using the existing displayed image, construct another statistical fractal image and overlay it on the existing display."

The computer constructed an artificial image based on the parameters of the one on the screen. When compared, the fractal image would show natural-appearing image segments, and these would be deemphasized to leave the unnatural images. It was a double check.

And it confirmed.

She punched up the connection to her superior officer. "Colonel, call up the image Magnum is presently displaying on my terminal screen," she told him. "I think we've found what we're looking for."

"If so, I'll buy the drinks," the colonel promised. "Huh! Okay, I see what you're talking about. Meet you in the Club at eighteen hundred hours."

It was only minutes before the same images were available on the display screens of the general officers involved.

"Best place on that big rock to put a clandestine facility," General Albert Murray of NIA mused as he studied his own display. "Look what happens when I take the point of view downwards."

On five different screens in five different offices, the image moved from a vertical display of the southwestern portion of Kerguelen Island as if the viewers were in an aerodyne descending. The viewpoint shifted to an oblique view to the northeast where the enhanced image of Port-aux-Francaise could be seen on the flats of eastern Kerguelen. Slowly, the legitimate French scientific station slipped behind a mountain ridge.

"So it's not a French facility," General Edward S. Carrington observed.

"Right! Plenty of other places on the island to put a facility where logistics would be easier," General Otis Brooke said. "Obviously, they're supporting it by bringing submarines up Baie de le Table to the Plaine Ampere. That fjord is over two hundred meters deep, which is plenty of room for a *big* submarine to maneuver. Furthermore, that fjord is also hidden from the French outpost at Port-aux-Francaise."

"Gentlemen, we should only assume that the hidden station isn't

French," intelligence director Murray told them bluntly, his years of experience in the intelligence business telling him that no best guess should be confused with reality until all the data were in.

"Well, if it's French, then General Jean-Francois Beaudry either doesn't know or is lying through his teeth...and I can't believe the latter," came the assessment of General Michael Chaffee, U.S. representative to the UN Space Security Commission.

"We'll find out soon enough," Otis Brook reminded them all then indicated a new face on the terminal screens. "I've asked Jake Carlisle here to take over as combined commander of Operation Tempest Frigid. You probably remember that Jake did an outstanding job in the Bastaard Rebellion when the French commander got himself trapped in Otjomuise. Jake, what's the situation?"

Major General Jacob O. Carlisle was in his office at the headquarters of the 17th Iron Fist Division in Fort Huachuca, Arizona. "The Washington Greys have been ordered to Wiesbaden, and they're currently deploying. The Air Force willing, the regiment should be at Rhine-Main tomorrow morning. Because this is a clandestine mission, I intend to use Wiesbaden as a staging base for the Greys. This move will draw less attention than deploying them to Bahrain and trying to outfit them there with cold-weather gear. Incidentally, Otis, I've had to detach a combat company from my Wolfhounds regiment to serve as tactical airlift drivers."

"How come, Jake?" Brooke wanted to know. "All RI regiments are supposed to have internal tac airlift capability."

"The Sierra Charlies don't," Carlisle pointed out. "When we reorganized the Greys at the first Sierra Charlie outfit, tactical airlift aerodynes were inadvertently dropped from the TO&E."

"How the hell did that happen?" the Army chief of staff wanted to know.

"We screwed up. Overlooked the obvious," Carlisle explained. "Since the Sierra Charlies showed they could move so fast on the ground, it was just assumed that tac airlift would be supplied by someone else. And the Sierra Charlies have been used in land operations where the Navy had to take them in, like Trinidad, or where the Aerospace Force had to carry out a long airlift, like Namibia. The Mexicans wouldn't allow our aerodynes into Sonora, if you recall, so that was strictly a land operation except when the Greys managed to commandeer that drug lord's Mexican-registration aerodyne and use it."

"Damn! With all the brainpower and computer power we've got, how the hell did we manage to overlook regimental airlift?" Brooke said vehemently.

"It's damned near impossible to think of all the ramifications of warfare ahead of time," Carrington pointed out. "If armed conflict were predictable, we wouldn't need to fight. It could be settled by computer gaming. The Brits found out the hard way in the Falklands that their low-level ship air defense had big holes in it, and our Navy scrambled like hell when the old Aegis system turned up with areas of no coverage or capabilities. We can't build perfect systems or military organizations."

"Fortunately, the Army remains flexible," Carlisle told them. "We can hack the mission of landing a combat team on Kerguelen to occupy the station and put it out of action. As usual, it's a patchwork. But we seem capable of sticking these patchwork operations together and muddling through to victory, as our Brit colleagues would put it. I presume, gentlemen, that we still intend to carry this off and then announce it and apologize after the fact?"

"I don't see any other way to do it without getting some other nation goddamned upset," Murray remarked. "And if we tip our hand, whoever is manning that station will be ready when the Greys assault it. I think they're going to have enough trouble with this operation as it is…"

Chapter Thirteen

"Well, they could have sent us to worse places than Germany in April," Lieutenant Kitsy Clinton observed as Carson's Companions dismounted from their vehicles in a Wiesbaden transient parking compound.

It was a cloudy day with a dull, gray overcast hanging at about a thousand meters, diffusing the sunlight so that nothing cast a shadow. It was cool but not cold. However, Wiesbaden had something Fort Huachuca did not: humidity. It was a damp cold. "Damn, I've gotten so used to a desert climate that I feel deprived if I don't see the sun every day!" Lieutenant Jerry Allen added.

"I don't much give a damn about sunlight right now" was the remark from Senior Platoon Sergeant Nick Gerard. From the irritated tone of his voice, Curt could tell the man was fatigued, which the sergeant confirmed as he went on, "I'm jet-lagged. I can't sleep for shit in an airplane. Never could."

"Sergeant Sampson, make sure everyone has their vehicles and bots powered down and closed up," Curt instructed his first sergeant. "Then muster the company with their individual gear ready to move to quarters. Lieutenant Allen, you're in charge. Lieutenant Clinton, please come with me and we'll see if we can't find someone on regimental staff who knows what the hell is going on here."

"Yeah, Major, we should have been met when we came through the gate, so I guess something's screwed up again as usual," Edie Sampson observed candidly. "So, what else is new? Okay, everyone, power 'em down...but not until you get 'em lined up nice and pretty! The Ready Rifles own Wiesbaden, and we don't want them to get the impression that the Greys have gotten sloppy just because we're getting all the glory as Sierra Charlies!"

"Glory, Sarge?" Tracy Dillon asked, but not until he'd started to mount his platoon's RTV. "This ain't the French army!"

"You'll be requesting discharge to join the French Foreign Legion if you don't quit yakkin' and get your ass in gear, Dillon!" Sampson threatened.

Curt knew he had a good first sergeant in Edie Sampson. She was a career soldier, hard as nails, and capable of whipping her weight in infuriated wildcats - as she'd proved over and over again in actual combat. She was one of that strange new breed of twenty-first-century woman who had found her place in life as a combat soldier yet could bring forth the unique form of femininity that goes along with real and total equality with the male half of the human race. The concept of the physically weak and mentally different woman of two hundred years ago had disappeared, at least in the Robot Infantry. God help the chauvinistic, idiotic brute who might either try to belittle or attempt to rape Edie Sampson - or any of the other women in the Washington Greys; Curt had the impression that such a man wouldn't live very long.

It was a job, however, to integrate new women replacements into the outfit. Some women came to the Greys with a very offensively defensive manner. Some of them wanted equality without the responsibilities and consequences of such treatment. Curt felt Kitsy Clinton had pretty much learned what it was all about, but she'd had a leg up because of four years of West Point. Dyani Motega was too new to the company for Curt to make such an assessment.

Curt motioned for Clinton to join him and began walking toward the nearest building.

He knew he was in Germany again. The long three-story buildings with their slate roofs anti substantial structure smacked of the usual Germanic thoroughness in design and construction techniques. The buildings, like everything else in Germany, seemed ages old to Curt because he came from a country that didn't build for the centuries but preferred to build, use, then rip down existing buildings for something newer.

All the deciduous trees were barely ready to break out in leaf for spring. Coming as the regiment had from Arizona, this was another change.

But the oppressive grey clouds and the lackluster colors depressed him. It didn't help that he was also suffering from what the biotechs called "circadian asynchronization" or, to put it more simply, jet lag. As far as his body was concerned, it wasn't early afternoon but early in the morning.

The first building the two officers entered was vacant. The second one was a madhouse of fast-moving, hard-working German contract support people conversing in the clipped; guttural sounds of the German language as they tried to get the building ready for the incoming Greys.

In the third building, Staff Sergeant Forest Barnes, Major Pappy Gratton's staff NCO, found them as they entered. He looked even more tired than Curt's troops, because the Headquarters Company had left Fort Huachuca on the first flight in order to get to Wiesbaden and prepare for the arrival of the rest of the regiment. And Barnes acted haggard, too. "Major, Lieutenant," he greeted them, saluting. "Where is your company, sir?"

"We pulled up in the parking area the MPs directed us to," Curt told him. "Where are we billeted? I've got some tired people."

"Yes, sir. I suspect you do, sir. We're all a bit bushed," the staff sergeant admitted. He pulled out a pocket notepad, turned it on, and punched something into its keypad. A base housing map appeared on its screen. As he spoke, he pointed to the little display. "We're here. Show me where you parked your vehicles, sir."

Curt peered at the display and indicated the parking lot.

"Goddamned MPs!" Barnes swore. "I told them that all the Greys' vehicles were to be sent to this lot here." He pointed. "You'll have to move them, Major."

Curt was pissed by then. "Goddammit, Sergeant, I've already ordered my vehicles powered down!"

"Sir, the Wiesbaden MPs fucked up. I guess I can change some parking locations around so you can leave your vehicles where they are, but your assigned quarters are over here about a kilometer from where you parked," Barnes informed him, indicating the display map.

"We haven't got that much gear to carry," Curt decided. "We'll walk."

"Very well, sir. Your choice," Barnes admitted. "Building P-ten-twelve is where the Companions are scheduled to be billeted. You'll be sharing the building with a CASS from the Wolfhounds which has been attached to the Greys for this exercise."

"A Wolfhound outfit 'attached' to the Greys?" Curt asked in disbelief. "On a redeployment exercise? That's unusual as hell!"

"Yes, sir. I thought so, too. Especially since they're coming in without their warbots but with all their aerodynes...which is why you weren't supposed to park your vehicles where you did. That area is supposed to be for the Warhawks' aerodynes. Now I'll have to figure out where I can put them instead."

"Whose company is the Warhawks?" Curt wanted to know.

Barnes punched another set of numbers into the notepad. "Worsham's Warhawks, Major. Commanded by Major Calvin J. Worsham. A combat air support company from the Wolfhounds..."

"Curiouser and curiouser," Kitsy Clinton remarked. "Why would a CASS unit be detached from a warbot regiment to the Greys?"

"Something is definitely screwy about this whole goddamned exercise," Curt admitted. "The short action time. The fact that the Greys don't need to have their rapid redeployment capabilities exercised. The high security classification. And now a temporarily assigned combat air support company."

"Doesn't add up," Clinton observed.

"Unless this isn't an exercise but the preliminaries of another one of those special little operations the Army seems to love to throw at the Greys," Curt told her. "I think I'd better rattle some cages over at regimental headquarters..."

"Won't do much good, Major," Barnes told him bluntly. "We've been thinking the same thing, and Rumor Control is running wild with guesses. But the colonel doesn't know anything more than we do..."

"Yeah, and he's a square shooter who'd tell us if he knew," Curt admitted. Once having been blooded at regimental command during the Sonoran operation, Colonel Bill Bellamack had carved his own niche in the Washington Greys as a commanding officer who was different from Belinda Hettrick but did it his own way - which was just as effective. "Well, shit, I guess we'll have to wait to be told on this one."

"Looks that way, Major," Sergeant Barnes said. "So maybe everyone ought to enjoy what rest we can manage to get while we can manage to get it. By the way, I did get the combat companies billeted close to the mess hall..."

"I appreciate that, Sergeant. Thank you. Which building will be regimental headquarters?" Curt wanted to know. He wanted to check in and find out where everything was.

"This one, sir. But the whole headquarters operation is still a sheep screw right now," Barnes admitted frankly. "Better wait until Major Hampton gets things settled down a tad."

Curt refrained from remarking that the situation seemed normal. Actually, Headquarters Company was well organized and operated in a competent manner by Major Wade Hampton. They did their job of making sure the administrative side of things was taken care of, and they stayed the hell out of the way. They also served as Bellamack's staff, with the exception of S-4 Logistics, which was taken care of by Major Fred Benteen and his Service Company.

"Thank you, Sergeant. You may report Carson's Companions on post and settling into quarters," Curt remarked to the staff sergeant. If Curt bitched about the fuck-up in parking, Barnes couldn't do anything about it; Curt would mention it to Hampton the next time the occasion arose and he could air what was really nothing more than a minor gripe. "Come along, Lieutenant," he told Kitsy Clinton. "We've got a hike or two ahead of us."

But something else was involved when Curt and his platoon officer got back to where the Companions had parked their vehicles.

Aerodynes were scattered everywhere - in the paved parking lot, on the lawns, and anywhere that an aerodyne could land. Lieutenant Jerry Allen was being confronted by a large, wiry man wearing major's gold oak leaves plus the winged ellipse of the Army's air support units. He was dressed in lightweight desert cammies. The leather helmet of the CASS with its built-in neuroelectronic pickups covered his shaved head. He was an unusual warbot brainy because he sported a thick, bushy handlebar mustache that made him look mean and nasty. Which he apparently was. The stranger was raising hell with Jerry and obviously trying to use his appearance and higher rank to intimidate the young lieutenant.

"I don't give a damn what your company commander *or* the fucking MPs told you, Mister Dumb John! Move those fucking vehicles the hell and gone out of here! This is my designated landing and parking area!" the major shouted in a rasping voice.

"Major," Jerry told him in a controlled, level voice, "I can't move without orders, and you can't give them to me. The MPs told us to park here. And although my ladies can probably out-curse you, I'll thank you to show a little respect for them by controlling your language . . . *sir*."

"I'll have your ass busted into a million fucking pieces for this, you smart-mouthed bastard!" the major shouted. "You may be hot-shit gravel grabbers who get down and dirty with mud shoved up your ass, but you're sure as hell not better than my aerodyne brainies...and that goes for your broads, too!"

Curt watched and listened unseen and motioned to Kitsy to cool it. Curt wanted to see how Jerry handled this situation.

He also saw First Sergeant Edie Sampson come up alongside Jerry. From the look in her eyes, Curt knew sparks would fly. He whispered to Kitsy, "Watch; this will be educational!"

Edie stood alongside Jerry and looked up at this imposing major. With her head shaved again, she looked almost masculine with her redhead's distinctive skull and cheek bones. She was pissed; it showed in the glint of her blue eyes. "Major," she said in a voice that was more of a growl, "you're wearing an officer's insignia, and by the regs I can't lip off to you. So, I won't. But I do want you to know that the ladies of this outfit ain't referred to that way by anyone who wants to keep his balls. And although we're all former warbot brainies like you haul around in your frisbees, sir, we're also Sierra Charlies who've learned how to kill with our bare hands if necessary. So, we're perfectly willing and capable of running a shiv in a messy way between the legs of any asshole who insults us."

"Sergeant!" the major exploded. "Are you threatening...?"

He didn't have the chance to finish before First Sergeant Sampson told him, "Not that we would, sir, but we're a little bit more than the usual female couch drivers of the regular Robot Infantry, and I've had my share of couch time. Now, I'm sure our company commander will have this straightened out, because that's why he went off to find someone who's in charge. And the lieutenant's right; he can't move from here without orders because this is where the MPs told us to settle in...sir."

"Sergeant, I'm going to pin your goddamned hide to the wall on an insubordination charge!" the major snarled.

"If you want a real fight on your hands, Major, go right ahead!" Curt suddenly snapped and stepped forward. "I'm Major Curt Carson, company commander and second-in-command of the Washington Greys. And who might you be, Major?" Curt slightly accented the terms of rank.

The major saluted. "Major Calvin J. Worsham, commanding Worsham's Warhawks, Combat Air Support Squadron, the Wolfhounds Regiment...sir."

Curt let him hold the salute for a few seconds before he returned it. "Oh, yeah, I've heard about you, Major. I understand you've been temporarily attached to the Washington Greys. Welcome aboard. And sorry for this little screw-up here, but we can blame it on the Wiesbaden MPs, who didn't get their instructions straight. I just returned from regimental headquarters with orders to leave my vehicles here. Colonel Bellamack would like to see you concerning your aerodyne parking arrangements and billeting. I suggest you go find him. Third building on the left. If you can't locate him, ask for

Regimental Sergeant Major Henry Kester and tell him Major Carson sent you."

That would take care of this loud-mouthed aerodyne squadron commander, Curt knew. Furthermore, Major Worsham would have no one to blame but himself now for starting out his own temporary tour of duty with the Greys in deep shit with this rather tight-knit regiment unless he shaped up. It was probably tough enough on the man for him to realize his aerodyne drivers were going to serve with a new outfit made up of Sierra Charlies...and no one yet knew why.

Curt began to wonder about the morale and *esprit* in some of the other warbot regiments. This wasn't the first time he'd tangled with defensive and offensive company officers from other outfits. That sort of thing usually spelled insecurity. On the other hand, maybe Major Worsham was another Captain Marty Kelly, a brass plated son of a bitch who probably would have been more at home in the Marines if the Marines hadn't been cut to hell as a combat force by the usually pinch-penny congress.

But, no, Worsham couldn't be another Marty Kelly, Curt told himself. First, they broke the mold, then they'd made Kelly. There couldn't be two of the same in the same army. Or could there?

"Thank you, Major. And my apologies for coming on a bit strong with your people," Worsham said. The words were apologetic, but his tone of voice wasn't. It was as though the words counted more than the way he said them - in a flat monotone of the same sort used in air-to-ground communications. "My 'dyne drivers have a tendency to be sort of...uh, spirited, if you know what I mean. I have to be reasonably rough to keep them in line. And we've just had a two-day cross-country coming from Bahrain...and I'm just a little bit on edge. So, by your leave, Major," Worsham said bitterly and saluted.

"See you around the Club, Major," Curt told him, returning the salute. "If you're going to be attached to the Greys, we should get to know one another a lot better...even though we don't know what the hell we're going to be doing together."

"Hell, Major, I thought you knew," Worsham remarked. "We're going to be your tactical airlift, your personal trash haulers…"

Chapter Fourteen

Curt's body felt a lot better after a good, long sleep that allowed his biological clock to get in synch with the local one. But he didn't feel any better about the whole "exercise."

From the looks on their faces, both Jerry Allen and Kitsy Clinton thought the same way when they showed up for breakfast the following morning.

"The hot skinny," Lieutenant Jerry Allen reported, "is that we're going into Kurdistan to act as a third force between the Sovs and the Iranians, both of whom seemed to be more than a little interested in that oil pipeline through there."

"Kurdistan?" Lieutenant Kathleen Clinton responded with surprise. "Rumor Control says we're going south of Tunisia to keep the natives from raiding the new oil fields there. And with summertime approaching, too!"

"What do you think, Major?" Jerry asked his CO.

Curt shrugged as he sat down with them. He didn't answer for a minute while he surrounded some of the food on his plate. It was almost an American breakfast, but not quite. Obviously, it had been prepared by German Commissary cooks who'd put their own little twists into it. The hash browns were a little heavy. The scrambled eggs were a touch too firm. The sausage was a bit greasy. And the pastry was definitely German. But it was a good try, and it was close enough that Curt didn't complain. It wouldn't have done him any good anyway; mess food is mess food, and sometimes the Army wasn't able to hire contract cooks as good as the Germans. Recalling his days in the Middle East, he knew the Arabs had never managed to get it just right...

"You can play the Rumor Control game for all it's worth," he told the two young officers, "and you'll always lose. The Army loves to play surprise party."

Regimental Sergeant Major Henry Kester walked through the mess room and stopped when he got to where Curt was sitting. "Good morning, Major," the old soldier greeted his former commanding officer. "I understand you had a little set-to with the 'dyne drivers yesterday, sir."

Curt looked up at him and grinned. "I take it that Major Worsham found you, then?"

"Yes, sir. He was both pissed and surprised," Kester reported. "He suggested bringing charges against Sergeant Sampson, but Colonel Bellamack told him there wouldn't be time."

" 'Wouldn't be time'? Something going on, Henry?" Curt wanted to know.

"Oscar meeting at oh-nine-hundred," Kester announced. "And, no, sir, not even the colonel knows what it's about. But we've got a three-dee holoconference circuit reserved for it at the request of divisional headquarters."

"Hot damn! Carlisle doesn't play games with us. Never has," Curt observed. "Okay, we'll be there, Henry. At least, the suspense will be terminated..."

"Maybe it will, sir, and maybe it won't," Kester informed him.

"I like a nice, definitive answer like that," Curt muttered as Kester walked off. He didn't interrogate his former first sergeant beyond that point; if Henry Kester had known, Henry Kester would have told Curt.

"Well, Major, I hope one of the first things we do is swap these light desert cammies for some warmer gear," Jerry Allen remarked with a shiver.

"Plus something a bit more substantial to cover our heads now that we've shaved them again," Kitsy Clinton added. "What do the warbot brainies wear over here?"

"Blue berets or service caps," Jerry told her.

"No good," Kitsy decided. "Doesn't keep your head warm and doesn't distinguish us from regular warbot brainies. Major, we've got to find some sort of unique headgear for us Sierra Charlies."

Curt finished off his plate and put his hands around his coffee mug to warm them. "Agreed, but we've got a hell of a lot more important things to do. I think. Maybe we'll find out what the hell they are today..."

"Well, Major, this whole maneuver makes sense if we're in a staging area preparatory to moving into action somewhere," Jerry guessed, putting his hands around his own coffee mug in unconscious imitation of his company commander.

"But where is any trouble within a thousand klicks of here?" Kitsy asked, then went on to report, "I managed to pick up Armed Forces Communications before breakfast. Nothing much of anything seems to be brewing anywhere, at least not of the sort of intensity that would justify hauling us halfway around the world. The usual sheep screw in the Middle East, of course, which is why we've got troops in the Persian Gulf. Elsewhere, the Chinese are acting mean and nasty in the Spratly Islands, and the Sovs are arguing with them about possible border troubles in the Lake Alakol region. But that's been going on for decades. Even Yemen's quiet right now. A short report on Berber guerilla attacks in the Tunisian area, which is why I think Rumor Control is right."

"The thing I don't like about tight security such as this," Curt interrupted her, "is that the troops waste so goddamned much time in speculation when they're not told. So I suggest we knock off the guesstimates of the situation. We'll know more in an hour or so. In the meantime, Jerry, how's your new squad leader fitting in?"

"Dyani Motega is doing fine," Jerry reported. "She was a little upset about shaving her head but went along with it because everyone else had done it. I wish to God we weren't saddled with this crazy experimental gear!"

"Maybe we won't be for long," Curt wished aloud, then continued, "How's Tracy Dillon handling it?"

Allen looked up in surprise and replied, "Dillon? Fine! In fact, he and Motega are having breakfast together over yonder. She's kinda intense and doesn't put up with any bullshit, Major. And she's trying hard to come up to speed in the platoon as quick as she can. Frankly, sir, I think she's pushing Dillon to the limit, and he's got to put up or shut up when it comes to training her up. Are you still worried about the situation?"

"No, Lieutenant, not worried, but I'd be a damned poor company commander if I didn't continue to remain concerned about it until I sense complete integration or we've been through a shooting operation," Curt admitted. He looked at his watch. "Okay, time for a shit, shine, shower, shave, and shampoo, then hit the Oscar briefing. Let's go!"

The briefing room at Wiesbaden was a regular Robot Infantry snake pit, with linkage couches, a holographic projector in the center of the pit, and no provisions for the sort of Sierra Charlie briefing that the Washington Greys had developed.

As Curt and the Companions entered, Colonel Willa Lovell came up with an anxious look on her attractive face. She was so concerned over her equipment and experiment that she neglected the usual formality of a morning greeting and simply asked Curt, "You brought your experimental harnesses, didn't you, Major?"

"Good morning, Colonel," Curt greeted her, observing proper manners. "Glad to see you here. Yes, we were ordered to bring them. Tell me something, is Exercise Rapid Reformer part of your experiment?"

"Oh, good heavens, no!" she replied quickly. "We didn't know about it, either. It's been difficult to get all our equipment together and get it over here with the regiment. I had to call in some favors to get airlift priority. It was a very busy two days…"

Colonel Willa Lovell could become obsessed with her work to the exclusion of consideration for people, and this was one aspect of her personality that bothered Curt. In fact, she was ignoring her own people at that very moment; Curt recognized the face of an old friend standing behind her. "Captain Pendleton!" Curt called out and thrust his hand toward the tall, gangling, rather plain man. "Haven't seen you since the Zahedan affair! How are you?"

Captain Owen W. Pendleton, Jr. had been one of the Zahedan hostages who hadn't gotten airlifted out and had thus been forced to stay with Curt and Edie Sampson until the Greys could mount the second rescue mission. An expert in artificial intelligence design and programming, properly referred to as an AI mentor, Pendleton had been a frustrated ROTC officer who'd happily accepted a brevet to lieutenant from Curt and helped the group fight its way out of that isolated eastern Iranian town.

"I'm fine, Major! Good to see you again, sir!" Pendleton replied affably. Gone was his shyness and apprehension; working on military AI research had apparently been good for him, because it had brought him out of his shell. Curt thought he knew what had done it. Military discipline and protocol eliminated the problem of what to do and what to say in a social situation; it was all preprogrammed, and all anyone had to do was to follow procedures. Curt had seen it turn shy people into quite social people. Pendleton was no exception.

But an additional bond existed between Curt and Pendleton: They'd been shot at together. Willa Lovell was also a member of that exclusive club because of Zahedan, but apparently, she didn't know to call upon it, or her high-level R&D work had again effectively isolated her from the real world of the military service. Curt guessed the latter had taken place.

"I see you qualified for a set of railroad tracks," Curt remarked, referring to the captain's insignia on the man's collar tabs.

"Actually, I'm supposed to have gold oak leaves like yours," Pendleton remarked, "but there was a screw-up in the Pentagon somewhere…Where's Sergeant Sampson?"

"Right here, Owen!" Edie called out and stepped forward. She saluted him unnecessarily. He returned the salute and did something quite unmilitary; he embraced her, and she returned it. "Boy, they've turned you into a man!" she told him.

"And they've turned you into a first sergeant," he replied. "I'm glad I'm not serving under you! If my recollections of Zahedan are ungarbled, you're one person I wouldn't want to get crossways with!"

Curt felt he had to step in. "Look, Captain, I'm glad to see you again. Let's get together tonight at the Club and get caught up. Right now, we've got an Oscar briefing coming up, and everything else is going to have to wait. Including reunions of old comrades. Captain, I take it you're involved with Colonel Lovell's work?"

"Yes, sir," he replied brightly. "You can blame me, Major. I got the idea in Zahedan and discovered later that the colonel had, too. So, we put together this human factors data acquisition project."

"Okay, we've got to talk to you and the colonel about it," Curt said. "But later. Right now, we've got to be in position. See you later, Colonel! Captain! Companions, let's take our places..."

As they settled into linkage couches, Jerry Allen asked, "Hard linkage?" He was inquiring whether or not full neuroelectronic linkage would be required for this briefing.

"Negatory," Curt informed him, then explained, "That's for warbot brainies. We're Sierra Charlies, and we get briefed the old-fashioned way. But...let me double check."

He walked over to where Colonel Bellamack was standing. "Colonel, I take it this is going to be a standard Sierra Charlie briefing?"

"That's right," Bellamack snapped. "I don't want anyone to get the idea that the Sierra Charlies can slip back to being warbot brainies at a moment's notice, regardless of the whim of some superior officer. We're trained and ready to act according to the doctrine we've worked out at a cost in time and lives. Go back and sit down. General Carlisle knows the Greys use the new briefing procedures."

With a slight smile on his face, Curt returned to his company and sat down on the edge of a linkage couch. He pulled his notepad from his belt, powered up, and got ready to take any notes necessary. His two officers and his sergeants took their cues from him.

However, it was going to be a "duplex" briefing that was both neuroelectronic in the standard Army fashion and visual-verbal for the Sierra Charlies. Curt noticed that all forty people of Worsham's Warhawks, the new Combat Air Support Squadron temporarily assigned to the Greys, had settled into linkage.

Well, one pilot couldn't fly the UCA-21B Chippewa assault troop carrier aerodynes alone without being in complete linkage with the circuits of the craft's artificially intelligent robot pilot. And the Sierra Charlies didn't have regimental airlift capability yet, although commercial aerodynes were available that could fill the requirement. But they were commercial vehicles, not military. It took six to eight years for the Army to go from a new vehicle proposal to hardware in the field, and the military R&D and procurement cycles hadn't caught up to the Sierra Charlies yet. As a result, the Sierra Charlies had to make do with mods of existing equipment or foreign buys of things they couldn't get through normal RI logistics channels. Someday, perhaps, the Sierra Charlies would have their own airlift capabilities. However, save for Namibia, where airlift would have come in handy and saved a long overland march, airlift hadn't been required in the sort of operations the Greys had gotten involved with.

Curt wasn't expecting what happened next.

A full colonel whom Curt recognized as the chief of staff of the 17th Iron Fist Division walked into the stage of the snake pit and announced, "Ladies and gentlemen, the division commander!"

Major General Jacob O. Carlisle, commander of the 17th Iron Fist RI Division, walked into the snake pit in person.

It was a surprise because the general had a full division to command. Curt immediately wondered why Carlisle had come to Wiesbaden for a mere training exercise, if that was indeed what Exercise Rapid Reformer was all about. Curt now seriously doubted it. Carlisle had been expected to communicate, if at all, via holographic teleconferencing from Fort Huachuca. But he'd come in person. Then why the holographic telecommunications channel that Kester reported?

It didn't make sense.

But nothing about this "exercise" was making sense.

"Take your seats and couches. Carry on," Carlisle announced and stepped to the center of the projection stage. He appeared normally to the Washington Greys, but neuroelectronic sensors picked up his image, computers processed it, and his visual and audio image was projected into the minds of Worsham's Warhawks who, as the CASS unit of a Robot Infantry division, were in linkage as usual for the briefing.

Carlisle clasped his hands behind his back and spread his legs in the classical stance of a general briefing his troops. "Congratulations on the successful completion of Exercise Rapid Reformer. And I would like to extend a formal welcome to Worsham's Warhawks, the Combat Air Support Squadron on temporary detached duty assignment from the Wolfhounds. Now that Rapid Reformer has been completed, we shall move on to Exercise Mighty Heidi."

The general smiled. "Yes, the computers sometimes come up with the damndest names for our activities! This will, however, be a training exercise. No, I didn't know about it until this morning." He did not reveal that he knew the ultimate destination of the Washington Greys or why they were *really* in Wiesbaden.

"Exercise Mighty Heidi will begin immediately following this orders briefing.

"This morning, the Washington Greys will muster by companies, and the combat companies along with the CASS will draw arctic clothing. The remainder of the day will be spent in reconfiguring all equipment for an arctic environment. Be prepared to operate where it gets very cold..."

Chapter Fifteen

"That was the goddamndest Oscar bash I ever sat through!" was First Sergeant Edie Sampson's evaluation after they'd been dismissed and mustered again in the temporary orderly room on the second floor of the Wiesbaden barracks to which they'd been assigned.

"An alpine airborne assault exercise against a redoubt defended by the Second Robot Cavalry Regiment?" Lieutenant Jerry Allen remarked as if he had a lot of trouble believing it. "They haul our asses all the way across the Atlantic to play war games?"

"Something isn't right," Lieutenant Kitsy Clinton maintained. "Something sure as hell isn't right!"

Curt Carson let the Companions bitch and moan and complain for a few minutes to get it off their chests. It wasn't sniveling or groveling, but good old Army complaining about the mission, something that's taken place probably ever since young Egyptian Pharaoh Thutmosis III briefed his troops before the Battle of Megiddo in 1469 B.C. This was the first recorded battle in history, but no one thought to document the feelings of the troops. Hence, the supposition of a precombat gripe session is probably very speculative. But such a session has its utility in helping to reduce tension, apprehension, and anxiety. Enough of those emotional factors would be present before the exercise anyway, and in actual combat they were even more intense.

Finally, Curt stood up and looked around. The Companions fell quiet. "Okay, Companions, we don't know why the high brass want us here in Germany playing war games. We aren't privileged to know the Big Picture. I agree: Something is brewing somewhere in a cold climate. The Army probably has been told by the politicians and diplomats to be ready to do something, and it wants to make sure that the Sierra Charlies of the Washington Greys are ready to go in and take care of whatever the trouble happens to be. Could be east Asia; Sakhalin and Korea can get pretty damned cold until late May. Could be Iceland or even Spitsbergen because the Russkies never liked those bases that could choke their naval operations. We don't really know what's going on because we don't see the classified diplomatic and national security messages and reports. But remember this: Wherever we're sent, we'll be ready. So..." Curt started to parcel out tasks by giving orders to various people. "Sergeant Sampson, see to it that the Companions have a pickup sked for the arctic gear we're supposed to have. Sergeant Gerard, Alpha Company will be first to pick up arctic gear; Sergeant Dillon, Bravo Company will follow. Sergeant Hale, as our new company biotech, I want you to be sure that all issued arctic gear is proper and fits; since we don't know where we're going, I don't want to have anyone suffer from trench foot or frostbite."

Curt turned to the warbot maintenance technician who'd been assigned to the company. "Sergeant Vickers, you're to see to it that all our warbots are modified for cold weather operations."

He turned to his officers. "Lieutenant Allen, you're responsible for the hardware; organize the servicing crews for the warbots and make sure Sergeant Vickers' instructions are followed. Lieutenant Clinton, you'll be in charge of training activities. And, as usual, since I'm your peerless leader, I'll exercise Army doctrine that requires every job to have a supervisor; I'll see to it that everybody stays busy. Actually, I'll go over this morning - or what's left of it - and try to break ground with Major Worsham so we mesh in with the Warhawks' training flight schedules. The next four days are going to be on a tight sked if we're going to be ready to go with Exercise Mighty Heidi on Monday morning next."

He looked down at the small display on his notepad. "Colonel Bellamack's staff training syllabus requires that we undertake a minimum of three training flights with the Warhawks before Friday evening," Curt pointed out. "I want every Companion to get to the nearest terminal and download the orders file ASAP. Study it, I want to make damned sure every one of you understands our training orders and the orders posted for Exercise Mighty Heidi, especially the Rules of Engagement for the exercise. Tomorrow morning, we'll hold a quiz session right after breakfast to go over all the data."

Kitsy Clinton raised her hand. When Curt recognized her, she asked, "Major, what's to train? We load 'dynes. We unload 'dynes. We've done that before."

"Well, Lieutenant, you're right in some respects," Curt told her. "Sure, we unloaded from Aerospace Force aerodynes against possible resistance at Swakopmund in Namibia, and we pulled off an airlanding strike in Sonora with a commandeered aerodyne. But that doesn't mean we know what the hell to do when we try a vertical envelopment under combat conditions! Look, in Exercise Mighty Heidi, we'll be loading up aerodynes under pressure of time and schedules. And, more important, we may be unloading in combat conditions, possibly under simulated fire from laser-designated weaponry. And we'll be doing that in unfamiliar arctic gear and with modified bots. Well, we've got four days to train with these things first, which is better than no training time at all. And we'll be flying in someone else's 'dynes. Next week, we'll be heading for the Bavarian Alps with orders to 'capture' a defended redoubt. Let's take advantage of the training time and consider the exercise as if it were the real thing."

"Yeah, Major, but *why*?" Sergeant Sampson asked the crucial question. "How come the sudden interest in training for an environment where no American troops are currently stationed?"

"I told you before, Sergeant, I don't know. But *something* is brewing, or they wouldn't be chasing us all over the world; that costs money. They wouldn't be issuing special gear, because that drags down emergency stocks here in Europe that are held as insurance against the Big Red Tide coming through Fulda Gap at umpteen-hundred.

"And they wouldn't be mounting an expensive and possibly hazardous mountain training exercise," Jerry Allen added. "It's got to be similar to something maybe we'll have to carry off. That's why we go through training exercises..."

"Right on, Lieutenant!" Curt complimented him. "We've got the chance to do a little training before this one...which is one whole hell of a lot better than some of the operations that have been dropped on us in the recent past. Yeah, Mighty Heidi will be an exercise. But think of it as if we're going to be going into actual live combat with people or bots actually shooting at us with intent to do bodily harm. Sergeant Gerard?"

Nick Gerard asked in an irritated tone, "Major, what about the goddamned experimental sensor harnesses?"

"You got yours?"

"Yes, sir! Brought it all the way from Huachuca because you told me to, sir."

"Then wear it."

"Under body armor and arctic gear, Major?"

"Damned right," Curt told him vehemently; "Colonel Lovell and Captain Pendleton will be taking data on this exercise. You might think their experiment is just a bunch of bot flush. But since Captain Pendleton is on, the project I can assure you it isn't any boondoggle thought up by the tech-weenies just to make us uncomfortable. Pendleton is a tech-weenie who's been shot at and who's shot back and killed people. He's one of us."

"Even though we're wearing a modified linkage harness now, it cuts down on freedom of movement, Major;" Sergeant Dillon pointed out.

"Excuse me, Major," Edie Sampson broke in and turned to the NCO. "Quitcherbitchin! Soldier, shut up and soldier!" It was First Sergeant Sampson's favorite phrase, one that she used to tell another NCO, in effect, to shape up or she'd pull the plug on him. The Companions had respected Henry Kester because he was an old soldier who knew it all and had seen it all; they respected Edie Sampson because she was tough and didn't take any shit from anyone, even though she hadn't been over the course the way Kester had.

She'd also raised a few lumps on some macho male bodies during unofficial and unreported sessions in the gym. Unlike her Biblical namesake, Edie Sampson didn't get by with sheer physical strength;

she fought smart when she fought and thought smart at other times.

Nick Gerard had been pissed when Edie had been bucked up to first sergeant upon Henry Kester's promotion to regimental sergeant major. He thought he should have gotten the job. But Sampson had Nick's number, and he didn't give her any bot flush about it as a result. Few things went as expected in the Army, lending an aura of truth to the old expression, "Shit happens."

Curt looked around. "Any more questions? Not bitches or snivels, but questions? Okay, move 'em out! Lieutenant Clinton, come with me."

"Yes, sir!"

Kitsy Clinton had worked into the Companions quite easily as a result of the Sonoran operation. Every Companion knew the pert little officer had managed to fill the slot left vacant by Alexis Morgan's promotion to captain and her resulting assumption of command of another company of Greys. But only the more juvenile minded Greys played the game of keeping score, and Kitsy Clinton had confused all of these small minds. Kitsy didn't play favorites, and keeping track of her was more than a full-time job. Unlike Alexis Morgan, who had given her full and complete loyalty to her company commander - except for some extracurricular activities in Namibia - Kitsy enjoyed playing the field.

This was a relief to Curt because he still had a very strong attachment to Alexis and wasn't ready to let the new lieutenant completely occupy Morgan's former place in the Companions.

As they left the barracks, Kitsy asked, "Major, may I plug into you?"

"Lieutenant, Rule Ten is operative," Curt reminded her. He wasn't horny right then, but he knew that. Kitsy Clinton often approached matters by going around the barn to get there.

"Yes, sir. I meant: Can I download the orders from your notepad to mine while we're en route here?" she clarified her request. "It would save some time, which we don't seem to have very much of."

He handed her his pad. She plugged it into hers and did a data dump. "Hope you didn't have your personal diary in there, too,

Major," she quipped.

"You're out of luck today," he shot back. Kitsy had overcome the initial shyness of a newcomer to the outfit; however, there were times when her pert sassiness wasn't cute. Although she seemed to sense when these times existed, she also had the tendency to push just a little bit. This was one of them. But Curt didn't reprimand her; she had spirit, and sometimes a combat outfit needed someone with a positive outlook like Kitsy Clinton's.

They found Major Cal Worsham in the temporary flight ops the Warhawks had set up in one of the barracks' orderly rooms. Without the luxury of a wall-projected display, the Warhawks had rigged an old-fash-ioned write-on wall board for their flight ops skeds. A slender woman wearing first sergeant's stripes and rockers was busily filling in all the space on the board.

"Major Worsham, Curt Carson, Carson's Companions," Curt reintroduced himself to the mustachioed man. "I don't believe you've met my Alpha Platoon commander, Lieutenant Kathleen Clinton."

Worsham looked up dourly, got to his feet, returned the salutes, then shook hands with Curt and Kitsy in turn. "I didn't realize that the Sierra Charlies had women in combat positions," Worsham remarked.

"A holdover from the days when the regiment was a full warbot outfit," Curt explained. "We just sort of transitioned without any of the high brass realizing it. Right at the moment, they're still wondering how it happened and still hesitant about posting the women to other full warbot units because of the hell the girls would raise. After all, our women fought with honor in our last three operations."

"Damn, we need to talk, Carson!" Worsham explained. "I've got some good female pilot material in the Warhawks, but the high brass won't let me schedule them to fly in combat conditions."

"Well, maybe if you were part of a Sierra Charlie outfit, things might be different," Curt ventured to guess. "In any event,

Lieutenant Clinton is in charge of our company training, and we came over to see if we can schedule our required three exercises with you."

"Jeez, the damn board's getting filled up pretty damned fast!" Worsham growled. "Major, meet my first sergeant and crew chief, Sergeant Tim Timm."

She turned, saluted, and took Curt's hand, then Kitsy's. She seemed to be a pleasant person, but there was no smile on her face. She said defensively, "I'm one of those the major referred to. I have a commercial ticket, but I get to fly only the trash-haul missions, and the Army won't give me wings because NCOs don't rate them. And, by the way, sirs, in case you're wondering, my first name is indeed feminine. It's a diminutive of Timothea."

"Why the hell do you stay in, Sergeant?" Curt asked bluntly.

"Because I like it, sir," she replied. "Why does any woman stay in this man's Army?"

"Because, Sergeant," Kitsy Clinton put in quickly, "the military services are socially advanced organizations where people are equally treated regardless of race, reli-gion, origin, or sex."

"Maybe that's what they taught you at West Point, Lieutenant," Sergeant Timm replied, "but that's not the way it is in Army aviation!"

"Sergeant, your feelings are well known to me, and I empathize with you," Worsham told her in a gravelly voice that betrayed the fact that the rough-hewn pilot commander was indeed on her side but hadn't figured out a way to do anything about it yet. "Let's see about squeezing this man's outfit into the sked."

As they began to work out the details, Curt noticed something was missing in the planning. He brought this up to Worsham. "I notice you've scheduled thirty minutes for a company to load up in your aerodynes and nearly the same length of time to unload, Major. Why so long?"

"Standard warbot practice, isn't it?" Worsham came back.

"That's what I thought. But we're not a regular warbot outfit, Major. The Sierra Charlies are lean, mean, and move faster than hell because someone is usually shooting at our pink bods. And we can move faster because out bots aren't so big and clumsy."

"I think we'd better hold to a thirty-minute loading and unloading sked until we see how much faster you can haul ass," Worsham told him.

"Tell you what," Curt offered. "Give us this afternoon to get our gear and bots in shape according to orders, then we'll slide into an oh-eight-hundred slot tomorrow, and we'll show you how fast we are."

"Takes us little time in the morning to get the Chippies checked out, Major," Sergeant Timm pointed out. "We rarely start training missions before ten-hundred hours."

"We're usually up at dawn," Curt pointed out, "and under combat conditions we like to strike earlier than that...about an hour before dawn. Of course, Major, if your hot pilots like to stay in the sack, they're likely to have to change their ways with the Sierra Charlies..."

Worsham stood up and put his hands on his hips. "Are you implying that the Warhawks are sack hounds, Major?" he asked defiantly.

Curt shook his head. "Not at all. But we like to get started in the morning. And we've got four combat companies that have to make required training flights...preferably before the end of the month. We can load fast so you can lift out, fly us around the patch, and land us under simulated combat conditions...when we'll move fast, too. Major, I'll bet by Friday afternoon Carson's Companions will have this drill down cold and be able to get into and out of your 'dynes in ten minutes...or *less*."

Worsham looked levelly at Curt. A smile flicked around the corners of his mouth, making his handlebar mustache turn up at its ends in a wicked, evil-looking manner. But Worsham wasn't trying to be difficult; he just appeared fearsome. "Are you saying you're willing to put your money where your mouth is, Major?"

Curt nodded.

"A hundred dollars says you can't beat ten minutes by Friday," Worsham went on. "In fact, I'll give you the benefit of the doubt. I'll give you fifteen minutes!"

"Don't stretch your luck, Major," Curt said smoothly. "I offered ten minutes, and I let it stand at ten. And a hundred sounds a little wimpish, sir. Let's make it two fifty…"

It was too steep for the airman. "Let's make it a hundred, and the winners buy the drinks for the losers in Rudesheim Saturday night. And the Warhawks will buy dinner, too, if you beat fifteen minutes. Deal?"

"Deal! Nothing like a little bet to stimulate an operation," Curt pointed out. "But there's one thing, Major: We're going to haul ass, and if any of your people drag ass or get in the way, they're likely to get run over. And if we detect any foot-dragging, the deal's off."

Worsham shook his head. "Negatory! We've got to have an independent umpire if those conditions hold."

"Got anyone in mind?"

Worsham nodded. "I've got some Luftwaffe buddies at Rhein-Main."

"No good," Curt told him. "Your buddies, not ours. Let's get the MPs to do it. They'll be there anyhow…"

"And they hate both our guts because of their screw-up yesterday," Worsham added.

"Oh-eight-hundred tomorrow?"

"You're on!"

Chapter Sixteen

"Major, I'm really confused. I don't understand why the Warhawks think we can't load our warbots and personnel aboard four Chippewas in less than thirty minutes," Lieutenant Kitsy Clinton remarked as the two of them walked across the compound back to the Companions' quarters.

Major Curt Carson smiled knowingly. "Major Cal Worsham doesn't realize all the consequences of dealing with Sierra Charlies, Lieutenant," he told her.

"Excuse me, Major, but I'm having a little trouble following the thread," Kitsy admitted.

"Tell me: What's the main difference between a regular RI company and the Companions?" Curt asked her, using his usual procedure of education and training by asking leading questions.

"We fight alongside our warbots," she replied without hesitation.

"True, but maybe I should have worded my question differently," Curt remarked, realizing that his control of the English language had probably slipped a bit since the company had become Sierra Charlie about two years ago. Running a neuroelectronic warbot required the use of specific and unambiguous thinking that was far different from the thought processes of everyday verbal communication. Kitsy Clinton had answered his question quite correctly, because she'd been recently trained as a warbot officer at Fort Benning following her graduation from West Point. "Let me put it this way: What are the equipment differences between the TO&E of a regular warbot company and a Sierra Charlie company?"

Kitsy caught on immediately. "A regular RI company has a hundred-forty-four warbots. We have twenty-seven," she replied quickly.

"And are the Sierra Charlie warbots - the Jeeps, Mary Anns, and

Hairy Foxes - different from ordinary M-twenty-twos or especially M-tens?"

"Damned right! They're a hell of a lot bigger and heavier…"

"So, what is Major Worsham expecting?"

"Uh, he thinks we'll be using seven people, some who have boarded ahead of time and taken up to fifteen minutes to get into linkage. Then these warbot brainies will have to load more than a hundred big, heavy neuroelectronic warbots into his Chippies while other members of the company dog them down to the cargo decks to prevent them from moving around in turbulence and violent combat maneuvers…"

"And?"

"And we'll be using twelve Companions to load up twenty-seven small, compact, voice-commanded warbots, no linkage time, and no heavy dogging down," she finished brightly.

"Glad to see you can think well in idiot mode," he told her lightly, using a compliment normally given to actual warbot brainies.

"Thank you, sir," Kitsy replied as she walked alongside him, unconsciously staying in step with him. Curt noticed this and unexpectedly performed the little jog skip used to change step. She suddenly looked at him and did the same.

"And glad to see you're still what the liberal news media calls a 'typical West Point military automaton,' Lieutenant," he told her with a grin.

"Sir, habits picked up during those four years are damned hard to break," she reminded him.

"Yes, I know. But the Companions are succeeding in that regard," he pointed out, "because I've noticed that your language has gotten a great deal saltier."

Kitsy sighed. "Yes, sir. Sorry, sir. It's just difficult *not* to pick up the vulgarities of combat soldiers when you live and work among the actual thing. It's tough to remain a lady…"

Curt had to laugh at that remark. "Lieutenant, in my experience, you have never once ceased to be a lady...even in some rather intimate circumstances when Rule Ten wasn't in effect. You have never once been rude unintentionally...at least in my presence, at any rate. So, don't apologize to me. Apology not necessary; therefore, apology not accepted." He started up the stairs to the Companions' barracks. "Now let's get with it. We've got a hell of a job to do in about sixteen hours..."

Platoon Sergeant Nick Gerard was supervising Kitsy's Alpha Platoon in checking out and becoming familiar with the arctic gear they'd just received from the quarter-master warehouse. Gerard looked like a fat, furry white teddy bear when he met them as they entered the day room, but he wasn't very happy.

"Lieutenant, I got the platoon kitted out, but you're going to have to go over to QM yourself to be sized," he explained to her. "They won't issue arctic gear unless it's configured to the individual."

"What the hell? Why not, Nick?" Kitsy wanted to know.

"Well, come here and I'll show you, sir. Actually, we've got a couple of bitchy problems with this stuff, and I need some advice on what to do about it all," Gerard remarked. Curt and Kitsy followed him to where both Charlie Koslowski and Jim Elliott were struggling with clothing and equipment.

If Nick bitched or sniveled about something, Curt listened. Gerard was a blooded combat soldier who'd been shot at and wounded several times. He'd been the mainstay of Alpha Platoon and had held it together after Alexis Morgan had been promoted to the command of her own company and while Lieutenant Clinton was getting up to speed. Since Clinton was a new young officer less than a year out of West Point, it was Nick Gerard's experience and savvy that still counted in the running of Alpha Platoon.

Gerard indicated the clothing that Koslowski and Elliott were working with. "Major, this is old, outmoded, obsolete gear. We could get better stuff if we went down to the local ski shop."

"That's what I thought," Curt said, because the arctic kit worn by

Gerard, Koslowski, and Elliott looked very familiar to him. "The Army hasn't fought in a cold climate for a couple of decades, and it doesn't pay much attention to the needs of troops that are only garrisoned and not expected to get into the field and fight. That's what warbots are for, or so the Army policy has dictated for the last twenty or so years."

Curt knew what he was talking about. Not only was the U.S. Army, in the cut-down, lean, mean, robotic military style of the twenty-first century, smaller than it had been after the Civil War in terms of ratio of military personnel to the general population, but the personal combat clothing needs of the individual soldier had been ignored until the Sierra Charlies had come along. No justification could be found to appropriate the funds for properly attiring combat field troops fighting in various climates; warbot brainies fought from comfortable neuroelectronic warbot control couches inside climate controlled armored vehicles. Save for noncombat every-day clothing such as overcoats and such, the Army's battle clothing needs and supplies were extremely old fashioned. In actuality, the Aerospace Force had far better field gear for its flight line personnel, who did indeed have to brave the vagaries and extremes of weather, and for its flight crews, who needed gee-suits, flight gear, and even space suits to protect them from obviously hostile environments.

The battle clothing of the Sierra Charlies thus far had been fairly simple, since the operations in Trinidad, Namibia, and Sonora had taken place in tropical or semitropical climates where fatigue or work cammies sufficed.

Therefore, the arctic gear that had been issued to Alpha Platoon was turn-of-the-century stuff.

The first layer was white thermal underwear, which the members of Alpha Platoon were trying to put on over their McCarthy experimental bioelectronic harnesses and the required body armor. The thermal undergarment was thin, with multicellular structure designed to retain body heat while at the same time permitting sweat to be transported away by capillary action so it could be evaporated outside the thermal protection and thus not permitted to cool the wearer. The thermal underwear also doubled as a chafing layer to protect the skin.

The second layer had a soft, porous inner surface to also trap heat and allow perspiration to migrate outward. This was followed by a thin integral structural fabric that also served as a chafing layer to prevent outside objects from rubbing or tearing the thermal underlayer. Its external surface was white and furry. The fur served not only to provide additional insulation but was also camouflage which would match the white background of arctic conditions while breaking up and softening the human outline. Although it was loose-fitting, it was tight around the neck, wrists, and ankles to prevent the escape of body heat.

With it were worn one or two sets of gloves and one or two pairs of boots, depending on the ambient temperature and the work to be done. A parka-like hood could be pulled up over a skintight balaclava and face mask; both were fabricated of a hydrophobic fabric that wouldn't hold water so that the wearer's breath would not freeze to ice around the edges.

All of this was old hat. Ancient technology. Curt winced inwardly. Nick Gerard was right: They could have gotten better, lighter, and more effective gear in the civilian ski shop in Wiesbaden - gear which, however, couldn't be used in combat because of its intentionally bright colors.

So, the old Army gear would work, even if it wouldn't work as well as modern high-tech cold-weather clothing.

"We've got a real problem, Major, and we're gonna have to figger out a way to make do," Nick explained. "We can't wear our combat helmets easily over the balaclava and under the parka hood." He pulled up his parka hood and had trouble getting it over the large Sierra Charlie combat helmet.

"Sirs, what the hell are we gonna do? We've been issued this gear and were told that it's right because it fits," Jim Elliott complained.

"Take this junk back," Kitsy Clinton suddenly said.

Curt was rather taken aback by this sudden outburst from the platoon's commanding officer. It certainly hadn't been characteristic of her somewhat tentative leadership to date. Maybe she was learning to be decisive and to put her neck out for her troops. Curt hoped so. She was a good fighter.

"Lieutenant? What the hell? This is what they gave us," Gerard complained. "The QM people said it fit properly."

"I said take it back," she repeated firmly. "I'll go with you, and I'll insist that everyone be given a larger parka that will fit over a combat helmet." She looked around at her platoon. "All right, everyone out of those sweat suits. Get back in cammies. Then come along and bring your helmets. I'm going to see to it that QM does its job and we're fitted out properly. Damned if I want my platoon to go into a frigid operation with gear that isn't right!"

"I'll come, too," Curt told her, encouraged by her reaction and wanting to be there to back her up if she needed it...though in her present state of mind, Curt felt she probably didn't need backup. Kitsy was small and lean, but she was a ball of fire and a tough lady to tangle with when she wanted to be. "Sergeant Sampson and I need to be outfitted. By the way, where is Sergeant Sampson?"

"Out in the parking lot with the RTVs, Major," Nick reported. "They're trying to get all the bots arctic-configured."

"Any word on how they're coming along?" Curt asked. "No, sir, except that regimental supply hasn't been able to get some of the cold-weather lubricants and heat blankets required by the AI cubes," Nick reported.

"Shit, this is going to be a real sheep screw," Curt muttered. "We may not have time to get things ready for an oh-eight-hundred load-up exercise tomorrow morning."

"Major, Alpha Platoon will be as ready as Supply will allow us to be," Kitsy promised, "even if we have to work all night."

"If I can get this organized, you won't have to" was Curt's reply.

That was his first priority after getting himself out-fitted, which was at the top of his "must-do" list at the moment. He had no doubt that the Companions would be able to put their twenty-seven warbots and twelve people aboard four Chippewas in ten minutes; the warbots weren't that large and were not difficult to strap down for flight. But they'd have to be ready with all warbots at least functional if not cold weather configured. They had at least several days to carry out the servicing of the bots. Curt figured they could work that in between their training flights, which were already tightly scheduled with Worsham's Warhawks.

But Curt Carson had a sneaking hunch that something else was in the works, something that might not give the Washington Greys time to do much of anything.

He was right...and he was wrong.

Chapter Seventeen

It was 0700 on another wan, gray, cloudy day in Germany. Carson's Companions, Alpha Company of the 3rd Regiment (Special Combat), the Washington Greys, gathered around their commanding officer, Major Curt Carson, in the day room of the Wiesbaden barracks.

Everyone was dressed in sensor harness, body armor, thermal underwear, and arctic white furs. The windows of the day room were wide open, and the heating system was turned off. Yet the Companions were sweating. None of them were wearing their parka hoods or gloves. They wore their helmets and carried their personal weapons.

Four other persons were present that morning: Lieutenant Colonel William Bellamack; his chief of regimental operations, Captain Hensley Atkinson; Regimental Sergeant Major Henry Kester; and Captain Owen Pendleton on hand with his portable recording equipment.

"Attention to orders," Curt snapped, standing before them. "This is a training exercise. Ammo has not been issued. Laser fire designators have been fitted to all weapons. If you haven't already done so, activate your experimental sensor harnesses and transmitters now so that Captain Pendleton may commence taking his data. Our objective today is to mount Chippewas flown by Worsham's Warhawks and proceed to Training Area Lima, located here in the Taunus Mountains." He indicated a map which he'd taped up on the wall although any of his company could have called it up on their helmet visors. Some did if for no other reason than to check their own equipment.

"The landing zone will be located here at coordinates five-Bravo-one-zero, seven-Delta-four," Curt indicated on the map. "We will have no tactical air support. We will dismount the Chippewas and immediately clear the landing zone area by moving under cover to the west. The company will then form up with Alpha on point and Bravo in maneuver position. We will proceed one-seven-point-zero kilometers on a heading of two-four-five to secure Hill Papa-Four, which is reportedly being held by a Red Force company of airborne armor.

"Ess-two reports that this Red Force company consists of four officers and twenty-seven men accompanied by three BMD-niner-niner armored support vehicles and one ACRV-two-four command vehicle. We can expect the usual sort of small-arms fire we'd get from a Red Force company-five-point-five-six-millimeter rifle and squad automatic weapons fire. They may have some RPG-eighty shoulder-fired antiwarbot missiles." Actually, no one was on Hill P-4; they were going up against a simulated enemy force.

"Alpha will probe for them. When we discover their disposition Bravo will lay down a fire base while Alpha maneuvers: We should be able to wrap up this exercise in less than an hour.

"Following the exercise, we will call for extraction by the Warhawks, who will return us to Wiesbaden." Curt paused and looked at Jerry Allen. "Lieutenant, what is the status of our warbot complement?"

"Sir, we have twelve Mark Sixty Mary Anns ready to go," the young first lieutenant snapped back. "Two of the Mark Forty-four Hairy Foxes developed glitches in their Mark Five AI units last night; replacement cubes are being flown in from Fort Huachuca but will not be here until noon tomorrow. Therefore, we have only ten Hairy Foxes active. All three Mark Thirty-three jeeps are operational and ready, sir!"

"Very well! Balance your squads in Bravo Platoon, Lieutenant. Otherwise, we will proceed nominally." Curt paused for a moment, then added, "We have a target of ten minutes' time for mounting and dismounting the Chippies. Alpha Platoon will mount Warhawk One. The first squad of Bravo Platoon will mount Warhawk Two. The second squad of Bravo Platoon will mount Warhawk Three. Warhawk Four will carry Colonel Bellamack, Captain Atkinson, Captain Pendleton, Lieutenant Allen, Sergeant Major Kester,

Sergeant Sampson, Sergeant Dillon, me, and the three jeeps. Colonel Bellamack, Captain Atkinson, and Sergeant Kester are observers and, in a way, umpires. I have a small bet with Major Worsham of the Warhawks that the Companions can mount the Chippies in ten minutes or less. If they lose, they buy the drinks tonight. If we lose, I buy the drinks. You have nothing to lose and everything to gain, so let's hustle!"

"Yo! Hustle!" called out Kitsy Clinton.

"Hustle!" echoed Jerry Allen.

"Very well, any questions?" Curt looked around. "If not, then form up and move out to the Warhawk parking lot. We've got to be a ready steady with a heady teddy at oh-eight-hundred, so don't be late! Move out!"

The company broke and ran for the RTVs parked about 500 meters away. They had twenty-seven minutes to power up, move the warbots, and be ready to mount up. So, they moved.

"What the hell is this about a bet?" Bellamack asked Curt as they moved toward the aerodyne area.

"Worsham didn't think we could mount our company in less than thirty minutes," Curt explained. "He's used to dealing with regular RI, not the Sierra Charlies."

"He'll learn," was Henry Kester's brief comment.

"Don't let the betting part get out," Bellamack warned. "If the high brass at Wiesbaden gets wind of it, they could make things muddy for me. By the way, why'd you do it?"

"Motivated the shit out of my company, Colonel," Curt explained.

"Good man! And, by the way, I never heard about the bet..."

Curt grinned. "You mean you don't want to take your share of the winnings?"

"I'm not supposed to be involved," Bellamack said.

"The hell you're not," Curt reminded him. "If you drag your ass mounting an aerodyne, you could cause me to lose that bet!"

"Carson," Bellamack said with mock frustration in his voice because he really supported Curt's little motivational scheme, "you're a troublemaker. What the hell am I going to do with you?"

The two men had a contract of mutual support which was unwritten and in some ways unspoken. In spite of formal military discipline, it made relations between the two of them more personal. "Maybe buy me the first drink tonight, Colonel?"

Twenty minutes later, Carson's Companions with their warbot complement waited quietly alongside the parking lot where four of the Warhawk aerodynes stood on their landing legs with their hatches closed and secured.

Curt was boiling mad. "Shit!" he muttered. "Here it is two minutes before oh-eight, and no one from the Warhawks has bothered to show up yet!"

"Don't sweat it, Major," Henry Kester advised and pointed. "Here they come now."

At precisely 0800, four aerodyne crews stepped into the parking lot. Curt was pleased to see that Major Cal Worsham was one of the pilots.

There was no small talk among the Warhawks. They moved with precision. At each of the four assigned Chippewas, a sergeant crew chief stepped up to the aft end of the 'dyne, plugged in an intercom headset, flipped up a weatherproof cover on the lip of the saucer shaped vehicle, and threw a switch to deploy the access hatch. The aft lip of each Chippewa opened into two segments, one swinging upward to provide cover for the cargo hatch and the other moving downward to form a loading ramp.

The UCA-21A Chippewas were the first of a new design intended for easier loading and unloading. They squatted almost on the ground; other 'dynes Curt and his troops had worked with in the post had stood aloft on spindly landing legs and used vertically moving loading and unloading hatches that went up into the belly.

The instant the aft cargo hatch was open, a pilot moved quickly into the Chippewa. Within a minute, sounds began to come from each aerodyne. Whines, whirls, and finally the muffled boom and roar of a starting aux power unit indicated the pilot had powered up.

The crew chief at Warhawk One was familiar to Curt. She was the Warhawks' first sergeant, Timothea Timm. She turned to face Curt, saluted, and called out, "Colonel, Major, the Warhawk Chippewas are ready to mount!"

Curt returned her salute and sang out, "Companions, mount up!" He punched the tab on his stopwatch as he gave the command.

It was quick. Although the Companions had never before loaded into Chippewas, they moved with speed and with little hesitation. They were used to working together as a team. A few blunders occurred, such as the one where two Hairy Foxes almost ran into one another trying to get into Warhawk Three. The Warhawk crew chiefs watched intently, trying to make sure these gravel crunchers and their beefy warbots didn't damage their aerodynes. Bellamack, Atkinson, and Kester also watched.

Eight minutes and fifty-six seconds after Curt had given the command, he was the last one to step into Warhawk Four and tell Sergeant Timm, "Companions are mounted, Sergeant. Inform the major that we are ready for lift."

Timm checked her watch, then looked at it again. "Yes sir! My compliments, sir! I honestly didn't think you could do it this fast!"

"SOP for Sierra Charlies, Sergeant," he remarked off-handedly to her and proceeded forward into the cargo bay, where he passed under the flight deck and called up, "Major, we're mounted and ready!"

Worsham's round face scowled and the tips of his mustache twitched. "Everyone aboard, Major?"

"I repeat, Major: The Companions are mounted and ready for lift!"

"Son of a bitch! You won this one, Carson! Let's see how you do on the recovery! Might as well come up and rock on the front porch with us during the inbound. I'll be in partial linkage and not very good company, but maybe you can see where we're going."

"Good idea. I might have some definite ideas about the landing point when we reach the LZ." Curt clambered up the access ladder and slipped into a seat. "I hope to hell you can get some air moving inside this frisbee, Major. With this arctic gear, we're sweating our buns off."

Worsham smiled his evil-looking smile, which Curt was rapidly coming to know as the man's non-evil trade-mark. It was just the way Cal Worsham looked. "As soon as we get airborne, Major. Goddammit, I figured you for at least twenty minutes, so we're fifteen minutes ahead of our clearance sked. Lemme see if I can negotiate an early release." He got the faraway look of a person who's in partial linkage, aware of his surroundings but using his brain waves to control his robotic flying machine and to communicate through its computers with the airspace control computers and their personnel.

While Curt was waiting in the meantime, sweat began to run down his back and sides, further irritating the linkage harness that was there by order of the commanding officer.

Finally, the Chippewa's turbines began to spool up. With no advance warning, the assault transport aerodyne suddenly surged vertically aloft. Through the flight deck windows, Curt could see the other three Chippewas also lifting off.

The vertical flight ceased at about 100 meters' altitude, and the four Chippies began moving northeastward toward the military maneuvering area.

Curt watched the moving map display on the console and soon oriented himself with regard to the outside terrain. About three klicks from the LZ, the Chippewas slowed their forward speed, lost altitude, and began to approach the LZ in assault mode at treetop level.

Something unusual caught Curt's eye. In the thick April vegetation below, he thought he saw a camouflaged aerodyne. It was gone as suddenly as he got the image in his mind. But a second one appeared, and there was no doubt. But he couldn't identify it.

Two aerodynes and maybe more down there on the ground. Well, maybe they had nothing to do with this exercise. After all, Training Area Lima was used by American, British, Canadian, and German ground forces.

However, when he compared the location of what he'd seen with the Chippewa's location on the map display, the camouflaged aerodynes were on the other side of Hill P-4.

There wasn't time to think about it.

Following assault doctrine, Worsham's Warhawks brought the Chippewas in low and fast, right over the treetops, and touched down on the landing zone.

Within seconds, the aft hatches popped open quickly as the lift flow over the upper surfaces of the Chippewa eased.

By the time Curt had clambered down from the flight deck, the Jeep had already debouched. He unslung his *Novia* assault rifle and let the Sierra Charlies out of the hatch. Bellamack, Atkinson, Kester, and Pendleton followed.

Bots and Sierra Charlies from the other three Chippewas were moving quickly toward the cover of the thick woods. Curt followed his Jeep, which was operating under the voice control of Edie Sampson at the moment.

Under the thick vegetation cover of the woods, the Companions grouped while the Chippewas lifted off and withdrew to a holding area where they would await the recall signal.

Curt knelt in the thick underbrush and keyed his helmet tacomm. "Alpha, report!"

"On the ground and moving toward objective!" came Kitsy Clinton's reply.

"Bravo, report!"

"On the ground and moving toward objective behind Alpha!" was Jerry Allen's answer.

"Let's go!" Curt said to Sampson. "Move that Jeep out in front!"

He stood up along with Edie Sampson.

"Incoming! Incoming! Was the sudden call from Kitsy Clinton.

"What the hell? Nobody else was supposed to be here!" Jerry Allen yelled.

And a bright red spot suddenly appeared on the white fur front of First Sergeant Edie Sampson's parka.

Chapter Eighteen

"My God, I'm hit!" First Sergeant Edie Sampson shouted.

"Like hell!" Curt yelled back. "That was a laser designator! We aren't supposed to have live opposition out here this morning! Someone has screwed up! Proceed!"

"Major Carson, attention to orders!" It was the voice of Colonel Wild Bill Bellamack in his tacomm. "The nature of this exercise has been changed. Your company is now deployed against a simulated force armed with laser designators. Captain Atkinson, Sergeant Kester, and I have become exercise umpires. I therefore rule that Sergeant Sampson has been hit and is out of action. Sergeant, you've got the next hour or so to relax."

"*What?*" Curt exploded, then realized that the United States Army was playing "surprise-surprise" with him again. He should have anticipated it, but he'd concentrated his attention on what he'd thought was the major purpose of this exercise: aerodyne operations.

Someone had turned it into a combat exercise.

"Jesus Christ, Colonel! If you knew this was going to turn into a shooting match, why the hell didn't you tell me?" Curt yelled. He was pissed off - really pissed off - that his regimental commander hadn't warned him. It wasn't like Bellamack to do this sort of shitty thing to his people.

"I couldn't," Bellamack admitted. "Talk to you about it later!"

Okay, goddammit, if that's the sort of fucking little game you bastards want to play, we'll play the shit out of it! Curt thought violently because he couldn't say it, at least not to Bellamack. Then he keyed his helmet tacomm and called, "Companions all, this is Companion Leader! Assume we are actually under fire! Some bastards are out there shooting at us with laser targeters ! Where the hell are they?"

"Companion Leader, this is Companion Alpha!" Kitsy Clinton's voice came back. "We've got our sensors up and functioning now! I have about two dozen targets, bearing two-eight-five magnetic, range three-zero-zero! They appear to have human characteristics insofar as thermal signatures and radar returns indicate. No warbots detected! At least, I don't think so! The targets don't look like warbots to me!"

"Companion Leader, this is Companion Bravo!" Jerry Allen reported. "Companion Alpha, we see our targets!"

"Bravo, are you in a position to engage?" Curt wanted to know.

"Affirmative! Affirmative! We're opening fire with Hairy Foxes!"

"Alpha, disengage! Flank right!" Curt snapped.

"Companion Leader, this is Companion Alpha! The going is bitchy! These thick woods make it difficult to move fast!"

"Do it, dammit! Do it!" Curt urged. "Alpha, can you report casualties?"

"Sergeant Kester just showed up as our umpire," Kitsy reported.

"Any casualties?" Curt repeated.

"Negatory! Uh, correction: Sergeant Kester just informed me I lost Sergeant Elliott and a Mary Ann!"

At this casualty rate, the Companions couldn't maintain the fight very long. That was a major concern to Curt at that moment, so he called, "Companion Bravo, any casualties?"

"Negatory, but I can't find Corporal Motega!"

"What do you mean, you can't find her?"

"Her beacon has disappeared off my display!" Jerry Allen reported.

Curt checked his own tactical display and confirmed it. "Equipment malfunction?" he wanted to know.

"I don't think so. When a beacon fails, I usually get some warning because it goes intermittent first. Motega's went off like it was hit hard or turned off. But that's not my major problem at the moment!

I'm taking heavy incoming! The trees around me are lit up with red spots! Whup! Just lost a Hairy Fox! And I've got targets! Lots of them! Company level! Maybe battalion strength! Some of the targets are just below the ridge this side of Hill Papa-Four!"

Curt took a few seconds to study the tactical display projected on his helmet visor. It looked like a full enemy platoon deployed between Bravo and the hill. On the hill itself, he saw about twice as many targets, all apparently firing on coordinates supplied by the enemy platoon ahead of Bravo. Alpha was moving to the right flank, but they weren't moving fast enough.

The fire laid down by the Hairy Foxes must be having some effect on the enemy, because the amount of incoming began to decrease.

"Companion Leader, this is Companion Alpha! I've come upon a road through the forest! I can follow it to flank the hill to the north!" Kitsy Clinton called.

"Negatory! Don't do it!" Curt warned her quickly. "Don't step out on that road! The enemy may have it covered with light automatic weapon fire! Don't take the chance! Move under cover alongside it!"

Damn! He needed Sampson to help run this sheep screw! But she was officially KIA according to the umpires.

What he needed to do and do fast was to maneuver. That was the secret of success for Sierra Charlies. If he didn't, the defending force - whoever they were - would probably move on him because it looked like they had no warbots.

That in itself was strange.

Who could they be?

The Germans were roboticized. So were the Brits and the Canadians. The only other NATO unit in this area was the U.S. 26th R.U.R. Robot Infantry Division, and it sure as hell wasn't a Sierra Charlie outfit!

Whoever was out there was good. They'd pinned down Allen's platoon with an enormous volume of fire totally uncharacteristic of a nonrobot Sierra Charlie outfit. And they appeared to be familiar with fighting in this sort of terrain.

Curt decided to move to the right with his Jeep and join Alpha Platoon's flanking movement. The going was indeed difficult through the thick underbrush of the German forest.

He wanted to get a visual on the enemy. He wanted to identify them. No nonwarbot units existed in the European theater. So, it seemed impossible to him that the Companions were suddenly up against a nonwarbot unit in the forests of the Taunus Mountains of Germany on a cold, damp spring morning.

"Companion Leader, this is Companion Bravo!" Jerry Allen called in.

"Companion Leader here! Go!"

"Major, I just got a report from Corporal Motega! You've got to listen to what she has to say!"

"Where the hell has she been?"

"I'm going to have to raise hell with her after this is over, Major," Allen replied in hurried tones. "She took off on her own to the left flank on a scouting jaunt..."

"Shit! Corporal Motega, this is Companion Leader! Major Carson speaking! What the hell did you think you were doing? And what have you got to report?" Curt asked over the tacomm link.

"Major, this is Corporal Motega reporting. I'm over on the left flank about halfway up Hill Papa-Four. I have the enemy in visual contact, but they don't see me because my beacon is off and I'm playing hard to see. Our enemy is a German warbot company using the new Krupp Mark Ten Super Tiger miniature warbots that are stealthed and spooked so they appear to be human troops, but there are no humans out there," the Crow Indian girl reported.

"Say again? Warbots?" Curt asked.

"Roger, sir. German Super Tiger warbots. I see no human troops," Dyani Motega repeated.

"What the hell are you doing, separated from your platoon? And what the hell happened to your beacon?"

"Major, I received no orders to the contrary, so I went on a scouting patrol," she replied. "Bravo Platoon is short a Hairy Fox, and it was the only warbot Sergeant Dillon assigned to me because this was my first field exercise. So, I turned off my tactical beacon to prevent the enemy from possibly snooping and finding me. I'm moving in stealth, creeping and crawling so I'm below the normal warbot sensor sweep zone. So, they'll have trouble picking me up visually unless they see my beacon return."

"Can you find their cee-pee?" Curt suddenly asked, realizing that he had a critical piece of information that might allow him to salvage this ambush.

"I'll try, sir!"

"Do it! Report on this channel when you have something!" Curt ordered. The new Companion had certainly acted with initiative in her first combat exercise, but Curt wanted to have a few words with her later about informing her platoon leader about what she was doing.

"Companions all, this is Companion Leader!" Curt snapped orders. "Tactical beacons *off!* Bravo Leader, maintain your position and continue your fire. Alpha Leader, I'm joining you! Alpha will proceed toward Hill Papa-Four until fired upon; when that happens, we'll put the Mary Anns and Jeeps in stationary return-fire mode and proceed to the hill on our hands and knees. Alpha Leader, how many M-one-hundred tube rockets you got?"

"Everyone is carrying two," Kitsy reported.

"Okay, we'll use them against the warbots from behind when we get into a position where we can't miss with those bumpers," Curt decided. "Unless Motega finds the cee-pee first. If she does and if we can get to it, we'll take it out with the M-one-hundreds instead."

"Without beacons, how are we going to know where our own forces are, Major?" Kitsy wanted to know. "We could fire into our own troops!"

"Not if we maintain tacomm contact," Curt advised her, "and let each other know where we are. The enemy can't track tacomm. It's a pseudo-random frequency hopper, and no one has enough computer power to break that program in less than an hour or so." At least, Signal Corps had finally gotten something right for the Sierra Charlies, Curt said to himself. Then he ordered, "Okay, move and keep moving! Alpha, I'm trying to find you."

"I hear you to the southeast of me, very close. Keep coming. I'll sit tight and wait for you, Major."

"Negatory! Keep moving! I can move faster than a whole platoon!"

But he couldn't. He came to the narrow road through the forest, was careful not to step into the open, and decided he could move faster if he didn't have to wait for his jeep. So, he put the warbot into standby/self-protect mode and forged westward alone through the pines.

Somewhere in the sweeping right wheel that he'd made with his jeep, he'd left Colonel Bellamack, his umpire, behind. Actually, Curt's stealthy moves through the forest had served to shake Bellamack, who wasn't used to operating in such terrain.

So, Curt suddenly found himself moving parallel to the road all by himself. It was a lonesome trek. He realized how alone he really was. As a combat soldier and a former warbot brainy, he was used to being a member of a combat team. This was the first time he'd been out in the field on his own since his early days at West Point. It was a funny feeling.

He hoped he'd catch up with and find Alpha Platoon. But he couldn't see them anywhere.

He wasn't fired upon, but he crossed the north side of Hill Papa-Four. "Companion Alpha, this is Companion Leader. I'm in the saddle between Hill Papa-Four and Papa-Three. Where the hell are you?"

"Companion Alpha is on the ridge of Papa-Four and we're waiting for you to catch up. We're behind the entire warbot outfit," Kitsy Clinton reported. "We can open fire on them whenever you get here..."

"Commence firing!" Curt snapped. No sense in holding up the show just because he wasn't there.

A red laser spot suddenly appeared on the tree next to him.

He dropped to his belly on the soft carpet of pine needles and tried to determine where the shot had come from.

When he saw, he let out a sharp whistle.

Corporal Dyani Motega suddenly turned, and Curt caught her movement in the bushes.

"Don't shoot at your company commander!" he said in a quiet voice which was suitable for the silence of the German pine forest.

She swung and saw him, then relaxed. "Major! How did you get here?"

"Same way you did. I walked," he told her. "Don't tell me you came all the way around the south side of the hill?"

"Yes, sir!"

"Did you find the German cee-pee?"

"Maybe, sir. That's where I was headed when I ran into you," she told him. "I saw something in the woods a couple of hundred yards west of this position."

"Let's go have a look," he suggested.

Dyani Motega was a born soldier. She moved smoothly and quickly from cover to cover in a motion that was liquid and silent. She made no sudden moves that would attract the eye. It was apparent that slow but decisive movement was part of her nature.

Curt remembered his West Point training class in which Colonel Ned Vaughn had told them, "Move slowly. Rapid movement attracts the eye, whereas slow movement doesn't. How many of you noticed that I swung my pointer slowly from left to right in front of me just now? Answer: None of you. Here, I'll do it again. Now I'll move it quickly. See?" It was a demonstration Curt would never forget.

Together, they came upon a camouflaged Armored Command Post Vehicle parked under the trees.

"Companions all," Curt announced into his tacomm "Corporal Motega and I have located the enemy command post. Hang on, because this will all be over in less than a minute…" He turned to Motega. "Let's take it!"

ACPVs are designed for warbot warfare and have no defenses against mere combat soldiers. Curt and Motega walked up to the aft ramp hatch. Curt grabbed the handle and turned it, pulling on the door as he did so. It swung outward. In a smooth motion, Motega stepped through, followed by her commanding officer. Curt reached up on a lighted control panel and punched a switch labeled *ausser Gefecht.*

"Achtung! Achtung!" Curt barked. *"Entschuldigen sie, meine Herren, aber stehengeblieben! Ergebt Euch! /hr seid vollstandig eingekreist ! Wir sind Amerikaner Kampf lnfanterie!"* Then he returned to English and added, "Nice work, but you Germans have a lot to learn about Special Combat Infantry operations!"

With the exception of the biotechnicians, all the German officers and NCOs in the van were in deep linkage and could not reply. But they heard Curt through the ACPV's internal audio pickups, and the biotechnicians certainly heard and raised their hands.

"Put your warbots into passive mode and recall them!" Curt told them. "We've captured your command post, so you've lost this exercise!" He turned to Dyani Motega. "Keep an eye on things. I'll go outside and sound the victory signal so we can get an umpire in here for a call!"

She smiled broadly. "Yes, sir!"

"By the way, nice work for your first time in the field."

She smiled again. "Major, I've been playing cowboys and Indians ever since I could walk…except I played on the opposite side from most people. It's nice to know that those tactics work so well against robot infantry!"

The tension was gone, and Curt could suddenly laugh. "We're all on the same side here, Motega…thank God!"

Chapter Nineteen

Colonel Wild Bill Bellamack showed up alone on foot a few minutes later. "I'll be a son of a bitch!" he cursed under his breath when he saw that Curt and Motega had indeed captured the ACPV of the opposing *Bundeswehr Robotinfanterie* company. "You got the hell away from me when you took off into the woods, Carson. I hope you did this all fair and square. And I wouldn't believe this if I hadn't seen it! Dammit, Hettrick warned me about this sort of thing! You and your Companions have a disturbing tendency to raise holy hell with war games and training exercises. I don't know how you did it this time, but I've got to award you the green banana sandwich. You won the exercise!"

Curt and Dyani Motega were sitting together on the steps of the German ACPV. There was nothing further they could do inside. The *Bundeswehr* warbot brainies were recovering their warbots and preparing for their own trek home. The commander of Carson's Companions grinned and explained, "We did what we've always done, Colonel: Go for the head, the brains, the command post, the headquarters. Capture the brain, and you've got the rest of the body. What else can human soldiers do against warbots? I could hack away at individual warbots and waste my people until hell freezes over - which it may do tonight if it gets much colder here. Or I could use the natural advantages of the Sierra Charlies to overcome the disadvantages. Warbots are big, powerful, and clumsy; people are small, fast, and versatile. So, we moved in on this German ACPV and took it by hand."

"But only two of you?"

"Only two of us, Colonel," Curt admitted. "Corporal Motega spotted the command post on a self-instigated personal recon sweep...for which I fully intend to chew her out because she broke away from her platoon and went charging all over the countryside..."

"What the hell prompted you to do that, Corporal?" Bellamack asked.

Motega got to her feet and came to attention, "Sir, I was assigned two Hairy Foxes because this was my first exercise and Sergeant Dillon didn't think I could handle six of them. Then one went toes-up before departure and Captain Atkinson declared the other one destroyed in the opening minute of the battle. I was let with nothing to run because my voice print had been introduced to only those two Hairy Foxes. I wasn't going to lie there on my belly in the mud and get shot at. So I took off to find out where the enemy was."

"You should have told Sergeant Dillon you were heading for the puckerbrush." Curt reprimanded her, making a mental note to do a little chewing on Dillon and Allen for being stupid and not programming all their Bravo Hairy Foxes to respond to the voice prints of all platoon members. This was an example of what could happen when voice-commanded warbots were assigned exclusively to individuals.

"Sir, Sergeant Dillon was declared out of action by Captain Atkinson," Dyani Motega explained. "Lieutenant Allen and Sergeant Cole were too busy trying to run four Hairy Foxes and a jeep under fire. So I faded into the underbrush and went scouting because it was apparent I was about as useful as tits on a turret at that point..."

"Well, thanks to the initiative of your troopers, Carson, you won this one," Bellamack admitted reluctantly.

"Colonel," Curt pointed out, "you sound like you didn't think we would."

"It was fifty-fifty," Bellamack said.

"Fifty-fifty? Hell, against a full Robot Infantry outfit, the odds have always been better than that! But I've got a heavy bitch to lay on you, Colonel," Curt remarked, standing up to face his regimental commander. "The Germans are inside the ACPV busily recovering their Super Tiger warbots; they can't hear us. And Motega here is going to forget this conversation because I tell her to. So I'm going to take this opportunity to yammer."

"Yammer away. Maybe it will do some good. Maybe it won't."

"Let's find out. We came into this goddamned 'exercise' this morning because for some reason unknown to us at the time, we have to get practice getting in and out of the Chippewas fast. Well, we did what we were expected to do, Colonel. But we sure as hell didn't expect to be shot at, even with laser targeters. Why the hell wasn't I notified that we were stepping into a war game?"

"Come on," Bellamack motioned, "let's walk back over the hill to the recovery zone, and I'll tell you what I know."

"Not until I take this goddamned parka off!" Curt complained and squirmed out of it.

Motega chose to continue to wear hers.

"You're right," Bellamack agreed as they walked. "The primary purpose of this exercise was to train for getting in and out of Chippewas fast. But Colonel Lovell also saw it as an opportunity to gather data."

"Aha!" Curt breathed. "I should have suspected that! But what they hell kind of data was she after?"

"The response to a surprise in the field under simulated combat conditions," Bellamack explained. "I had to keep it from you. Otherwise, no surprise, and the data would have been invalid. But you handled it real well. You recovered your balance and had the situation under control within minutes. Incidentally, Captain Pendleton told me he got outstanding data!"

Curt glanced down at Motega, who glanced back and said nothing. She was low on the totem pole and completely new to the sort of military informality that characterized the Washington Greys in action. She didn't know how to react to this, so she revealed nothing and kept on listening.

They passed a line of warbots heading toward the ACPV. These were warbots that were new to Curt's experience. The Germans had made significant progress in robotics since he'd fought in

Munsterlagen during the German Reunification skirmishes. The Krupp Mark Ten Super Tigers had a particular Toutonic appearance to them - an angular, powerful, no-nonsense functionality with all the subtlety of a *picklehaube* or classical Ger-man spiked helmet which had again come into fashion in the *Bundeswehr*. The Germans had done their usual thorough job on the Super Tigers; they were spotted with radar-, lidar-, and infrared-absorbing material in such a way as to mask their true identity to sensors and to possess the signature characteristics of human beings. Well, this had fooled Curt and the Companions until Motega had gotten a visual on them. It might have won the skirmish for the Germans if visual contact hadn't been achieved until later on.

Down the other side of Hill Papa-4, Curt's troops were collecting their voice-commanded warbots and preparing to move to the pickup area. Tech Sergeant Vickers, the warbot maintenance specialist assigned to the company, was checking each bot while Biotech Sergeant Shelley Hale made sure the human element of the company hadn't been hurt during the fracas.

The white fur on the parkas of the Companions was filthy with mud and stains from the pine needle carpet of the forest.

First Sergeant Edie Sampson wasn't dirty, since she'd been hit early and been forced by the umpires to sit out the skirmish, much to her disgust - which was why she was now taking some of her frustrations out on the troops by reminding them, "When we get back to Wiesbaden, get those uniforms cleaned up pronto! We ain't gonna get any others, so these have gotta last! If them stains set, the parkas won't be any good for winter environments. You'll stand out against snow like a rock! I want us to form up clean and sharp for tomorrow morning's exercise, so everybody *will* wear their arctic gear to the Retreat ceremony tonight! Clean! Hear me? I'll be inspecting for dirt and stains!"

"Aw, Sarge!" Charlie Koslowski complained. "Just because you didn't have to crawl on the ground and get your parka dirty! If I have to wash this, it won't dry out for days!"

"Don't snivel to me, damn it! FIDO!" Sampson told him. "Get it clean by tonight!"

Biotech Sergeant Shelley Hale went over to him and brushed her hand across the fur. The dirt fell off, leaving the white fur clean. "That's what I thought," she remarked. "This material is hydrophobic so that the moisture in your breath won't freeze to ice around the edges of the hood. It doesn't like water, and it won't bond with mud or other material containing water. Same stuff that's used in the dressings I've got. Just wait until the mud and dirt dry, Charlie, then brush the fur clean."

"Are you sure about that, Shelley?" Edie Sampson wanted to know.

"Sergeant, I'm sure," the biotech told her.

"Flush and brush," Koslowski remarked, originating a term that was thereafter applied to the arctic gear as "F-and-B."

When everyone was ready, Curt had Edie Sampson transmit the recall and recovery signal to the Warhawks.

The Warhawks flew the Chippewas with professional precision as they wafted in and settled to the ground in a random pattern intended to present a difficult target to any ground fire or tacair. No one needed to urge the Companions to move rapidly in loading up. The weather had turned foul, and a few spits of rain had started to fall over the hazy, foggy forests. They were more than anxious to get out of the weather and back to Wiesbaden, where they could get rid of their stifling arctic gear, weapons, equipment, and experimental harnesses.

In spite of the fact that they were tired after an intense training exercise under fire, the Companions got everything into the Warhawk Chippewas in less than nine minutes.

Major Cal Worsham didn't say anything on the ride back. He was busy flying the Chippewa at low altitudes under the sort of instrument meteorological conditions common in Europe most of the year. Popping in and out of areas of fog and rain made flying a Chippie far more difficult than driving one of the big cargo 'dynes on long-distance runs at higher altitudes. A pilot always opts to go high and fast in instrument conditions; under low and slow operations, a pilot runs a much higher chance of hitting a rock-filled cloud-commonly referred to as *cumulo granite* - even with the help of sophisticated sensor systems.

But when the Warhawks had set the Companions back down in the parking lot at Wiesbaden and the Companions were taking their time unloading, Cal Worsham approached Curt. The air support squadron commander had delinked in a short time - too short, Curt thought. But that was Worsham's problem, if it really was one for the big, rotund man.

"I had the opportunity to chat with some of the *Bundeswehr* boys on a linkage command net after you creamed them and they were waiting for their pickup," Worsham remarked, running his hand over his smoothly shaven head and plopping a service cap atop his skull to keep the rain off. "I ought to warn you. A *Robotinfanterie hauptmann* is very unhappy that you and Corporal Motega had the gall to capture a command post by hand without warbots! The Germans sure as hell weren't expecting that."

"Tough shit," Curt Carson replied with a grin. "Winning in combat means taking advantage of something the enemy doesn't expect. It's called the principle of surprise. The *Bundeswehr* ought to know something about that. Their *blitzkrieg* doctrine depended on surprise and movement, and it was one of the last times doctrine converged with weapons systems."

"Shit, they forget. We all forget," Worsham observed. "I'd forgotten that you Sierra Charlies didn't have to move a lot of big warbots around. That cost me."

"So, I guess the Germans aren't the only ones pissed off right now," Curt suggested.

Worsham leered with his evil expression. He clapped Curt on the shoulder and said in his loud, parade ground voice (probably caused by a progressive loss of hearing from flying 'dynes for years), "Who's pissed, Carson? Not me! You won fair and square. Both loading and unloading. Never cracked ten minutes max. I dunno how you Sierra Charlies do it, but you've sure as hell got my respect!"

"As I recall, we won more than your respect, Cal," Curt reminded him. "Something about buying drinks and dinner…"

"Yeah, you got it. But not this crappy junk they try to cook up as American food and throw at us here in Wiesbaden. Let's do it in Rudesheim Saturday night," Worsham offered.

"Along with all the happy German drunks?"

"Sure! Why not? Better food and better beer!"

"Do you want to hit up the colonel for passes?"

"You know him better. He's your full-time CO. So why me?"

"Don't call it a bet," Curt cautioned. "It was a motivational incentive to enhance troop performance."

"Whatever you say, Carson." He turned to go, then paused in midstep, whirled around, and cam back to say to Curt, "Goddamm it, I thought you Sierra Charlies were going to be a bunch of muddy gravel-grippers. But you're all right. Yeah, you're all right. The Warhawks will fly you anywhere any time you want to go."

"Thanks, and the confidence is reciprocal," Curt told him. "But we're both going to go where they tell us to go…and damned if I know where the hell that's going to be…"

Chapter Twenty

Rudesheim can probably best be described as a place on the Rhine River that's a resort town, a drinking town, and a happy town. Generations of Germans have come to Rudesheim on weekends to relax and enjoy life. It's also been a playground for the various military forces that have been present in Mittel Europa from prehistoric times onward. And it's been part of military history, too. Here the final collapse of the Roman Empire began when the Vandals crossed the frozen Rhine on the last day of 406 A.D. and continued moving westward into the defenseless province of Gaul under pressure from the invading Huns in the east. And in 1945 Patton's Third Army went through going the other way and forcing the collapse of yet another empire.

And here at Rudesheim played the American troops stationed in Europe as part of NATO to deter yet another invasion, again from the east.

But military history was farthest from the minds of Carson's Companions and Worsham's Warhawks on Saturday afternoon as they went into the happy town of Rudesheim on the banks of the Rhine for two days of R&R.

It had been a rough week during which the Companions had come from half a world away on an 'exercise' they *knew* was leading to a mission. But no one would tell them what the mission might be. The Warhawks had flown their Chippewas on a series of cross-country hops from Bahrain to Wiesbaden, again with no information as to why they were being redeployed to Europe except as tactical airlift for the Washington Greys.

It had also been a week of work, training, and occasional danger.

Major Cal Worsham was good to his word. He not only managed to get passes for the Companions but also for the First Group of his Alpha Flight, whose four Chippewa pilots, himself included, and crew chiefs had worked with the Companions over the past three days training on vertical envelopment techniques using Warhawk Chippewas.

Worsham even managed to finagle transportation from Wiesbaden to Rudsheim via an Army tour bus. When Curt asked him about this, the squadron commander merely grinned his evil-looking grin with his mustache tips quivering on each side of his mouth and remarked, "An acquaintance in the motor pool owed me a few. And the Chippie can carry about six tons and flies better when loaded."

"What the hell were you carrying as a favor?" Curt wanted to know.

"Don't ask," was Worsham's blunt reply.

So, Curt backed away from the subject.

But Curt knew damned good and well it had to be alcoholic beverages because beer, wines, and liquor were the *only* chemical substances tolerated by warbot brainies and the Army. Anything else - pot, hashish, coke, crack, peptides, or even nicotine - produced effects that could be quickly and easily picked up by the linkage computers and intelligence amplifiers. The computers were programmed to reject warbot branies trying to enter linkage with any intoxicating or narcotic chemical substances in their systems other than a minute trace of alcohol.

On the other hand, the Army had to tolerate some form of social relaxation for its troops, and the use of beer, wines, and liquor in moderation historically had produced few long-term effects. Furthermore, modern biotechnology knew a great deal about the effects of alcohol on the human mind and body. The biotechnology circuits could easily handle the physiological effects of a mild hangover and would report any physiological problems or symptoms that might indicate a warbot brainy was becoming an alcoholic.

But warbot brainies were careful about linking with a hangover because it was rough going in and rough coming out. There rule was simple: "Eight hours debauch to couch." Longer if it had been a very good party. Which is why most of the hard drinking took place during Stand-to on Friday night.

Thus the American military services in the twenty-first century were probably the "cleanest" ever. Soldiers weren't prudes or straights, but they know damned good and well they'd be caught or that their performance would be so degraded that they might be killed even in the simulator if they weren't sharp and on top of everything.

Linking with a computer had its advantages and disadvantages. One of the disadvantages was that the system sometimes killed the stupid.

Therefore, Curt knew what Worsham had been up to. Some Aerospace Force outfits ran German or American beer to various places, and bottles of good Scotch and Tennessee sippin' whiskey were always at a premium. Curt guessed that Worsham had gathered favors by transshipping stuff from Aerospace Force bases to the troops in garrison. It was a commonplace run-run activity.

The Companions and the Warhawks, and Lieutenant Adonica Sweet of Frazier's Ferrets because she went everywhere that Lieutenant Jerry Allen did, essentially took over a small inn on the back street in Rudesheim with the intention of staying Saturday night. But they gathered in a little *bierstube und café* nearby.

The beer was good because it was good German beer. The meal was good because it was hearty German food cooked for Germans to German tastes, not German food cooked American-style in an attempt to cater to American tastes. And the wine was good because Rudesheim is one of the win centers of the Rhine River valley.

The Warhawks got along well with the Companions, and twenty-one people can have a pretty good party.

However, the Warhawk women were envious of the female Companion troopers in a strange way. As Warhawk First Sergeant Tim Timm had remarked several days before, the situation of women in the Army Air Service was different from what it was in the Robot Infantry. AAS women weren't allowed to fly tactical aerodynes because of the long-standing Army tradition and congressional ban against women serving in direct personal combat assignments a tradition followed until the Washington Greys converted from Robot Infantry to Sierra Charlies. As it was, the women in the Greys were continually fearful that their backdoor entrance into personal combat assignments would draw reaction from Congress that would overwhelm the positive acceptance women combat troopers had gained as a result of Namibia and Sonora. At the moment, Congress was deliberately ignoring the situation, waiting to learn what the ultimate reaction of their constituents would be.

It wasn't that the Warhawk women weren't ready and willing to fight, however.

When the party broke up late in the evening, the Companions and Warhawks found themselves trying to proceed down a narrow Rudesheim street filled with carousing Germans.

And, as it turned out, carousing Sierra Charlies, too.

The American troops were conspicuous because they were in uniform. Both the Greys and the Warhawks had been deployed so quickly that no one had had the opportunity to bring along civvies.

Most of the happy German drunks ignored the uniformed Americans.

"Stay together, but don't worry about being mugged," Curt told his Companions. "Rudesheim is a safe town. The local *polizei* see to it that it stays that way so business isn't affected."

"Yeah," Major Cal Worsham added, "just act as drunk as the German next to you, and everything will be okay...Who needs to act drunk, by the way?" The last was addressed to no one in particular.

The Americans felt a lot better when they ran into another dozen Sierra Charlies.

"Well, goddamn if it isn't the Army's answer to the war-comic heroes!" came a call in Curt's ear. "Good evenin', Curt!"

Curt turned to see Captain Alexis Morgan and her Marauders.

The Marauders were in uniform, but all of them wore on their shaved heads a blue tam o'shanter with a yellow pom in the center.

"Well, Captain, that attire certainly looks fetching, but what's the blue cow pie on your head?" Curt asked with a grin. "Sort of nonreg, isn't it?"

"Ellie Aarts found them in a haberdashery!" Alexis bubbled. "We thought they'd be the sort of orgasmic caps the Sierra Charlies should wear!"

"Well, I guess the colonel will have the final say about that," Curt told her. "Come on, stick with us. We're heading back to our hotel!"

"But the evening's early!" Alexis complained.

Someone deliberately and rudely bumped into Curt.

"Entschuldigen sie, bitte," Curt responded automatically.

But the man who bumped him hard turned to face him, and Curt thought he recognized the young German. He was a typical Teutonic giant with a handsome, round face. If he hadn't sported the shaved head of a warbot brainy, he probably would have had a thatch of blond hair.

"You are *not* excused, American!" the German snapped at him in defiant tones. "Not only do you take far too much room on our German streets, but you insulted the *Bundeswehr Robotinfanterie* by your unforgivable actions in capturing my command post!"

Curt took a closer look. The young German was the company commander of the robot infantry unit he and Dyani Motega had captured on that first exercise Tuesday last.

"I offered you my apologies, *mein Herr,*" Curt told him firmly, "and the military exercise was only practice."

It was patently obvious that the young German captain wanted a confrontation then and there. He'd been well fortified with alcohol, and Curt noticed that there were more than a dozen more young Germans with him. Both the alcohol and his companions gave the captain courage to stand up to Curt. Furthermore, he stepped forward in an attempt to get Curt to step backward. "You did not have to embarrass us by capturing my command post without warbots!"

"If that was your first encounter with special combat troops," Curt pointed out, not backing off an inch, "then how the hell do you expect to defend *der faderland* against Soviet motor rifle divisions?" He knew he'd hit a sensitive spot there because of the way the German flinched.

"Far better than you will be able to do it with your Valkyrie women! Women should be kept at home having babies! How can an army fight with women?"

It was Captain Alexis Morgan who stepped between. Curt and the drunken German officer. "I wouldn't stay at home to have your babies on a bet! And we fight pretty damned well! Or haven't you noticed?"

"Perhaps we see how well you fight," the German growled and swung at her.

Alexis responded so quickly and smoothly that the German hardly knew what hit him. Certainly Curt, who wasn't expecting it either, really didn't see what happened. Alexis easily deflected the wild swing and brought her knee up fast and hard. She caught the German squarely in the testicles.

The other German warbot brainies saw their officer go down and heard his scream of agony. They charged through the crowded street to get at the Americans.

The German crowd of happy drunks scattered as quickly as the narrow street would permit, leaving the battleground to the adversaries.

But it was a matter of warbot brainies against Sierra Charlies. The former were used to fighting from linkage couches. The Sierra Charlies were physically fit and trained for hand-to-hand combat. Nationalities had nothing to do with the brawl that suddenly erupted.

And it was somewhat one-sided with thirty Americans against that number of *Bundeswehr* robot infantry-men.

Curt managed to get in only one solid punch. The five women of the Companions and the Marauders - nobly assisted by Adonica Sweet and the three "non-combatant" crew chief sergeants of the Warhawks who'd complained earlier about not being allowed to fight - proved to be the American street fighting shock troops.

In the first place, the Germans who'd been spoiling for a fight that night came from a culture where, indeed, the women were supposed to "stay at home and have babies." They were more than a little surprised to find themselves confronted by violent American women who not only knew how to fight but had no compunctions about fighting to win as dirty and quickly as possible.

In the close quarters of the narrow street, speed and deceit were more useful than sheer strength.

The American women were well trained in the martial arts, and they didn't even try to use their fists. They used their hands in chop strokes, their feet in versions of *la savate*, adapted to the circumstances, and slammed their knees into groins when they could close with their adversaries. They struck in ways that incapacitated men much larger and heavier than they.

And it was over in less than thirty seconds.

Curt didn't have time to hit more than one man. And he hadn't even lost his breath.

Alexis Morgan took the blue tam from her head, dusted it off, and perched it back. "I think," she said carefully, looking around at the number of prostrate and moaning forms lying on the street, "that we'd better get the hell out of here before the *polizei* show up, which should be pretty damned quick."

"Agreed," said Kitsy Clinton. "Where can I get a blue tam?"

"Tomorrow morning. I'll show you," Alexis promised.

"Son of a bitch!" Cal Worsham exploded. "Remind me never to tangle with one of you girls!"

Lieutenant Ellie Aarts, a tall blond woman of substantial proportions, smiled at him and remarked, "Major, you don't have to worry about it unless I want to tangle with you...and it might be fun under much more comfortable conditions, I assure you."

The Americans managed to get to their hotels before the German police showed up to quell the reported riot. That sort of thing didn't often occur in Rudesheim, which was usually full of happy German civilian drunks, not unhappy and, drunken German soldiers. Thus, their only job was to pick up the unconscious and otherwise badly hurting bodies and see to it that they got medical attention.

No one knew who paired with who, but it seemed that the women were the ones who did the choosing and inviting that night. It seemed there was nothing like a good fight to arouse other urges as well.

Chapter Twenty-One

"It's the third time, Mister President, and the Soviets are getting somewhat antsy," General Edward S. Carrington, chairman of the joint chiefs of staff, reported.

"So, what do you want me to do about it, General?" the President replied in a vexed tone of voice. This emergency meeting with the JCS chairman and the chief of NIA had interrupted what the President had considered a very important weekend study session with two members of his cabinet on the military commitment of the United States. The President was looking for ways to reduce the national commitment and thus reduce the defense budget which, in turn, would free up funds for social programs.

The President of the United States wasn't exactly antimilitary, but he'd ridden into office on a platform of peace-making, arms reductions, internationalism, and many of the classical policies of New Millennia Liberalism that were so different from those of his losing opponent, the former President. He knew that military surveillance satellites and spacecraft were essential in allowing him to keep up-to-date with potential military threats in other parts of the world so that he might move in with his charismatic personality and diplomatically settle them before shooting broke out. So, he wasn't convinced that the infection of a third Soviet Red Sentry surveillance satellite was a big crisis.

Carrington had felt the heat of the new President's wrath in the wake of the highly successful American intervention in Sonora, Mexico, and the subsequent damage done to a major drug lord's empire there. In spite of the fact that a private Mexican army had shot up the border, killed Americans, and destroyed property, the President had hoped he could avoid a full shooting war with Mexico by calling on his only alternative: ordering American troops into Mexico under the auspices of an old and forgotten treaty. It hadn't turned out exactly that way, and the President hadn't been prepared for the additional killing and destruction that resulted from his go-order. Thus, Carrington had privately taken it in the shorts from the President as the most convenient fall guy. Carrington didn't lose his job; he knew where too many bodies were buried. But this time the JCS chairman was a bit more cautious.

As a result, Carrington was accompanied on this Saturday afternoon visit to Camp David by General Albert Murray, chief of the National Intelligence Agency. The secretary of defense and the secretary of state were already at Camp David for a weekend of talks and study regarding American Persian Gulf and North African military protection policy, what there was left of it in the wake of the new President's fifteen months in office and a major Army arms scandal in Bahrain.

The beauty of early spring in the mountains of northern Maryland belied the ugliness the President felt in his soul. The world was turning out to be a much more dangerous and vicious place than he'd thought it to be...and even rougher than his advisors had warned him. In spite of his beliefs, he was being forced to make decisions that went more and more against his personal philosophy. He'd discovered that the people of the world were more like a bunch of rowdy adolescent street gangs out to control turf which could take the form of money, markets, people, land, or ideologies.

"Mister President, it's the recommendation of the joint chiefs that you approve Ex Op Ord Thirty-one-dash-four," Carrington advised him in steady, quiet tones.

"What the hell is that?" the secretary of state asked, belying his confusion and ignorance of military terminology. "I wish you military types would learn to speak English."

"John, my dear, I'll translate for you," the secretary of defense told him bluntly, ignoring the fact that he wouldn't take kindly to a woman knowing more about something than he did. She considered him one of the last male chauvinists, and she never missed the opportunity to goad him in a polite manner that belied her inner toughness gained from several years on the judicial bench.

She'd gotten the job after the recent cabinet shake-up, not because she was ex-military but because she'd served a hitch in the ROTC once to help pay her way through law school and two years in the Judge Advocate General's Corps. "Edward is talking about an order authorizing Army Robot Infantry special troops to land surreptitiously on Kerguelen Island and destroy the secret satellite infection base there."

"General, I still don't understand why the United States has to take this military intervention on its shoulders," the President broke in testily, because this whole thing, to say nothing of the military and naval activities of his administration thus far, wasn't going the way he liked or wanted it to go. He was a positivist; he honestly believed that if he worked hard enough, he could make the impossible become reality. But the Presidency itself wouldn't allow that to happen; as in the past, the office molded the occupant, not the other way around, unless the occupant was far stronger and more tenacious than the bureaucracy that had grown up around the Executive Branch. "Look, dammit, the Soviets are losing satellites, not us. This discovery of the secret base on Kerguelen Island should be reported back through the UN Space Security Commission so that joint international action can be taken."

"Mister President, the last time we got involved in an international operation, we took high casualties and ended up saving both the French and the British contingents," Carrington said, reminding him of the Namibian operation. This may have been unnecessary but it was certainly to the point; however, the President really didn't wish to be reminded of it because it hadn't happened on *his* watch. Carrington went on, "Sir, I briefed you last week on the reasons why we believe this should not be brought before the Commission...at least until we have the opportunity to act."

"Just because you believe that one of the Commission nations may have established the station?"

"Yes, sir. I'm not the only one who shares this viewpoint. General Murray of NIA has something of his own to say about it, and I won't try to take words out of his mouth. I can't anyway; in spite of intelligence briefings, he knows far more about the black side of this than I do. But I sincerely believe that bringing it before the Commission will not cause the offending nation to withdraw the station, even if it's done quietly. It will cause someone to lose face, and that's a serious matter in international affairs," Carrington pointed out.

"You speak as if the offending nation were Oriental," the President snapped.

"No, sir, I have no information that such is the case," Carrington replied quickly. "But it makes no difference whether the offender is Oriental or not. Let me put it this way, Mister President. Suppose the infetion station on Kerguelen had been placed there by the United States..."

"Ridiculous! We wouldn't do such a thing!" the President snorted.

"*You* might not, Mister President, but many of your predecessors did similar things," Carrington reminded him. "If we'd done such a thing, and if the Soviets discovered it, what would we do if the Sovs brought it before the Space Security Commission?"

"Well, we sure as hell would have worked through the various scenarios before we did such a thing in the first place," the secretary of state observed profoundly.

"Some nations are highly opportunistic and *don't* work through best-case and worst-case scenarios, John," the secretary of defense observed. "Most of the armed conflicts around the world wouldn't even begin if nations did that sort of thing. I'm no student of military history," she admitted, "but nations aren't very much different from individuals when it comes to opportunism. If they think they can get away with it in such a manner that the gain is great or the penalties for getting caught are minimal or nonexistent, they'll do it. Otherwise, lawyers like myself would be out of work...Actually, Mister President, I can tell you exactly how you or any other President would act if the Kerguelen station were ours and we were discovered: You'd behave like a kid caught with his hand in the cookie jar. Or have you forgotten Watergate, Iran, and Montevideo? Except in this case, announcing the discovery of the Kerguelen station before the Commission might be an early trigger to a major war."

"War? Explain!" the President snapped.

"I defer to my esteemed colleague of the NIA, who briefed us on the possibilities yesterday, which is really why I neglected my husband and children on this lovely weekend and came up here instead, your request notwithstanding, Mister President," she told him frankly but respectfully. She turned to the intelligence agency chief. "Al, run your rationale past the President, please."

General Al Murray had sat quietly in the background on the porch while the conversation ran its course. He had the latest input from NIA agents around the world. He had no specifics yet, but he did see a pattern emerging. "Scenario Number One is the obvious one. A possible reason a nation would want to blind another nation's surveillance satellites would be to hide something," the intelligence chief began slowly, wishing that he'd had the luxury of spending weekends with his family while he'd been working up the promotion ladder in the Aerospace Force. "But why would a country want to hide something? Answer: probably because they were getting ready to do something someone else might not like. It's been two weeks since the first Red Sentry was knocked out. The third one was hit last night. Three times the Soviets have put a Red Sentry up; three times it's been infected and essentially disabled or killed. Now, it takes about two to three weeks to amass enough troops for a really major land operation. So, I think something is about to break. What could it be? The first place I'd look is for a pattern that indicated the People's Republic of China going after the Soviet Union in eastern Asia…"

The secretary of state snorted in derision. "Low probability, Al! What you're talking about is a replay of the 1968 border incident and the Sino-Soviet Space War. No one won those except the Japanese, who eventually got Sakhalin back with our help…and we're still there helping them hold it as a nearby military base against anything happening in the Amur Peninsula."

"Oh, a replay of the Sino-Soviet incident is realistic enough," Murray insisted firmly. "The Chinese are patient and persistent. If they lose one, they pull back, analyze what happened, and wait for the next opportunity, during which they don't make the same mistakes again. All of us here know the Soviets are strung out along that border. They're scared to death that the legendary Mongols and Huns are going to erupt over the face of Asia as they have in the last thousand years; I doubt that they will, because the Chinese are not the Mongols or the Huns, and the situations are different. But, on the other hand, the Soviets are scared because they can't match the Chinese manpower...and we won't sell them the warbot technology they need to match the Chinese."

"Damned good thing we keep warbot technology so secure!" the secretary of defense snapped. "With our limited budgets and manpower, that's the only way we can match the overwhelming Soviet manpower in Europe!"

"Please, please! All this talk of war!" the President objected. "There has to be an alternative to war. How can we handle this situation with that in mind?"

"Mister President, I understand your beliefs quite well, but I ask that you respect mine as well because I've devoted my life to the defense of this country and the maintenance of peace in the world. I believe these Soviet satellite incidents are indeed a prelude to war," General Carrington told him bluntly.

"You would! That's your job! You can't justify your pay or a defense budget unless you have a war now and then!" was the emotional outburst from the President one which he immediately regretted.

"Mister President, all of us abhor war," Carrington said quietly in deliberate counterpoint to the Chief Executive's statement. "The soldier abhors war most of all because the soldier is the first one to face death in a war. The job of a soldier in the twenty-first century - at least in the leading countries of the world - is to keep the peace so that wars don't have to be fought. I wish the radicals and religious fanatics in other countries shared the same outlook..."

"I've heard that before, General. I wish I could believe it, but it's my job as the commander in chief to do the same thing. Therefore, I'm willing to listen and perhaps be convinced." The President breathed, getting himself back under control again. "General Murray, you said that was but one scenario. Assign a probability to it and apprise me of some of the others."

"I can't assign a hard number probability to my first scenario because some of the other scenarios are equally as probable and may even have a higher level of possibility," the intelligence director explained. "Another serious scenario can be labeled, 'Let's you and him fight.' In short, a third party instigates an action that's blamed on one of two potential adversaries who have been close to fighting for years and may be looking for a convenient excuse to go at one another anyway. This means that almost *anyone* with the money to buy the technology could have established that infection station on Kerguelen to kill Soviet satellites so the blame might fall on the Chinese...or even the United States!"

There was silence among the group sitting around the porch in the April sunshine. The dogwoods were just beginning to bloom, and some of the birds were back from their winter habitats half a world away. But none of the conferees noticed. Each of them felt an enormous weight on his shoulders. They felt like Atlas supporting the world. One bad move might bring it crashing down in pieces.

"Another scenario," Murray then went on, "can be called 'See what you've done to me?' Maybe the Soviets themselves established and operate that station. Maybe they're killing their own satellites. Why? So they can lay the blame on someone else and thus have an excuse to seek retribution by diplomatic *or* military means. Maybe the Soviets have decided to go after the Chinese while they still have some chance of beating them. Maybe they've decided to try getting us out of the game in Europe as a prelude to getting NATO off their backs so they're free to handle the Chinese."

The intelligence chief paused and did indeed look out on the budding springtime of Camp David. Then he went on, "But what worries me most is that *someone* has worked out *one* of these scenarios - or perhaps another we haven't discovered yet - and then taken the time, trouble, money, effort, and risk to *go ahead and do it!* Maybe they're just trying to learn whether or not they can get away with something like this. If so, the next thing they try may be far worse. Which is why, Mister President, the United States *must* step in and covertly attempt to eliminate this factor, which amounts to an insidious threat because *we don't really know why someone is doing it!"*

Silence fell on the gathering. A slight breeze blew coolly through the trees. Finally, the President asked, "What happens if we fail?"

"No one will know if we fail," General Carrington said. "But we won't fail. We'll be sending in the best people we've got, the Robot Infantry's Special Combat troops."

"How can warbots handle this?" the secretary of state wanted to know.

"These aren't warbot brainies," Carrington explained. "They're the people who did the job in Trinidad, Namibia, and Sonora. They're the controversial personal combat soldiers who fight alongside their warbots."

"The Washington Greys," the secretary of defense added.

"The one with the women combat soldiers?" the President suddenly asked.

"Yes, Mister President, and don't worry," the secretary of defense added. "They're not likely to be shot at, and the women have shown themselves to be more than up to the job...as we might expect."

The President looked at her. "I suspected you'd defend them. Very well, activate the operational order, and keep it at the highest possible level of secrecy. And keep me advised of everything that happens! Understand? I don't want this to be another wild foray into unknown territory like the Sonoran operation. And, John, I want your people to be ready with diplomatic actions if the military operation succeeds or fails...both."

He didn't mention that he also reserved the right to change his mind.

Chapter Twenty-Two

It was sheer, unadulterated pleasure, the sort of thing that didn't come very often in the life of Major Curt Carson.

The room was dark and cozy.

The bed was warm and incredibly soft so that he sank deeply into its mattress.

Clean sheets and warm blankets covered his body.

And it was doubly pleasurable because he was shattering it with someone else.

Which is why he didn't pay a great deal of attention to the bell.

When he finally realized that it was the unfamiliar, strange, almost Teutonic ring of a Continental telephone, he moaned.

"I hope to hell you weren't stupid enough to leave a wake-up call," he murmured to his companion.

"I'm not stupid, just sexy," Alexis Morgan mumbled sleepily. "So forget it. I've got other things for us to do."

"Forget it? Are you kidding? The Germans are goddamned thorough in their design of telephone bells, too. They make them deliberately as annoying as possible!"

"If you won't pull the humper off the wall, I will," she promised.

Years of ingrained habit got the better of him. All his life, he'd been carefully trained to answer a telephone when it rang, first by a very demanding father, who was an Army officer, and then by countless upperclassmen, instructors, and superior officers. He couldn't understand people who would calmly allow a telephone to ring unanswered until it finally stopped ringing. To grab a ringing telephone only to discover that the caller had hung up...Well, in his book that was failure to act quickly and decisively.

The caller was Captain Hensley Atkinson, regimental chief of staff. "Sorry to break up your weekend, Major," her voice came to him in apologetic tones, "but the colonel has just announced that all leaves and passes are canceled. He requests everyone to return to base before twelve hundred hours to attend an Oscar briefing at thirteen-hundred."

Curt grunted, then said curtly, "We'll be there..."

"Thank you, sir, and please inform any other Greys you may happen to see in Rudesheim," she added diplomatically, knowing full well that few Sierra Charlies willingly spent overnight passes alone.

After she'd hung up, Curt slammed the receiver viciously into its cradle, missing and causing it to fall to the floor. He didn't bother to pick it up. "Goddammit!" he swore softly. "This is getting to be a regular Sunday morning happening!"

"What time is it?" Alexis wanted to know, not raising her head from the pillow.

"Oh-seven-thirty," Curt reported when he checked his watch on the bed-stand.

"More than four hours before we have to report back," she noted, suddenly not sleepy any longer. "Plenty of time. Come here!"

"Listen, by the time we get up, get cleaned up, get dressed, grab something to eat, round up everyone, and find transportation..." he began, starting to get out or bed.

"Come here! That's an order!" She reached out and grabbed him. "I may not outrank you, but I can sure as hell outlast you!"

He relented, but only because he knew Atkinson had given them ample time. "We'll see about that," he promised her. "You waste a lot of energy being rough."

"You haven't seen what rough is," she promised him. She was a strong woman with an ample body that was quite in contrast to Lieutenant Kitsy Clinton's spare, slim, almost girlish one. She could and did play rough when the spirit and her partner moved her.

That morning, however, she was only very, very thorough.

When she was finished being thorough with him and they were merely lying there, she remarked, "It may be a long time before it gets this good again."

"That depends on how long we're in a situation where Rule Ten is in effect," Curt pointed out.

"Oh, since when does Rule Ten have anything to do with it? I noticed it didn't have very much effect on you when it came to Zeenat Tej on Trinidad...or Fredrica Herrero in Sonora..."

He shrugged. "You tell me. I seem to recall a news hawk in Namibia," he reminded her. "Can't remember his name, so it couldn't have been very important. Or very long-term..."

"I thought we agreed that we were even on that score," Alexis suddenly said.

"I don't think the two of us had better keep score...ever, Allie," he admitted. "The potentials are far too great within the Regiment itself when Rule Ten isn't active."

She was quiet for a moment, then snuggled against him and asked coyly - or at least as coyly as she was able, "Certainly Kitsy Clinton doesn't have either my experience or my bod, but Willa Lovell might have the advantage in the experience category...and God knows she's got the medical know-how as well as a mature body and approach..."

"One more word," Curt warned her, "about situations that are obvious and natural and completely within the bounds of propriety, my dear, and I'm likely to be the one who gets a little rough..." Curt wasn't taking any of this pillow talk seriously, and his tone of voice projected that. But he wasn't sure that Alexis was taking it as lightheartedly as he.

She sighed. "Well, even in the twenty-first century Army with its all-around equality, I guess a girl often has to settle for what's available..."

As they were dressing, Alexis perched the blue tam o'shanter on her head. Curt remarked, "Don't tell me you're really serious about that thing! It's totally non-reg, Alexis!"

She smiled and pulled it from her head. "Why not? Here! Check it out." She tossed it to him.

"Well, you certainly chose quality," he said, looking it over and noting that the black leather band around its bottom as well as the yellow pom in its center were good quality and well made. "But you said you cleaned out the shop where you found these. If the colonel and the other high brass buy off on it, where can we get more of them?"

"Oh, I suspect we can write the manufacturer," Alexis remarked in an offhanded fashion.

Curt looked inside the crown and found a label. *Maori, Limited. Aukland. 100% wool. Made in New Zealand.*

"I'll check out the firm next time I'm in the neighborhood," he promised. Then, in a moment of rebellion against the Army for disrupting two weekend passes two weekends in a row, he put it on his shaved head at a jaunty angle. "Makes me look like someone in His Majesty's Royal Scots Fusileers," he observed.

"No," Alexis corrected him, "if you recall from Namibia, the Royal Scots wear the Stuart plaid, a white pom, and a gray feather on the right brim. Except when they're wearing the black beret all of the Brits have taken to. There! I'll bet you thought I was so busy noticing Len Spencer all the time that I never noticed anyone else! Well, I did! But those Scots warbot brainies were all too shocked at us Army girls in spite of the fact that they were handsome devils! Too bad. They never learned what they were missing...Gimme. Go get your own..."

Curt asked the concierge to wake the rest of the Companions, then found Sergeant Koslowski in the lobby and sent him to another hotel to roust the Marauders. But the Companions and the Warhawks were already in the dining room having a Continental breakfast-and complaining about how they'd eat a real meal when they got back to Wiesbaden. Worsham remarked to Curt that transportation back to Wiesbaden had been requested and was on its way.

"I see," Alexis remarked as they finished, "that your new squad leader seems to be getting along quite well with her platoon sergeant." She nodded her head toward a window table where Sergeant Tracy Dillon and Corporal Dyani Motega were sitting together.

"Interesting" was all that Curt had to say about it at that moment. In a way, he was glad to discover the two of them together on their own. He filed away his concerns about how Dillon would accept her. On the other hand, Motega was new to the Regiment and Dillon had come in as part of the conversion of the outfit from a Robot Infantry unit to a Sierra Charlie group. "I was a little worried."

"About what? The fact that Dillon is a Westerner and might harbor some traditional dislikes about Indians?" Alexis guessed.

"Partly. They're both new to the Greys since we went Sierra Charlie," Curt pointed out. "They don't have the RI traditions between men and women warbot brainies that you and I got used to from the day we got our commissions and were posted to the Greys."

"Oh, you were afraid that Dillon wouldn't consider Motega a real fighter, huh?"

"That will come in time all by itself, if Motega is as good as I think she is...which she started to prove this week during those exercises," Curt explained. "I guess it's always a big question mark to me whether or not new troops are going to absorb the sort of mutual respect that you and I, for example, have for one another as combat soldiers."

Alexis grinned and laughed. "What you're really trying to say, Curt, is that you hope to hell some new-comer doesn't screw up a good thing, right? Well, let me tell you that since taking over the Marauders, I've gotten a little different perspective than I had as a mere platoon officer. I know you think we're pretty nice to have around, even on the battlefield, but I've got to tell you that from my point of view - and I probably share the viewpoint of the other girls in the Greys - I enjoy being around real men..."

"You mean," Curt replied in a light mood, "that you don't really like what we like, the urge that comes as a result of being shot at and missed?"

"Quit while you're winning, Major," she told him bluntly.

By 1000 hours, everyone had gathered in or around the front door to the little hotel, waiting for transportation back to Wiesbaden. As the Companions, Marauders, and Warhawks stood around killing time in idle conversation, four German *Schutzpolizei* in their olive-green uniforms with their barrel-shaped shakos and silver gorgets of authority stepped up to Curt. One of them wearing the collar patch of a *Haupwachtmeister* flashed his silver warrant identity disk and spoke in perfect English. "Major, I am *Wachtmeister* Mueller and I require your cooperation. We are searching for a number of American soldiers who were engaged in a street fight last night. They were wearing blue hats like those I see in this group. I ask that all of your people wearing the blue hats please come with us to the *polizei* casern for questioning."

Curt looked coolly at the German policeman. It had been several years since Curt had served in Germany with the Greys when the regiment was RI, but he knew the rights and privileges of treaty troops that had been hammered out over decades. So, he replied calmly, "*Wachtmeister*, you will probably see a lot of blue tams around Rudesheim from now on. These are new head-gear of special American Robot Infantry troops. I don't know how many blue tams were in Rudesheim last night when the alleged fight supposedly took place. I admit that I was jostled a bit by the street crowds but that hardly constitutes a street brawl. Therefore, unless you have positive identification of the supposed miscreants, I suggest you register an official complaint with the provost marshal at Wiesbaden and allow the American military police to investigate the matter further." Curt had deliberately used long and obscure American words; the Germans often had a tendency to do the same thing because both languages encouraged the creation of linked words to describe things.

The *Wachtmiester* looked around at the blue-hatted Marauders and the otherwise ordinarily attired Companions and Warhawks. Not only was his four-man unit badly outnumbered, but he could not admit either to himself or to these Americans that he was really looking for women wearing blue tams. At least, he'd been told to detain and interrogate American women soldiers wearing blue tams. He'd told himself it was ridiculous to consider that women would have started a street brawl, much less completely decked a large number of *Deutschland's* finest robot troopers.

So, he touched his patrol stick to the visor of his shako and replied, "You are right, Major. I shall do that. Thank you for your assistance." In an irritated fashion, he motioned the other three *polizei* to follow him down the street.

"Very smooth, Major," Kitsy Clinton remarked.

"Shucks, Lieutenant, as Sergeant Henry Kester would say, ' 'twarn't nothin'.' " He smiled at her. "Would you have gone along with them if I hadn't advocated your cause?"

"No," she replied curtly, then cocked her head to one side and added pensively, "I believe we girls could have handled them quite well. By the time they woke up, we'd all be in Wiesbaden...By the way, sir, where did Captain Morgan get that hat? I want one! We found out it sure sets the Sierra Charlies apart!"

Curt turned to Alexis. "Captain Morgan, is the shop where you bought these close by?"

"Yes, Major. Right around the corner, I think."

"Did you clean him out of these tams?"

"He told me I did, Major."

Curt pulled out his military credit chit and handed it to her. "Would you see if he's open? It's Sunday morning, but this town doesn't have any blue laws that I remember. It caters to tourists and is happy at any time to separate them from their hard-earned or borrowed money. If he's open, buy every blue tam he's got. Your wool cow pie got us through one fracas, and maybe it'll do the same again in the future. Can't take a chance it isn't good luck for us

Sierra Charlies. When our transportation comes, I'll hold it until you get back...And don't tangle with any *Bundeswehr* or *polizei* en route!"

Chapter Twenty-Three

"One of these days...*One of these days,*" Captain Joan Ward complained as they stood around the Wiesbaden snake pit waiting for Colonel Bill Bellamack to show up and get the Oscar brief started, "I'm going to get a weekend pass and be able to spend the whole damned weekend doing what I want."

Curt knew Joan Ward wasn't much of a looker, but she was a lot of fun to be with on a pass. She'd been one of his plebes, had found his soft spots - Curt would never tell - and henceforth had used them artfully to keep his hazing level well below normal insofar as she was concerned. When she was no longer a plebe and the two of them could legitimately be together off post, they'd taken a few leaves together. But once they'd joined the Greys, they'd found others to play with. But they still had a strong friendship and a healthy respect for one another. "Ah, but we staunch defenders of freedom are on constant call to protect the world from evil and destruction," he said humorously. " 'Ours is not to reason why...Into the valley of death...' "

Joan Ward snorted. "Alexis, where the hell did you get that hat?"

Alexis told her.

"That figures. You're the only one with enough pure brass to wear a piece of nonreg gear to an Oscar brief," she remarked lightly.

"Want one?" Alexis asked.

"Do you have another one?" she suddenly asked anxiously.

"For a price."

Ward sighed. "I'm not sure I want to pay your price, but it's worth asking. How much?"

"Consider it a gift for old times' sake," she told Joan, extracting one from the cloth bag she was carrying just for that purpose. "See if it fits."

It did. "I'm not sure I want it as a gift," Ward told her. "It might cost me more later. My momma always told me to beware of soldiers giving gifts…"

"Just wear it. If every Sierra Charlie company commander wears one, maybe Wild Bill might have a chance to slip it past the Pentagon staff stooges so it could become a piece of regulation gear for Sierra Charlies," Alexis explained her strategy. "Matter of fact, I got an extra one for the regimental commander. If he calls me on the carpet for wearing one during the Oscar brief, I'll present him with his personal tam."

"You're a sneaky individual, Alexis, and you'll come to a bad end," Captain Joan Ward predicted.

"I hope so. Anyhow, Joan, on you it looks good! Maybe you should be the one to hit up Wild Bill!"

Joan Ward looked at Alexis Morgan levelly. "Thanks for the tam, but up yours," she told her.

Chief of Regimental Staff Major Joanne Wilkinson stepped onto the snake pit stage and called in a loud, clear voice, "Ladies and gentlemen of the Washington Greys, the regimental commander!"

A quick flurry of activity took place as people found their places. Bellamack was actually watching from the door and didn't step in until everyone had hit their marks and was standing at attention. Then he walked in and mounted the stage. "Be at ease. Take your seats," he told them. He looked around carefully, noting the blue tams he'd been warned about…and chose to ignore.

"At oh-four-thirty-five this morning, local time, the regimental computer received Div Op Ord Thirty-one-dash-thirteen. The order was then confirmed by ciphered reiterative procedures and was determined by me to be legitimate. The orders are brief and succinct. The Washington Greys are hereby directed to commence redeployment no later than eighteen hundred hours today from Rhine-Main Air Base to Muscat in the Sultinate of Oman. The combat companies will deploy with weapons and warbots in accordance with the Minimum Required Equipment list to be discussed later; the support units will deploy with full support, maintenance, and supply facilities and vehicles. I have been advised that further orders will be issued after we reach Muscat."

A ripple of muttered comments ran around the snake pit.

Curt was astounded. The regiment had been issued arctic equipment and had reconfigured their warbots for cold-weather environments. Now they'd been deployed to the eastern tip of the Arabian peninsula in a definite desert environment.

It didn't make sense to him.

The other members of the regiment obviously felt the same.

Curt couldn't tell from Bellamack's voice whether the commanding officer was also perturbed about these orders.

"The regimental staff," Bellamack went on, "has been working on the necessary arrangements for the redeployment. If some of you were upset about having weekend passes canceled and being recalled to Wiesbaden, shed a tear for the staff who got rousted out at dawn today and have been hard at work ever since. So, let's hear from them. Major Gratton, the S-One briefing please."

Major Pappy Gratton took the stage. "All personnel will be involved with the redeployment. The entire regiment will be out of here within thirty-six hours. The Combat Air Support Squadron, Worsham's Warhawks, has been assigned to the regiment until further notice. All leaves and passes are hereby revoked and canceled. And the base is sealed. Colonel." He stepped down. His was the easiest job of the redeployment.

Captain John Gibbon, S-2 staff man in charge of communications and intelligence, took his place. "As Major Gratton remarked, the regiment is in secure condition at this time. Other than official communications, no one will be allowed to communicate outside the regimental compound. We will be redeploying to the Sultinate of Oman, an absolute monarchy tightly ruled under Muslim customs and law. Company commanders will ensure that their personnel become current with the latest information in this regard, which is posted in the database. The United States Navy maintains a fleet support station at Muscat to support Persian Gulf operations; we will be utilizing American naval facilities in Muscat. Colonel."

Captain Hensley Atkinson, chief of the operations staff, looked tired and haggard as she stepped to center stage to present her briefing. She and her staff were the ones who'd had to work the hardest thus far. "This is not a combat mission," she stated. "Therefore, Headquarters Company will deploy first in order to ensure proper facilities are in hand at the Muscat naval facility for the remainder of the regiment. The combat companies will deploy in the second wave, taking only weapons, warbots, and supplies specified in the MRE lists. Plus, for some unknown reason, the arctic equipment previously issued along with the experimental equipment from McCarthy Proving Ground. Combat vehicles will be left here at Wiesbaden in secured compounds. The Warhawks will deploy separately, flying their Chippewas cross-country to Muscat by way of Tunis, Cairo, and Bahrain. Yes, Major Worsham, the Chippewas will be ferry-mode tanked for two-thousand-kilometer maximum range. Colonel."

Last but not least, Major Fred Benteen spoke for S-4 Logistics. "As previously mentioned, the vehicles of the combat companies will be left here in Wiesbaden. The regiment will deploy the rations and supplies for three days and with a full complement of ammunition. As soon as the Aerospace Force can gather up whatever airlift equipment it has on the lot, we'll know who goes when and in what aircraft. Watch your company terminals for load-up orders. Colonel."

Bellamack stood and faced his regiment again. "To stem a tide of questions: I have been given no reason for this movement, nor have I been told where we go after Muscat. Apparently, *someone* knows what's going on, but we're not being told, probably because of security. We must assume that this isn't insanity running amok, because it's costing a hell of a lot of money to move the Washington Greys and the Warhawks around the map like this on very short notice. We'll find out soon enough what's going on and what's expected of the Washington Greys. So, let's squelch the sniveling and whining, quit wasting time working for Rumor Control, and get this outfit in the air and down to Muscat on the bounce! Carry out your orders! Dismissed!"

"Companions!" Curt called out. "Assemble in our orderly room immediately!"

Other company commanders were likewise gathering their people for low-level briefings and operational planning.

Once in the orderly room, the Companions were full of bitches and guesses.

"Arctic gear? In Muscat? Jesus, the damned tech-weenies want to test us for heat exhaustion!" Platoon Sergeant Nick Gerard exploded.

Tracy Dillon shook his head. "Naw, Nick, you got it wrong. We'll be staging at Muscat for an operation in Antarctica..."

"Antarctica?" Edie Sampson asked incredulously. "Listen to me, youngsters! Antarctica is over ten thousand kilometers from Muscat! And it's all ocean in between. What the hell are we gonna do? It's a long swim..."

Curt listened and let the Companions blow off steam for a few minutes. He'd checked the terminal upon arriving in the orderly room, and no load-up orders had yet been posted for his company. He knew they could be ready in an hour or so, so he didn't fret. Better to let them get the gripes and guesses off their chests.

"If you want my opinion - and I thought about this on the way over from the snake pit," Sampson went on authoritatively, "we're headed for Tibet and the Himalayas!"

"What the hell is going on there, Sarge?" Tom Cole wanted to know. "I heard of nothing happening there. Are the Chinese and Indians going at it again?"

"What do you mean, again?" the Companion's first sergeant asked rhetorically. "India and China have been nose-to-nose in the Himalayas ever since China invaded Tibet back in nineteen-and-fifty-one. And they've been squabbling in Kasmir and at Karakoram

Pass ever since...in spite of the road they jointly put through there..."

"Maybe you're right, Edie," Gerard admitted. "Maybe we're going on a third-party truce operation..."

"Caught between two outfits shooting at one another? Great!" Charlie Koslowski muttered.

"Yeah, but whose side are we *really* on? India's? Or China's?" Nick wanted to know.

"If it's a truce operation, we're not supposed to be on anyone's side," Sampson told them.

"Kind of hard to swallow that one," Tracy Dillon observed. "Why would the United States get in the middle of regional fracas the hell and gone up in the mountains where the friggin' land is useless because it stands on end? It sure as hell isn't a UN operation. We haven't been issued UN brassards or repainted our warbots or helmets..."

"Maybe it's a fight between India and Pakistan up there in the hills," Tom Cole ventured a guess. "Maybe we're being sent in to keep the Chinese out of the fight."

"Oh, shit! If that's the case, we're in deep slime," Nick Gerard muttered loudly.

"Yeah; and if that's the case, why are we leaving our command and transport vehicles here?" Edie Sampson pointed out. "Why are we depending on Chippies to get us around?"

"Rugged country," Gerard pointed out. "Maybe the high brass learned something from the Sonora operation, where we crawled through the hills for days and finally had to use a captured 'dyne for the final assault."

"Well, what's your best guesstimate, Major?" Sampson finally asked the company commander.

Curt shrugged. "I don't know. Could be Antarctica, although that's a military-free zone. Not supposed to put combat troops in there. But it could be Tibet, too. However, ladies and gentlemen, I'm not paid to conduct strategic analyses. And I don't have enough data to make what I would consider to be an honest guess. We'll know soon enough. I do know that whatever we're going to be doing is highly classified. Otherwise, we wouldn't be given the mushroom treatment - kept in the dark and fertilized often. General Carlisle has never been secretive with us, and he won't start now unless he's been deliberately told to keep quiet. Same holds for Colonel Bellamack, except I'm positive that the colonel doesn't know any more than we do. He's a straight arrow."

Of this last, Curt felt absolutely certain. He and the colonel had an unwritten contract between them. As the regimental second-in-command, the highest ranking officer with a combat-rated position code, Curt would have expected to be briefed by the colonel separately, even if the operation was classified, if Bellamack knew anything more than he'd told the troops.

"But this redeployment is going to be a lot different than getting here from Huachuca," Curt went on. "We're going to be stripped to what we can carry, or the warbots can store. So, the first order of business is to get to our ACVs and RTVs, get the warbots out, then go through all the crap most of us have stashed away in the vehicles for possible combat use. We're going to Muscat with only what we can carry. Sergeant Sampson, do you have the MRE lists?"

Edie looked down at her notebook and scrolled a few pages on the small display. "Yes, sir! All downloaded, sir!"

"Okay, the rest of you do the same," Curt snapped. "Platoon leaders, check your people to make sure they've got everything on the MRE. Anything else they want to take out of the vehicles is additional…if they can carry it."

"Oh, shit!" breathed Nick Gerard, looking at the MRE list on his own notebook. "If I gotta carry all this stuff, it may mean I'll have to toss out my deck of cards…"

"Well, Nick, you can probably lighten your load enough if you'll throw away the joker," Edie Sampson told him.

Chapter Twenty-Four

It was a bitching time, and the troops of the Washington Greys were bitching.

"I'm getting goddamned tired of seeing sunrises from different parts of the planet," First Sergeant Edit Sampson complained.

"Well, don't snivel that the Army hasn't allowed you to see the world," Platoon Sergeant Nick Gerard retorted. "What jerks me off is busting our buns to get here, then having to wait around for the Chippie drivers."

The Washington Greys had trickled into Muscat all day on various Aerospace Force Airlift Command flights from Frankfurt. Now the whole regiment was on hand...waiting and confined to the Wadi Akhdar Naval Auxiliary Station.

"Yes, but why are we waiting for them?" Sergeant Tom Cole wondered. "In fact, why are we waiting anyway?"

"It's the Army way of doing them?" Sergeant Tom Cole wondered. "In fact, why are we waiting anyway?"

"It's the Army way of doing things," Lieutenant Jerry Allen interjected, trying to make the situation a little more bearable. "Any by now, Tom, you should know the three ways of doing things: the right way, the wrong way, and the Army way. Besides, what the hell are you sniveling about? Nobody's shooting at us. And we've had all day to rest."

"Rest, Lieutenant? Since when have you given us any time to rest?" Corporal Dyani Motega observed. "Not that I'm complaining, mind you. I'd rather be busy than sitting around doing nothing. It could be worse." It was very unusual for the newest Companion to talk that way. Motega was usually quiet, reserved, and even stoic. It meant that this operation was getting deep under everyone's skins.

"I agree. It could be worse," Lieutenant Kitsy Clinton observed, looking out the window at the sunset over the western hills. The exterior surface of the window was covered with dripping condensation caused by the very humid outside air being cooled by contact with the glass. The ancient air conditioner in the Navy building was working hard at maximum capacity.

"How could it be worse?" Allen wanted to know.

"It could be raining," she pointed out.

"Lieutenant, it ain't rained here for years," Sergeant Tracy Dillon told her. "Just like some places in Montana."

"Oh, it rains to beat hell here," Kitsy said. "They catch the ass end of the Indian monsoon. Why do you think this place is so fertile? And wet?"

"It reminds me of Yuma," Major Curt Carson said adding his two cents' worth to the post-dinnertime gabfest, "during the monsoon season there."

"Yeah, I thought Arabia was supposed to be a desert," Nick Gerard muttered.

The view out the window wasn't desert like except for the barren hills far to the west. Beyond the fenced perimeter of the Wadi Akhdar Naval Auxiliary Station and as far as the eye could see, fields of cotton and wheat lay shimmering in the late afternoon heat.

"Reminds *me* of Kansas, except for the ocean," Corporal Dyani Motega put in. "Same heat, same humidity."

"And here we are with our furry arctic whites," Tracy Dillon reminded them.

Curt knew his company was tired. It had been a busy few weeks with the rapid redeployment to Wiesba-den and then an equally quick transfer to Muscat on the Oman coast of Arabia. What made it even worse was the fact that they didn't know why they were here, where they'd be going, or when they'd by going there. And they didn't know what they'd be doing once they got there. Or if anyone would be shooting at them. To Curt's operating and command style, this was no way to treat good, seasoned, and loyal people.

But the Army had its reasons for doing things. Sometimes they were rational. Sometimes they weren't. For his own morale, Curt had to continue to believe that someone somewhere knew why the Washington Greys were sequestered in Old Naval Auxiliary Station buildings on the eastern tip of the Arabian peninsula. Because security demanded that the Greys be confined to the naval base, there wasn't very much to do. So the Greys had gotten bored once they'd checked and rechecked equipment, configured not for heat and humidity, but for cold weather operations, and found that the old naval base offered absolutely nothing in the way of off-duty recreation.

The Wadi Akhdar Naval Auxiliary Station was a third-level facility that had once been a major naval base supporting U.S. Navy operations in the Persian Gulf and the Gulf of Oman. And it was still a naval base because it had the three requirements for such: a coffee pot, a loudspeaker system, and officers' country. Its location was such that military and naval control could be exercised over the whole Persian Gulf theater from Wadi Akhdar.

But it was potentially vulnerable to air attack from the Iranian air and naval base at Chah Bahar a mere 300-kilometers northeast across the Gulf of Oman. So it was relegated to auxiliary status when the Navy got its submarine carriers, which could lurk beneath the water and still control the sea lanes when they launched their air groups.

A disgruntled Lieutenant Junior Grade was in "command" of Wadi Akhbar. Curt didn't know if the man's surly manner was the cause of him being here or a result of being here too long. The half-dozen other Navy types were merely supervisors overseeing the typical lazy Arab housekeeping force. They were also supposed to keep the locals from pilfering the base down to nothing. They hadn't totally succeeded, and Curt suspected that some interesting cumshaw deals took place regularly between the Navy ratings and the Muscats.

But although the Navy had allowed Wadi Akhdar to run down, the Navy-constructed buildings remained almost untouched, even with the heat and the humidity chewing away at them. The Navy always seemed to build buildings to last forever. The big empty hangars on the edges of the wide concrete tarmacs and long, hot aircraft runways as well as most of the barracks buildings were either solid reinforced concrete or well bonded block construction. Thus, the buildings were marginally usable for the Greys, but the rest of the place had been allowed to deteriorate badly. The plumbing worked - just barely. Most important, the old air conditioners still worked. But the furniture, what was left of it, was beat, and the whole place could have used a coat of paint.

The accommodations, spartan and disheveled as they were, wouldn't have been bad if the Greys had popped in and out on their way to wherever. But no one knew when they were going to get out of this place, they were discovering to be a stinking hellhole.

"What happened to the Warhawks?" Kitsy Clinton asked Curt. "I thought they were due to show today."

"Yeah, Worsham told me they'd scheduled a sixteen-hour flight with two stops, which would make their total time en route something around eighteen hours," Jerry Allen remarked. He checked his watch. "They should have been here by now."

"My guess is that they had equipment trouble at some point and got delayed" was the remark from Tech Sergeant Bob Vickers, who, as the company's warbot technician, had a very low professional opinion of the reliability and maintainability of flying machines.

"I'll feel better when we get some orders and know what we're supposed to be doing," Sampson muttered darkly. "Bored, bored, bored, bored, bored…"

"It's probably a good thing we're confined to the base" commented Biotech Sergeant Shelley Hale. This remark was met with a chorus of complaints from the rest of the Companions, which prompted her to add, "Look staying on base forces us to eat and drink the stuff we brought along. This part of the world is not only rife with cholera, but I don't want to have to spend time trying to treat you for dysentery caused by strange food and drink."

"No chance for you to practice your profession, Shelley," Charlie

Koslowski told her. "Even if we were allowed to go into Muscat, none of us brought any money along because we're stripped for combat. And I'm not sure the Bank of Muscat will accept a military credit card with a request for cash advance. I don't think any Americans except the Navy's housekeeping contingent have been here for years..."

Curt could feel that the morale of the Greys was slipping. Certainly he was doing his best to maintain it in the Companions, but it was difficult.

From down the hall in the direction of the orderly room used by Morgan's Marauders came the sound of two men singing a duet. Curt knew it was Sergeants Billy Ed King and Joe Jim Watson, two squad leaders from Dixie who were inveterate songsters. Kmg had brought along his compact electronic guitar, and Watson had done a nonreg programming job on Lieutenant Ellie Aart's jeep so it could synthesize the sounds of a complete country-and-western band to accompany them.

They were now singing a new ditty that Kind and Watson had obviously put together today to relieve the boredom of sitting around and waiting. They sang it to the tune of "On Top of Old Smokey."

"Now gather round closely from near and from far,
We'll sing of old Muscat and Wadi Akhdar.
While we sit here a-sweating, wondering why we are here,
The salt from our teardrops makes our hot beer taste queer.
There's not enough whiskey to grace this fair land,
But there's plenty of flea bites, of dung heaps and sand.
It's so dirty and humid with the heat and the smell
You'll think you've been buried and gone straight to Hell.
Each Charlie then swears they've been wrongly assigned
And the regimental commander has gone out of his mind;
But with all of our bitching, there's one thing that's clear:
Sure, it's rough in old Muscat, but there's no shooting here."

Over the roar of the air conditioning blowers, Curt heard another sound and looked out the window in the direction of the base airfield.

Sixteen Chippewas accompanied by two Tonto support 'dynes were hovering over the ramp near one of the hangars and landing there.

And out on the airfield itself, a white VC-39 Sabre-dancer utility command transporter was just touching down.

"Heads up, Companions," Curt called out. "The Warhawks have arrived. And a VIP transport just touched down. I *think* we're about to get the scoop with the group here."

Kitsy Clinton, Jerry Allen, and Edie Sampson were beside him at the water-covered window.

Edie peered through the glass. "I'd swear that Sabre-dancer has five stars on it. Only one general officer in the Army has five sparklers."

"Carrington. Joint chiefs," Kitsy muttered.

"Right!"

"Shit! No sleep tonight!" Allen remarked in a disgusted voice.

"Why the hell do you say that?" Curt asked his platoon leader.

"Major, my guess is that we'll be briefed and on our way tonight," the young officer said. "I hope so. We don't have enough supplies to last here very long, and I noticed no logistical 'dyne airlifting food in for us. They sent us a general instead."

"I can hear Sergeant Manny Sanchez over in Supply bitching about having another damned mouth to feed," Edie Sampson remarked.

"That's an interesting bit of deductive logic, Lieutenant. You, too, Sergeant," Curt complimented them. "I agree. So, let's stand by for a call to an Oscar brief."

It came in fifteen minutes.

And the Companions found themselves in what was left of the base movie theater, which had been stripped of its seats, video projection screen, and video satellite downlink equipment. But it was the only place large enough to hold the entire regiment.

The air conditioner worked, but not very well. And it roared loudly.

It was a hell of a place to have an orders briefing.

Cal Worsham and the Warhawks came in looking hot, sweaty, disheveled, hungry, and at war with the world in general.

"Good flight?" Curt ventured to ask the Combat Air Support Squadron commander.

The reply was a string of invective and profanity that emanated almost effortlessly from the square-headed bald man with the handlebar mustache. Cal Worsham wasn't a happy man. When he had apparently ex-hausted his vocabulary of curses and vulgarity, he snarled, "Not only no, but hell no! Fucking Arabs in Tunis tried to give me shit about military overflight permission, so I decked a customs official and took off anyway. Bastards scrambled Gaspard X-wings on us, and we had to jink our way out of their airspace down on the deck where they couldn't hit us. So, the fucking low altitude sand screwed up our filters, and we lost a turbine on one ship, so we had to lay over two hours in Cairo while Ron and his troops cleaned filters and replaced an engine. Now we get here and find it's hot and damp and miserable. And no fuel and no food and not even a goddamned place to sit down! Jesus, what a sheep screw!"

Lieutenant Harriet Dearborn of the Supply Unit overheard him. Actually, it was difficult *not* to hear Cal Worsham when he was pissed off like this and spoke in a voice suitable for marching a whole division around a parade ground. "Major," she told him quickly, "I'll get some chow in here for you. It won't be haute cuisine. Just Mark Ten field rations. But they'll be hot meals, and I'll get something cool to drink for you, too."

Cal Worsham's demeanor immediately changed. In a very polite tone of voice, he replied, "Lieutenant, thank you. We'd appreciate that very much. We've just had flight rations since leaving Rhine-Main early this morning. At least, I think it was this morning..."

"Well, we've been sitting on our asses sweating since we got here at dawn, so you aren't the only one who's had a bad day," Curt admitted. "But it looks like maybe we're going to get the straight shit here at last. Who was in that Sabre-dancer that followed you in?"

"Don't know," Worsham replied curtly. "We weren't talking to him. He was maintaining radio silence and Level Two stealth."

"Goddamn!" Curt burst out at hearing this. "Whoever it is, he doesn't want the world at large to know he's here! I saw five stars on the nose."

"Carrington?"

"He's the only five-star."

Worsham shook his head, not in negative response but in disbelief. "I'll be damned surprised if it is. We're too low on the totem pole for his personal attention."

"Unless whatever he's going to tell us to do is god-damned important," Curt reminded him.

Their questions were suddenly answered. It was Colonel Bill Bellamack who stepped up on the low stage in front of them and announced, "Ladies and gentlemen, the division commander!"

Clad in combat cammies, Major General Jacob O. Carlisle stepped from the wings and called out, "At ease! Sit down. Looks like you've got only the floor but sit anyway. This hasn't been an easy operation thus far." When everyone was seated on the floor, the commanding officer of the 17th Iron Fist Division (RI) went on, "Unfortunately, this operation is cloaked in the highest possible security. We cannot afford to have the slightest leak. Therefore, I apologize for not being able to give you a complete briefing, even at this time. But I did want to see you and to explain the situation in person as best I can under the security circumstances before you make the next move in this game.

"I cannot yet reveal to you where you are going and what you will be doing when you get there," Carlisle went on. "I promise you that a full briefing will be given to you within the next twenty-four hours. I'll be with you, but only as the overall commander in chief of the operation, not as your division commander. Colonel Bellamack, you will remain fully in charge of what the Washington Greys will be assigned to do.

"But I'm here tonight merely to brief you on the next move and to coordinate your activities with the other elements that are involved. Major Worsham, what is the fuel status of your Chippewas?"

Worsham got to his feet in a manner that told the world he was very stiff from having sat in linkage at the controls of a Chippewa for many long hours. "Sir, I believe we were ordered to top everything in Cairo and burn off the ferry tanks first. So, we have approximately ninety minutes of fuel aboard all Chippies."

"How quickly can you shit-can the ferry tanks?" Carlisle's use of soldier vernacular was deliberate. He knew he was facing weary, confused troops. In spite of their discipline, they would be harboring a natural resentment against the high brass for keeping them in the dark and moving them here and there all over the world. "How soon can you be lift-operational to move the Greys?"

"Sir, it's twenty-hundred hours now," Worsham observed. "If we bust our butts, which we will, we can be airlift-configured by zero-one-hundred hours."

"Very well. Please make it so," Carlisle told him in easy tones. "You will be given flight plans and frequency utilization for direct entry into the airbot controllers of your Chippewas at that time. Understood?"

"Yes, sir!"

Carlisle looked at his regimental commander standing on the low stage next to him. "Colonel Bellamack, prepare the Washington Greys for departure beginning at oh-one-hundred hours local. Understood?"

"Yes, sir!"

"And I'll carry through on my promise. After this move, you'll all be briefed within twenty-four hours concerning this operation. Dismissed!"

Chapter Twenty-Five

The bitching, griping, sniveling, and whining were no more: The Washington Greys, the 3rd Robot Infantry Regiment, now knew that their colonel was as much in the dark about their mission as they were and hadn't stonewalled them. They knew that their division commander was familiar with the secret mission and that he hadn't told them because he had to keep it a secret. They trusted Major General Jacob Carlisle because Carlisle had never let them down in the past. They knew that they'd soon find out what the Big Secret was.

The only Companion who was slightly out of shape, but only slightly, was Lieutenant Kitsy Clinton, who remarked to Major Curt Carson as they were completing move-out arrangements, "Nuts! I was looking forward to maybe taking a quiet stroll on the beach tonight..." Kitsy had never been forward or pushy, probably because she was fully aware that her company commander outranked her. Therefore, she tended to be somewhat obtuse. "I was hoping that maybe you'd like a walk, too," she added hesitantly.

Curt simply turned his head and looked at her a moment before answering, "That would have been fun...except that Rule Ten is in effect because it turns out we're in mid-deployment."

"Uh, Major, what's the longest the regiment has operated under Rule Ten?" she then asked after another moment of hesitation.

"About a week."

She sighed. "Well, if the other gals can, so can I."

"I've usually had more problems with the men. They tend to act more aggressively," Curt admitted, "but the women are more persistent and tenacious. But both sexes seem to suffer equally, Lieutenant, if that's any consolation..."

"No, sir, it isn't, but I guess I'll have to live with it..."

The Companions were all business with little conversation and banter as they powered up their warbots shortly after midnight and formed ranks on the hot concrete tarmac where the Chippewas rested. Curt made his usual preflight inspection.

He looked up and down the line. Some of his Companions were wearing blue tams. Bellamack had noticed back in Wiesbaden but not commented, so some of the Companions - along with the Marauders and those of other companies who'd managed to obtain them - were wearing their distinctive tams tonight. Well, if Bellamack hadn't raised hell about it, and if Carlisle didn't - wherever he was going with them - Curt would take the chance, too. He didn't have his tam yet, but he let the Companions who had them continue to wear them. This was no time to play around with morale…

"Did we get everything, Sergeant?" he asked Edie Sampson. "We didn't leave anything behind, did we?"

"No, sir. Not even our good will. Everyone is damned glad to get out of this stinkin', sweatin' hole." She paused for a moment, then added, "And please thank the colonel for letting us pack our arctic gear in our duffles."

"No sense in wearing it here," Curt told her. "The colonel didn't want his troops passing out on the ramp before lift-off. And neither do I." He turned to the Companions. "Stand at ease! You look sharp! I don't know what we're getting into. Like the man said: Follow the sun and follow the moon; we don't know where we're going but we'll get there soon! Relax until we get the order to load. Any questions…except I'll cream the idiot who asks where we're going and what we're going to do…"

The Companions relaxed. The squad leaders put their warbots into standby mode, and little conversation took place among the Sierra Charlies. It was early in the morning, Muscat time, and it had been a long day without enough sleep in a rather crummy environment. They were all tired.

Curt turned and signaled with a green blink from his flashlight toward the Chippewa loadmaster, First Sergeant Tim Timm, who was standing by, reading for the signal from her squadron leader that preflight checks were complete, and the flight plans had been loaded into memories. She flashed him a response, a yellow blink. Soon the tarmac would be full of the noise of turbines spooling up and life air roaring out of slots, so this colored light signal procedure had been worked out during the three days they'd had to practice in Wiesbaden.

Several questions gnawed at Curt, probably the same ones bothering most of the Greys that night on the hot, steamy old Navy air base tarmac on the eastern tip of the Arabian peninsula.

Where were they going with only 90 minutes' fuel?

And with only warbots, weapons, and minimum personal gear including arctic clothing?

Curt thought he knew where their first destination would be. Had to be. Every other possible destination was more than 90 flight minutes away.

And it wasn't across the Gulf of Oman in Iran, either, because there wasn't the slightest hint that such an operation into that militant Muslim country was even in the wind right then.

Curt followed world affairs when the occasion permitted - and the occasion had permitted it in Wiesbaden. He felt it necessary part of his job as a military man to know what the hell was going on in the world because he might be called upon to go out and put his pink bod on the line somewhere because of world affairs that affected the United States or its partners. Or to lead his Companions in doing that. If he was going to willingly place himself and other people in danger, he wanted to know why. In that regard, he was like all American soldiers since the Revolutionary War. Of all the soldiers in the world, the American soldier had always needed a reason to fight. Wars had been lost when this was ignored.

Nothing but nothing was really boiling or even simmering in this part of the world. Which led him to the conclusion that their next destination was a temporary one, too. He thought he knew what it would be because he'd been there before. But he kept counsel only with himself. Let the troops monger rumors and play guessing games; that was part of soldiering. But a leader of troops shouldn't do that sort of thing, Curt believed, unless it was absolutely necessary - in order to salvage morale, for example. To Curt, a leader should be positive and not speculative. Or, if he speculated, he should make it clear that's what he was doing.

At 0100 on the dot, he saw a green flash of light from Sergeant Timm. He responded with a green flash, then called to his company, "Companions, load up as planned! Head for your aircraft! Move it out!"

He turned to his jeep as Edie Sampson switched the warbot to full power. "Isaac, keep your weapons stowed! Follow me!" he told his Mark 33 General Purpose warbot, using the familiar name he'd assigned to it.

"Follow you! Roger!" the warbot answered with its synthesized voice.

Aboard Warhawk One, Curt helped Edie dog down Isaac on the cargo deck; then he went up to the flight deck to take what had become his usual flight post behind and to the right of Cal Worsham.

Worsham was in linkage with his Chippie, so he wasn't conversational.

No course or destination data were showing on the displays.

Curt was surprised when First Sergeant Tim Timm showed up on the flight deck and took the right seat.

"Decided to come along this time, Sergeant?" Curt asked.

She turned to him and nodded. "We're leaving the Service Unit behind," she told him. "They'll be on their way back to Bahrain by sunrise."

"How does the major plan to maintain or repair the Chippies if something goes wrong?"

"Nothing will go wrong," Timm stated flatly. "If it does, I'll have help."

Curt thought he knew what she meant.

The Combat Air Support Squadron was stripping for action. They were leaving their technicians behind. The Greys did the same thing when they went into combat; they left the Headquarters and Service Companies in the rear and out of harm's way.

He never heard the lift-off command, but the Chippewa spooled up with surprising speed, then lifted off the tarmac with the usual wobbling motion of an aerodyne just getting airborne while its computer sought out the stability parameters to match its load and the environmental conditions.

The tarmac hadn't been brightly lighted in the first place, and now it disappeared from view as the Chippewa tilted and began to pick up forward speed. The lights of the city of Muscat - actually, Curt would have rated it as merely a town - were on the north, and they soon slipped behind.

Without cockpit lights to bother him, Curt's partially dark-adapted eyes quickly became totally adapted. And he could see absolutely nothing outside the Chippie's cockpit. It was pitch black. No points of light on the ground below. No running lights or formation lights on the other Chippies.

But Curt could see the stars through the clear canopy, and he oriented himself.

The Chippewa was heading eastward out over the dark waters of the Gulf of Oman.

Over the muted roar of the slots and the whine of the turbines, Curt asked Timm, "Where are the other Chippies?"

"In formation behind us."

"Can't see them."

"Of course not. But the major can. He's linked with One's i-r sensors."

He had to be. And Curt wasn't.

It made Curt feel a little uneasy being in a robot and not being part of it. He hadn't gotten this unusual feeling during the daylight exercises in Germany.

But he knew there was nothing under them but a few hundred meters of air and a lot of water.

They had never practiced over-water emergency evacuation of a Chippewa. So, Curt asked Timm, "How the hell do we get out of this thing if the major has to put it in the drink?"

He didn't like the answer she gave him. "We don't. If it lands on the water, we'll have to keep the cargo hatch closed; otherwise, it'll fill with water in seconds and sink like a rock. We'll just have to hope that it doesn't leak too damned bad before the other Chippie drivers find out or our emergency beacon is picked up."

"Can we get out at all on the water?"

"Certainly, sir. Major Worsham will simply blow the canopy, and we'll go out the top. But you'll have to leave your warbots behind."

"Any life rafts aboard?"

"No, sir. We didn't know we'd need them, and we didn't have time to install them anyway."

Usual Army sheep-screw operation, Curt thought. As much as hard-working and long-suffering staff stooges tried to plan a mission in as much detail as possible, they could never catch everything. Usually, it was something simple but absolutely essential that they missed.

The Chippewa suddenly surged upward.

Curt then knew that Worsham was flying about ten meters above the water and had pulled up another ten meters to miss a ship.

The only reason why the Chippewa was at ten meters, totally dark, no running lights, and probably stealthed against other sensing devices as well was straightforward: This was a clandestine operation. Granted that the Gulf of Oman was a busy place with lots of ships and usually lots of aircraft patrolling the sea lanes, The United States obviously didn't want the presence of the sixteen Warhawk Chippewas to be readily noticed, probably by the

Iranians across the Gulf.

He checked his watch. They were now 30 minutes out of Wadi Akhdar. About 150 kilometers if his dead reckoning was correct.

With only 90 minutes of fuel aboard, the Chippewa had to be making its rendezvous very soon lest it run out of reserves that would get it back to Wadi Akhdar.

His dark-adapted eyes caught it in his peripheral vision.

It was a smudge of almost-light.

Two rows of smudges.

Two rows of smudgy targets aligned like a runway heading away from the Chippewa.

Long ultraviolet approach and landing indicators on the water.

Curt knew his guess was right.

He felt Worsham slow the Chippewa to a near-hover. Or maybe it was on full autopilot now and receiving landing data. He didn't know and he didn't care. Worsham had made his rendezvous.

The Chippewa slowly began to descend from a hover.

Curt could only sense the huge black hulk on the water.

Then he saw the black shadow of its sail and vanes against the starry sky.

And the Chippewa suddenly bumped to a landing not in the water but on something very solid.

As the turbines spooled down, he sensed frantic activity outside the 'dyne. He felt it move again, but it wasn't in flight now. Then there was another downward surge and the sail and vanes disappeared. In fact, the whole starry sky disappeared.

More motion on the sides.

Sergeant Timm began ministering the delinakage of her pilot, Major Worsham.

"Are we where I think we are?" Curt asked her.

She merely threw him a quick glance, went back to her pilot, and said, "Yes, sir, I think so. We're on the U.S.S. *McCain*."

Chapter Twenty-Six

"At last!" Lilutenant Kitsy Clinton exclaimed with a broad, happy smile on her pixie face as she sat down at the table in one of the passenger wardrooms of the U.S.S. *McCain* SSCV-17. She set the tray of food on the table and looked at it. "Good food!"

"Navy food," Lieutenant Jerry Allen corrected her, sitting down across the table from her. "But excellent quarters!"

"Begging your pardon, Lieutenant," First Sergeant Edie Sampson said, looking up from where she was tackling the Navy food. "Better chow than the Army swill in Wiesbaden."

Major Curt Carson sat down at the same table and placed his tray before him. "That was German food disguised as American food by German contract cooks. We do just as badly trying to cook German food for Germans."

"Well, this is American food disguised as American food by Navy robocooks," Alien amended his earlier statement.

"What did you expect in a submarine that spends months at sea without replenishment?" Curt asked, digging into the first hot meal other than field rations that he'd had in almost two days.

In spite of the fact that he was sniveling a bit about the food, Allen was eating it with relish and didn't reply until he'd stuffed several more bites into his mouth. "As I said, Major, the quarters are excellent, as usual."

Kitsy interrupted eating to add, "I'm surprised. I've got plenty of room in my quarters. I always though submarines were cramped. But I've never been on a submarine carrier before."

"Well, Kitsy, I admit everything's probably more your size than the major's," Jerry told her, referring to the comparison between her petite size and Curt Carson's robust 185-centimeter frame. "But, Kitsy, don't *ever* let one of the Navy files hear you say you're *on* a ship The proper and correct naval terminology is *in* a ship."

"And, Lieutenant, only the old Navy types are permitted to refer to a submarine as a *boat*," Edie Sampson added to those instructions.

Kitsy thought about this for a moment, then said, "always thought that a submarine *was* a boat."

"Well," Curt advised her, "the old surface Navy used to refer to submarines as 'pig boats,' and that led to calling them 'boats,' but the new submarine Navy prefers to call these submarine carriers 'ships' - and because they are indeed the modern ships of the line think they're justified in doing so."

"So do I! My God, it's *big*!" Kitsy breathed in wonderment.

But Curt, Jerry, Edie, and Nick Gerard took it ii stride. They'd been in the McCain for the Zahedan hostage rescue mission. However, Curt had never lost all of his "sense of wonder," and he inwardly marveled at both the engineering and the technology that had, gone into this huge 275-meter 35,000-ton submersible, aircraft carrier. True vertical-takeoff-and-landing aircraft like the aerodynes and the Cheetah strike fighters had made submarine carriers possible, and the high probability of nuclear warfare at sea had made them inevitable and indispensable. Composite engineered material and nuclear power had made them technically feasible

Furthermore, the SSCVs were an integral part of "power projection." Many critics had reviled "gunboat diplomacy" and the concept of sailing a battleship into a harbor in order to restore order by its mere presence or to create awe because of its huge size and capabilities. But having a battleship or a *Nimitz*-class surface aircraft carrier suddenly steam into a harbor had actually stopped many brewing wars and forced diplomats to begin talking again.

It was even more impressive to have one of the *Raborn*-class submarine carriers suddenly surface in a harbor, its enormous black bulk breaking the smooth water surface and adding the element of surprise to "gunboat diplomacy." No one could fail to be impressed by a 275-meter black whale suddenly appearing, ready to launch strike aircraft, where nothing had been a minute before.

Was this the kind of mission they were on now? A power projection operation to some southern hemisphere country or island where something more than the submarine carrier in the harbor might be required in order to restore peace and order? A possible airborne operation to reinforce an embassy or to rescue trapped diplomats as the Greys had done in Namibia?

Curt didn't know, and he didn't want to guess aloud. However, the news media were carrying no stories or reports of any problems with any southern hemisphere country far enough south for the Greys to have to use arctic gear in order to operate there.

When Curt was an ordinary warbot brainy fighting through warbots from a comfortable linkage couch far enough to the rear of the action so that he didn't have to worry about being hit or killed, he hadn't paid very much attention to world affairs. But now that he was a Sierra Charlie who might have to put his own body in jeopardy doing what neuroelectronic warbots had proved they couldn't do, he'd started to pay attention to what was going on in the world.

The reality of death had returned to warfare.

"Yeah, it's big. It has to be," Curt reminded them all, then turned to the business at hand. One of the big problems any commanding officer has with troops prior to an operation is to keep them busy enough so they don't individually get battle anxious. Everyone gets apprehensive prior to action; some with imagination are affected more than others. But keeping the troops busy without resorting to obvious make-work required a lot of creativity. And matching preops work with the need to have rested troops was a balancing act as well. He addressed his First Sergeant. "Edie, make sure all the warbots we left in the Chippies are topped off with power and ammo. I want them hot to trot when we get the orders to move, and I *don't* want to leave any warbots behind! Without the heavy weapons on our vehicles and the Saucy Cans on the LAMVs, we're short on firepower, particularly the heavy stuff. Make sure Vickers fixes anything that's even marginal. If any bot even *smells* like it might need some rear echelon patch-up, have him get with Sergeant Ray Wolf."

"If we can find Wolf, Major," Edie Sampson replied. "This sewer pipe is so damned big that the maintenance unit may be bunked half a kilometer away!"

"Then have Vickers *find* him, Sergeant! We're going to be plenty short of bot support as it is. I repeat: I don't want to leave any warbots behind in a tits-up condition on the *McCain* when we get orders to go somewhere and make a nuisance of ourselves," Curt told her firmly.

"Yes, sir! Our bots will roll when we do, Major! And shoot when we want them to."

"Make sure the Companions are in equally good shape," Curt went on. "We should all get as much rest as we can under the circumstances. I don't know how much time we'll have in the *McCain*, but I want everyone to catch up on snore-shelf time. If someone has trouble, have Shelley Hale get with them to help them out with a sleepy pill or bioelectronic therapy, preferably the latter."

"Are we on duty?" Jerry Allen asked suddenly.

Curt knew why his senior lieutenant had asked that question. Lieutenant Adonica Sweet was also aboard with Frazier's Ferrets. The two young officers had a very torrid romance under way. It had been that way since Trinidad. But the two of them were punctilious in observing Rule Ten. Both of them knew a good thing and didn't want to screw it up. "I don't know how long we'll be in the *McCain*. It could be one day, or it could be several. While we're aboard, duty hours will extend from oh-eight-hundred to sixteen-hundred hours, ship time, including chow time," Curt advised. "We'll be on duty for Oscar briefs and whenever we must be in order to carry out whatever the hell mission we're on. Otherwise, it would be goddamned stupid of me to try to restrict everyone."

"When do you think we'll get an Oscar brief on this, Major?" Jerry Allen asked.

"General Carlisle promised one within twenty-four hours," Kitsy added.

"Then we'll get one within twenty-four hours," Curt told her. "The general and the colonel can be counted on to do what they say they'll do. Always. Count on it. And don't ever forget it."

"Never crossed my mind otherwise, Major," Kitsy admitted.

Curt turned in his chair to Platoon Sergeant Nick Gerard, who was seated at a table behind him with Tracy Dillon, Dyani Motega, and Tom Cole. "Nick, how are you doing?" Curt asked. He was a little worried about the man. During the Trinidad operation, Nick had toggled over to panic mode inside the submersible landing craft, exhibiting latent claustrophobia that hadn't manifested itself before.

Gerard looked fine, although his eyes betrayed the fact that he was tired. But he wasn't alone. All the Companions were tired. The last 48 hours had seen little time for sleep, much less for rest. "Major, if you're sweating over me because I might go ape-shit in this sub, don't worry. This is no different from being in our old Diamond Point headquarters under that mountain. Being in this big son of a bitch doesn't shake me at all. After all, I've been here before."

One thing Curt didn't like about naval vessels was the public address system. It was a Navy tradition. It was pervasive. It was everywhere. It was capable of breaking into any other activity. He knew that a PA system had to exist and that it was absolutely necessary in an environment where it might be critical to have everyone aboard informed at the same time of something important, like the ship sinking for example. But Curt never got used to the piercing whistle of the traditional boatswain's pipe that preceded every announcement except the General Quarters call.

The whistle penetrated the farthest nook and cranny of the huge vessel and had enough of an on-edge pitch to wake the dead.

"Hear this! Hear this! Personnel of the Third Infantry Regiment will attend a briefing in the ship's auditorium at sixteen hundred hours!" an impersonal voice announced.

Curt looked at the bulkhead clock. "Okay, we've got a little more than eight hours," he observed.

Edie Sampson picked up on it. "Roger! Okay, Companions, the quicker we finish the work we've got to do, the more time we'll have to shelf out and get to log some sheet time before maybe we get told to mount the Chippies and go do something nasty to someone. So, let's get with it!"

But Curt didn't get the chance to log any of that sheet time and get rested. He was kept busy checking and inspecting the Mary Anns, Hary Foxes, and Jeeps dogged down and ready to go inside the Chippewas on the hangar deck. Then he checked with each Companion to make sure everyone had the Minimum Required Equipment called out for this operation back at Wiesbaden. He checked and doubled-checked with Major Cal Worsham to ensure that the loads were properly distributed between the four Chippies assigned to the Companions, that everyone had a seat on a Chippie, and that everything was aboard each Chippie and properly tied down. He spent several hours with the regimental staff, especially Captain John Gibbon's C-cubed people, making sure that communications and data links were set up, checked out, and ready should the Companions leave the *McCain* for any operational reason; he had to be able to talk to Bellamack and the other company commanders if they went into combat.

The eight hours were intensive work and involved checking not only the equipment itself but the paperwork in the form of computer displays.

Some company commanders would have left some of this up to subordinates and, although Curt did indeed let his lieutenants and NCOs carry out their assign-ments, he personally checked each one. He'd been in combat both as a warbot brainy and as a Sierra Charlie. He knew there was no such thing as being "too ready" and, once committed to action, no chance to go back and cover something that had been overlooked. In the past, forgetting something important had almost lost the fracas. He knew he couldn't cover every base, but he also knew he could minimize the panic that ensued when they discovered the inevitable screw-up.

Besides, it kept him and his Companions busy and didn't give them a lot of time to worry about what the hell they might be getting into.

At 1600 hours, he found himself dragging into Compartment Delta

24, the *McCain's* snake pit briefing room. Curt remembered it from the Zahedan operations. It was still configured with linkage couches and terminals arranged around a holographic projector in the center of the amphitheater. The Navy wasn't as hot for bots as the Army, but it had embraced neuroelectronic robot technology where it felt it would help its officers and ratings run the extremely complex naval vessels of the twenty-first century.

The Companions were also bushed. They took their positions without a lot of chatter or bulling with the other companies. Captain Alexis Morgan did come over to Curt, however. She looked haggard. "I was going to suggest maybe a quiet, unwinding evening together because I've got some very nice quarters this time," she told him openly. Alexis had never been shy. "But I'm not sure I could turn anything on tonight. In short, I'm sorry but I've got a headache."

"Likely excuse," Curt returned lightly. "But acceptable under the circumstances."

"It had better be, because that's the only one you're going to get," she warned him, the joviality gone out of her voice and replaced with a weary note. "Besides, we may be in action before tomorrow's dawn."

"Where?" Curt wanted to know. "We're out in the middle of the Indian Ocean heading God knows where…and sure as hell nothing worth fighting over within thousands of kilometers."

"Damned Army will probably create a place!" Alexis claimed, then rejoined her Marauders.

It started as usual. A 17th Iron Fist divisional staffer stepped on stage and announced the division commander, Major General Jacob Carlisle, who walked on and told everyone to sit down.

"Last night in Muscat, I promised you I'd tell you what the hell is going on," he began, his hands clasped behind his back as he strode around the platform, looking at everyone in turn. "We are now on the submarine carrier *McCain*, where there is no chance that security might be compromised in the slightest. It was vitally important that security on this mission be total and complete. You'll understand why when you learn the details.

"It has taken an incredibly complex series of moves to get an entire regiment and a combat air support group on this submarine carrier without drawing attention to what we were doing," Carlisle went on. "To get the Greys out of Fort Huachuca, it had to appear as a regular European emergency redeployment exercise. The same excuse was used to cover the movement of the Warhawks from Bahrain. Then there had to be nothing unusual about pulling the Greys and the Warhawks out of Wiesbaden; the movement of the Greys had to appear to be ·a nominal reinforcement of the Middle East theater, and the Warhawks had to appear to be returning following exercises with the Greys.

"The most critical point in the mission thus far was the layover in Muscat. That, too, was designed to appear as a nominal Middle East training exercise, but we didn't dare allow any contact between the troops and the locals," the experienced leader of the Iron Fist division explained.

"We pulled it off, all of it, thanks to your cooperation and long-suffering patience. No one, not even our NATO allies, even suspects that anything is going on or that we are now in the final stages of mounting Operation Tempest Frigid."

Carlisle chuckled. "Yes, I know the computers come up with some amusing operational designators occasionally, and this one may be a tongue twister for some people. Never mind. It describes our mission quite well.

"We are indeed going into cold weather. We are headed due south from the Arabian Peninsula and will continue southward through the Indian Ocean. Our destination is more than eight thousand kilometers away in a place where winter is just beginning. Ladies and gentlemen, Operation Tempest Frigid is a search and destroy mission on the island of Kerguelen."

Chapter Twenty-Seven

"Has anyone here ever heard of Kerguelen Island?" Major General Jacob Carlisle asked, breaking the silence that followed his announcement. "Show of hands, please...I thought so. I hadn't heard of it either before the operations orders for Tempest Frigid came in. Very well. Georgie, attention to orders," the general said, addressing the invisible division megacomputer.

By means of low-frequency radio, satellite transmis-sions, optical networks, and other modern telecommunications technology, a wideband data link existed between the submerged *McCain*, running at 100 meters beneath the Indian Ocean, and Georgie, whose picoelectronic innards were ensconced in the bowels of an Arizona mountain on the other side of the world.

"I'm here, General," replied the synthesized male voice of the megacomputer.

"Georgie, project a three-dee hologram of Kerguelen Island and give me a one-minute encyclopedic synopsis of data concerning the island," Carlisle ordered, being careful to phrase his order in such a way that Georgie didn't spill his enormously detailed guts and thus spend a long time reporting all the data about Kerguelen that was in the accessible memories of the world data base.

The lights in the snake pit dimmed, and a three-dimensional hologram of a rocky, rugged, barren island built up like a model on the stage.

"Kerguelen Island," Georgie explained, "is the largest above-water portion of the Kerguelen-Gaussberg Ridge and is located approximately forty-nine degrees south latitude and seventy degrees east longitude. It is a rocky volcanic island approximately one-hundred-thirty kilometers east to west and one-hundred-twenty kilometers north to south. Its climate is maritime polar in nature. It supports few trees or other vegetation other than the sort one might expect to find in a subpolar biome."

As Georgie described the island, the hologram was highlighted to show what he was talking about. "The island has a mountainous west side and a low, tundra covered east side. The highest point on the island is Mount Ross with an elevation of one-thousand-eight-hundred-fifty meters. A large area of the western portion of the island is covered by Cook Glacier, which is a miniature continental glacier having many moraines and outwash plains feeding into narrow fjords. The glacier itself has not been sounded but is considered to be extremely thick since its dome has an elevation of more than a thousand meters and its moraines are at or near sea level.

"Kerguelen Island is typical of most near Antarctic islands. Its indigenous life forms are limited to a few insects, penguins, and some species of sea birds. The island belongs to France and is uninhabited except for a transient population of approximately thirty French oceanographers, biologists, and meteorologists who live under rather primitive conditions in the tiny village of Port-aux-Francaise here on the east side of the island. Port-aux-Francaise consists of eleven buildings and a radio station. The main street of the village is the only road on the entire island. Port-aux-Francaise is visited by a French oceangoing vessel twice a year to resupply the scientific outpost and rotate personnel. The last ship visited on March tenth of this year. The island has no industry, but some fishing is carried out by various French companies in the Indian Ocean around the island." Georgie then paused and asked, "I have more data in greater detail should you wish to have it."

"Thank you, Georgie. Leave the hologram up and stand by for further requests," Carlisle replied quickly, then addressed the Greys. "That's enough for right now, but all of us are going to become much more familiar with Kerguelen in the next few weeks because we've got to make a covert landing on the island in a search and destroy mission. Why? It's rather ironic that an isolated, out of way, primitive island such as Kerguelen happens to be the scene of an extremely high-tech military activity: Georgie, please illustrate what I'm going to talk about."

"Standing by."

"On the fifth of this month, less than three weeks ago, a Soviet Red Sentry military surveillance satellite was infected with a virus program transmitted to it from an unknown ground station." Carlisle continued his briefing while Georgie displayed a hologram of the Soviet satellite which hung in the air over the hologram of Kerguelen. "This was detected by an alert Aerospace Force officer as American computers downloaded the Red Sentry data in full accordance with various international agreements which allow such things. This officer also detected the virus program before it infected the entire United States national command computer network. But the program did take out the Soviet counterpart when the Soviets attempted to download their surveillance data later in the same orbit. In accordance with protocol, the United States reported this to the UN Space Security Commission, whose members disavowed any knowledge of the ground station transmitting the virus program. The subsequent disablement of a second Red Sentry allowed the Aerospace Force to pinpoint the location of the transmissions as coming from Kerguelen Island. An overflight by a highly classified vehicle produced the following images. Georgie, please overlay the last refinement of the Albatross data on the Kerguelen Island holo."

Carlisle didn't know how the Aerospace Force and the NIA had gotten the overflight data; he hadn't been told and only knew that the data was called the Albatross data. The SRO-17 Albatross was a very black Cosmic Top Secret vehicle, and its operations were heavily shrouded in security. But he wondered at the extreme clarity, definition, and resolution of the data.

"What appears to be a manned station was found to exist on a ridge called la Mortadelle here at the south end of the Cook Glacier." The general pointed out the spot as Georgie highlighted it. "Georgie, please magnify the image. There! That's good! No, we do not know who built this station, but we do know that it's being used to disable Soviet surveillance satellites. We don't know if it has the capability to disable or infect other satellites. The third Red Sentry was infected on Saturday, the nineteenth. As a result, your training exercises were terminated, your leaves and passes canceled, and your regiment redeployed from Wiesbaden. The President, the National Security Council, and the joint chiefs believe that we must move rapidly to learn whose station this is and to take it out of action as quickly as possible. If we don't, we're likely to have a thermonuclear war on our hands at worst. And the worst is what we must prevent."

This assessment fell like a bombshell on the Washington Greys.

General thermonuclear war had never taken place. Classified data would reveal that several isolated nukes had been popped in isolated skirmishes over the past eighty years. Other very secret information told of nuclear weapons being seized or destroyed in both covert and surprise assaults on Third World countries and, in at least one case, on a terrorist organization that had quietly assembled all the necessary components save one. This information was kept in deep, dark highly guarded vaults and known only to a few people. No one wanted to panic the world's population, and the new media would have gone into a feeding frenzy over the information had it leaked. The only way to keep the most powerful explosives under control was to keep the lid on, freedom of information notwithstanding.

In the decades since the Manhattan District and the Little Boy and Fat Man bombs, enough information about simple nuclear weapons had appeared in the unclassified literature that nearly anyone could easily find enough data to permit the design and construction of a nuclear weapon using U-235 or plutonium implosion squeeze. Getting the hot stuff was no real problem; kilograms of both elements had disappeared over the years. The key piece of information needed to make a nuclear weapon go bang instead of making a messy and deadly melt had never been disclosed and was known to very few people. In short, anyone could make a nuclear weapon, but very few people knew how to make it go off. But there was always the chance that *that* bit of information had also leaked...In time, anything will leak.

Carlisle looked around and decided that this was time to break for comments and queries. "Questions?" he asked the assembly.

Colonel Bill Bellamack raised his hand, was recognized, and spoke up. "General, why is the United States taking unilateral action here? Why isn't this a joint mission carried out by the combined forces of those nations represented on the UN Space Security Commission? Or by the Soviets? Why us?"

"Because the Kerguelen station may belong to the Soviets."

"Excuse me, sir, but that doesn't make much sense to me," Bellamack observed. "Why would the Soviets knock out their own surveillance satellites?"

"Maybe to have an excuse to go to war, or to put diplomatic pressure on us," Carlisle explained. "Or perhaps the station is manned by forces from a nation that's a member of the Space Security Commission; if that's the case, they might try to delay any action, but it's certain that an announcement of the station's discovery and of any possible search and destroy mission would give the offending nation time to do something about it."

Carlisle paused before discussing the next possibility, primarily because it was a very touchy and delicate one. But he felt the Washington Greys should have all the data that might possibly affect Operation Tempest Frigid. So, he added, "Or maybe it's a ploy to infect American security computers and those of other nations with a virus program that would render them inoperative a plan which has probably backfired if there was indeed such a plan. If it was a Soviet plan and we confronted them with the knowledge of it…Well, the Russians are running the show in the Soviet Union, and they've always been an extremely paranoid group of people. I, for one, would hesitate to predict what the Soviets might do. They could toggle over into a very nasty and vindictive attitude. If we keep quiet about it, they may continue their current cooperative stance and may even help us with the post-mission diplomacy…which is something we don't have to worry about, thank God, because it isn't our job!" Carlisle said with relief.

"Be that as it may, ladies and gentlemen, I understand that the President and his aides debated this issue and all the scenarios quite passionately before the commander in chief authorized a unilateral strike. And we have been given operational authority to make a covert landing on Kerguelen, confirm the location of the station, occupy it, put it out of commission, take into custody the operators, and get off the island. We must do this without being detected by the French scientific contingent at Port-aux-Francais or by any of the space surveillance facilities. So, we'll go in and do it." Carlisle looked around and told Georgie, "Remove the hologram but make sure it's stored in the *McCain's* tactical computer memories so it can be called up quickly without bothering you, Georgie."

"It's done, General, and it's really no bother to me. After all, I am only a tool for you to use…"

"Thank you, Georgie. Please continue monitoring and recording," the commanding general of the 17th Iron Fist Division told the megacomputer. "Ladies and gentlemen of the Greys, you've been given an overview briefing of Operation Tempest Frigid. You've been told what must be done, but I haven't told you how to do it. And I don't intend to do so. Those of you who know me also know I'm a firm believer in the advice of General George S. Patton, who told his officers and staff, 'Never tell people how to do things. Tell them what to do and they will surprise you with their ingenuity.' So I do not intend to micromanage Operation Tempest Frigid. I've been assigned the overall responsibility of commander of the combined forces; it's my task to ensure that the Army and the Navy - and even the Aerospace Force, if we need to call it in - work smoothly together and that Operation Tempest Frigid is completed successfully and within the bounds of the rules of engagement. Therefore, Colonel Bellamack, you and your officers are responsible for working out the detailed tactical plans."

"General," Bellamack said, "you've just saddled me with a hell of a big responsibility. I'll take it, of course, but how much time do we have to develop our tactical plan for Kerguelen?"

"I'm told by Captain Joseph of the *McCain* that we'll be underway for three days en route to Kerguelen. So, you don't have to get on it right away," Carlisle told him easily. "A good commander should see to it that his forces don't get worn out and beat down before the action starts. Fortunately, you've got three days' time here while the

Navy gets us to where the action will be. You've all been under the stress of not knowing what you were being ordered into, and you've all busted your asses for days in a row, so I don't expect instant planning. Enjoy the Navy's hospitality tonight; I understand the officers of the Greys and Warhawks are invited to a dinner given by Captain Joseph this evening in the senior officers' mess."

"How about my NCOs?" Bellamack wanted to know. "We don't observe any social stratification between our officers and NCOs."

Major General Jacob Carlisle nodded in agreement. But he'd had to deal with the Navy on their terms in this case, and the ship's captain was theoretically in complete charge until the *McCain* reached Kerguelen, whereupon the submarine carrier would become a staging base and Carlisle would resume actual command. "Sorry, but the Navy is a bit more tradition-bound in this respect than we've become in the Iron Fist Division. I brought this to the attention of Captain Joseph, who then informed me that the NCOs are invited to the *McCain's* petty officers' mess. We're basically guests aboard this ship, Colonel, so we must conform to the customs of our hosts."

"Yes, sir, but I have some officers who may decide to party with the NCOs," Bellamack informed him, anticipating some problems there.

"Colonel, any officer who would do that would be insulting the captain of this vessel," Carlisle reminded him. "This sort of interservice diplomacy is sometimes more difficult to manage than international protocol. I've done both before, which is why I was assigned the job of joint task force commander. I agree: The Navy is a bit backward in this regard, but they probably have their reasons. Try not to gloat over the fact that our Army is a bit more socially advanced than they are…probably for the first time in this nation's history! If I have to adjudicate any difficulties that might arise, I'm going to become a real bastard because the big fight may be on Kerguelen, not in the *McCain*. I hope everyone understands that."

"Yes, sir, we do. This isn't a party," Bellamack admitted. "Even so, we're not exactly in partying condition after the past few days…"

"So I'd advise all of you to get some rest tonight," General Carlisle suggested. "We'll resume normal duty hours while we're underway, and our clocks will match those on the *McCain*. I'll be available tomorrow for consultations and questions. I expect Colonel Bellamack to inform me the day after tomorrow concerning the tactical plans for carrying out Operation Tempest Frigid. Captain Joseph informs me that the McCain will be in the vicinity of Kerguelen Island on Monday, April twenty-eighth. But if we haven't developed what you believe to be a workable tactical plan by then, we don't have to mount the strike until we're ready. Operation Tempest Frigid must succeed without fuss or fan-fare. Too much depends upon it. If there are no further questions...? Good, but I expect you to have a few tomorrow, or the next day! Dismissed!"

Chapter Twenty-Eight

"A dinner? A full, formal dinner?" Jerry Allen wondered, shaking his head in disbelief as he read the invitation given to him by a yeoman as they left the Oscar brief. "What the hell are we supposed to wear, Major? We only brought combat gear along."

Curt had selected the best set of combat cammies in his duffle and put them on in the confines of the stateroom he shared with his senior platoon officer. "So, we wear combat gear, Lieutenant. The captain doesn't expect us to have dress blues along."

A discreet knock on the compartment door was followed by Lieutenant Kitsy Clinton's voice. "Major?"

"Come in, Kitsy," Curt told her. He thought he knew what it would be about, but he was only partly right.

Kitsy looked distraught. "Major, I realize that this is Navy protocol, but I'd sure like to tender regrets, sir," she told him, rustling the hard copy of the captain's invitation she held in her hand.

Curt shook his head slowly. "Only if you're on the sick list, Lieutenant."

"Sir, I'm tired and I haven't got a thing to wear but grungy old combat cammies, and…" Kitsy Cinton started to complain.

"Stop sniveling, Lieutenant! I can't make excuses for you," Curt snapped. Kitsy looked like a little girl who'd just been told she had to go to the grown-ups' party, but she was squeaky clean and fluffed, so he told her, "You're wearing a clean set of cammies, and you've washed your face, so you're perfectly proper and respectable for this evening. If you don't show up, you'll insult Captain Jospeh, who just happens to be by Navy regulations the closest thing to an absolute monarch."

"No, sir. Yes, sir. Very well, sir. I'll go. And I had no intentions of insulting the captain, sir. I would have sent my written regrets,"

Kitsy admitted sourly. "But I'm sure a lowly shavetail lieutenant won't go missed."

"Yeah, Major, we're going to be in this tub for only a few days," Allen pointed out. "And we're coming up on possible combat! I can't understand why the captain would be throwing a dinner for us under these circumstances..."

"Wrong, wrong, wrong, lieutenants," Curt told them, straightened up, and faced the two of them. "We may be in this submarine carrier for weeks, maybe longer. We don't know. Look around you. What do you see?"

"A naval vessel," Allen replied.

"A sub carrier," Kitsy Clinton added.

"Don't ever call it a 'sub carrier' in front of a member of its crew," Curt admonished her. "The abbreviation 'sub' means 'inferior,' and this ship certainly isn't. It's a 'carrier' or a 'submarine carrier.' But that isn't why I asked the question. Do we go into combat in such luxurious surroundings? Hell, no, we don't! When a Navy man dies, he's slept between clean sheets and his belly full of hot food and hot coffee beforehand. The Navy considers their service the only civilized one, and there may be some truth to that. It's also a different sort of 'club' than ours. Different rules. So we'll respect their rules."

"Sir," Allen said as Curt paused, "why is the captain holding a social affair this close to a combat situation?"

"It's not purely for social purposes," Curt explained to the two of them. Although Allen had been in the *McCain* before, it had been during the very rushed, busy, and frantic Zahedan operation, where there wasn't time to do anything more than eat, sleep, and use the ship as a portable airfield. Furthermore, Jerry had been fresh-caught in the Companions back then, and they had all still been pure warbot brainies at that time. "We're going to be living in these close quarters with the officers and crew of the *McCain*, sharing their wardrooms, and depending upon them to get us to Kerguelen and back...as well as probably having to work damned closely with them while we're there. The officers of the *McCain* want to know the officers of the Greys and Iron Fist, and we'd damned well better know them, too. So that's why this is essentially a command performance before an absolute monarch. Besides, it's a way for Captain Joseph to show proper respect and honors to a general officer of another service. Have you ever thought that this dinner might be in recognition that there's a two-star aboard in flag country?"

Kitsy Clinton perked up. Some of her spark came back when she realized that this was just another bit of Army nonsense that she was expected to carry through in a rote performance like a social call. So, she smiled and said, "Very well, sir, I'll be there with bells on! Maybe I should wear my furs!"

Curt looked her up and down. "You're fine the way you are, Lieutenant."

"May l put on some makeup sir?"

"As I said, you look fine, Lieutenant. And I hereby decree that Rumanian orders are in effect," Curt stated firmly.

"Sir?"

"When Rumania declared war in 1916, the first order to their army decreed that only officers above the rank of major were thereafter allowed to use makeup," Curt told her.

"But they didn't have women in their army then," Jerry Allen put in.

"That's right! We have fifteen minutes to find the senior officers' wardroom. Let's go!"

The senior officers' mess in the *McCain* was large as wardrooms went, but when almost fifty people get together in any submarine's compartment, it's likely to be a bit crowded. Surprisingly, a reception line was in operation with Captain Kim Blythe, Carlisle's aide de camp, announcing each officer's name to General Carlisle, who then made the introduction to Captain Joseph. To many combat officers, this sort of thing might seem to be overpoweringly stuffy, especially on a combat mission. But the *McCain* was safe beneath the sea and underway, Kerguelen was three days away, and this provided an opportunity for people to get to know one another. It was semiformal because of the circumstances. The naval officers wore what was for them the equivalent of combat cammies of the Army officers: khaki shirts and pants with black tie and black shoes.

Curt and his two lieutenants went speedily through the reception line. A visual sensor picked up each person's image, and Georgie then identified the officer through a tiny earphone in Captain Blythe's ear. But Curt needed no introduction to Kim Blythe, whom he had from time to time dated at West Point, and General Carlisle knew Curt from past operations.

Carlisle's introduction of Curt to Captain Lewis Joseph was also unusual. "Captain, this is Major Curt Carson, my second in command. He's probably one of the finest combat officers I've ever known and is the man responsible for the new Sierra Charlie doctrine."

Captain Lewis Joseph was a small, spare, trim man with dark hair and intense blue eyes under rather bushy black eyebrows. He was also a very animated man. "Really!" he said as he shook Curt's hand. "What prompted you to suggest that the Army get away from total robot operations, Major?"

Curt returned the man's handshake just as earnestly. Knowing that he couldn't and shouldn't become involved in a long conversation in a reception line he merely said, "Captain, it happened on this ship, as a matter of fact, back when we went into Zahedan after those Orient Express hostages."

"Well, I hope I get the chance to talk to you about it sometime while you're aboard," Joseph snapped back, his eyes flashing. "Please feel free to drop by when you have the time. Just check with my orderly. Major, permit me to introduce my executive officer, Commander Tom Weaver." Joseph smoothly passed Curt along to the next officer in the line.

Weaver was a quiet, horse-faced man who reminded Curt a little bit of Bill Bellamack.

Curt was most impressed with the officer he figured he'd have to work most closely with, Lieutenant Commander Rebecca Buell, the air officer. She was a small, slender, dark-haired woman with an amazing superstructure. To Curt, she looked like she was streamlined for about Mach 5 with all the necessary accessories. Curt mentioned that he looked forward to working closely with her for the airlift portion of the mission, whereupon she replied politely, "Well, I hope your Army 'dyne drivers can get on and off the flight deck fast; we had to leave a strike fighter squadron and an antisub flight at Bahrain in order to accommodate the Warhawks. We may be a tad shy on shooting capabilities..."

"Well, Commander, Major Worsham's Chippewas can shoot, too," Curt reminded her pleasantly.

The last man in the line was Major Howard Pence of the United States Marine Corps, a proud, square headed little man with a voice that sounded like sand-paper going over glass. He wore a full chest of ribbons, including two Expert Marksman medals. Although the Marines were now mostly a guard force for the Navy, it was apparent from the man's ribbons that Pence had seen some action, perhaps on exchange duty with the Army. "Major," he rasped to Curt when they were introduced, "I'm glad to see the Army getting' down and dirty again!"

"Well, Major, we discovered that warbots couldn't do it all," Curt told him.

"The Marines told them that twenty years ago, but no one listened," Pence said through gritted teeth as he smiled.

The reception was over as soon as all the Greys and Warhawks had been formally introduced. Since Navy regulations forbade alcohol, smoking, and almost every other sort of social relaxant aboard a submarine, there was little to do except to stand around chatting while waiting for the general and the captain to take their places at the head table. Once they started in that direction, everyone began the ordered search for their place tags based on the customary seating arrangements of senior officers being closest to the head table and seats thereafter being assigned in order of descending rank. Wherever possible, the navy protocol officer had seated a male Army officer between two Navy women officers and a female Army officer between two male naval officers. Thank God for computers! Curt told himself. It would have been an impossible sorting job otherwise.

Curt found himself seated between the operations officer, Lieutenant Commander Loretta Ara, who was a petite brunette, and the navigator, Lieutenant Commander Doreen Weber, an attractive woman who had shaved her head like a warbot brainy so that she could link better with the computers and intelligence amplifiers of the *McCain's* computer network. Across the table were other naval officers interspersed between officers of the Greys.

It was a convivial meal that accomplished its mission. Furthermore, it was just the sort of R&R that Curt and the rest of the Greys really needed at the moment, although they were reluctant to admit it to themselves.

"You've been in the *McCain* before," Commander Ara said. It was almost a question yet also a statement of fact.

Curt nodded. "Yes, ma'am, but it was somewhat of a matter of in and out," he admitted. "I never got the chance to meet any of the *McCain's* officers except a doctor."

"Were you in sick bay?" Commander Weber wanted to know.

"No, that was in the middle of the Zahedan hostage rescue operation, and I had to interview a couple of Iranian natives we had to bring back."

"I seem to remember something about it," Ara remarked. "Well, I'm glad we have an opportunity to get to know one another. The Sierra Charlies are the hottest military news around in a long time!"

"I understand you fight in the field alongside your warbots," Weber said.

"That's right. We use our warbots as stupid grunt infantrymen with lots of firepower and the ability to take incoming. The human half of the Sierra Charlies does all the thinking and is maneuverable, fast, and versatile. I think we can probably learn something from the Navy because you never went full robotic," Curt told them.

"There's too much human equation in what we do; we discovered years ago that it can't all be automated," Ara admitted. "The old Aegis system was probably as close as the Navy will ever come to full automation."

"The Army didn't go totally robotic," Curt pointed out. These two Navy ladies were bright, intelligent, and interesting; he was enjoying talking with them. "Like your aviators, our combat air support people went only part way. Major Cal Worsham and his Warhawk pilots still put their pink bodies into those Chippewas every time they have to go somewhere. I've driven a few 'dynes myself, and I know it's almost impossible to get full situational awareness in an aerial combat situation if the 'dyne is a full warbot."

"You'll get along fine with Jugs Buell," Weber remarked.

"Excuse me?" Curt was somewhat taken aback by the apparent nickname that obviously referred to Buell's spectacular superstructure.

"Her call sign," Ara explained with a grin.

"My God, I'd think the top brass would have a shit fit over that!" Curt blurted, then realized that maybe these Navy ladies didn't talk that way.

"They may not like it, but there ain't one goddamned fucking thing they can do about it," Weber shot back quietly in equally vulgar terms, which put Curt at ease a bit. "It's probably embarrassing - it seemed to be that way to you, Major - and it's sure as hell tasteless. But I wish I had that call sign, sir!"

"Yes, it's right for Buell," Ara agreed. "She's a shit hot pilot, and that call sign is her badge of acceptance among all the jocks. Jugs is one of the boys..."

"But, Major, you'd better not call her that," Weber warned.

"I think I know why," Curt guessed.

Ara nodded. "Yes, you don't qualify yet. She'll let you know what you do, and there will be no question about it when it happens…"

Curt was beginning to both admire and respect these naval officers. In many ways, they were similar to their Army counterparts. And in other ways they weren't. Given the different circumstances present in the submarine Navy, Curt thought he could understand the difference. But again, he was surprised.

"Don't tell me how to qualify," he remarked, then added, "I suspect naval regulations have something similar to Army Regulation Dash-Ten?"

"Yes and no," Commander Ara told him with a slight impishness. "

"We're always on duty, so our regulations have to do with being on watch. And officers must follow slightly different requirements than our petty officers."

"What's that?" Curt asked, aware that he might be stepping in it.

"We are always required to act like ladies and gentlemen…"

"Which means that one is never…"

"…Unintentionally rude to anyone," Ara finished for him. "Although there have been times when I was intentionally rude…"

"And damned lucky you weren't caught," Weber told her. "Although I don't believe the captain has ever meted out boot discipline to the ladies in his command."

Curt was feeling much better now. He'd been well fed. The Navy knew damned good and well what it was doing by inviting its Army guests to dinner, and they'd choreographed it in such a way that it was a pleasant evening designed to provide a bit of respite from the constant, nagging worries and fears of forth-coming combat. But Curt had also discovered that these naval ladies were like the ladies in the Greys - persons of the opposite sex who were not to be trifled with and the sort you'd be glad to have at your back or even fighting alongside you.

Operation Tempest Frigid could become a real up-tight sheep-screwing squirrel cage, but he knew he was with the right kind of people if things really went to slime.

And he'd been on enough missions to know that they probably would.

But he didn't know how it would happen yet.

Chapter Twenty-Nine

"We have some information that may be critical to the operation," Lieutenant Commander Loretta Ara reported. She looked down at the hard copy in her hand. "We're monitoring the meteorological reports broadcast by the French from Port-aux-Francaise. The oh-eight-hundred local observation shows sky partially obscured, ceiling one thousand ragged, temperature minus-two Celsius, dew point the same, winds two-six-zero at one-five meters per second, gusts to two-two, barometer nine-eight-seven millibars and falling. Snow showers over the mountains to the west."

As openers in the tactical planning meeting, that news wasn't very good as far as Curt was concerned. But it was Lieutenant Colonel Bill Bellamack who asked the *McCain's* operations officer, "What's the latest forecast?"

The petite naval officer checked her hard copy. "Colonel, conditions are not expected to improve during the three-day extended forecast period."

"Do we have a current weather satellite image?" asked Lieutenant Commander Rebecca Buell.

Ara keyed a terminal, and it flashed on the big display screen of the *McCain's* operational planning center. Ara punched up commands which displayed the temperature and altitude of the cloud tops.

The assembled commanders and staff of the Greys, the Warhawks, and the McCain didn't like what they saw. A huge comma-shaped cloud mass covered the southern Indian Ocean and extended westward. The satellite animation showed it slowly drifting eastward at the urging of the polar jet, which had swung northward in a huge loop.

"Goddamned weather never cooperates on these panic missions," Major Cal Worsham growled, the tips of his mustache drooping slightly.

"Major, can you put your Chippewas on the island under those conditions?" Bellamack asked.

Worsham nodded his shaved head. "No problem. We can handle the wind if we've got visual or i-r data. As long as we can get some idea of where the hell the ground is, we're fat."

"I won't put 'dynes of any sort up in Force Nine wind conditions," Buell advised them. "They'll have hell to pay when they try to trap on the recovery, and I'll have bolters all over the sky. I'll launch A-forties because they're Vee-stol airframes and can maintain reasonable relative speeds coming into trap. But I'd still worry because of the sea conditions. Loretta, any data on sea states?"

"Negative, Becky. Port-aux-Francaise doesn't report sea states. And we're still too far from Kerguelen to make a good guess on sea state there from an observation at our present position."

"Commander," Bellamack said, addressing the *McCain's* air ops officer, "you just made a comment which may strongly affect the conduct of Operation Tempest Frigid, especially any air support we may request from you while we're on the island. Will you please clarify the conditions under which you won't authorize an air launch? What is a Force Nine wind condition?"

"Force Nine relates to the Beaufort wind scale, Colonel. About twenty meters per second minimum. And if we've got twenty meters per second up on the surface, we've also probably got sea state Hotel-One or at least Romeo-Four," Buell told him in no nonsense tones. "That's marginal for launching aerodynes and damned difficult for their recovery. I can get Commander Weaver to run downwind if necessary, provided he has sea room. But if the sea state is bad enough to cause waves to break over the flight decks, we'll ship a lot of water. If that happens, we may not be able to dive again. Or we'll have to dive with aircraft on an open deck and lose them. I'm not going to take that chance."

"Are we going to be able to launch this mission at all?" Bellamack wanted to know.

"Not if the weather's bad," Buell stated. "At least, I'd advise against it if conditions near Kerguelen don't improve. Sea state permitting, we might be able to launch, but I have to have in my hands a good forecast of the expected weather at recovery time. I won't risk my pilots and aircraft."

The exchange between Bellamack and Buell snapped back and forth between them.

"What are your limits of risk, Commander?" Bellamack pressed her. "What are the worst conditions in which you'd authorize operations of your aircraft?"

"Naval regulations say Force Eight winds and sea states Mike or Bravo," Buell shot back without hesitation.

"I didn't realize you were so weather-limited," Bellamack shot back, intimating by his tone of voice that he wasn't very happy with the Navy at this point. "The Army has to fight anywhere at any time in any weather if it's ordered to do so…and we were ordered to do so on Kerguelen!"

Buell caught the innuendo. Every officer in the room suddenly realized that this planning meeting had become a face-off between Buell and Bellamack. When two strong people went at one another, junior officers stood back. "Colonel, we're in a submersible ship at sea, and I have the safety of my air group in my hands. You may be willing to take chances, but I'm not. I'm well aware that the Army has different limitations than we do. After all, the Army has never had a parade ground sink…"

I wasn't aware that you might have to pay for the *McCain* if you risked her doing what she was designed to do," Bellamack replied slowly in an acidic tone. "Let me get this straight for my own planning purposes, Commander. You have a standing policy that you won't launch your aircraft if the surface wind is twenty meters per second or more. Correct?"

"Navy regs are one thing, Colonel. I'm will to do better if the situation warrants. I have some leeway under emergency conditions unless the captain overrides me. I'll authorize launch in Force Nine winds."

"How about recovery?"

"I won't let aircraft go in the first place if the forecast calls for Force Nine at their recovery time."

"You would attempt to recover them in an emergency, however?"

"Hell, yes! I'd have to check with Tom Weaver to ensure we weren't risking the ship, but we'd get them aboard if we had to."

"Good! I just wanted to clarify that point. Major Worsham's Chippewas were purchased on an Army appropriation, and they'll be carrying Army personnel. May I ask General Carlisle for a command decision concerning who has the authority to approve the launch of the Chippies on any Kerguelen mission?"

"Colonel, if the Army is willing to accept responsibility, I see no reason to call for a command decision on this," Buell said, backing down slightly. "As air officer, I'm here to work with you. I've told you the situation in which I wouldn't launch Navy aircraft. If you pilots are crazy enough to try it with your 'dynes, I don't imagine I can stop them. But Commander Weaver might not allow the ship to surface or, if it's on the surface, might not permit the flight deck hatches to be rolled back if the sea state might sweep us."

"Colonel. Commander." Curt suddenly spoke up, aware that he might have just stepped into the ring with two pit bulls. "The general is expecting us to report to him tomorrow with a tactical battle plan, and we're here to work on that. May I suggest that we develop Plan A that assumes acceptable weather and Plan B that can be carried out if the weather turns to slime?"

Bellamack and Buell turned to look reproachfully at him, and Curt thought for a minute that he'd really stepped in it this time.

But it was Wild Bill Bellamack who suddenly realized that the argument was getting nowhere and that his second in command had done the proper, if risky, thing by subtly calling it to their attention. "I'm willing to proceed in that manner," he said, satisfied that he'd clarified a point rather than gotten a concession. It had been obvious to him that Commander Buell had always operated under the assumption that any aircraft in the *McCain* was her responsibility. "A lot of things could happen between now and when we get to Kerguelen. We must develop plans that will take care of the need to get a strike off fast regardless of the weather. Commander, I'm sure you've heard of Shangri-La?"

"Can't say that I have, Colonel."

"Perhaps I phrased that wrong," Bellamack admitted. "As a naval officer, I'm sure you remember the Dolittle raid on Tokyo during World War Two?"

"The one where they launched land-based bombers off a surface aircraft carrier? I've heard of it."

"I might recommend that you check it," Bellamack advised her. "They launched sixteen land-based Mitchell bombers off a carrier deck in the teeth of a North Pacific storm."

"Yes, Colonel, but they didn't have to worry about recovering them," Buell reminded him, "or about the U.S.S. *Hornet* foundering as a result. But if that's the sort of operation you're anticipating, the Navy will come through again..."

"Good!" Bellamack was aware that the Navy might not want to take the same sort of risks that he'd grown used to accepting as ordinary since he'd taken command of the Washington Greys. As far as he was concerned, the Navy was perhaps a tad too conservative when it came to letting it all hang out. On the other hand, he understood the reluctance on the part of naval personnel to risk a multi-billion-dollar submarine carrier and a thousand people aboard her. "Now, how close in shore can you get us?"

"As close as you want," Loretta Ara said. "Just give us diving room and seaway to maneuver. How close do you need to be?"

"Major Worsham?" Bellamack indicated that he was tossing the question to the combat air support squadron commander.

"A hundred klicks would be great, but we could work out to five hundred if necessary," Cal Worsham admitted.

"I don't want to be five hundred kilometers from the action," Bellamack objected. "We need to get as close as possible for maximum communications capability, especially if we have to operate any neuroelectronic birdbots by linkage from the *McCain*."

"Colonel, may I suggest that we undertake a reconnaissance mission first?" Curt put in. "We really don't know what the hell we're getting into on Kerguelen. The only real data we have are some French maps, some satellite photos made under lousy weather conditions, and some close-in quick-look data taken on two passes of some superblack Aerospace Force machine. Let's see if Gibbon can put up some recon birdbots and have a real-time look at the place. We'll also get some idea of what's there and where it really is. Might even discover a quick way to get to it without having to crawl all over a glacier first."

"Commander Ara, could you come to periscope depth a couple of kilometers off the west side of Kerguelen so our intelligence people could control a birdbot on a recon flight?" Bellamack wanted to know.

"Depends on what sort of sensors are painting us at the time, Colonel," Ara told him. "This is supposed to be a covert operation, and we sure as hell don't want to get caught with our hands in the cookie jar." The operations officer was considerably less formal and redoubtable than the air officer. And she was a lot more cooperative while still maintaining a modicum of conservativism.

Buell had been right: The Army was a good deal more willing to take a chance because its warbots wouldn't disappear beneath the waves if something went to slime. Both Bellamack and Curt realized that their biggest problem thus far - and probably during the entire mission - was going to involve a confrontation between the Navy's conservative approach to combat versus the Washington Greys' willingness to be audacious with their Sierra Charlies and warbots.

"Very well. Let's outline an overall plan," Bellamack proceeded, trying to get the planning meeting focused on what it was supposed. to be doing rather than fencing between two services. "First, we get to Kerguelen, come to periscope depth, and check for sensor sweeps. If no one is watching, we launch one or more birdbots for a recon swamp of the target area on the south side of the Cook Glacier. Based on that data, we'll either put a manned recon mission ashore in Chippies to scope out the situation or launch an all-out strike mission with all four of my combat companies. Following the strike mission, the ball is in the Navy's court again in order to get us all the hell and gone out of here. Does that sound like a reasonable overall plan?"

"Buyable," Buell said, nodding.

"Colonel," Curt put in, "that's a manned station we're going after. I'm sure you don't want us to use Kelly tactics..."

"Kelly tactics?"

"Sorry. I was referring to a company commander in the Greys who was transferred out before you assumed command," Curt apologized. "His combat policy was simple: *Kill 'em all, let God sort 'em out.* Got him in a heap of trouble several times. In short, we're certainly not expected to assault that station and slaughter everyone there, are. we? Do we take prisoners? How do we handle them? Is the *McCain* prepared to handle them? If so, how many?"

"We will not slaughter whoever is manning the station," Bellamack stated. "Since we'll destroy the station, including its life support systems, anyone manning the Station would either die or be in serious difficulties if we left them there. So, we'll do the humanitarian thing: We'll rescue them and return them to the *McCain* so the powers that be can decide what to do with them. Commander Ara, how many prisoners could you handle?"

The petite operations officer thought about this for a moment, then replied, "About fifty. Maybe less if some of them require medical attention, which is likely to be the case if any fighting takes place. But we can always arrange to transfer some of the prisoners to the other four ships in the task force..."

"You haven't mentioned other ships before," Bellamack told her.

"Colonel, any time the Navy sends a ship as big and expensive as the *McCain* anywhere in the world, an escort always goes along. Four attack submarines are accompanying us - *Shark, Barracuda,*

Nautilus, and *Guppy.* With the *McCain,* they make up Task Force Tango Foxtrot."

"Tango Foxtrot?" Bellamack asked.

"The Navy doesn't like the D-oh-D game of letting a computer generate fancy names for operations," Rebecca Buell added. "It could cause confusion when giving or receiving orders because of code names that might sound similar to commands. So, we automatically translate to the phonetic alphabet."

"Very well, Major," Bellamack remarked to Curt, "any 'rescued personnel' can be taken care of. Now, since we have an acceptable overall plan, let's get down to the details. We need to lay all this on the general and the captain tomorrow at the latest. And be ready to pull it off in two days. So, we have to go with what we've got and hope to God it's adequate."

Chapter Thirty

"My apologies, General, Captain," Commander Loretta Ara remarked deferentially as she entered the planning compartment where General Carlisle and Captain Joseph were listening to the detailed Tempest Frigid tactical plan developed by the Washington Greys and the division chiefs of the *McCain* and being presented by Colonel Wild Bill Bellamack. "I have information that may impact the plans for Operation Tempest Frigid."

Carlisle looked up from the three-dimensional holographic display of Kerguelen Island projected on the large horizontal table. "What do you have, Commander?"

"Sir *Barracuda* has received passive signals indicating the presence of three submarines approximately five-zero-zero nautical miles' range, bearing zero-two-one, course parallel to Task Force Tango Foxtrot. The preliminary estimate of destination is Kerguelen Island," she reported. "Preliminary signature analysis indicates two Soviet attack boats and one Soviet transport boat."

Captain Lewis Joseph sat straight up.

Major General Jacob Carlisle paused and thought about what he'd just heard. Finally, he spoke up by addressing the voice-actuated terminal before him. "Georgie, did you receive that verbal report just now?"

"Affirmative, General," came the slightly garbled synthesized voice of the 17th Iron Fist Division's megacomputer half a world away. The garble was apparently caused by the pseudo-random noise introduced into the network by the *McCain's* underwater telecommunications system, a highly classified technology based on some esoteric principles of quantum mechanics; no one liked to talk much about that, even if they could pretend to understand it.

Carlisle then turned to the *McCain's* operations officer and asked, "How good is this data? What sensors were used?"

"The data is considered reliable, General. As for the sensors used, I am not at liberty to discuss them," she told him bluntly, "without receiving confirmation of a need to know from JCS or from Captain Joseph."

Carlisle turned to the Captain, "Lew?"

Captain Lewis Joseph looked directly at Carlisle and told him, "General, be assured this is not a Navy plot to withhold information from the Army. At the range she mentioned, we have only one sensor system capable of obtaining that information from multiple targets. And, believe me, it is indeed highly classified. I can also confirm that the data Commander Ara quoted from this system are accurate and reliable."

"Georgie, do you know anything about this Navy system that was used?" the general asked his computer.

"Affirmative, General. Captain Joseph and Commander Ara are correct. Although I can access that information, I am not at liberty to reveal it even to you, sir, without receipt of need-to-know signal from Jericho," Georgie replied, referring to the master executive defense computer sequestered at Camp David, Maryland.

"Soviet submarines..." Carlisle mused. "Well, that certainly adds a certain spice to this mission! We're due at Kerguelen at dawn tomorrow. Strange that the Russkies would choose to be slightly behind us at this point...assuming they know we're here. If we can detect them, Lew, can they detect us? Do they know we're out here?"

The wiry little naval captain picked up his service cap and put it on his head. "No, I'm sure they don't, General. We're running too deeply for them to pick up surface turbulence on side-looking Doppler radar from any ocean-surveillance satellite they've got. And we're too deep to leave any detectable thermal wake in spite of this cold water we're in."

"Unless the Russkies have stolen what you just used to find them," Carlisle remarked.

Joseph shook his head. "I seriously doubt that."

"Do they know we're out here?" Carlisle repeated.

"I don't know for certain, but my initial reaction is that they don't," Joseph remarked curtly in deadly serious tones, then added, "But I want to find out. And I want independent tracking on them. I'm going to talk on ELF with Norfolk and get some satellite, aircraft, and deep ocean tracking of those bogeys. Maybe Nav Ops is already on top of the situation and hasn't signaled us yet. If so, they may have data we don't at this point. I intend to find out and request that they share it with us if they have it."

"Let me see if I can save you some time, Lew," Carlisle told him, then turned to the terminal again. "Georgie, does Jericho or Tiffany know of any Soviet submarines within a thousand kilometers of our present position in the *McCain*?"

"Affirmative, General. The three Soviet boats spotted by the *McCain's* systems are known to have departed Cam Ranh Bay in Amman three days ago," Georgie told everyone after a slight hesitation which indicated he had accessed the data base in both Jericho and Tiffany before replying.

"Thanks for the hot skinny," Joseph remarked. "I'll confirm it. In the meantime, General, the tactical plan looks good thus far, and I'll buy off on it if Commander Buell does so. Please excuse me. The three Soviet submarines constitute a potential major external threat to this ship and Task Force Tango Foxtrot. I have work to do. Commander Ara, please come with me." And he was gone, obviously deeply concerned as the ranking naval officer of Task Force Tango Foxtrot and therefore de facto task force commander. It was also obvious that he didn't relish the idea that the Task Force now had company in the Indian Ocean.

"General Carlisle," Bellamack spoke up, "I suggest that we'd better develop Plan C on the basis of this new information."

"Agreed! Georgie, does an alternative contingency Plan C appear to be a reasonable approach at this time?" Carlisle queried his computer, using it as he usually did as a quick-look, quick-answer, quick-evaluation member of his staff with access to an enormous data base.

"I would recommend two contingency plans, General," Georgie replied.

"Specify and justify," Carlisle ordered.

"Yes, sir. If the three Soviet submarines are also on a strike mission to take out the Kerguelen ground station with Spetsnaz troops, one sort of contingency plan will be required. If the three Soviet submarines are a task force to reinforce and reprovision the Kerguelen station already emplaced by the Soviet Union - if the Soviets are indeed the owners of the Kerguelen infection station - yet another contingency plan may be required."

"General, we should keep the number of contingency plans to an absolute minimum," Colonel Bill Bellamack pointed out anxiously. "If we get too goddamned many contingency plans here, it could turn the whole mission into a confused sheep screw."

"Georgie, you didn't justify your two speculations," Carlisle reminded his computer, temporarily ignoring Bellamack's recommendation.

"The first scenario is based upon a highly likely assumption. I calculated the probabilities as zero-point-nine-two with a confidence factor of point-eight-seven. Thus, the Soviet Union is sending its own Operation Tempest Frigid for exactly the same reason we are," Georgie hypothesized in unemotional tones. "I find the second scenario much less probable because the Soviets are not that devious, the Soviets don't like to waste resources because they don't have them to waste, and the Soviets don't play the sort of international chess game in which they would throw away a pawn of this sort without excellent chances that the expenditure would buy them something they couldn't otherwise obtain. I have attempted to analyze what they might be trying to acquire that would be worth this scenario, and I cannot come to any logical justification that would also satisfy the Soviet way of thinking or fit in with their present doctrine. I furthermore…"

"Thank you, Georgie," Carlisle interrupted his megacomputer, which, like all computers, attempted to give a total and complete assessment when called upon to do so…which is what Carlisle had ordered. Georgie was often pedantic to the point of being an irritant. Turning to the human beings in the planning room, Carlisle stated, "I agree with Georgie. I don't think the Kerguelen station is Soviet. So, I don't think the second scenario - which I hereby tag as Plan C-two is viable. I've been trained to 'think Soviet' in situations like this, and Plan C-two just doesn't sound like something they'd do. Art, you have a comment?"

"Yes, sir. I agree. But for different reasons, perhaps. If the Soviets have somehow detected Task Force Tango Foxtrot..." Colonel Arthur Eastwood, Carlisle's G-2 staffer, began.

"I don't think that's a viable assumption. To detect this task force, the Russkies would have to be good...Goddamned good!" Commander Buell interrupted him.

"Yes, of course," Eastwood continued diplomatically, "But if they somehow managed to detect us, Plan C-two could lead to a shooting fracas, and I'm not convinced that the Soviets want it. They would have put to sea with far more submarines if that was the case...and they have the submarine fleet to mount a much larger operation than they apparently have."

"If the shooting takes place at sea, that's the Navy's pigeon," Carlisle pointed out.

"And I'm short my submarine warfare flight," Buell admitted. "It's back at Bahrain. Had to make room for the Warhawk Chippewas. So, it would be a submarine-to-submarine affair, which means that Captain Joseph would withdraw the *McCain* to a position where it won't be endangered."

"Which means no land operations until it's over," Carlisle surmised, knowing that the Navy would have to withdraw the multi-billion dollar *McCain* out of possible danger. "Well, Commander, that scenario is the Navy's. I won't worry about it. Besides, it's low probability. Plan C-one is something else. Georgie, I assume that you have computed that the Soviets appear to be carrying out a mission parallel to ours?"

"Affirmative, General. That is the variable that falls out of that scenario as a given for tactical planning."

"And what is your recommendation for action in Plan C-one?"

"No change of present plan recommended," was Georgie's immediate assessment.

General Carlisle obviously didn't agree with his megacomputer. "How about it? Anyone have any different ideas on that one? I'm calling for inputs."

And that's what Curt Carson was waiting for. "General, if the Soviets intend to put a Spetsnaz battalion ashore on Kerguelen, we should get there first, do our job, and get the hell out before they arrive. In short, I agree with Georgie. I suggest no change in the tactical plan except to expedite it."

"Would you be willing to go in there without the reconnaissance you're insisting upon?" Colonel Eastwood asked pointedly.

"We may not have to give up the recon...if we can pull it off fast without wasting time, Colonel," Curt told the staff man. "The Soviets are trailing by five hundred nautical miles...Let's see, I don't remember the old English measurements very well, but if the Soviets can move at nearly the speed of this task force, that gives us about a day's lead time on them. Commander Buell, do the Soviets have submarine carriers? Could they airlift a Spetsnaz battalion into Kerguelen? Or are they going to have to carry out an amphibious operation and put men on a beach somewhere?"

"The Soviet Navy is a strike force intended to interdict shipping routes at world choke points," Buell pointed out. "Their naval air arm is land-based, and they've never developed the submarine carrier as we have. They do have some very large transport submarines - and one of the Soviet boats has been tentatively identified as a transport boat. Which means they'll most likely carry out a beach landing using submersible crawlers."

"If the Greys are on Kerguelen and the Soviets attempt a landing, Commander, can you make the Soviets keep their heads down by using your tactical strike squadron?" Bellamack asked her.

"If I can launch and recover the A-forties, I'll try."

"I want to keep that option open," Carlisle remarked quietly, "but only as an option, because I suspect I'll be receiving some rules of engagement now that the Soviets are likely to become involved. I shouldn't second-guess JCS, but they'll probably get orders from the White House that will translate into an ROE prohibiting us from taking any overt action against the Soviets, including shooting, unless they shoot at us first...and even then we may not be allowed to shoot back until we've identified ourselves..."

"General, with all due respects, sir," Bellamack broke in, "I don't think I'll be able to enforce that sort of a rule of engagement among the Sierra Charlies who'll be ashore on Kerguelen."

"Colonel, I understand the situation...I think," General Carlisle replied firmly. "I haven't received new ROEs yet. So, don't get your water hot about any potential ROEs. Do keep one thing uppermost in your minds, however: This looks like it's going to turn into one of the most ticklish missions we've ever been involved with. It could escalate quickly if it got out of hand. If the Kerguelen station is Soviet, that's one thing. If a third nation is involved, that's something else. Either way, it's touchy, regardless of what Georgie or I think. We must be prepared for any eventuality at this point. But I don't want you and your tactical troops worrying about it. I'm the man on the international hot seat in this one. I guess I shouldn't have done such a good job in Namibia. At any rate, I'm going to be a frog-holler type on this one. Understand?"

Bellamack and Curt understood. Commander Buell did not. "Frog-holler type, General?"

Bellamack turned to her and explained, "The general is being quite diplomatic with the Navy. It means that when he hollers 'frog,' everyone had damned well better jump right now because he may not be able to explain why."

"Yes, sir," Buell said, nodding. "I'll pass that along. When it comes to frog hollering, General, you'll find that the Navy are frog jumpers, sir."

"Good! I'm buying off on the basic tactical plan," Carlisle announced, standing up. Everyone else in the planning compartment stood up as well. "Art, Zeb,"' he said to his G-2 and G-3 staff men, "I want you to work with Commanders Buell and Ara...and anyone else who needs to be involved. I want contingency operations laid out for Plan C-one *and* Plan C-two, JIC. If the data on the Sov task force becomes firm enough later today, I'll want to go over your plans this evening. Otherwise, tomorrow morning."

"Sir, we launch our first recon birdbots tomorrow morning," Bellamack reminded him, "and the first recon mission as quickly as we recover the birdbots."

"I'm aware of that," Carlisle told everyone. "We may cancel the first manned recon mission if the birdbot data is good enough or if circumstances push us into making the full assault ASAP. This is going to be somewhat hectic, but if we've done our homework right in a professional manner, it won't turn into a panic. Carry on!"

Once Carlisle had left, Colonel Zebulon Morris turned to Colonel Arthur Eastwood and remarked, "Let's get on it, Art. The difficult we do immediately; the impossible takes a little bit longer."

"And you don't need to tell me which this is," Eastwood replied. "Bill, if you want to stick your oar in the water here, feel free to stay around. Otherwise, basically, this is just nit-pickin' little detail stuff, minor changes in the overall plan to accommodate the potentials of the various scenarios."

"Curt, what do you think?" Bellamack asked.

"Colonel, this's fine by me," Curt remarked to his regimental commander. "But if I'm going to have to land on Kerguelen tomorrow morning, I want to make sure my people are ready. May I be excused, sir?"

"Of course," Bellamack told him. "By the way, Sergeant Kester wanted to speak with you."

"I want to speak with him, too," Curt said, paused, then went on, "Colonel, Henry Kester is a wily old son of a bitch, and I'd like to request that you reassign him temporarily to the Companions for this action."

"Negatory," Bellamack told him, but there was a twinkle in the man's dark eyes. His voice also had a slight chuckle to it. "He's working for me now. But he was getting damned antsy about the possibility of upcoming combat. And he's been bugging the hell out of me. So, at his request I've assigned him a job with the landing force. He's going to be the official regimental penguin counter…"

Curt grinned. "Yes, sir!"

"You're dismissed, Major. Oh, by the way, I know this is going to make you happy as hell, but the experimental sensor harnesses are considered to be on the minimum required equipment list for this mission."

Curt gritted his teeth. If this turned into real, shooting combat - and it was looking more and more like that - those experimental sensor harnesses and Captain Owen Pendleton's data base were going to be a royal pain in the ass. But Colonel Willa Lovell obviously had a hell of a lot of clout. And Curt wasn't going to argue with it and come up a loser. He didn't want to be a loser at *anything* for the next couple of days. He didn't feel he could afford it.

Chapter Thirty-One

"What a godforsaken place!"

Curt's exclamation was tacitly and quietly agreed with by everyone from the Washington Greys who was present in the snake pit of the *U.S.S. McCain*.

On the flat display was projected the video view through the *McCain's* periscope. It showed the rugged western coastline of Kerguelen Island around Baie Bretonne, where the submarine carrier floated unseen just beneath the surface of the heaving sea. The ambient early morning sunlight was the dull, subdued glow of the long winter twilight in the Antarctic regions. It was so diffuse that no shadows were cast anywhere. The world above the ocean surface was a study in various shades of gray. And the ocean surface was a maelstrom of spray-capped waves that occasionally broke over the periscope's visual sensor.

In spite of the size and mass of the *McCain*, the huge submarine carrier rolled and pitched in the heavy seas as 3-meter waves dashed themselves against the periscope, whose sensor was gyrostabilized in order to provide a picture that wouldn't create vertigo in the viewers.

Off to the west, what appeared to be a group of whitish islands weren't. They were Antarctic icebergs, their strange, hulking shapes scattered over the ocean's surface all around the seaward side of the bay. This was the first time Curt had seen such huge ice mountains. They helped him realize that the ship wasn't very far from the ice-bound continent of Antarctica, where the bergs had broken off the ice shelves and been transported to Kerguelen Island by the westerly ocean currents that circled the globe at these high southern latitudes.

The coastline was rugged and swept rapidly upward from the sea. Gray waves beat against the rocks, throwing spray skyward where the wind picked it up and drove it again against the rocks.

Peak after barren peak of volcanic rock speared into the dull gray, leaden sky where snow showers swept down to hide the tops of some of the mountains.

Not a scrap of vegetation was to be seen, although the data base claimed that many species of hardy subpolar shrubs and grasses grew among the rocky slopes and crags where patches of snow didn't cover the black rock.

Peeking around a conical volcanic peak were the two limbs of the Cook Glacier named Glacier Descartes and Glacier Levoisier. Their ragged faces fell to the moraines and glacial outwash plains.

"The infection station is hidden behind the bulge of the Cook Glacier and this conical peak called le Podium," began the ongoing commentary from Colonel Art Eastwood, Carlisle's G-2, who was lying in a linkage couch in the snake pit operating in soft linkage with the *McCain's* computer as well as with Georgie. "We have about a hundred-fifty meters of sea depth at this position, which is as close as the captain and the navigator care to take the ship in this weather. The beach where the two arms of the Cook Glacier come to meet the sea is called Sea Lion Beach. Let's see if I can get a magnification on this. Maybe some sea lions are there this morning."

Because of the fact that even an experienced warbot brainy like Colonel Eastwood always had a bit of trouble linking with a new and different computer not totally familiar with his neural signatures, the scene zoomed and expanded giddily until the Greys were watching gray and brown lumps of something moving slowly where the glacial outwash plain met the ocean.

"Well, we've got some sea lions there this morning, but they don't look very active," Eastwood went on. "But 'National Geographic' this isn't. Thought you might like to see, but there was nothing really there to look at. Captain Gibbon will have the birdbots aloft at any time, and I've arranged to patch into the visual sensor circuits. The relay is going through Georgie because it takes a hell of a lot of computer power to translate those birdbot visual sensor signals into raster type video signals capable of being projected like this. So, we'll have about two seconds' delay due to both signal transmit time to and from the United States and the computer processing time."

"Good God almighty!" Jerry Allen breathed. "That looks colder than a witch's thing!"

"Cold enough to freeze the balls off a billiard table," was Kitsy Clinton's comment.

"Yeah, we'd better not take any brass monkeys along," First Sergeant Edie Sampson remarked.

"Sergeant, I hope you and Vickers get the bots ready for this weather," Curt asked anxiously.

"Yes, sir. Heaters around the power packs and critical AI circuitry. Low viscosity lubricants in every Zirk fitting. They're as ready as we can make them for this sort of crap," Edie Sampson replied, aware that Curt still counted on her as the company's warbot expert as well as the new first sergeant.

"Henry, are you sure you want to expose your pink bod to that weather?" Curt asked Regimental Sergeant Major Henry Kester.

"I been cold before," the old soldier replied laconically. "Someone has to keep the rest of you tenderfeet from freezin' your parts off. Sampson, I sure as hell wouldn't count on the heaters keeping all the AI and robotic circuitry warm enough to operate. Those heaters are an additional drain on the power packs..."

"I know that," Edie Sampson replied. "But Vickers and me, we worked some unauthorized mods. We doubled the power packs in each bot."

"Ain't room for that, especially in the Jeeps," Kester reminded her.

"Plenty of room if the heat pipes are removed."

"The heat buildup will fry the AI cubes," Kester warned.

"At forty below? Hell, Henry, the problem with the warbots is keeping them *warm!*" Edie Sampson tried to tell him.

"It ain't the heat load itself I'm worried about," Kester admitted. "It's the heating rate. Don't make any difference how cold the outer hull is; if the heat can't get out fast enough - which is what them heat pipes were designed for - it can get pretty damned hot pretty damned fast in there."

"Is there any way we can install some heat reservoirs to hold that heat energy in a safe place, since it looks like the bots may need it?" asked Sergeant Nick Gerard.

"Yeah, if we had a full Level Four war bot maintenance and modification shop at our disposal," said Tech Sergeant Bob Vickers. "And if we had two full working days to make the mods. And if Captain Otis could get authorization to do it, which is probably the biggest hurdle."

"Screw the red tape!" Henry Kester growled. "I can cover that now. Vickers, could you do a lash-up on heat reservoirs? Maybe only in the Jeeps?"

Vickers shook his head. "No way, Sergeant. Not enough time. And I'm not sure the Navy has the right tools and stuff aboard."

"There was a time," Kester muttered loudly enough that Vickers and the others could hear him, "when we didn't need fancy shops and special tools for warbots. Give me a Phillips head, a knuckle-buster, and a Mexican speed-wrench, and I could fix or make mods on the bots…"

"Was that back during the Indian Wars, Sergeant?" Vickers asked the old soldier.

"No, about the time they was screwing the plug into your belly button to keep you from running out all over the floor," Kester snapped back without rancor, although he honestly felt that these new tech sergeants were horribly spoiled tech-weenies who couldn't fix things with only a screwdriver and a pair of pliers. As far as he was concerned, all they knew how to do was to find the busted module, unplug it, slip in a new one, and send the broken one back to Level Four maintenance, where another robot would look it over and fix it, calling for a human mechanic only to check that the fix had been done right.

"Snap trap!" Curt ordered, indicating the display screen. "Eastwood's got Gibbon's visuals from the birdbot!"

A lot was lost, Curt decided, in the computer processing of the visual image picked up by the birdbot and then transmitted digitally to Gibbon's IA and computer, then bridged off the data bus and converted by Georgie to signals that would activate the huge snake pit display. The image had a decidedly dreamlike nature to it, with sharp edges only in the center where visual fixation was greatest and smeared more and more toward the image periphery. Actually, this was the image characteristic of the birdbot's visual sensor itself, because it had been tailored to match the actual visual pattern of the human eye. But humans aren't aware that they see this way; the whole visual scene they see with their eyes always appears to be sharp because the human brain has learned to perceive it as such.

The motion of the birdbot was evident in the pitching and rolling of the image.

"Georgie," came the verbal command from Colonel Eastwood, "stabilize that image or I'll get vertigo. Or worse."

The divisional megacomputer complied immediately. In some ways, computers were the ultimate soldiers because they did exactly and precisely what they were ordered to do, and they did it at once. The only problem was that they did *only* what they were told to do unless the fuzzy logic of their artificial intelligence circuitry overrode the Boolean logic which governs all computer operations.

"That's good. Thank you," Eastwood muttered, then began a running commentary of what the birdbot was seeing. "Okay, there's the coastline...Ilots Max Cristensen just off Sea Lion Beach...the Place des Moraines...We might be able to put a landing party on the beach there if we had to..."

"Damned if I want to grind ashore if we've got Chippies to airlift us in," Curt growled to Jerry Allen and Kitsy Clinton.

"Colonel Bellamack, I can pass instructions along to Captain Gibbon in linkage," Eastwood remarked. "Let me know if you want him to direct the birdbot to have a closer look at anything."

"Roger, Colonel, I read you," Bellamack replied. "For now, let's let Gibbon fly it as he sees it. We're taping the birdbot visual, and we can go back and process any part of it to get a better look at anything that might interest us." Bellamack knew that Georgie or even the *McCain's* computer could carry out an ordinary fractal analysis and SPIT enhancement if necessary. He saw no need to hassle a warbot brainy in linkage.

"It's a wonder anything can live in that environment," Kitsy Clinton observed as the visual image showed the beach covered with the hulking brownish shapes of sea lions and seals. "Looks like nothing grows on this island."

"Not true," Jerry Allen replied, digging back into his encyclopedic memory. "There's one unique plant on this island found nowhere else. Called Kerguelen cabbage, of course."

"Is it good to eat?" Kitsy probed.

"Hell, I don't know. I've never seen one," Jerry admitted with a grin. "Maybe I'll get the chance."

"Just hope to God you don't get stuck on Kerguelen and have to find out whether or not it's good to eat," Curt told him.

Colonel Eastwood continued to give a wing flap by wing flap commentary, although the motion of the birdbot caused by its wing flapping had been edited out of the image by Georgie. "Looks like an outstanding approach for aerodynes if we wish to remain in defilade from the station on the east side of the glacier. We can probably come right up the valley ahead between the two hills and over the Lavosier Glacier arm. That glacier wall and dome puts about a six-hundred-meter hill between. Good approach right up a very narrow gorge..."

The image wavered. It was apparent that Georgie was having difficulty with it. This was confirmed a split second later when Georgie reported verbally, "The visual image from the birdbot is still a strong signal, but the birdbot is moving quite violently. I am having trouble keeping the image stabilized! Sorry, but I've lost the capability to stabilize it!"

The image began to gyrate and wobble and tilt. It was as though someone were trying to run with a video camera on his shoulder without trying to keep it steady. The image bounced and smeared from the rapid movements of the birdbot.

"Gibbon reports severe turbulence," Eastwood commented. "According to the positioning data, the birdbot is over the Plaine des Moraines, heading up the gorge to the Lavosier Glacier with le Podium and the Descartes Glacier on the left...The wind velocity is apparently quite high, although no apparent reason for this seems to be..."

It got worse.

Curt couldn't look at it. The motion of the image threatened to give him vertigo. "Look away," he directed his Companions. "First one who vomits on me is in for trouble!"

Eastwood was obviously having some trouble communicating with Gibbon at this point. "What?...Uh, why?...Hang on! Do a one-eighty, Captain! Get the shit out of there while you can!...Christ, he's losing it!...Gibbon, get out of there! Don't try to save the warbot! Withdraw! Biotechs, stand by Gibbon for possible quick withdrawal!"

Curt sneaked a look at the wildly swinging image. He knew what was going on. The recon birdbot was, for some reason, now out of control. It had hit such violently severe turbulence that its gyros had lost alignment...which means the turbulence was very strong indeed. But why? The sky state and the sea state gave no indication of violent weather right then.

"Gibbon! Get out! Now! Pull out of that warbot! Do it!" came the yell from Eastwood, who, being in parallel linkage with the intelligence officer of the Washington Greys, was seeing and feeling some of the same things as Gibbon.

"*Oh, shit!*" came the final cry of anguish followed by a terrified scream from Eastwood that was cut off abruptly.

Curt found he couldn't tear his eyes away from the final images.

The birdbot was going down. It was going to crash into the rocky slopes of the glacial moraine.

As Eastwood's scream cut off, so did the visual signals from the birdbot as the final view showed rapidly approaching rocks and ice.

Then nothing.

Surprisingly, the members of the Washington Greys in the snake pit suddenly either echoed Gibbon's scream or vented primal yells. Most of them were old warbot brainies; they knew what had just happened.

"We may have just lost John Gibbon," was the dry throated comment from Curt Carson, who also knew.

"Lost him? Lost him? Why?" Kitsy Clinton asked.

Curt knew she'd never experienced losing a warbot while in linkage and thus had never been KIA or "killed in action." Which is exactly what had just happened to Captain John Gibbon.

As a matter of fact, Curt had never before experienced the trauma of seeing what another warbot brainy was going through while being KIA. He'd been KIA himself while operating in linkage as a warbot brainy, and it had been months before he'd been himself again. This wasn't quite so bad, but it triggered a lot of deliberately sublimated memories - memories that post-KIA therapy had helped him put out of the way.

Curt ignored Kitsy for the moment. He was more worried about his former warbot brainies. "Jerry, Nick, Edie...You all right? Sound off!"

"I'm okay, Major" was Jerry's white-lipped reply.

"With you, Major," came the voice of Nick Gerard, who knew how to handle it, although it wasn't easy.

"Uh, yeah, uh, I'll make it," was the broken comment from Edwina Sampson.

"What happened?" Kitsy Clinton pressed.

"We may have suffered our first casualty of Operation Tempest Frigid," Curt told her. "You may have just watched what John Gibbon saw as he suffered a double-lobed Lebanese systolic stroke. Goddammit, this is a hell of a time to lose the officer who runs our cee-cubed-eye!"

Chapter Thirty-Two

"John is not in outstanding shape" was the report from Major Ruth Gydesen, the regiment's chief medical officer and commander of the biotechnology unit. "The new anti-KIA circuitry and programming worked. But, for some reason, John isn't responding to it as well as Curt did in Namibia."

"Jesus!" Colonel Bill Bellamack swore softly under his breath. It had been about an hour since Captain John Gibbon had augured-in the birdbot. "How come? I thought you had the anti-KIA procedure down cold."

"Colonel, it's still new. John is only the second person we've had to use it on," the doctor responded. "And when Curt threatened to KIA, he didn't fight the programming; he let it take him out. John stayed with the birdbot and fought to regain control right down to the last millisecond. He wouldn't turn loose. He was very tenacious."

"Damnation! How long will he be on the sick list?" Bellamack couldn't help but admire the zeal of his S-2 staffer, although that zeal might have cost the regiment its intelligence chief.

"Couple of days at least. Maybe a week," Gydesen told him. She was doing the best she could with the equipment, software, and other facilities of her medical unit, a novel and unique combination of old-time military trauma treatment plus the biotechnology related to robot warfare.

"Doctor, perhaps I can help," Captain Owen Pendleton tentatively spoke up.

"In what way, Captain?" Gydesen wanted to know. She immediately raised the defensive barriers that the medical profession unconsciously erected when its practitioners encountered an enthusiastic nonmedical helper. After all, Captain Owen Pendleton was only an artificial-intelligence mentor, one of that unique breed of human beings who could think like a computer and thus mentor or program AI systems. Furthermore, he wasn't even RA, much less a man with a combat-rated position code. He was a tech-weenie, an officer who'd gained his commission because of his expert knowledge of robotics technology. Gydesen didn't realize that she and her doctors in the biotech unit could also be considered as tech-weenies by that definition.

"Well, Major, McCarthy Proving Ground has been carrying out some experimental work on neuroelectronic trauma therapy for the past several years," the round-faced young man with the halting voice replied slowly.

"Yes, I know of it, Captain, but most of it has been involved with physical therapy," Gydesen reminded him.

"Not all of it, sir," he corrected her gently. "My current research into the neuroelectronic responses of combat soldiers is part of the work Colonel Willa Lovell is engaged in...which involves the application of electropsychotherapy to neuroelectronic delinkage trauma..."

The conversation between the two experts was quickly becoming an exchange riddled with the patois of biotechnology and bioelectronics. Bellamack was interested in the welfare of his traumatized S-2 staffer, but he didn't have the time to allow these two experts to carry on a debate in what was otherwise a tactical planning session. So, the colonel broke in, "Major, I hope there's something to Captain Pendleton's assertions. Please work with him to see if any of his ideas might be useful in bringing John Gibbon back to the world of the living as quickly as possible."

"Colonel, I won't place my patient in danger," Gydesen stated firmly.

"I'm not asking you to do so, Doctor. You have the ultimate biotechnological responsibility in this matter," the regimental commander reassured her, smoothing some of her ruffled medical feathers in the process. "But please listen to Captain Pendleton and allow him to try any procedures that you and your biotechnology staff believe might not be unduly hazardous..."

"Anything other than the well-proven procedures for traumatic delinkage therapy may be unduly hazardous," Gydesen maintained.

"Major," Owen Pendleton tried to reassure her, "I won't try anything unless Colonel Lovell and the people at McCarthy approve...and unless you also undestand and approve of the procedure. Don't you think we owe it to John to get him out of his living death as quickly as possible?"

"Of course. I just don't want to take unnecessary risks. We already handle far too many unknowns in biotechnology without introducing new ones," the doctor explained.

Pendleton resisted carrying the debate further at this time. He could have argued well that the biotechnologists along with the neuroelectronics and AI people were always working in a high-risk area because no one fully understood the human body yet, much less the human mind and the interrelationships between the two. Some doctors and biotechnologists thought they did; Pendleton was hoping that Gydesen wasn't one of those. Besides, he'd won his point, and there was nothing to be gained by prolonging the discussion at that moment. In fact, prolonging it could cause him to lose ground he'd already gained.

Captain Owen Pendleton might have been a bit shy and a bit introverted, but that didn't mean he wasn't bright enough to look after himself.

His research was going very well indeed. The forth-coming mission would add incredibly important information to his data base. Furthermore, he might be able to help Captain John Gibbon. Pendleton's cup runneth over. So, he sat back and listened.

"Where do we go from here, Colonel?" Major Curt Carson asked, bringing the meeting back to its original path of determining the next course of action in Operation Tempest Frigid.

"What do you think we should do next, Major?" Bellamack threw it right back at Curt. Although he had a very good idea of what should be done next, he also knew Carson and the Companions would be among those who'd have to land on the barren island of Kerguelen, so at this point he solicited their input.

"First of all, sir, I think we should try to learn what happened to the birdbot," Curt ventured. He, too, knew what would probably be done next, but it was also important to try to find out what happened to the birdbot. "If it was equipment or linkage-channel failure, that's one thing. If it ran into countermeasures of some sort, that's something else. What caused it to go ape-shit out there? And why couldn't John get it under control again? Who's got an answer? Or part of an answer?"

Captain Hensley Atkinson, who was renowned in the Greys for her intimate knowledge of the highly classified linkage technology of warbot operations - and who was perhaps the only one in the regiment entrusted with that highly classified information - piped up, "I've had the chance to make only a cursory examination of the data tapes from the mission, but I did check the recorded operational data. Although I may change my mind later when I've had time to make a thorough study of the data, I would say right now that nothing happened to either the uplink or downlink channels. I also saw no evidence of countermeasures...or at least no countermeasures that I recognized. I can give you a better answer tomorrow morning..."

"We haven't got until tomorrow morning," Bellamack remarked sourly, "so I'll just have to buy your quick look evaluation, Captain. And so will everyone else. Does anyone have any heartburn over that?" He looked around.

"I don't," Captain Alexis Morgan announced. "We're not going to be operating ordinary warbots remotely by linkage. So even if someone did have some sort of covert countermeasures, that won't affect our operation."

"Major Worsham, how about you?" Bellamack asked the combat air support squadron leader.

Worsham shrugged. "Colonel, we're hard-wired to our Chippies and our circuits are hardened because it's our own pink bodies riding in the 'dynes we're fling. No way any sort of link channel countermeasures could really screw up our operation. Don't worry about neuroelectronic countermeasures on our account. We'll get your troops in and out of Kerguelen."

"I have no problem," Captain Russ Frazier added. "Let's go in there quick and surgical. Get the job done and go home."

"But do you know what it is we're assaulting, Russ?" asked Captain Joan Ward. "All we've got to go by are those superblack recon images the Aerospace Force managed to somehow get with one of their superblack vehicles."

Frazier thought Joan Ward was being too cautious, and that would be natural for him because he'd served under the legendary Captain Marty Kelly when the Ferrets were called the Killers. He still had the tendency to be brash and bloodthirsty, something he'd inherited from his original company commander. "So? Do we know where it is? Sure do! Do we know how many buildings or structures are there? Sure as hell do! So we just go in and take them!"

"Against what sort of defending force, Russ?" Joan asked. "Are we up against company strength defenders? Or a regiment?"

"Joan, I know you're a careful officer," Alexis Morgan interrupted her, "but even a quick analysis of what we see on the Aerospace Force data tells me that the station couldn't support more than about a hundred people. Simple War College analysis."

"And how many warbots? And what sort of defensive firepower?" Joan came back. "A hundred people can operate up to ten times that number of remote linkage warbots. We used to do that in the Washington Greys before we became a Sierra Charlie outfit."

"Unless the station is Soviet. And they've managed to steal a hell of a lot of our warbot technology," Alexis observed. "I'll opt for a sit-guess that goes for zero warbots."

"Would you care to place a small wager on that?" Ward asked in reply.

"Ladies," Bellamack broke in, willing to let the dialogue run its course for the sake of getting issues on the table and then discussed, but unwilling to allow it to degenerate into Club Night, "we're wagering lives already. Let's leave it at that, please. Alexis, what would you do?"

"I'm with Russ Frazier. We go in now and hit them hard on the first try."

"Joan?"

"I'd really like to have more information."

"Curt?"

"I'm. with Joan," Curt replied, aware that they would be going into action with insufficient information if they proceeded now. He didn't like that. He remembered other times when they'd proceeded with poor or nonexistent intelligence data and ended up in deep slime. "We can't anticipate every contingency we might run into on any mission, but with the help of good spook data we can reduce the possibilities and thus the number of surprises. Can we put another birdbot up there real soon?"

"Sergeant Crawford, you're running the cee-cubed-eye operation until Captain Gibbon can resume command of the unit," Bellamack said to her. "How about it?"

"We have a smaller and less powerful birdbot, Colonel," Staff Sergeant Crawford reported. "I'll volunteer to take it up. But I should warn you that we may lose it the same way we lost the one Captain Gibbon was running. And we don't know what caused that. I'm willing to do it, Colonel, if you're willing to run the risk of losing another birdbot and possibly me, too."

"A birdbot is just a machine," the colonel reminded her. "You're not. How do you feel about the possibility of going into spasm mode out there?"

"Sir, I volunteered," Crawford pointed out.

"When can you launch?"

"In two hours, Colonel. By eleven hundred hours. I can be back aboard by thirteen hundred hours."

"And we could launch the assault shortly thereafter and have it on the ground on the glacier by fourteen hundred hours," Captain Hensley Atkinson added.

"We're talking," Bellamack mused, indicating the map projected on the display on the conference room, "about putting four combat companies on the ground on the Cook Glacier just to the northwest of this rocky outcrop called Mons des Lunettes Noire. That's approximately eight kilometers from the station. Captain Atkinson, what time does the sun go down here?"

Hensley keyed her hand terminal and called up the almanac data. Even she didn't like what she saw. "Fifteen-twelve hours, sir."

"You want to pull off a night assault on the station, Alexis?" Bellamack wanted to know.

"Not if I can help it, sir. But we can sure as hell put down on the glacier with the equipment necessary to overnight and then attack at dawn."

"You ever spent a night out on a glacier at forty below?" Curt asked incredulously. He hadn't, and he knew that no one in the Washington Greys had done so. "Look, Colonel, let's give it another try with a birdbot today, then launch a dawn assault based on the additional data we'll get from the birdbot."

"Under the watchful eye of the Soviets?" The question came from Commander Rebecca "Jugs" Buell, who, as the air group commander of the *McCain*, had thus far sat quietly listening to what her Army guests planned to do. "Don't forget, Colonel, our latest information indicates those three Soviet submarines will be in the vicinity of Kerguelen tomorrow morning. We know now that their flotilla consists of the attack boats *Kuznetsov* and *Bondarenko* escorting the larger patrol personnel carrier *Smirnov*. Naval Intelligence says *Smirnov* has at least one Spetsnaz battalion aboard either to reinforce the station if it is indeed Soviet or to assault it if it isn't. Now, the Navy will support whatever you want to do as long as it doesn't unduly expose Task Force Tango Foxtrot to possible conflict with the Soviets, and that includes spoofing or otherwise trying to intimidate them to stay the hell away from Kerguelen. But are you willing to take on a Spetsnaz battalion as well as whatever and whoever is in that station?"

"What are you trying to tell me, Commander?" Bellamack asked.

"Colonel, I can't tell you to do anything. But it's my suggestion that if you want to do this job and get the hell out of here before things get goddamned complicated, you'll launch your assault forces *now* and get the job done before the Sovs show up. I can give you air support this morning; I may not be able to do so tomorrow morning because all my aircraft may be involved over the Soviet boats. They don't have aircraft aboard, but they do have some SAMs, and my people will be busy even if they're not being shot at...which they may be."

That clinched it as far as Bellamack was concerned. "Major Worsham, can you get the Greys in and then recover them?"

"Yes, sir!" Worsham might have been overconfident, or he might only have been trying to maintain the reputation of his combat air support squadron. Either way, Curt thought, Worsham might have made the wrong decision right then, when the ultimate decision depended upon the capability of the air support squadron to do its job.

"Very well, let's not waste any more time, combat commanders, muster your units and prepare to launch the assault as quickly as you can get them in the Chippewas and off this ship! Move out! Meeting dismissed!"

Curt didn't have time to voice dissent. He knew it wouldn't have done any good anyway. Circumstances had closed in on them. They had to act to carry out the mission. Bellamack really had no choice. So, orders had been given. Now it was his problem to carry them out.

He knew it wasn't going to be easy.

But it rarely was.

Chapter Thirty-Three

"Damned good thing we trained up to load the Chippies fast," First Sergeant Edwina Sampson remarked as the Companions stood on the huge enclosed flight deck of the *McCain* and waited, as usual, for others to complete their preparations for departure. The Navy ratings were busy doing what had to be done to surface the huge carrier submarine and to open the overhead doors of the flight deck once on the surface.

The Companions were now completely kitted out in their arctic gear, well aware that although they might be sweating in the warm confines of the flight deck, the weather outside would soon make them damned glad they had cold-weather gear.

Captain Owen Pendleton busied up to Curt, checked the portable data logger in his hand, and remarked, "Curt, it looks like all your personnel are giving good readings at this point."

"I hope to God it's useful somewhere sometime," Curt growled. "These harnesses are a hell of a lot more comfortable than the original ones, but they're still a damned nuisance! You'd better understand we're giving a lot for science here!"

In all seriousness, Pendleton looked at Curt and replied, "Don't think of it that way, Major. Don't forget; I'll be monitoring all of you while you're on Kerguelen. That weather out there defies human reason. If I see any of you in physical trouble, I'll see if I can't get someone to go in and recover the person in trouble."

"Well, I never thought about these experimental harnesses that way," Curt admitted. "But, yeah, I can see that you'd be able to do something here if you spotted any of us in trouble out there. Thanks, Owen. By the way, you mentioned bad weather out there. What's it doing?"

In an indirect reply, Pendleton asked, "Notice the motion of the deck?"

In spite of the fact that four days in the *McCain* had made the usual ship motion commonplace to Curt, now he did indeed sense that the rolling motion was a bit more than usual. "Yeah."

"According to Weber, we've got sea state Charlie on the surface," Pendleton explained. "Jugs Buell had a hell of an argument with Wild Bill Bellamack a few minutes ago. She doesn't want to launch anything in this weather. General Carlisle had to intervene with Captain Joseph to get an order to launch."

"Orgasmic!"

"Yeah, I think so, too. Good luck!" And with that, the AI expert was off to check with Ward's Warriors. "Yeah, orgasmic as hell." Colonel Bellamack walked up from behind. He was accompanied by Regimental Sergeant Major Henry Kester. "If we weren't being squeezed by the goddamned Soviets, I wouldn't launch, either! You ready, Curt?"

"As ready as we'll ever be, Colonel," Curt told him. He noticed that the Colonel was kitted out in arctic gear and was carrying a *Novia*. Curt knew that Bellamack had taken a cue from others in the Greys and tended to accompany his troops into combat when he could. "Who you riding with?"

"In any Chippie where Worsham has room for us," Bellamack replied. He held up his tacomm unit. "Match and cross-check for freak and hop. Command net will be Channel November-one-seven. Hop crypto is Lima-four-Romeo-seven. Digital code and rate is Sierra-Lima-Zulu-four-two-zero. Got it?"

Curt had keyed the codes and sequences into his own portable tacomm unit as Bellamack announced them. So had Edie Sampson. As he activated the "execute" toggle, he remarked to his regimental commander, "Colonel, I don't like this one goddamned little bit! It has all the makings of a grand sheep screw. We don't know what the hell we're getting into!"

"Agreed," Bellamack said with a nod. "But we don't have a whole hell of a lot of choice."

"Why don't we lie still and wait to see what those Soviet

motherfuckers are up to?" Curt suggested.

"Because General Carlisle broached that possibility to JCS and requested a standby until things got clarified. But Old Hickory did a bunch of computations and combinations and whatever the hell else it does, and it belched forth the fuzzy logic that says it's a Soviet station and the Soviet pig boats are reinforcing it because Moscow somehow got wind of Operation Tempest Frigid," Bellamack shot back.

"We're going to let a goddamned war-plans computer under the Pentagon give orders on how to run an operation on the other side of the world?" Curt asked in disbelief.

"As I understand it, Major," Bellamack replied in a low, disgruntled voice, "General Carrington said no to the Old Hickory plan. General Brooke said no. But the commander in chief decided he trusted a multi-billion dollar computer because it couldn't make human-motivated errors."

"That's what happens when you wake a politician in the middle of the night and ask him to make a decision," grumbled First Sergeant Edie Sampson.

"Sergeant," Curt immediately rebuked her, "I did not hear that! And you'd better hope that the colonel didn't either!"

"So, we go, Major," Henry Kester added. He was pissed, too, but his distaste for politically motivated stupid orders was mitigated by decades of successful service to those same politicians. He knew who paid his salary, and he also knew - and had taught Curt - to go in and do an outstanding job in spite of the stupid orders. Or maybe because of them. "Okay if I ride with you and the Companions?"

"I couldn't stop you if I wanted to...which I don't." Curt observed. "Stick yourself in ranks somewhere and stand by, Henry."

"I'm riding with the Marauders," Bellamack told him. "Monitor the command freak once we get airborne, Curt. We're going to have to play this one strictly by ear. Communications are key."

"Roger, Colonel."

After Bellamack walked away and before Kester faded back into the ranks of the Companions, the old soldier nodded to Curt and took him aside. "Major, I ain't got nothin' against the colonel. He was real tactical at Bisbee and Douglas in the last fracas, but something's eating him on this operation," Kester confided to his former company commander.

"Any idea what it is, Henry?"

"No, sir, none. But I almost had to shame him into accompanying the troops and commanding from the field on this mission," Kester admitted.

"Did he forget to wear his thermal socks?"

Kester shook his head. "No, but something about this mission bothers him. I don't know what it is."

"Maybe I ought to warn Captain Morgan."

"I already have," Kester put in. "But I thought I oughta warn you, too, since you're second in command."

"That bad, Henry?"

"Well, a second in command has to be prepared to take over if the commanding officer can't hack it, sir."

Curt was worried about what Kester had just told him, but there wasn't time to do anything more than note the worry and file the data against the time when it might become critically important. But he was grateful to Kester for warning him that he might have to take command. "Bad weather up there?" Curt wondered.

"Yes, sir. Colder than a witch's thing. And blowin' to beat hell. The captain wants to get us Army types the hell and gone off his ship before it takes on too much water and founders," Kester explained. "I heard Commander Buell and Colonel Bellamack go at it a while ago. Although I might have some concern about the colonel, I gotta tell you he stood his ground real well with the Navy..."

The flight deck bull horn interrupted the discussion. "Hear this! Hear this!" it demanded. "Army units board your aircraft now! All personnel must be aboard the Chippewas before the ship surfaces and the flight deck doors are opened!"

The loading ramps opened on the lips of the Chippewas.

The Companions didn't wait for further orders. They moved. Fast.

Major Cal Worsham was in soft linkage with Warhawk One when Curt took up his position in the cockpit. Worsham's nervous system was linked with the Chippie's, and Worsham knew Curt was present, but the speaker on the instrument panel didn't greet Curt or acknowledge his presence. It was obvious that Worsham was deeply involved with prelift checks and probably monitoring the god-awful weather outside.

The *McCain* gave no indication of having surfaced, and Curt would not have known except that the huge submarine increased its pitching and rolling motions when it broached the interface between the sea and the air. The seals on the huge flight deck deflated, allowing cold seawater to cascade onto the formerly enclosed flight deck and run off through the scruppers back into the sea.

Waves broke over the upper edges of the doors, which had been opened to the vertical position to act as extended gunwales against the heaving ocean. Nevertheless, water did surge over the tops.

Worsham wasted no time spooling up the Chippewa's turbines. He'd been given some specific instructions by Commander Jugs Buell to the effect that he and his Chippie pilots had only one minute to get off the deck in this sort of weather. That much time Buell and Captain Joseph were willing to give the Army, regardless of how much water was shipped during the launch. But beyond that, Buell had informed Worsham that the flight deck doors would be closed no matter how many Chippies had managed to get off.

Spindrift - wind-driven ocean spray - froze on the surfaces of the Chippie as it struck them. Worsham was valving antifreeze around the turbine inlets and had activated anti-ice equipment everywhere, especially on the blown surfaces which were cooled by the expansion of the turbine exhaust roaring through the lift slots.

The leaden sky above wasn't a welcome sight to Curt. Ragged

clouds swept past. As the Chippie lifted off the *McCain* and climbed vertically, Curt saw the gray-black rugged coastline of Kerguelen. Clouds were topping the higher mountains, and other mountains were hidden in the white veils of snow showers. Curt could tell from the motion of these clouds and snow sheets that the wind was blowing hard.

The outside air temperature gauge on the Chippie's panel registered -28°C.

The air density was therefore very high, and the Chippewa thus had a lot of lift. But this didn't keep it from wobbling like a badly thrown Frisbee while Cal Worsham fought for control. Curt knew the man was totally engrossed in the job, because the pilot made no verbal comments while this was going on.

By looking around, Curt saw that other Chippewas just launched out of the *McCain* were having similar problems with the wind.

Curt never saw the *McCain*. By the time the Chippie had moved far enough away from the ship that he could see it over the lip, its flight deck doors had been closed and sealed, and the huge ship disappeared beneath the surface of the white-capped ocean waters.

Worsham got the Chippie moving eastward toward Kerguelen, but Curt still didn't like what he was seeing. The weather was shitty. There was no other way to describe it. It was so bad that you wouldn't even think of using the Latinized versions of the earthy Anglo-Saxon words of soldiers.

The only redeeming virtue of this weather was that whoever was manning that station on Kerguelen probably was staying inside and not expecting anyone to make an assault landing on the island. Maybe the Greys could manage to make their short trek across the Cook Glacier and carry out a surprise assault with no resistance.

The incoming Chippies were hidden from direct line of sight of both the station and Port-aux-Francaise by ridges of barren snow-swept peaks. The French scientific contingent on the eastern side of the island certainly wouldn't know of their approach. And the infection station was also out of sight.

Looking around at the approaching shore of Kergeulen, Curt thought it would have been a whole hell of a lot easier if Captain Joseph and Commander Weaver had brought the *McCain* closer to shore or even into one of the deep fjordlike inlets along the western marge of Kergeulen Island. Even flying 15 kilometers across the open waters of the Indian Ocean exposed the Chippewas to potential attack from an unknown enemy ahead. Curt felt uncomfortable. He didn't like being bottled up in the Chippie and thus totally at the mercy of someone outside shooting at him with no possible way for him to shoot back.

Now he was glad he was wearing arctic gear. It was growing cold in the unheated Chippie as the craft slowly lost what heat it had from the *McCain's* flight deck. The damned thing probably didn't have either a heater or a cooler, Curt thought; that sort of luxury was too good for fighting troops! He recalled the sniveling and groveling the Greys had had to do when they were trying to get ACVs and RTVs modified for Sierra Charlie operations.

Maybe they should have brought some of these vehicles along with them. They might have made the cross-island trek - only a few kilometers - a bit easier.

But when the Chippie swept in across Sea Lion Beach and Curt saw the face of the glacier ahead, he decided vehicles wouldn't have worked here. The ground was far too broken and rocky. Furthermore, the glacier itself looked formidable, far more than just a huge block of ice lying on the ground; Curt could see that it was cut with ridges and crevasses.

The Chippie began to pitch and yaw violently. Curt had been so intent on studying the terrain below that he hadn't noticed both Henry Kester and Edie Sampson standing beside and behind his seat, looking over his shoulders to see what he was seeing. The sudden motions of the Chippie pitched Sampson against him.

"Sorry, Major."

"What the hell is causing this turbulence?" Curt wondered.

"Wind," Henry Kester replied brusquely, indicating telltale plumes of snow and spray that had begun to appear on the slopes of the two mountains - le Podium and Mt. Gay-Lussac - as the Chippie began to fly between them up the gorge toward the Glacier Lavoisier arm of the Cook Glacier. "Coming around the hill on the left and also blowing like hell down this canyon."

The Chippie seemed to have lost a good deal of speed. Curt didn't bother Worsham; the pilot would be very busy indeed now. "Goddamned wind must be more than a hundred klicks on our nose!" Curt exclaimed, guessing at their loss of speed.

"More than that," Kester opined. "This ship has slowed to a walk. Closer to one-fifty."

"What the hell can cause winds like that?" Edie Sampson wanted to know.

Curt suddenly knew as old lectures on meteorology from West Point came back to him. Weather has always been a factor in combat and warfare, and Major Mount-Campbell at the Military Academy had always stressed this, backing up his contentions with numerous historical anecdotes.

"It's that damned Cook Glacier!" he suddenly realized and vocalized his thinking. "We've hit a down-slope wind. A katabatic wind. Like a chinook wind over the Rockies, except this is a little different. Cold air over the glacier's dome naturally flows downward. But it's so damned cold outside that even compression warming from altitude loss doesn't change its temperature much. So, it just keeps right on blowing. And it's funneled through these canyons here like Venturi tubes. Christ, we're going to have a hell of a time with this wind! We didn't count on it!"

He *knew* the Greys should have gotten more data before launching this assault.

And he also knew what had hit Gibbon's birdbot in about this same area.

A birdbot just isn't equipped to handle the sort of severe high-velocity turbulence that was now tossing the multi-ton Chippewa around the sky.

The rocky outcrop of Mt. des Lunettes Noires appeared through the icy surface of the Cook Glacier ahead. Then it disappeared momentarily in a white veil.

White-out! Curt thought.

The computer-generated voice of Major Cal Worsham came from the panel loudspeaker. It was absent of emotion, but its emotional content was present in the pauses and breaks that were sure indications that Worsham was under enormous pressure trying to fly the Chippie in these weather conditions. "Carson!...I'll try to put you down...where we're supposed to...but it may be a rough landing...so have your troops hang tight!...All my Chippies are having difficulty...but we'll hack it somehow...Buckle up!"

"Cal! Are you going to be able to get everyone down okay?" Curt asked anxiously.

"I think so!...I've got good pilots!...But this is a real bitch!..."

Nervously, Curt motioned the two sergeants to go back and strap down. He hitched his safety harness a little tighter. Already, the straps were cutting into him through his arctic gear, soft body armor, and experimental biotech harness as the Chippie lurched in the turbulence.

Worsham approached a level spot on Cook Glacier just west of their landmark outcrop. Slowly, he brought the Chippie to a hover, which was really not a hover in this wind but a zero-ground-speed condition flying against a 150-kph wind.

As the Chippie settled slowly with Worsham feeling for the white ground below without any vertical clues to guide him, the craft suddenly heaved, and the bottom seemed to drop out.

"Brace for crash!" was all that Worsham was able to get out.

Chapter Thirty-Four

Curt instinctively knew that it couldn't possibly be a bad crash, not at the low altitude and minimum hover air speed of the Chippewa. But it could be a very hard landing, so he held on tight and braced.

But the crash never came.

It was totally impossible to see what was going on. The world outside the cockpit bubble was a whirl of white caused both by the white-out and by the down-ward blast of the aerodyne slot flow kicking up loose snow on the surface of the glacier.

In fact, the Chippewa didn't even make a very hard landing. But it was firm and solid. And surprisingly mushy.

Curt heard the turbines spool down to idle and felt the Chippewa settle slowly into a slightly tilted ground angle.

"We're down," Cal Worsham's voice announced from the panel speaker. "Get your troops unloaded, Carson!"

"Are you going to be able to lift out of here?" Curt asked anxiously. If Worsham couldn't, it was a long, cold, wet walk back to the *McCain* for the Companions.

"Hell, yes! That is, if the goddamned weather doesn't get any worse!"

The white outside slowly began to turn to gray. Curt looked around, trying to spot the other Chippies. "The rest of your squadron on the ground?"

"Negatory! Shut up, Major! I'm trying to get a sit-rep from my pilots! Get your people the hell and gone out of here!"

Curt unstrapped and called out loudly over the rumble of idling turbines, "Companions! Anyone hurt?"

"I'm getting' too old for this kind of crap" was the reply from Regimental Sergeant Major Henry Kester.

"You volunteered," Curt pointed out. He pulled the protective face mask down and lowered goggles over his eyes. Outside at -40°C the windchill would make it seem -100°. Exposed flesh would freeze in less than a minute. "Edie?"

"Yo! No one hurt down below! Jesus, close that friggin' door! It's cold out there!" his first sergeant called back as Worsham opened the lip cargo access doors and the numbing wind of the Cook Glacier blasted in.

Curt toggled his helmet tacomm unit and called out or "thought" to his helmet's neuroelectronic circuits, "Companion Alpha, are you on the ground?"

"Companion Leader, this is Companion Alpha," came Lieutenant Kitsy Clinton's voice through the neurophonic circuits of Curt's battle helmet. "Roger! Grounded! But, goddamn, that was rough! We're debouching now!"

"Cover up! No exposed flesh! Rendezvous on my beacon as planned! Don't go wandering off! You could get lost out there in this white-out!" Curt snapped. He was partly relieved; his Alpha Platoon and their Mary Anns were on the ground.

Lieutenant Jerry Allen touched Curt's shoulder and told him directly by speaking through the fabric of the face mask, "Bravo Platoon is in trouble!"

As Curt beat his way against the wind to the cargo hatch, he asked directly in reply, "How? Where? Be specific, Allen!"

"Warhawk Two hit the ground nose-down and flipped," Allen reported.

"Oh, shit! Why didn't Worsham tell me?"

"Just happened. Motega in Warhawk Three saw it and just reported it on my platoon freak. The pilot hit the white-out with some forward speed, misjudged the wind vector, and plowed the Chippie in. I've gotta find it! Tom Cole was aboard! Dillon! Where the hell are you? Join me! Oh, there you are! Hard to recognize people wearing masks..."

Curt was out of the Chippewa now and wished he wasn't. Even with his heavy arctic clothing, he knew it was cold. Damned cold. He could feel it on his face even through the cloth mask that put a protective layer between his flesh and the wind. Without the mask, he knew his skin would freeze solid in less than 60 seconds. The moisture in his breath quickly froze on the open-weave fabric of the mask and made it increasingly difficult to breathe. He saw through the white-out the belly of a Chippewa not 30 meters away. Both Allen and Dillon headed for it, leaning against the terrible force of the wind.

"Bravo Three is here!" came the voice of Corporal Dyani Motega on the company tac freak. "I'm in Warhawk Two! I can't find Cole! He must be on the control deck, and it's underneath at this moment! I'm working my way through the wreckage of two of my Hairy Foxes that broke loose and rattled around in here. I'll have to leave them aboard! Get me some help finding Cole!"

"Hale!" Curt called his biotech. "Get over to Warhawk Two! Cole may be hurt! Dillon, knock it off, get over to Warhawk Four, and unload the rest of Bravo's Hairy Foxes! Vickers, where the hell are you?"

His warbot tech sergeant didn't answer. Instead, Jerry Allen's voice sounded in Curt's head. "Cole and Vickers are in Warhawk Two. The Chippie is bravo delta, totally out of action!"

Curt turned to locate Henry Kester, but the sergeant major wasn't there, so he put out the general call for him on the tacomm.

"Grey Major here," came the calm but hurried voice of the old soldier. "Sorry to bug out on you, Major, but Warhawk Eight bought it. Looks like it hit a snow-covered boulder with a little forward velocity when it landed. It's bravo delta, too. I'm trying to get the colonel out!"

"Grey Head, this is Companion Leader!" Curt called, hoping against hope that Bellamack was still alive and functional after the crash described by Kester.

No answer.

"Companion Leader, this is Grey Major. I hear you. Be advised Grey Head is trapped in the crashed Chippie," came Kester's reply. "I won't know his condition until we can get a can opener or something to bust into Warhawk Eight."

Then and only then did Major Cal Worsham's voice come through on the tacomm frequency. "Warhawk Eight is out of action! If you want in, find the rescue panel and pull the handle!"

"It's under about a meter of ice," Kester replied.

"Then bust the canopy! Warhawks all, this is Warhawk One! Lift out of here when able!"

"Negatory, negatory!" Curt fired back. "Warhawk One, this is Companion Leader! Until we hear from Grey Head, I'm assuming command! We may have injured Greys! You may have to evack them back to the ship!"

"I'm not sitting on my ass here! The way this snow and ice is blowing around, the turbine inlets could ice over! Then we don't go nowhere!"

"How's your anti-ice consumables?"

"Passable."

"Then stay the shit here!" Curt ordered. "Greys all, this is Companion Leader!" Curt put on the regimental freak. "Grey Head may be temporarily down. Assemble on my beacon! We may have to load up for injury evack before we proceed!"

"Companion Leader, Warhawks are outta here!" came Worsham's warning.

"You do that, Worsham, and I'll have your fucking hide for a wall ornament!" Curt growled.

"We're icing up!"

"Squirt your goddamned anti-ice fluid! That's what it's for! I'm not going to argue with you, Warhawk! I've got other things to do right now!" Curt told him firmly. "Greys all, this is Companion Leader! Target the Chippies with your Mary Anns and Hairy Foxes! If any of them lifts without my clearance, shoot!"

"You son of a bitch! You wouldn't!" Worsham put in. He meant it. He didn't believe that the Army would shoot at its own aircraft.

Curt wasn't sure that the Greys would. But he wasn't about to let the Warhawks abandon the Greys in this situation, regardless of how badly Worsham wanted to save his ass and his Chippewas. "So, stay on the ground and don't force my hand, Worsham! I don't know what freezing soldiers will do in this situation!"

Against the intense cold and the hurricane force of the wind, it took long minutes before things got sorted out and people were pulled from the two crashed Chippewas. When Curt began to get a picture of the situation, he didn't like it.

Bellamack was injured and unconscious; he'd have to be airlifted back. to the *McCain*.

The Companions had lost six Hairy Foxes in the crash of Warhawk Four. Sergeant Tom Cole and Tech Sergeant Bob Vickers had been injured in that crash and required evack.

Morgan's Marauders were on the ground with no accidents or injuries.

Half of Frazier's Ferrets were down, but two of the Warhawk Chippie pilots, knowing of the crashes of the two Chippewas, flatly refused to attempt to land Russ Frazier and his company command. Two Chippewas carrying the Ferret's Bravo Platoon and their Hairy Foxes were on the ground...barely. Lieutenant Adonica Sweet had gotten her troops and warbots out and assembled.

The four Warhawk pilots flying the Chippies carrying Wards' Warriors flatly refused to land and were already on their way back to the *McCain*. Curt was furious with them and with the two aerodyne drivers who'd opted not to land Frazier and his Alpha Platoon. There wasn't a whole hell of a lot that Curt could do about it except threaten; the pilot of any aircraft is solely responsible for the safety of his craft and its occupants, and if a pilot decides against doing something, he can't really be overruled, even by a five-star.

Allan Williams of the Marauders and Shelley Hale were the only two biotechs on the ground at that point. "Major," Hale told her company commander, "we've got the colonel and the other injured soldiers and pilots aboard Chippies. Major Worsham can get them out of here…"

"You're not going with them?"

"No, sir. They're less than fifteen minutes from biotech help on the *McCain*, and we've got them stabilized. No one is in critical condition. Maybe some broken bones. Concussion maybe. Nothing really serious. They don't need us. On the other hand, you'll need Al and me here."

Curt blinked behind his goggles. He knew his own biotech was a dedicated person, but it took real dedication to both her people and her profession for Biotech Sergeant Shelley Hale to stay in this frigid, miserable, unreal environment when she could have easily accompanied the injured out.

"Warhawk One, this is Companion Leader," Curt called the squadron leader. "Okay, Cal, you're clear to scram. Shit and git!"

Worsham was eager to depart. He didn't waste words. "Okay, Carson, get your troops out of the way. We're gonna blow snow!"

"I owe you a drink or two when this is over."

"You damned well owe me the economy six-pack of fifty-five-gallon drums of something expensive," Worsham fired back. "Up ship!"

The lift-off blasts from the Chippies were nothing compared to the katabatic wind that tore at the Greys on the glacier.

"Tango Foxtrot Head, this is Grey Head," Curt called the *McCain*, hoping that he had critical communications.

"This is Tango Foxtrot Head," came the reply from the submarine carrier 10 kilometers away.

"Warhawks are coming back with injured," Curt reported. "Please refuel the Warhawks immediately. They may have to come get us. We'll do our best, but this weather is unbelievable!"

"Roger, sir, I'll report that to the captain and Air Ops," came the reply. "Captain Pendleton wants you to know he's reading your data signals and will be watching your physical conditions. He reports that the injured Greys' conditions appear to be stable. I'll be monitoring this frequency constantly, so don't hesitate to call if the Navy can be of help..."

"Turn off the fucking wind," was Curt's reply.

"Sir?"

"Never mind. Where's the Red task force?"

"Five-four klicks northeast. We're tracking."

That was an unusual way for a group of submarines to approach Kerguelen Island, Curt thought. Maybe the station was indeed Soviet. Maybe the Soviet submarines planned to come around the eastern side of the island and land whatever they had on the south coast. Maybe they already knew Task Force Tango Foxtrot was off the island's west coast.

But that was something for General Jacob Carlisle and the Navy to worry about. Curt had enough on his hands right then, a lot more than he'd bargained for because of Bellamack's accident landing. The whole show was now his responsibility.

So, he cleared the frequency with the *McCain* and spoke via tacomm to the Greys who were gathered around. Some of them were huddled in the lee of their warbots, trying to stay out of the wind. The big Hairy Foxes made the best windscreens. The Mark 33 Jeeps with their oil-drum bodies were far less protection.

"Greys all, this is Grey Head," he broadcast. "Align your positioning systems on mine, channel one-India-seven. We're going to navigate strictly by inertial units since a compass is less than useless in this sort of weather because it can't be held steady in this wind. Everyone has the destination coordinates uploaded; if you don't you haven't followed orders. So, we're moving out. We've got ten klicks to go, and the quicker we get there the quicker we get in out of this wind and cold. Anyone in distress at this time? Signal me on the emergency freak if you are...or any time you get into trouble, as a matter of fact."

He paused, but no distress signal came from any of the Greys around him. He knew they were cold and miserable from the wind, but none of them was in deep trouble at the moment.

"Warbots?" he asked, needing a status report on their condition. It was Edie Sampson who replied. "I'll do double duty with Bob Lait of the Marauders as warbot tech," she said. "The bots are cold but serviceable thus far. Power levels holding about as expected."

"Watch those power pack levels, Edie," Henry Kester warned her. "They could start droppin' kinda fast as the bots really begin to get cold..."

"Okay, we're moving out as planned. Fill up the gaps caused by the inability of the absent units to land," Curt went on. "Companions in the lead followed by the Marauders. Sweet, attach yourself to Morgan's company. Alexis, any heartburn about that?"

"Negatory, Major, but goddamn it's cold!" was the reply from Alexis. "I don't think I'll ever get warm again."

Curt wanted to tell her he'd give a try at it later, much later; but he said nothing. Private communication on the regimental tac freak didn't exist. And he had now to carry off this mission in the absence of the regimental commander. So, he said, "The quicker we get to the station, the quicker we'll get warm again. We've got twenty-four people and sixty-one warbots. The go/no-go plans say we can carry out the mission with this strength. But we've got to emphasize surprise and mobility. So, let's move it! Mush!"

Slowly, fighting every second against the vicious wind, the Greys ordered themselves for the 10-kilometer trek across the southern edge of Cook Glacier.

The going was extremely difficult. In fact, it was nearly impossible.

If Curt had ever bothered to read the diaries of Peary, Scott, and the other polar explorers, he would have anticipated this. But he hadn't. No requirements existed for him to read those diaries. Troops of the United States Robot Infantry hadn't fought in cold conditions like this for decades. Even in Alaska, the warbot brainies sat warmly inside and let the warbots brave the cold.

The hurricane-force wind was almost directly against them. It was difficult to move. Toking each step required pushing against an enormous force.

If it hadn't been for eye-protective goggles, eyes themselves would have frozen. As it was, tears became so cold that they were almost painful instead of lubricating the eyes as they normally did. The goggles couldn't be sealed; body moisture would condense on their inner surfaces and freeze instantly into ice on the lenses. The main function of the goggles was to eliminate the windchill which would freeze eyelids and eye-balls within minutes.

Visibility wasn't very good because the white of the glacier blended into the whitish gray of the skies, making the horizon extremely indistinct. Occasional and frequent white-outs of blowing snow forced people to simply stop because it was impossible to see the ground directly ahead. When the white-out cleared, progress was resumed.

Curt's breath froze into crystals of ice on his face mask, making breathing difficult. He had to continually brush his heavily gloved hand over the mask to clear it of heavy ice crystals.

It was impossible to talk because every bit of effort had to be put into staying erect against the wind and taking slow and hesitant steps forward on the irregular and rugged ice of the glacier. Curt wasn't even sure his tacomm unit was still working, because it was silent. No one was talking. Curt forced himself to speak occasionally, calling Alexis Morgan, Jerry Allen, Kitsy Clinton, and the other officers and leaders to ensure that his own tacomm as well as theirs were still working.

An hour of strenuous effort produced progress that dismayed Curt when he checked the inertial positioning unit display on his helmet visor.

The Greys and their warbots had advanced only 1,200 meters from where they'd landed in the Chippewas.

In a brief moment of marginal visibility in between blasts of snow and white-outs, Curt saw his point elements vaguely against the white ahead.

The two white-garbed human forms of Platoon Sergeant Nick Gerard and Corporal Dyani Motega battling the wind ahead of him vanished, disappeared in an instant.

A scream cut through the silence of the tacomm frequency.

Chapter Thirty-Five

Two Mary Anns following Gerard and Motega also disappeared.

"Crevasse!" came the call from Lieutenant Jerry Allen on the tacomm.

"Jesus Christ, Dyani's fallen into the goddamned glacier!" The anguished cry came from Platoon Sergeant Tracy Dillon.

"Gerard! Montega! Do you read me?" Allen called.

The reply was weak. It was Gerard. "Yeah, Lieutenant, I read you. I'm wedged between a couple of chunks of ice. What the hell happened? Where am I?"

"Montega?"

"Corporal Motega here," came the cool reply. "I'm in a crevasse. I've got some foot on a narrow ledge, so I'm not about to fall any further. I can see the edge of the ice above me. I probably fell less than three meters…"

"Don't move!" Allen cried. "I've got your beacons! We'll get ropes down to you!"

"Gonna take more than ropes, Lieutenant," Gerard replied. "I'm wedged. If I wasn't, I'd fall a hell of a long ways…I think. But I can't wiggle out upward either. I think a bot is wedged in above me. As long as it don't fall or this ice don't move, I'm not going anywhere."

"Stay still!" was Allen's advice. "Let's get a rope around you, Nick. Then you won't fall and we can see about hauling you out."

"You can't drop a rope to me without getting that bot out of the way first. But be damned careful you don't cause that number to fall on me!"

"Montega, can you see Sergeant Gerard?" Allen asked her.

"Yes, sir," Montega replied. Her voice was surprisingly calm and collected.

"Can you get to him?" Allen wanted to know.

"No, sir, not without a rope to keep me falling further. But get a rope on me and I'll try to get to Gerard," she told her platoon officer. "That Mary Ann is wedged in a meter or so above him. I can probably attach a grapple or two on it if I can get over there. So, get me a rope, sir. In the meantime, don't rush it; nothing's going to happen. And we're out of the wind down here. It's almost pleasant...but scary."

"Marauder Leader, this is Grey Head," Curt called Alexis. He couldn't see three meters in the blowing snow and ice. "I don't want anyone else to fall into a crevasse. Halt forward movement!"

"Halt, hell! We're making about a hundred meters per hour, that's all!" Alexis's voice came to him in his helmet. "Have we got anything that will help us make ice soundings so we don't have people and warbots falling into crevasses?"

"No, dammit! When we get Gerard and Motega out, we're goin to have to proceed in a double skirmish line with the leaders proving the ice and roped to a safety man in the second wave," Curt decided. "We'll have the Jeeps follow, then the Mary Anns, then the Hairy Foxes."

"If we keep up this blistering pace, we're not going to make it to the station by sundown," Alexis warned.

"So we take it by night assault," Curt told her.

"Goddamned risky."

"Goddamned long, cold night if we don't," he reminded her.

"We should have risked direct airborne assault."

"Maybe. Maybe not. We don't know what triple-A defenses they've got."

"If any."

"Want to take a chance they don't have any?"

"Might be better than freezing our asses off crawling across this goddamned glacier in the world's coldest weather."

"Might. But we don't have much choice," Curt told her. "Here we are. So, we push ahead as vigorously as we can. In the meantime, order everyone to crouch down or find shelter behind a warbot. If they hunker down, they can get in the boundary layer of the wind blowing over the glacier. Like staying out of the wind on a cold day at the beach." He wished he were on some warm beach as he keyed his company's tacomm channel. "Companion Bravo, Companion Leader here. Sit-rep please."

"We found the holes where Gerard and Motega fell through, plus the holes where the Mary Anns went in," Jerry Allen replied. "Sampson's trying to get a rope lowered to Motega now. We can't get a rope to Gerard because the Mary Ann is wedged above him."

"Ident your beacon so I can locate you," Curt ordered him. "I'm coming over."

"Identing, sir. But I suggest you stay the hell away from this crevasse. We don't know the extent of it, and I sure as hell don't want you to fall through the ice!"

Allen was right, so Curt overcame the urge to be present at the rescue. "On reconsideration, I'm holding position," he told his lieutenant. "But I'll be monitoring your tacomm channel."

Jerry Allen sounded busy and distracted. He was basically running the rescue, and he was trying to devote his full energies to it while at the same time trying to keep his superior officer informed. "Thanks, sir. If I run into trouble, I'll yell."

"I'm sure you will," Curt told him and remained silent to listen to the conversation on the tacomm. Curt decided it was probably time he stopped trying to hold Jerry's hand on everything. The lieutenant was an experienced Sierra Charlie now and had shown that he could lead his platoon well.

Regimental Sergeant Major Henry Kester stepped out of the white world around Curt and motioned that he'd like a private confab. The two men drew close enough together to they could talk over the howling wind.

"Major, this is the shits. I think we can make faster time if you don't mind the possibility of losing a coupla warbots in the process."

"Hell, Henry, warbots are supposed to be expendable, or have you forgotten what it says in Field Manual One-hundred-dash-fifty?" Curt replied, referring to the old warbot brainy's battlefield bible of warbot procedures, tactics, and doctrine. "I'd rather lose a warbot than a trooper. Warbots are just machines and it takes a hell of a lot longer to make and train a soldier."

"I was hoping you'd say that," the old soldier replied, his voice cutting through the heavy layer of frozen breath on the front of his face mask. "Once we get Gerard and Motega out of the glacier, why not put the Hairy Foxes in front? They're big and heavy. We got a lot of them, far more than we'll probably need in a close firefight. If the Hairy Foxes don't bust through the ice, the Mary Anns and us can sure as hell get over. If they do bust through, they may not fall completely in. They'll probably get stuck. Then we'll know where a crevasse is. Maybe we can get the bot out, and maybe not. If not, we forge ahead and let someone else worry about recovering it later."

"Henry, how come you know so goddamned much?" Curt asked him lightly.

"Hell, Major, I don't know very much. I just watch and listen to what other people do and say...then I steal it and use it myself," Kester replied frankly.

The chatter on the tacomm frequency was graphic.

"Okay, Motega, Sampson's got a flashlight on the end of a rope and is lowering it in your vicinity," Jerry Allen explained. "Lemme know when you see it."

"Got it, Lieutenant. It's about a half meter above me and a meter to my left."

"I don't know where you left side is, Dyani," Edit Sampson told her.

"Move the rope to one side, and I'll tell you if you move it nearer or further away."

"How's that?"

"Closer. Okay, down a bit…Got it! Thanks for the light. I can use it down here. Lots of dark crannies…Okay, I've got the rope wrapped around me, I won't fall. Drop another rope alongside the first."

"Here it comes!"

"Got it! Okay, keep slack in the second rope but stand by on the first one. I'm going to attempt to move toward Gerard. I may slip. If I do, snub the first rope so I don't fall."

"Understand."

"Easier to move than I thought. I can wedge myself against the sides of the crevasse and get suitable purchase. Howdy Sergeant! You are stuck, aren't you?"

"Yeah, I can't move my legs. They're jammed."

"Okay, let me try to sling my *Novia* so I don't lose it. Hang on to yours. Slip this under your arms. Okay, Lieutenant, I've got the second rope around Sergeant Gerard now."

"Want another rope for the Mary Ann?"

"Negatory! It's dinged pretty bad. Really not worth trying to recover it. Let's not waste time on it."

"How about putting a line or two on it so it doesn't slip and fall on you?"

"That's going to take some time. I'm not sure I can shinny up the crevasse enough to do it. On the other hand, I've got Sergeant Gerard secured. I'll take the chance that the Mary Ann isn't going to fall on us. Sergeant, you got your boot knife?"

"Yeah, but I can't reach it."

"I can. Here, take it. And help me chip away at the ice wedge down by your thighs and knees. I'll work chipping away below. You work close to yourself."

"Want me to knife myself, huh?"

"Yes, because if that happens, you'll know right away and won't have to yell to me. Know how to split ice?"

"You bet! Worked in an ice house during the summers when I was a kid. Coolest job in town! Hey, this stuff doesn't split and flake right."

"Not man made. Got a different crystal structure. More like pressure ice."

"Where did you learn to work ice?"

"Used to go ice fishing with my father in Minnesota. Whups!"

"Gotcha! Be careful, Dyani! Some of this ice crumbles under pressure."

"Thanks. It's a long fall. Dropped my knife, dammit! I'll bang on the ice with the butt of my *Novia*. Shock may make it easier to fracture it."

"Ow! Goddammit!"

"Stabbed yourself?"

"Yeah, right through the trousers. Okay, left leg free. Hit that chunk where my knife is pointing. Good! Hey, that busted it! I damned near fell!"

"This time I got you."

"That you did."

"Okay, Sergeant, move toward me. Push against the crevasse walls with your arms, legs, and butt."

"Shit, this is like running stuck elevator rescues!"

"Easy! Push! Where did you do something like that?"

"The summer before I worked in the ice plant. Assistant elevator inspector in a skyscraper. I quit. Job was too damned scary and hot. Besides, I don't like tightly closed places like elevator shafts...or glacier crevasses."

Curt recalled that the platoon sergeant suffered from claustrophobia which didn't affect him except under severe mental stress. Why Nick wasn't in panic now confused Curt until he realized that

Gerard was probably too damned busy trying to save his hide to worry about being terrified of the closed space he was caught in.

"Okay, easy, here's the ledge. We're out from under the Mary Ann. Lieutenant, take slack on Gerard's line. I think you can probably lift him up now. Sergeant, get your feet on that little ledge below us and turn loose of me so they can hoist you out of here…Sergeant?…Lieutenant, Sergeant Gerard just panicked. I had to smack him with my *Novia*. He's out cold. Go ahead and lift while I guide his body."

"What happened?"

"Gerard went ape. Got round-eyed and stiff. Scared the hell out of me."

"His claustrophobia got the better of him once he knew that bot wouldn't fall on him," Allen put in, but he said nothing about the one other time in the past when the platoon sergeant had freaked out under stress.

"Hold it! He's limp and can't maneuver his body through the cracks. Lower him about a half meter so I can get my line around him. That will allow you to swing his bottom part sideways through some of the openings above."

"You'll be without a rope!"

"True, but I'll wedge myself so I won't fall. Unless you've got another rope. That would make me feel a whole lot better about this."

"I can't get it down to you past Gerard."

"Okay, then lift him out. I've got my rope around his knees now. Be careful. He may not have noticed it, but his left leg may be broken. It's got a funny angle to it."

"Here he comes! Okay, we've got his head and shoulders…Yeah, he's out cold, but his leg looks okay. Medic! Hale, Williams, can you see my beacon? We need you over here!"

"Hale here, Lieutenant. Right behind you. I agree. I don't think his leg is broken, but it's hard to tell through the arctic gear. Someone break out a shelter half and get it under him! We can sledge him on it until he's conscious and ready to walk...if he can."

"Rope coming back down to you, Dyani!"

"Got it. Okay, please get me the hell and gone out of here!"

Curt looked at Kester and Alexis. Neither of them said anything. Curt was impressed. At no time during the incident had there been the slightest hint of fear, panic, or any emotion other than concern in the voice of Corporal Dyani Motega. She had remained cool, calm, and rational during the entire dangerous affair. Curt hadn't seen it, but he felt in his gut that one slip could have either injured her or caused her to fall until the slack in the line was taken up. He had noticed that the proud young woman had remained relatively aloof since she'd joined the Companions. He had attributed that to the usual newcomer's reluctance to become fully involved in the affairs of the platoon and company, the classical "new kid" or replacement's syndrome. But maybe her aloofness was part of her personality, a semi-stoic and cool-headed outlook on the world. He didn't know how wrong he was at the time, of course, because he really didn't understand this young Crow Indian girl's background. But he did know that he'd certainly put in a citation for Dyani Motega for displaying outstanding courage in a potentially deadly situation.

They left the Mary Ann in the crevasse, noting the inertial coordinates so that perhaps it could be retrieved during the pull-out from this operation if the weather got better. Curt didn't really want to leave any of their warbots on Kerguelen if he could help it; they were probably the newest war robots in the world, although they were basically cobbled-up makeshift units put together in a hurry in order to support the Sierra Charlie concept.

The assemblage of soldiers and warbots was reorganized as Henry Kester had suggested and resumed the trek across Cook Glacier. Nick Gerard regained consciousness and insisted on walking rather than being hauled across the snow on the makeshift sledge of a shelter half.

The trek moved a little bit faster, but Curt kept watching the sky -

when he could see it - with a great deal of concern. He knew that they were going to have to continue during the oncoming night. By the time 1600 hours rolled around and the landscape began to grow dark with the coming night - the sun had never once broken through the leaden overcast - the Washington Greys contingent had traversed only 4-kilometers of their planned 9-kilometer march.

The wind never let up. It blew cold and strong against them, although it now came from their left as it roared down off the glacial dome to the north.

When the blowing snow and ice permitted it, Curt could see an ice ridge about 1,000 meters ahead. It was unanticipated, although the map display on Curt's helmet visor indicated that the French had mapped the ridge many years before, but it was far more prominent now due to movement of the glacier. Huge blocks of ice reared up, forming a veritable wall in their path. The Aerospace Force images hadn't shown this. And the aborted birdbot recon hadn't got this far.

Bad recon. Poor intelligence data. Curt realized that the chances of getting through that ice ridge and assaulting the station were pretty low right then. The amount of effort it would take to get through that ridge would be intense. If his own physical condition was any indication, his troops were pretty well exhausted by the demanding job of fighting the bitter cold and the roaring force of the wind. He was tired. He was hungry. He was intensely cold. He wasn't sure the Greys could tackle the rest of the trek.

And the light of the sun had started to fade.

Which meant they'd have to be recovered from the glacier within an hour to so.

Or they'd have to spend the night out there.

Chapter Thirty-Six

Spending the night on a glacier with a windchill factor nearly 100 degrees below zero wasn't Curt's idea of a good thing to do. He quickly reviewed the choices he had and was forced to the conclusion that they'd blown the original mission plan.

His first move was to check with his field commanders.

"Companion Leader, Grey Head," he called Lieutenant Jerry Allen, now in command of Carson's Companions. "How are the troops?"

"Companion Leader here. Nick Gerard is having trouble; he tore the left leg of his pants getting out of that crevasse, and that compromised the thermal integrity of his equipment. He was bleeding, but that's been stopped now by Shelley Hale. Motega's okay except she's very tired. Clinton and Sampson are holding up well. Better, in fact, than Koslowski and Elliott. Our third platoon, Ferret Bravo, is having slow going with their Hairy Foxes, and Adonica reports some of her troops are dragging. We're having a hell of a time against this wind, and we're reaching the end of the rope. So, the overall picture isn't real encouraging, Major."

To have Jerry Allen report that negatively meant that the Companions were not in good shape. Allen was an optimist. He was eager, gung-ho, a ready teddy. He always tried to give the best report he could. Curt mentally gritted his teeth; his real teeth were chattering from the cold behind his face mask. He hoped the rest of his truncated command was doing better. So, he called Alexis Morgan. "Marauder Leader, Grey Head. Sit-rep, please."

"Marauder Leader here. We've got only about five klicks to go. I think we'll make it," she replied. Funny, but in this tough situation, Alexis was strangely more gung-ho than Jerry Allen. And her voice seemed to have a dreamlike quality to it.

So, Curt asked her, "Got any ideas how to tackle that ice ridge ahead?"

"Uh, where?"

"About a thousand meters at twelve o'clock."

"Can't see it."

"Looks like it's thirty meters high with few passages through it."

"Uh, got it on my display, but only as a topo map. No visual yet. Uh, do you think it's going to be a problem for your forward movement?" Alexis's voice was thick and slurred. Since it wasn't really her "voice," but the computer reconstruction of her voice picked up from her verbalized thought processes, Curt knew right away that she was getting into trouble with hypothermia.

"Williams, check your company commander for signs of hypothermia!" Curt snapped.

"Williams here! I'll home on her beacon."

"Uh, why? Hypothermia? Hell, Curt, I'm okay. Just cold," Alexis objected.

Curt made a quick decision. It was time to bug out. *Have no pride when it comes time to get the hell out of Whiskey Creek!* was an old warbot brainy truism. In short, don't hesitate to abandon a bad situation when continuing to push might cause unnecessary casualties or losses. So, he toggled his tacomm over to the mission frequency and called, "Frigid Head, this is Grey Head."

"Frigid Head here. Go ahead, Grey Head," came the reply from the mission operations center in the *McCain*, submerged off the west coast of Kerguelen.

"We may have a problem making our objective before dark," Curt reported. "The wind is intense, and the cold is unbelievable. My troops are nearing exhaustion. And we've got an unsuspected ice ridge in the glacier ahead of us. The situation isn't good. Request immediate air evack."

"Wait one, Grey Head. We're informing Frigid Leader," the voice of an unknown division staffer said in his head.

"Goddamn it, you don't understand! Get an evack flight in the air!

We're in deep shit here!" As Curt said it, he suddenly realized that it was very uncharacteristic of him to say things that way, especially to higher command. The cold and the intense effort were taking their toll on him as well.

"Grey Head, stand by, please. We understand the nature of your situation."

Like hell you do, you fucking staff stooge! Curt thought savagely. *You're sitting on your fat ass in a nice warm room with a cup of hot coffee at your elbow!* Again, something inside his head told him that he was reacting to emotions and feelings that were welling up from deep within the uncontrolled and undisciplined depths of his mind because of fatigue and thermal stress.

While he was waiting, he took a piss into his piddle pack. It felt good. He hoped he hadn't filled the container yet because that would mean he'd have to breach the thermal integrity of his arctic gear. Exposing any part of his body to these environmental conditions could cause freezing in less than a minute, and Curt wasn't about to risk that! He hadn't yet used his "fecal containment device," which the Army had borrowed outright from the Aerospace Force space suits. The Sierra Charlies didn't give a damn about fancy, inoffensive names, so they'd simply called it the shit bag. He suspected that some other troopers had used it. They'd been away from the *McCain* for more than 6 hours now. But none of them were willing to freeze their asses off, either. All of which meant they couldn't stay out here much longer without literally freezing their buns off or getting into deep shit.

"Grey Head, this is Frigid Head," the voice of General Carlisle came to Curt. "Sit-rep, please."

"General, we've managed to make six klicks," Curt told him. "You should be able to locate us by our beacons."

"Roger. I see you."

"We've come up against an ice ridge. The light is failing. This weather is incredibly bad. My troops are nearing exhaustion. It's already affecting the mental abilities of my field commanders...and my own as well. We can't get through this ridge in darkness in our present condition. And if we stay out here in these conditions overnight, we're going to take losses which we can't afford at this point. Therefore, as the commander in the field, I'm aborting the mission and requesting immediate air evack," Curt reported bluntly.

The brief pause told Curt that he was in real trouble. "Grey Head, bad news. Tango Foxtrot reports sea state Romeo and wind force eleven on the surface. Warhawk is willing to fly an evack, but Tango Foxtrot declines to surface and open flight deck doors for fear of foundering in heavy seas."

Curt was growing increasingly cold, and therefore he wasn't exactly thinking straight. He broke procedures by stating, "General, if you can't get us out of here, I'm probably going to have some people die tonight!"

The reply was equally terse. "Curt, I know your situation. Pendleton is monitoring you. He reports no one in serious trouble yet."

"Tell Pendleton to stuff it! We may be okay at the moment, but I don't know how the hell we can last for another eighteen hours out here!"

"You've got to!"

Curt breathed heavily. The moisture from his sigh condensed on the open-weave cloth of his face mask. That flat statement of fact from the commanding general of the 17th Iron Fist Division, a man who knew and understood his people and who could be counted on to do everything possible for them, yanked Curt back from his irrational fear that they'd blundered into the final deadly situation. He started to think again. That saved him, and it saved his command. "Okay, General, if we've got to, we will. But I want some data on the physical conditions of Captain Morgan, Lieutenant Clinton, Sergeant Gerard, and anyone else - including myself - who looks like they're deteriorating and getting near the danger point."

"I've notified Pendleton. He's on top of the situation. He's noted some irrational patternn coming from both you and Morgan. He doesn't exactly know what they are, but he'll stay on top of the situation and notify you if anyone else begins to exhibit the same patterns."

"Tell Pendleton those irrational readings are because we're going into the initial stages of hypothermia," Curt snapped.

"What do you want to do, Grey Head?"

"Get the hell out of here," Curt repeated, knowing as he said it that it was going to be impossible. Then he went on, "But since we can't, we've got to stop, circle the wagons, and look for a place to spend the night. We'll try to find somewhere that's sheltered and out of this goddamned wind. We've got inflatables with us; they can serve two people for bundling heat if necessary. We've got catalytic heaters. We'll do our best." He knew the Greys would have to.

"Good! Hang in there," the general advised him. "In the meantime, Joseph will try to get inshore to find conditions where he can surface, open, and launch."

"Can Worsham get in here in the dark?"

"He says he'll try. He may have to use lights."

"That will compromise security! He could be seen from the station!"

"I'll risk that possibility if we can get the Warhawks airborne. I don't think anyone at the station is looking for anything tonight with the weather the way it is."

"God, I hope so, General!"

As Curt toggled off, he saw Henry Kester alongside him. "Did you hear that, Henry?"

"Damned right...sir!"

"Suggestions?"

"Just exactly what you said, Major...and as quickly as possible before someone goes into hypothermic shock or worse."

"Do you feel up to going ahead and running a quick recon of that ridge to see if you can find a place for us to get the hell out of this fucking wind?"

"Yes, sir, but I'll be damned if I'll go alone in this weather with all these crevasses around," the old soldier told him frankly. "Can you spare Edie Sampson and Tom Dillon?"

"Find them and go!" Curt told him.

Then he toggled the general regimental freak and explained to his troops what they were going to do.

"Orgasmic!" was Alexis Morgan's comment. "But it's better than trying to make the objective in this stuff. I've got one, maybe two, people who may have frostbite. I need to get everyone under cover and have them check themselves."

"Okay, so don't drag ass, anyone! The quicker we find a place to winter over tonight, the better. Does everyone have Kester's beacon on their display? Home on that."

A few minutes later, Regimental Sergeant Major Henry Kester's voice came, "Grey Head, Grey Major here. Ain't a whole hell of a lot to choose from. The ridge runs downhill parallel to the wind flow. But we've found a couple of outcrops that can give us some protection."

"Roger! Homing on you! Greys all, this is Grey Head! Proceed as rapidly as feasible to Grey Major's beacon. Once you get there, prepare to bivouac. Pick a buddy and tag your inflatables together; you'll stay warmer tonight."

Someone - Curt could not identify the voice - suddenly asked, "Rule Ten in abeyance tonight?"

"Not only no, but hell no! Goddammit, I don't know how anyone could even think of such a thing in this cold weather!" Curt fired back. "Okay, I'll relax it insofar as bundling goes."

"Bundling?" was the question from Lieutenant Adonica Sweet.

"Yeah, Lieutenant," came the comment in a nasal New England accent that told Curt that the. speaker was Sergeant Jim Elliott. "I don't 'spect you people from down south would know of things like that. Old Puritan tradition. Means occupying a bed with someone else without undressing. Believe me, a couple of New England winters would convince you it's a good way to stay warm..."

At the base of the ice ridge, Kester had worked with Sampson and Dillon to locate the bests spots. The ice ridge wasn't smooth. It had breaks and outcrops along its north-south axis. The katabatic wind still roared through these irregularities, but it wasn't quite as strong as it was out in the open.

"Line up your bots so they act as a windscreen," Curt advised his troops.

"Better use them as makeshift snow fences," Sergeant Tracy Dillon added, calling upon his experience growing up in Montana. "This wind is carrying a lot of snow with it. You could wake up in the morning and find yourself buried."

"Marauder Leader, this is Marauder Fix," came the voice of the only warbot technician left with the Greys, Tech Sergeant Bob Lait. "These bots are getting loggy and slow. All of them. Some more than others. I don't know how many of them are going to be operational after a night at these temperatures."

First Sergeant Edie Sampson, known in the Companions as an expert warbot tinkerer, told him, "Get 'em in position, Lait, then shut down everything except heaters on the critical computer cubes."

"Lait, I'll help you as soon as I get my inflatable secured," Kester put in. "We oughta try to reprogram the power pack loadings so that the outer units are used first because they'll get cold first. Once they're dead, they can act as a heat barrier for the inner units."

"Henry, take care of it as quickly as you can get your own comfort assured," Curt told him. "Same goes for everyone else. First priority is to keep your own ass from freezing. Second priority is to save someone else who may be in trouble. Third priority is saving warbots. And last is saving weapons."

Setting up camp under the extreme weather conditions wasn't easy. In fact, it was almost impossible. Each person carried an insulated, inflatable tube tent built like a thermos bottle; its outer layer was separated from its inner layer by an airtight compartment which was inflated with a small pressure canister. The pressurized layer of air acted as insulation. It was possible to Velcro two of them together end-to-end to make one long tube tent and thus allow two people to contribute their body heat toward maintaining inside temperatures. In worst conditions - and these were worst conditions - two people could occupy the same tube tent while saving the second one for additional living space if needed.

But the inflatables had to be pegged down to the ice to keep them from being blown away.

And that was nearly impossible in the strong wind that blasted and gusted around the ridge.

About one third of the inflatables were literally torn from the hands of the Greys by the howling gale and blown away down the glacier's slopes toward the sea.

Some Greys were so exhausted by this time that they could only flatten themselves against the walls of ice and try to stay out of the wind.

Nearly half the warbots - mostly the Jeeps and smaller Mary Anns - simply quit, their power packs drained because of the effects of the cold weather. A few Greys had the strength left to manhandle these dead warbots into position where they could serve as primitive snow fences.

Even at that, blowing snow began to pile up around those inflatables that had been pegged down.

Curt stuck his *Novia* into the snow to mark his inflatable, then went looking for people to herd into shelter. He moved in a daze, hardly recognizing anyone behind their face masks. Curt literally drove himself past the point of exhaustion because he kept telling himself, *I'm the CO here. It's my duty to make sure my people are taken care of first! Get them under cover! Get everyone in an inflatable! Move, man, move!*

He finally crawled back into what he thought was his own inflatable, sealed the opening against that of another pegged down head-to-head, and stripped off his ice-covered face mask. He was shivering uncontrollably.

He discovered it wasn't his tent. The tube was occupied by two people already. One of his tent companions for the night had already broken a light-stick, which shed its cool orange glow dimly through the tubular enclosure. The other already had two catalytic heaters going to provide some warmth.

"Major! You look terrible!" Dyani Motega exclaimed.

"Goddammit! Wrong tent! I'll go find mine," Curt muttered through lips that were blue with cold.

"The hell you will, Major!" snapped Biotech Sergeant Shelley Hale. "You'll be in even worse shape before you find your own tent out there tonight. We've got room in here."

"Cozy, but room," Motega added.

In the dim light of the chemical light-sticks, Shelley Hale immediately saw Curt's blue lips and noticed his uncontrollable shivering. "Major, I've got to get you out of deep trouble right now," she replied in her calm, professional voice. "Get your gloves and shoes off...now!"

"No, I'm okay. Just a little cold. My hands and feet aren't cold at all."

She didn't bother arguing with him but reached out and stripped off his heavy gloves. "Dyani, get his boots off!" she snapped.

"Doing it," was the brief reply. "No, Major, keep your headgear on! You've shaved your head and you haven't got any insulation up there! And that's where you'll lose most of the body heat you've got left!"

Curt was at that point too cold and too exhausted to care. The vicious wind rippled the inflatable tent fabric, but the double layer of cloth and its air cushion gave it enough structural integrity combined with flexibility to withstand the blow. He was cold, very cold. He couldn't stop shivering. So, he just lay there and winced at the sudden feeling of pain that ran through his left hand as Hale began to warm it.

"Dyani, what have you found?"

"Shelley, some of his toes are cold and white. Frostnip. I'll warm them by friction massage. And breathing on them."

"Damn, I never thought about breathing on frostbitten parts!"

"Old trick my grandfather taught me. Used to get pretty cold out on the plains of Montana during a blizzard."

"Indian lore, huh?"

"You bet! If it works, I'll use it!"

"Hey, if it worked for him, it'll work for us!"

Hale put something warm in his left hand. "Hold this," she told him. It was a catalytic hand warmer. Feeling slowly began to return to his hand. Funny, he hadn't noticed that it had become numb. But when he looked at it, he almost got sick to his stomach. Some of his fingers were white. Others were just beginning to turn blotchy red. One was swollen. The red, swollen one began to hurt.

"Frostbite?" he asked.

"Maybe just frostnip," Hale replied, continuing to warm his other hand. Anticipating his question like the good nurse she was, she told him, "I don't think it's very bad. We caught it quickly. We'll keep you warm tonight, and by tomorrow morning we'll know if there's any residua."

"Goddammit!" Curt exploded wearily. "Pendleton was supposed to keep me advised of any potentially dangerous physical situations!"

"Captain Pendleton isn't a biotech," Hale reminded him.

"So? Jealous of your professional know-how?" As he said it, he knew he shouldn't have. But he was still so damned cold that it didn't seem to matter.

"Not at all. But I don't think Captain Pendleton, or any other warbot expert has ever seen any linkage data from a warbot brainy suffering from cold injury."

Curt suddenly realized that he'd sloughed off some of his responsibility to someone else who wasn't at risk and who was sitting comfortably in the rear echelon. He was angry with himself for letting it happen. But he was too tired to do much about it. And the pain from his hands and feet was growing greater now.

He didn't notice when Shelley Hale gave him an analgesic.

He did remember Dyani Motega feeding hot soup to him and insisting that he drink it. She had a no nonsense, quiet, stoic, almost unemotional way about her.

He must have fallen asleep still cold, because he was shivering. But at some point, he realized that he wasn't cold any longer.

Two warm, soft bodies were on either side of him.

He fell back into sleep.

Chapter Thirty-Seven

Curt awoke to the smell of food.

In the wan yellow-orange glow of a light-stick, he saw Corporal Dyani Motega brewing something on the catalytic stove-heater unit down by his feet.

"Ah, good! You're awake, Major!" she noticed. "Got some hot soup here. And hot tea, too. Shelley says the hot tea is more effective than hot coffee." She filled a plastic cup and reached down to him. "Here. Drink up!"

"Thanks. Where's Hale?" Curt wanted to know as he gratefully sipped the hot soup. His fingers were no longer tingling, although they were red and a little swollen. His toes had feeling in them again, and he noticed that someone had put his boots on.

"She's out keeping the snow off us," the Crow Indian girl explained. "We took turns all night. Otherwise, we would have been buried this morning."

"Well, the two of you sure as hell had time for a ménage a trois," Curt muttered with a slight smile. "Too bad we weren't in a situation where we could make the best of it!"

Motega looked at him and replied levelly, "Major, it wouldn't have been right to do anything other than that to get you warm again. Hale noticed that you weren't getting any warmer when we bundled with you. So, we had to go a little bit further."

"Thank you. I'm glad you did."

"But that's as far as it's going to go, Major. Beyond that, it wouldn't be right…"

"I understand. Dyani, you have a commendable set of standards."

"Well, Major, I was raised by a family that believed in the strict rules of our past because those rules worked very well for untold generations," Dyani Motega told him bluntly in her calm, stoic voice. "The Crows may have been considered savages to Europeans two centuries ago. But that doesn't mean that we didn't have and still don't have moral standards. But keeping you from hypothermia last night wasn't an immoral act."

"Sure as hell wasn't, and I'll see to it that a commendation is forthcoming."

"If we get out of here, Major."

"We'll get out."

A blast of frigid air blew into the inflatable as the seam separated and Biotech Sergeant Shelley Hale crawled in. She sealed the seam and saw that Curt was up. "Good! How do you feel, Major?"

"Tired, but not as tired as I was. Cold, but not as cold as I was," Curt admitted.

"Great! Well, the good news is that you had mild frostnip, and we got to it in time to keep it from disabling you," Hale reported. "The bad news is that the weather hasn't improved, and we've got some Greys who weren't lucky enough to have a biotech sergeant in their inflatable with them. We have some frostbite cases, and they need to be evacked."

"How many?" Curt wanted to know.

Hale shook her head. "Four that I know of. Probably just as many that I don't know. about. Lieutenant Aarts. First Sergeant Carol Head. Sergeants Koslowski and Saunders."

Curt reached over, grabbed his helmet, and fitted it over his head. Its circuits, powered again by his body heat, came on line as he checked their telltales on the visor display. A repetitive all-call was echoing in the tacomm. "Grey Head, this is Frigid Head by recording. Please reply by keying your transmitter twice in two seconds. Grey Head, this is Frigid Head by recording. Please reply by keying…"

He toggled the transmit switch twice.

The recording kept sounding in his head.

"Dammit, I'm not getting through. Shelley, how much snow is on top of us?"

"Very little. Dyani and I took turns every hour last night shoveling it off."

"You must be exhausted," Curt observed.

Hale shook her head. "Tired, but we got some rest. That's what counted."

"Okay, please move to the other inflatable and let me out of here. I've got to be on the surface so I have enough signal strength to punch through with this low powered helmet tacomm," Curt told her.

"Don't stay out too long," Hale warned.

"Dammit, we can't stay in here all day!" Curt muttered.

"You may think differently when you've been outside for a while, Major," Dyani said.

She was right.

The wind hit him like a physical blow and the cold cut like a jagged knife.

The same wan sunlight illuminated the scene.

Some of the warbots were buried. Most of the tents were secured and uncovered. Curt saw no one else.

Curt knew they couldn't stay here. The weather and the ice environment had beaten them. It would have beaten anyone. The Greys would have to be airlifted out. Soon.

He keyed his transmitter twice. The recording stopped. So, he transmitted, "Frigid Head, this is Grey Head." He sent the call several times, knowing it might take a few tries before someone woke up to the fact that he was communicating again.

"Grey Head, this is Frigid Head. Two Star is speaking." It was General Jacob Carlisle. "What's your situation?"

"Not good, General," Curt replied, giving as succinct and accurate a report as he could at the moment. "We made it through the night, but we've got four people with frostbite who need to be evacked ASAP. At this point, we have an undetermined number of others who may have frostbite or hypothermia. The weather hasn't improved. I haven't had time to check out the warbots, but I suspect at least fifty percent of them have inoperative power packs or are frozen up. My initial estimate of the situation hasn't changed since last night. In fact, we're probably worse off because of the continued exposure to the weather. We can't carry out the mission in our present condition, and I'm officially aborting. Request airlift ASAP, sir."

"Okay, Curt, get your troops together," Carlisle told him, saying words that made Curt feel better than he had in hours. "We've tracked the Soviet submarines into Table Bay south of the glacier. We've picked up a fourth submarine, identity unknown, also approaching Table Bay from the east. Joseph is sticking his neck out a hell of a long way, but he's bringing *McCain* to the surface and coming inshore on the surface to Melissas Bay. Buell thinks the sea state and wind there may be more conducive to launching the Warhawks.

"How soon, General?"

"We were standing by until we heard from you," Carlisle replied. "Now that we have, Joseph is going to surface and run in. I suspect it will be about two hours before we can launch. Monitor this freak, and I'll keep you advised."

"General, with the Sovs so close by, is it advisable to converse in plain language like this?" Curt worried.

"I wouldn't have done it if I didn't think we'd be okay, Curt. It takes a lot of computer power and a long time to break a skip code like ours."

"Yessir. I'll monitor this freak, General."

When Carlisle switched off, Curt went to work trying to roust the Greys from their tents. It went slowly until he found Kester and Sampson in their combined tent. After that, he left the reveille call to them, thinking that the situation had made for some strange and interesting bundling last night. But much of the pairing had probably taken place purely by accident as it had in his case. In any event, it didn't concern him. If the Greys had made it safely through the Antarctic night, he didn't much give a damn right then how they'd managed to do it. Maybe he'd find out later. Maybe he wouldn't. The Greys were very discreet people.

It took real guts and determination to get out of those warm tents and brave the frigid gale that continued to blow down off the Cook Glacier. But the Greys slowly emerged and began checking their warbots.

Curt told everyone that the Warhawks would be coming for air evack within a few hours. That news cheered them and helped keep them going. They were fatigued troops. Curt knew that yesterday's exertions and the uncomfortable night spent in the howling wind had whupped the Greys. In spite of all the emphasis he and Colonel Bellamack had tried to place on physical fitness, and the fact that the Washington Greys were probably in better condition than any regiment in the entire United States Army, they still weren't fit enough to survive *and* fight in this environment.

Curt wondered why the Army hadn't brought in warbot troops from Alaska. He got his answer very quickly that morning. No soldiers in the world save perhaps the Mongol troops of the Red Army, and certainly no military leaders, would have planned a mission in the sort of weather that the Greys had run into on Cook Glacier. Not even arctic warbot brainies would try to fight in such an environment.

And that became evident as Curt began to get re-ports back from Kester, Sampson, and Lait.

The Jeeps were out of it. The blowing snow had driven into their turret and gun mechanisms, jamming the works. It had also dropped the temperature of their computer cubes, a factor which changed electrical resistances and rendered them inoperative. The Jeeps were mindless machines now.

The Mary Anns had frozen up and their power packs had died

because of the extremely low temperatures and high rate of heat flow from their interiors. They were so cold that they wouldn't even begin to function when some of the power packs from disabled Hairy Foxes were jumped to them. Even their low temperature lubricants had become too viscous, turning into gooey glue instead of slippery lube.

The Hairy Foxes were big and had managed to have enough heat sinks and heat retention so that their power packs weren't dead. But some of their AI circuitry was too cold to operate, and their travel gear was jammed with snow and ice that would require being melted off for them to operate. With the possibility of their heavy 50-millimeter recoilless tube cannons being subjected to insane commands from very cold AI computers, no Grey wanted to risk turning on the Foxes for fear they might somehow open up at will on random targets.

The personal weapons were in somewhat better shape, except for the ones that had been inadvertently left outside during the night to mark the location of various tents. Sergeant Jim Elliott came up to Curt and Henry Kester with his *Novia* in his arms, voicing the complaint, "Major, the action's frozen solid!"

"Piss on it," Henry Kester told him.

"Huh?"

"You heard the Sergeant Major," Curt told him.

"But make sure you shoot a ten-round burst right after you do it," Henry went on advising him. "That'll blow most of the water and piss out of the action and boil off what don't get blown out. Check it again after a minute or two and if it acts like it's starting to freeze again, blow off a few more rounds. But shoot it into the snow, Elliott, not into the air."

Elliott must have passed that information along to other Greys who had the same problem. Within a few minutes, the sound of random rifle fire cut through the howling wind.

"Grey Head, this is Warhawk Leader!" came the call in Curt's helmet tacomm.

"Go ahead, Warhawk Leader! This is Grey Head!" Curt replied at once.

"We're airborne and heading for you! Get ready to load up!" were Cal Worsham's instructions.

"Got our beacons?"

"Roger that! We'll be there in seven minutes! How's the weather?"

"Snow and blowing snow. Some random white-outs. Temperature about as cold as it's always been, and the goddamned wind blowing like hell out of the north off the glacier," Curt told him. "Sorry I can't be more specific, but I haven't even got the luxury of a wet finger to test the wind; it would freeze off."

"Okay, I've got only three Chippies," Major Cal Worsham informed him. "That's all we could get out of maintenance after putting you down. Snow and ice raised hell with the systems. So, we'll have to come back and get the warbots later. First priority is to get your troopers out of there."

"Jesus, should we leave these warbots here?" Curt wondered aloud. "Suppose the people at the station come out and get them?"

"Chance we'll have to take. It's been approved by Carlisle, so your ass isn't in a sling for abandoning them," Worsham pointed out. "If the weather holds, we can get the warbots out later today...Six minutes!"

"Hey, Cal, we're waiting!" Curt announced, switched over, and told the Greys, "Six minutes to recovery! Only three Chippies heading in! Nine of us in each! Leave everything else! Power down the bots; we're not taking them! We'll come back for them later!"

"Major, they've got the latest classified Mod Five AI circuitry in them!" Tech-sergeant Lait complained.

"So we'll come back and get them later. Nobody is going to swipe them off *this* glacier today!"

"Forget I mentioned it, Major!"

"I can't wait to get warm again!" Captain Alexis Morgan remarked.

Curt sensed the morale of his troops had improved 105% in the last minute. No one wanted to stay on this glacier a minute longer than necessary. Now the evack airlift was on its way.

Worsham brought the three Chippewas in high at about 100 meters. Curt could see them, black holes against the gray overcast.

"I know I'm over you because I've got your beacons," came Worsham's voice in Curt's head. "I'd like some infrared as a cross-check."

"Okay, we'll give you a parachute flare, then a couple of ground flares and some smoke for wind detection," Curt replied.

"Screw the smoke! I can see the snow blowing! My guess is fifty to seventy knots right out of the north! Confirm?"

"You've got it!"

"Okay, this is going to be touchy as hell," Worsham's voice told them. "I'm going to send one Chippie down at a time. That way, if we bend one we don't run the risk of driving it into another one. Carson, I hate to tell you this, but we may not be able to get all the Chippies down in this crap!"

"Just do your best, Cal!"

"That's a given. Okay, Captain Bob Pond has volunteered to take the first Chippie down. Give us those air and ground flares now!"

A bright red parachute flare arced into the sky, popped its chute, and began to blow with the wind. But Worsham saw it. The Greys lit six ground flares and tossed them out on the glacier.

One Chippewa started to descend from hover. It Frisbeed and wobbled as it came down, fighting the strong, gusty wind off the glacier.

At that moment, a white-out hit. The horizon vanished in a blowing cloud of snow and ice particles. Even with his radar altimeter working, the loss of visual reference in such gusty conditions caused Captain Robert Pond to lose it. Flying an old helicopter or an aerodyne without outside visual references was always a tough job, even for trained instrument-rated pilots. When caught by surprise as Pond was, a pilot could easily lose his floor in an instant.

The Chippewa fell out of the sky. Pond pulled it up just short of the ice. The howling gale got under its lip and suddenly flipped it over. Pond made a visible attempt to stop the flip, but the Chippewa hit the ice and crumpled. As Curt and the Greys watched helplessly, pinned into near immobility by the wind and the white-out, they saw Pond blow off the cockpit canopy and an unsteady form crawl out. Pond wouldn't be in very good shape, having been yanked out of linkage with the Chippie on almost a moment's notice. But the man was apparently driven by sheer survival instinct because he got out of the Chippie before it blew apart as fuel hit the hot turbines.

"Hale! Williams! Get to that pilot as quickly as you can!" Curt called, then said to Worsham, "We'll get him okay, Cal. Are you still going to try?"

"Hell, yes! We won't leave you down there without trying everything!" was Worsham's reply.

Lieutenant Ned Phillips, flying the second Chippewa, watched and waited carefully, suddenly cut his power, and made a heart-stopping fall out of the sky, coming back into hover scant centimeters off the surface and letting the aerodyne slam down the final distance. The lip cargo doors opened.

"It's going to be a max gross lift-off," Worsham told Curt, "but Ned will try to get fourteen of you. Get over there!"

Alexis Morgan had taken the job of loadmaster and immediately herded thirteen Greys into the grounded Chippie.

The door closed. Over the howl of the wind, Curt heard the screaming whine of the turbines and watched the snow and ice billow up around the Chippewa.

It lifted into the air with the usually wobbling Frisbee motion of an aerodyne operating in a high wind.

Just at that moment, another white-out hit.

The loaded Chippewa vanished.

The sound of impact, tearing metal, and screaming turbines running out of control before they came apart…all assaulted Curt's ears over the roar of the glacial wind.

Chapter Thirty-Eight

It wasn't a hard crash. The Chippewa didn't have far to fall. And it was loaded, so it didn't blow around like the unloaded Chippie that had preceded it. But it was down permanently.

Before Curt and Alexis could react, the cargo doors blew off as Captain Ned Phillips activated the emergency egress systems, having seen what had happened to Captain Bob Pond's Chippie.

"Grey Head, this is Companion Head," came Lieutenant Jerry Allen's voice in Curt's tacomm. "Hey, we're okay! Shook up, but we're getting out!"

The Greys aboard the Chippewa were tired, but their discipline held. They didn't panic. They got out of the damaged Chippie quickly and in order as they'd been trained to do in Germany.

"Damn! And I thought we had it made getting out of here!" came the First Sergeant Edie Sampson's complaint.

The fourteen Greys who hadn't been in the Chippie now fought their way across the glacier against the wind to offer assistance if needed. But their comrades were only shaken and unhurt.

"Warhawk Leader, this is Grey Head," Curt called anxiously to Cal Worsham. "What are your intentions, Cal?" He was firmly convinced that the crash of two Chippies in these awful conditions would cause Worsham to abort his mission as well.

Curt was surprised when Worsham called back, "I've got plenty of fuel. I'm going to hover up here and burn some more of it off. I'll watch the weather. When I see it's clear to the north and no gusts coming, I'm going to drop it down there, load up, and git shit out of there. I want you to stand by, all the Greys. I want a fast load-up. I may not lift right away, but I want everyone aboard as fast as possible in case I get good lift conditions. But I won't lift until the conditions are right. You may not have much time to load, but you're pretty damned fast at that anyway. Or you were."

"We still are," Curt replied. "Cal, can you take twenty-seven people? In fact, make that twenty-nine with your two pilots."

"I don't know," Worsham admitted. "I'll try, if we can stuff everyone in."

"You'll be badly overloaded," Curt reminded him.

"So, this goddamned Chippie ought to do it in these low temperatures! I won't be any fucking tac assault 'dyne as performance goes, but I sure as hell ought to be able to get you all out of there! That's only about twenty-nine hundred kilograms…"

"Greys all, assemble on Grey Head!" Curt called on the tacomm. "We may have to move fast. Can the two pilots hack it?"

"They're both suffering from rapid delinkage," Biotech Sergeant Shelley Hale reported. "Disoriented, confused, denying reality. Williams and I have them in hand."

"Can you handle them along with the frostbite victims?"

"With some help, yes. But we've got lots of help," Williams pointed out.

The Greys were supporting one another as they usually did, whether in the field in combat or in the streets on R&R. Although they were primarily interested in saving themselves, they wouldn't refuse to help a fellow Grey.

The katabatic wind wasn't constant this morning. It was gusty. That had proved to be the undoing of the two initial Chippies. Cal Worsham knew it. He put his Chippie into hover, unwilling to make the same mistakes, waiting for a break between gusts, watching to make sure he wouldn't get caught in a white-out. He was in no rush.

He also knew that he was the last best hope of the Greys down below.

The Greys huddled together on the glacier.

Although the wind was still blowing hard, Worsham called to Curt,

"Okay, coming down! Stand by!"

"Still blowing here!" Curt warned as he saw the Chippewa start to drop out of the sky as Worsham brought its turbines back to high idle, killing the lift over its upper surfaces.

"Yeah, but by the time I get down there, the wind should drop. Look out because I may have to maneuver! Once I get on the ground, I'm okay. We can take our time waiting for the right conditions to lift again! Gotta toggle off! This is taking my full attention..."

It was a fantastic feat of flying. Curt wished it had been possible to videotape it. Cal Worsham knew exactly what he was doing and timed it precisely. As the Chippewa dropped out of the sky, the wind suddenly diminished and it became possible to see the rugged crags sticking up from the Cook Glacier to the west. Worsham compensated for the sudden drop in wind velocity, corrected his lift vectors, put the power to the turbines, and achieved enough blow lift to stabilize the Chippewa and set it gently on the ice.

As the cargo doors opened, the wind began to gust again.

Curt didn't lead in this situation. He was behind the Greys, making sure that they got aboard.

But as the Greys began to load the Chippewa, spots of snow and ice began to erupt around them.

Above the howl of the gale, they heard the snap of shock waves from bullets.

Then the reports of rifle fire reached them.

"Major! We're under fire!" came the cry from First Sergeant Edie Sampson.

Lieutenant Adonica Sweet and Regimental Sergeant Major Henry Kester had been urging others into the Chippewa. Along with Platoon Sergeant Tracy Dillon, who had turned at the sound of incoming, and Dyani Motega, who reacted immediately by taking cover and returning fire, Adonica and Kester spread out rapidly from the Chippie and began marching fire, shooting their *Novias* from the hip as they moved.

"Adonica! Henry!" Curt called verbally, forgetting that his voice wouldn't carry because of the wind noise and the turbine sounds. But his tacomm picked up the message and broadcast it. "Get back here! Mount up!"

"Major, it's a whole damned company!" was Sampson's report. "Can't identify them! They're coming in strength through the ice ridge! Get the hell out of here! I can make them keep their heads down until you do!"

"Edie's got help!" was the comment from Tracy Dillon.

"Curt, we've got them under fire!" reported Adonica Sweet. "Get that Chippie out of here!"

"Goddammit, all of you! Knock it off! Get the hell back here! We're not leaving anyone, firefight or not!" Curt yelled, although the tacomm transmitted it at normal levels.

"Make up your fucking minds! I'm taking hits and I hope to God one of them isn't a Golden BB!" Cal Worsham reported from the Chippewa. "Get aboard or be left!"

Curt saw that he wasn't about to get the five Greys back. They'd deployed into positions along the ice ridge.

"All Greys! Withdraw! Into the Chippie! Dammit, follow my orders!" Curt blasted into his tacomm.

"We can hold 'em!" was Edie's reply. "Get the Chippie out of here! Warhawk can come back and pick us up later!"

"I can't take many more hits! I'm outta here, Carson!" Worsham stated as the Chippewa's turbines began to spool up. "Ramp coming closed!"

The situation had temporarily gotten beyond Curt's control. It had happened fast. His people had reacted as they'd been trained: move, return fire, pin them down.

But they'd forgotten one important factor:

They no longer had the usual warbot fire support.

The warbots were out of action.

And Curt wasn't about to abandon them on the glacier. He turned his back on the Chippewa's gaping cargo door and started to make himself a poor target. "Go, Warhawk One! Get the hell out of here!" Curt told him.

The weather cooperated. The wind suddenly dropped. The badly overloaded aerodyne spooled up and broke ground, lifting slowly and ponderously. If there had been more wind, it might not have made it in those first few seconds of flight. But once airborne and in the atmospheric environment, Worsham rotated the Chippewa into the wind, tipped the craft down, and used the oncoming gust to produce some forward air-speed and additional lift.

In the covering white maelstrom of the Chippewa's lift, Curt zigged and zagged across the ice, trying to find cover. As he ran in a crouch, firing his Novia in single-fire semi-auto mode just to worry the enemy, he heard in his tacomm, "Grey Head, this is Frigid Head monitoring! What the hell is going on?"

"We've been ambushed by a company of troops firing on us with small arms!" Curt said between panting intakes of cold air that seared his throat in spite of the face mask. "Small arms fire. No warbots. Got four - no, five - people left here. They reacted by returning fire."

"Can you identify the enemy?"

"Negatory! Negatory! I'll try to get some ID when I can see them!"

"Can you hold them until we can get another Chippewa in to pick you up?"

"We'll do our damndest, General. But we could sure use some air support while we're waiting for Worsham to unload and come back!" Curt reported, trying to size up the situation, a difficult task since the world was ten shades of whitish gray out there.

"I've called for tacair from the Navy," Carlisle's voice told him. "Buell is hesitant…"

"Tell Jugs to get off her heinie and prove she's the hot pilot she thinks she is! It's time for her to stop mother-henning her pilots and aircraft and do something for a change!" Curt snapped, trying to find a target in the whitish gray ahead of him along the ridge.

A slight pause was ended when Carlisle replied, "Buell just left the CIC. She said to relay a message to you. She's personally going to lead the strike, so she says to tell you to keep your ass down so she doesn't shoot it off."

"How long before she gets here?"

"Twenty minutes! She's got to power up a flight and get it off..."

"General, we may not have twenty minutes!" Curt told him frankly. "Let me get some situational awareness here; then I can tell you what our chances are of holding out that long!" The Greys never surrendered, of course, but Curt had no illusions about how long they could hold out against a full company of regular infantry in these conditions. Six people were rather outnumbered and outgunned without warbot support.

"Adonica!" he called on the tacomm, "Where the hell are you and what's going on?"

Lieutenant Adonica Sweet had been the first one to react to the ambush. She had not hesitated to return the fire and put herself in a position that meant she'd be left when the Chippewa took off. She wasn't stupid. The regiment and its people were her Number One Priority. Although she was a stunningly beautiful young woman who seemed totally out of place on a battlefield, she had a family tradition of military service behind her and was also one hell of a fighter. She'd proved that on Trinidad when she'd served as their "native guide" and a field-breveted "third lieutenant." Her calm voice replied in Curt's tacomm, "Major, I can't see how many are out there, but from the quantity of incoming small-arms fire I'd estimate infantry company strength at least...about a hundred men minimum. Maybe more. But they're in this ice ridge, and that restricts their ability to maneuver."

Curt located her beacon on the tac display on his helmet visor. "Any ID on whose troops they are?"

"My guess is Chinese."

"Chinese?"

"Yes, sir! The small-arms fire sounds like seven-millimeter stuff from Chinese A-ninety-nine assault rifles."

"How do you know?"

"I've been in the pits marking targets when foreign technology officers demonstrated for us. Chinese ninety-nine has a definite muzzle bark, and its rounds warble because the ninety-nine doesn't have enough twist and the rounds sometimes tumble." Adonica Sweet knew small arms, and she had once demonstrated her expertise in the area.

In the back of Curt's mind, another piece dropped into the puzzle of the Kerguelen operation. It would make sense for the Chinese to have the satellite infection station.

But he couldn't worry about that right now. He noticed two beacons together where they shouldn't have been. "Okay, Adonica, coordinate our fire if you can. Henry, what the hell are you doing down by our tents?"

"Edie and I are jump starting some Hairy Foxes, Major," came the calm reply.

"Forget it! They're frozen!"

"No, sir, not if we pop the juice from enough power packs into them. We'll get 'em hot enough to shoot their fifties."

"Dammit, Henry, with their AI circuits possibly irrational, they're likely to fire on anything that moves…including us!" Curt objected.

"Negatory, Major," Edie Sampson replied. "We're also talking on another channel to Captain Pendleton. I took off my physical transmitter package and patched it into a Hairy Fox. Pendleton's monitoring the circuits in three of these Foxes by using a sort of primitive remote down link. He'll be able to advise us whether or not they'll be capable of shooting only on our command. Should be easy and simple. We're not going to ask them to move around, just to shoot where we tell them."

"Give us another minute, Major, and you'll get some light artillery support," Kester promised.

It was less than that. Apparently, the three Hairy Foxes could pick out the infrared targets that didn't correspond to the locator beacons of the four Greys out there - Curt, Adonica, Tracy Dillon, and Dyani Motega.

The *crump-crump-crump* of the 50-millimeters on the Hairy Foxes was music to Curt's ears.

A 50-millimeter round is a healthy piece of metal to hose downrange at high fire rates. The Hairy Foxes were launching AP rounds since the targets appeared to be grunt infantry. The air bursts were discernible even over the incessant noise of the wind.

The incoming suddenly ceased.

"What the hell?" was Edie Sampson's comment. "Why'd they stop firing on us?"

"We didn't hit 'em that hard," Henry remarked. "Major, this may be a break in the firefight. It gives us maybe a few minutes to organize and maneuver before the enemy does what he's setting up to do..."

"Adonica!" Curt snapped, realizing that Kester had voiced one reasonable scenario, one that might give the Greys time to do something more than return fire toward an unknown enemy. "Locate Tracy and Dyani! You're the maneuvering element! I'll coordinate with Henry and Edie to form a fire base for you. Find out where these enemy riflemen are, report to me, and prepare to flank 'em. Henry, suspend firing for the moment. Let's see if the cessation of incoming is significant."

"Yeah, it is, Major!" was Henry's reply. "I can now see someone in the open walking toward the old encampment here. He's got his rifle slung, and he's carrying a flag of truce. For some reason, the enemy wants to talk, but it can't be because we've whupped them. It don't make sense, Major!"

"It doesn't...which means we've got something confused or we've made some wrong guesses," Curt remarked. He knew what he was going to have to do, and it meant that he'd have to put his pink bod in the line of fire. He slung his *Novia*. "It's apparent the enemy wants to talk. So, I'm going to go talk with him...if I can. Henry, where is he with respect to your position? Anyone else see him, too?"

"Forty meters, bearing about zero-seven-fire from my position," was Kester's response.

"I've got him, too, Major!" was Adonica's input. "Range thirty meters, bearing one-one-zero. I've got him targeted! If you get shot at, I'll blow his shorts off!"

"Good! Cover me! Dillon! Dyani! Continue to move flankers and see if you can't get a better sit picture for me," Curt told his maneuvering unit. He needed better situational awareness. But he asked his helmet computer to run the triangulation and mark the target for him. He got a line of march on his visor display.

"Grey Head, this is Frigid Head. Tac strike is ready to launch. Do you want it now!" came General Carlisle's voice from the *McCain*.

"General, please hold them on the deck until we see what the hell is going on here!"

"Roger! We're monitoring you. Proceed."

Curt didn't have a scrap of white cloth to use as a truce flag. So, he kept his gloved hands in plain sight. Then he did what he really didn't like to do at all: He exposed himself to possible enemy fire.

The white-garbed form appeared in front of him when he got about 20 meters from it. Curt held his hands out to both sides and continued to walk. If the man was Chinese, Curt could talk to him; his language at West Point had been Chinese. But he hadn't used it since graduation, so he searched back through his memories, trying to put together the proper phrases.

When he got within five meters of the man, Curt took a chance that his face might freeze and pulled down his face mask to show his face.

"Nin haul Wo shr mei-gwo gung-min. Ni shwo ying-wen ma?" Curt addressed him, hoping that the proper inflections would be heard

over the noise of the wind.

The other man pulled down his face mask, too. Curt was surprised; the other wasn't Chinese. *"Zdrahvstvooy-tyeh! Yah rooskee! Gohvohreetyehlee vee poh-rooskee?"*

Chapter Thirty-Nine

Curt realized he was standing on the frigid Cook Glacier of Kerguelen Island face-to-face with a Soviet officer!

And probably the commander of a Spetsnaz battalion as well!

It made sense; the Soviet submarines had come inshore to the south. The Spetsnaz team could have made its way to this position during the night.

But were they here to reinforce the station? Or to assault it?

Curt wasn't fluent in Russian, but he knew a few phrases because the Army had taught its officers enough to allow them to handle some combat situations if the Big Red Tide ever broke through in Europe or Iran. So, he replied, *"Nyet! Yah amerhreekahnets. Gohvohreeyehlee vee poh-ahngleeskee?"*

"Dah! We soldiers of the Motherland are always prepared to meet with the hired minions of the capitalists!" the man replied in excellent colloquial American English. "I'm Major Dmitri Leonovitch Kurakin. And you might be?"

"Major Curt Carson. What the hell are you doing in Kerguelen, Major?" Curt asked bluntly.

Kurakin smiled. "Exactly what you are doing, Major. After all our *Chahssohvoy Krasneey* sputniks were the cosmic craft that were disabled."

"Then why the hell did you shoot at us?" Curt wanted to know.

"I am sorry. I offer my apologies. We believed your unit to be a patrol looking for us," the Russian explained. "I did not identify your aerodyne correctly. When your warbots began to fire upon us, I knew you were the American Third Robot Infantry Regiment of the Seventeenth Division which came here in the *McCain* from Muscat. We have no argument with Americans, Major Carson. Because we are both here on Kerguelen for the same reason, and because this matter is very secret in both our countries, we do not wish to harm Americans."

Curt didn't want to precipitate an international incident, either. And it was obvious that all the tight security precautions had peen of little use; the KGB and the GRU had both apparently found out about Operation Tempest Frigid…but probably at a very high level, not from observing the movements of the Washington Greys as they skittered here and there across the globe.

Curt also thought he knew why the Soviets were on Kerguelen, but he asked anyway: "I repeat my question, Major Kurakin. What are you doing on Kerguelen?"

"We are here to make certain that the job gets done thoroughly and completely," the Soviet officer replied candidly. "It is extremely important to continued world peace that this task be carried out thoroughly. When we learned that you Americans intended to eliminate the High Dragon stations on Kerguelen, my unit was assigned the task of making absolutely certain that it was done. I think you Americans have a saying, 'Always have Plan B.' There is also an old Russian saying, 'To make certain your pants do not fall down when dancing, wear both belt and braces.' "

"Yeah, we have the same old saying," Curt remarked. "Except we call it 'belt and suspenders.' The High Dragon station, eh? Whose is it?"

"*Zhong-hua ren-min gong-ho-kuo.* The People's Republic of China," the Soviet officer replied. "We have…problems with them for a long time."

"Yeah, you have," Curt agreed, knowing that the USSR and the PRC shared a long common border across Asia. He'd already figured out that the logical nation to have established such a satellite infection station had to be the PRC. And High Dragon was an obvious name for it. However, Curt pressed the Soviet by asking, "So why did you call this truce? What do you want?"

"It is nonsense to fight each other when we both came here to do the same job."

"Are you suggesting that we work together?" Curt asked.

"*Dah!* We must work together because we must work fast. The Chinese at High Dragon must have seen your aerodynes. We have no time to fight each other - and no good reason. We have little time to make our strategy for the assault on High Dragon."

"I don't know if the Chinese saw us. The weather's pretty bad for that," Curt pointed out. "I couldn't see you fifty meters away."

"Major Carson, do you want to take the chance that the Chinese did *not* see the aerodynes and do not know that we are here?"

"Okay, you have a point. And I agree with your assessment of the situation. If we've lost surprise, we're going to have to make it up in mobility, strength, and firepower," Curt remarked, pulling his face mask on again. "But I need to communicate with my superior officer about it. I'll call in my troops if you'll call in yours. Let's get everyone out of this cold wind while we talk about it."

Major Dmitri Leonovitch Kurakin understood perfectly - or thought that he did. Although he was a Spetsnaz battalion commander who was expected to operate independently, he had been educated and trained in the Soviet style of linear decision-downward command and control procedures. One *always* obtained the approval of superior officers before changing plans, even in a Spetsnaz unit. He also pulled his face mask on and replied, "I agree. But this is a nice spring day in Leningrad!"

"It might be for you, but we come from Arizona!" Curt reminded him.

"*Da!* Fort Who-a-chuck-oh! I know about Fort Who-a-chuck-oh!"

Major Curt Carson had never suspected that his military career would bring him face-to-face with a Soviet Spetsnaz officer in a situation where he had to laugh at the serious intensity of the Russian and his mispronunciation of a difficult Spanish word. "Greys all, this is Grey Head! Assemble on me!" Curt broadcast into his helmet tacomm as Major Dmitri Leonovitch Kurakin said something in rapid Russian into a portable comm unit.

"Curt, this is Frigid Head," came General Carlisle's voice in Curt's neurophonic pickups inside his helmet. He knew he couldn't be heard by the Soviet officer. "Talk with him. I'm holding the tac strike. I've got other problems at the moment, but we'll support you all the way from here."

Curt subvocalized his reply to Carlisle, knowing that Kurakin couldn't hear it. "If he wants us to fight alongside his Spetsnaz unit, I'm going to lose control when he discovers I've got only five other people, General!"

"You'll have the full Greys with you as quickly as I can get them there. I've got to get some things straightened out first. Stand by."

Curt didn't understand exactly what General Carlisle meant, but he wasn't in the CIC of the *McCain* at that moment.

Major General Jacob O. Carlisle was, and he found himself between two intense, adamant women officers who were disagreeing with one another. Carlisle was known for his carefully honed abilities as a negotiator and joint services commander in chief, a task he'd handled so well during the Bastaard Rebellion that it had earned him the Defense Distinguished Service Medal. However, being between two women officers was something new to him.

Even Captain Lew Joseph of the *McCain* stood there listening; he was trying to make sense out of the altercation so he could make the proper naval recommendation to Carlisle.

"General, we've unloaded all the personnel with injuries, frostbite, and exposure," Captain Alexis Morgan reported, then stated firmly, "The rest of the Washington Greys aren't getting out of Warhawk One until we're back on Cook Glacier!"

"General, Warhawk One won't power down, and I can't launch *any* naval strike aircraft until we get those Chippewas off the flight deck and back down on the hangar deck," snapped Commander Rebecca Buell. "I've got three patrol aircraft aloft at the moment, and I've got to recover them within the next thirty minutes before they go bingo fuel. And I can't launch the other patrol to keep track of that unknown submarine coming around the east side of the island! Or continue to track the Soviet submarines in Table Bay right now!"

"General, all we want is Warhawk One refueled while Harriet Dearborn of the supply unit hands some hot food up to us," Alexis broke in to explain.

"*Major Morgan!*" Buell admonished her, following Navy tradition of bucking an Army captain up one rank because there can be only one captain aboard a naval vessel. "I was speaking! Or is it commonplace in the Army to interrupt a superior officer?"

Lieutenant Kitsy Clinton was standing next to Alexis, and she shared the concern of the other company's commander. Bitterly, she put in, "In this case, maybe a captain and a first lieutenant equals a three-striper..."

Alexis Morgan looked at Buell and envied her spectacular figure even in its loose-fitting Navy flight gear. Alexis didn't even bother to respond, but she motioned for Kitsy to shut up, ignored Buell, and continued to address the general. "Sir, we had to leave six Greys on that glacier under fire from an unknown enemy of unknown strength and capabilities! They're still there! The Greys will *not* abandon their own, sir! We never have, and we never will!"

"Captain Morgan, Major Carson has made contact under a truce, and it's a Soviet Spetsnaz unit..." Carlisle told her quietly.

Alexis apparently didn't hear him, so preoccupied was she with the fact that her friends and comrades were still out there in that howling cold gale being shot at. "Sir, Warhawk Leader informs me that the squadron can lift in the rest of the Greys who didn't land yesterday now that the weather has improved marginally. That will give us a hell of a lot more manpower where we'll need it because the damned warbots froze up and are out of action. We can put in fresh troops and bots in addition to those of us who just came out of there. We can stomp those..." She paused, then exclaimed, "Oh, my God, *Soviets*! Did you say a Spetsnaz unit, General?"

"General, the Army won't be able to get in there with the Chippewas until we can mount an air strike first to sanitize the Sovs," Buell tried to point out. "The Chippewas will take ground fire and probably casualties and losses, as if they won't have enough to worry about trying to land in that wind with random white-outs! Tell this smart-mouth captain to shut up, get her troops out of that Chippewa, and clear the deck so the Navy can do its job! Right now, the *McCain* is sitting here almost blind with three Soviet submarines and an unknown in the vicinity, and three of my aircraft about to splash in the bargain! Captain Joseph, please help me out here!"

The wiry, dark-haired little four-striper with the intense blue eyes said nothing for a moment, looked at his Air Ops officer, and told her, "Becky, our primary mission is to land the Greys on Kerguelen and support them. So, fuel the Chippewas and get them out of here with the Greys aboard. Then recover your aircraft, launch their patrol replacements, and short-time the Hell Razors for possible strike."

"Captain, I'll have to recover the Chippewas at some point in that procedure," Buell advised him.

"The *McCain* has two flight decks, Commander," Joseph reminded her. "We're the biggest and newest SSCV in the fleet. We should be able to handle a simple air assault mission without risking the ship. So, we will handle the mission. Tom and Loretta will worry about the ship; you get the aircraft on and off as required, when required, and where required."

Rebecca Buell looked at her commanding officer, then at Alexis Morgan, who'd won this round. Jugs Buell had a strong, aggressive personality; with her established flying capabilities combined with her goal-oriented command experience, she always tried to get her own way when she believed she was right...and she never tried unless she knew she was right to begin with. Sometimes she discovered she was wrong, like now. She realized that the battle between the services was in a truce along with the war between the sexes. She had to perform. "Yes, sir," she said with a touch of edge still in her voice.

Joseph looked directly back at her and added brusquely, "Make it so, Commander."

"Yes, sir! May I be excused, sir? I have a lot of work to do." The edge disappeared from her voice. She also knew that she wasn't going to be able to take part in the air action, driving an A-40 Sky Devil over Kerguelen in the company of VA-174, the Hell Razors squadron; the launch and recovery of the necessary aircraft over the next few hours were going to require her full attention as Air Ops officer in the *McCain*...unless she *really* did an outstanding job. Which she decided she was going to do.

She decided she was going to make damned sure that every aircraft was launched and recovered properly, with no Chinese fire drill on the flight deck, hangar decks, or lifts. Her flight support people were good, and she knew she'd trained them well. Now they were going to have to perform miracles. But that's why she was Air Ops.

"Stick around, Becky," Joseph told her, deliberately not using her air call name. "Run Air Ops from here. This is going to be complex, and you'll need to be plugged in as the situation changes. And it's going to change, because we keep being handed little surprises when we least expect them."

Another one was handed to them at that moment.

"General Carlisle," came the synthesized voice of Georgie, the 17th Iron Fist Division's megacomputer in faraway Arizona. "Request for two-way from JCS."

"Go," Carlisle replied curtly.

It was audio-only, which told Carlisle that it was being set up in a hurry. "Jake, we just got your hourly sit-rep and heard the audio. The Chief doesn't want us to tangle with the Soviets. He wants to withdraw before we get in any deeper," came the voice of General Edward Carrington, CJCS.

Carlisle acted fast. He touched the squelch switch, turned to Captain Alexis Morgan, and told her with a quick motion of his arm, "Get the Greys back on Kerguelen...now! *Move!*"

Alexis didn't hesitate. She didn't know what her general was going to do, but she knew he'd cover her. With Colonel Bellamack injured and still in sick bay, and Major Curt Carson up there on the Cook Glacier, she knew she was the de facto officer in charge of those Greys now in the *McCain*, in spite of the fact that Captain Joan Ward had an earlier date of rank. She could work with Joan. And Joan Ward wasn't stupid; she'd pay attention to someone who'd been out there on Kerguelen overnight.

"General," Carlisle reported to his superior via audio comm, "two companies of the Greys are already on Cook Glacier, and we're engaged in sending in the other two companies that couldn't land yesterday. Major Carson is already working with his Soviet counterpart. We're planning to do the job together as Operation High Dragon."

"The President doesn't want to take the chance that this would cause an international incident," Carrington explained.

Carlisle knew that the commander in chief had acted quite characteristically and had gotten cold feet. "General, this was all worked out in the preliminary planning. One of the scenarios was an international incident, but it was afforded extremely low probability because it was determined that none of the participants would want to make an international issue of it."

"He's changed his mind."

Carlisle looked around the CIC at the faces of the men and women there, some of whom had put their lives on the line to get things this far. But they were considered expendable. Carlisle knew that his life was not the only thing that was possibly at stake; his career and reputation were also on the docket. If he withdrew from Kerguelen now with possible loss of life, *he* might be the one to take the flak if things ever came to a congressional investigation.

This was the sort of thing no one talked about at West Point, and no one taught it at the War College or the Command and Staff School. You had to learn it by watching others take it in the chops.

"General, I'll withdraw, but due to the nature of the situation I would like to have an official direct order in writing from the commander in chief himself."

"What! Why?"

"Sitting up on Cook Glacier are sixty-one of the latest warbots in the United States Army inventory," Major General Jacob O. Carlisle explained. "These warbots are fully operable; they're just frozen up because of the environment. They contain the latest Mod Five AI units. They contain auxiliary warbot linkage circuitry that can permit them to be operated by neuroelectronic linkage techniques. Therefore, they contain security-sensitive, classified, high-technology material. In my One-oh-one File is a personal security agreement which I've signed concerning the protection of classified material…"

"We all signed that sort of thing, Jake. What's causing you heartburn?"

"If I pulled out of Kerguelen now and left those undestroyed warbots out where a Soviet Spetsnaz unit could pick them up, someone very high up could nail me under Title Eighteen, U.S. Code, to say nothing of Title Fifty and all the mishmash of security acts and executive orders put on the books in the last hundred years," Carlisle reminded him. "If they were looking for a scapegoat, that is. And they might be if Operation Tempest. Frigid ever leaks…which it sure as hell could."

"I'll cover you, Jake."

"I'm sure you will, General. But who's covering you?" Carlisle wanted to know. "Look, I don't want to get my tit in a wringer…or my ass in a sling, either, for that matter. But you might want to get back to Sixteen-hundred Pennsylvania and ask a simple series of questions. First of all, do we want to let the Sovs get their hands on our warbot technology after we abandon it on Cook Glacier? Secondly, do we want to give them the High Dragon station with whatever computer virus technology is there? We've got a quiet situation with the Sovs right now but consider what their acquisition of unknown-to-us computer virus technology will do for them and to us."

There was a moment of silence on the other end, which was the Outer Ring of the Pentagon. Then the chairman of the joint chiefs replied, "Jake, thank you for bringing those matters to my attention. I'm going to wake The Man and tell him. But I also want to tell him what you're going to do about it."

"I'm implementing Operation High Dragon," Carlisle told him. "I'm sending the Washington Greys into the Chinese station with the Soviet Spetsnaz unit. Together with the Soviets, we'll take prisoners and destroy High Dragon, making damned sure the Sovs don't get anything. While we're doing that, we'll either bust those sixty-one warbots or recover them. Then we'll all go quietly home."

"Maybe. Maybe not," Carrington added somberly. "We've identified that unknown submarine approaching Kerguelen. It's the *Tang*, a PRC Dynasty Class attack submarine."

Chapter Forty

If General Carlisle was solving his problems, Major Curt Carson wasn't.

About ninety men came out of the ice ridge and gathered behind Major Dmitri Leonovitch Kurakin. Some were obviously Russians who looked little different from Americans. But Curt could see from the faces of the others that the majority of that Spetsnaz unit was made up of round-faced men with the typical epicanthic eye-fold of Mongols, men who lived and survived in the coldest part of the world. He also knew that the Russians were the officers and head NCOs, people who could keep the brutal Mongolian tribesmen under control because they were not adverse to using methods of discipline so brutal that they'd been outlawed in the American Army after the Civil War. This Spetsnaz battalion was a bunch of tough sons of bitches, Curt realized. Anyone who could make a night march up a glacier in this weather was one rugged bastard as far as he was concerned.

Only Regimental Sergeant Major Henry Kester and First Sergeant Edie Sampson joined him when he sounded recall and assembly.

"Sweet, where the hell are you? And where's Dillon and Motega?" Curt subvocalized into his tacomm circuitry so that the Soviet major couldn't hear him.

"Major, how many Russkies are down there?" Adonica Sweet's voice replied.

"About ninety."

"That Russkie major left about twenty-five men up here in the ice ridge," she reported. "We've got them spotted, and all three of us are in excellent positions to bring them under fire if they try something stupid."

Goddamned Russkies never trust anyone! And they're obsessed with power! Curt reminded himself. "Adonica, you stay where you are with Dillon and Motega. I'll keep my tacomm channel open. However, you can talk back to me on Channel Oscar Bravo. You're doing fine. Just keep on doing it."

"Yessir. I thought you might want us to stay up here JIC."

"You okay?"

"Roger, sir. Cold, but we're out of the wind. That helps."

The Soviet major tapped Curt on the shoulder, led him behind an outcrop of ice and out of the wind, and asked, "Major, where is the rest of your regiment?"

"The same place the rest of your battalion is, Major," Curt told him bluntly. "My people are up in the ice ridge with yours, and we've got your people targeted. And my troops will stay there until you bring your men down here, too."

Kurakin smiled. "I have stationed pickets to guard against a possible Chinese assault. Are these two people your only troops, Major?"

Curt shook his head and told him, "Of course not! I've left the majority of my soldiers up in the ice ridge to watch yours. And we're not the entire regiment, only a guard detail. We stayed on the glacier last night as an outpost. We'll be joined by the main body of my regiment in less than ten minutes." God, *I hope Carlisle can get those Chippies off soon!* he told himself. They were literally sitting ducks here, facing 115 Soviet Spetsnaz troops, all armed, all fresh, all inured to cold weather, and led by a Soviet officer who was the epitome of the Russian mindset.

But Curt had to cover...fast. And he had to take control of the situation and hold control, in spite of the fact that he was presently outnumbered ten to one.

So he tried to take charge. "Major Kurakin, when the Washington Greys show up in their aerodynes, it will be a dead giveaway to the Chinese. So, we must move fast once they're here. Now, we're only about thirty-seven hundred meters from High Dragon. Because of the rugged nature of this glacier, we won't be able to move our heavy-fire warbots much once they're down. We lost a couple of them in hidden crevasses yesterday. So, I'm going to have them put down here to provide a long-range fire base for us."

"Ah, yes! Your Mark Forty-four Hairy Fox warbots! You are right. Pity we don't have mortars with us; mortars are outstanding light battalion artillery pieces! But the fifty-millimeter weapons on your warbots will be able to serve as mortars by firing at high angles over the ridge and into the High Dragon area," Kurakin said, nodding. "Do you intend to have your Mark Sixty Mary Anns precede you in the assault according to doctrine?"

The remark told Curt that Kurakin had read or been briefed on the initial Sierra Charlie warbot assault doctrine developed by the staff stooges at the War College. It also told him that Kurakin wasn't aware of the current doctrine, developed by the Grey's in Namibia and hones in the battles of Bisbee and Douglas, which was far more flexible, allowing Sierra Charlies to move ahead of the Mary Anns when conditions warranted. It also permitted humans and warbots to move together in mutual support when advantageous. Kurakin did understand, however, that the Hairy Foxes were intended to hold the enemy with fire while the Sierra Charlies and Mary Anns moved to the best assault positions.

So, Curt took a chance and stated, "With our Hairy Foxes as the fire base, we need to coordinate your Spetsnaz troops with my Sierra Charlie forces and their Mary Ann light fire warbots...unless you brought warbots with you..."

Kurakin hesitated, then admitted, "We did not plan for an airborne assault. So, we brought no warbots on this mission. Our intelligence told us that the Chinese have no warbots at High Dragon. And we had to move quickly across the glacier. Our warbots are far heavier, larger, and more powerful than yours. They would only slow us down."

Curt cut through the fractured logic which Kurakin tried to use so he wouldn't have to admit that (a) the Soviets had no submarine air capability and (b) the Soviet warbots were typical of all Soviet designs copied from the West, being larger and with lower performance. "That confirms our own intelligence, which reported you had no warbots on this mission." It was a flat-out lie, but Curt wanted to put the Soviet major a bit off guard and perhaps convince the man to be a little less paranoid...although fear was an integral part of Soviet life, especially in the KGB and GRU, whichever organization was the parent of this Spetsnaz battalion.

"My unit is well equipped to carry out the assault on High Dragon. We have made a careful study of the operation. Therefore, the best plan is for your warbot regiment to provide the heavy fire support for my unit," Kurakin stated bluntly.

Curt shook his head and attempted to reach a reasonable compromise. "No, Major. Our two units should go into High Dragon together...because we're not going to flatten it like Warsaw or Berlin before we take it. My orders are to occupy the station, take its occupants alive, then destroy the facility. What do your orders say, Major?"

"My orders are nearly the same," the Soviet replied firmly. "I am to take whatever measures are necessary to eliminate this treacherous threat to the Motherland and restore our ability to conduct our peaceful space program. However, I am not required to take prisoners because we have no facilities for properly handling them or repatriating them to China."

Curt knew from that statement that Kurakin's orders told him to assault and destroy High Dragon with as much brutal terror as possible so that the Chinese, when they discovered what had been done, would be reluctant to do such a thing again. Curt could read that into Kurakin's response because he knew that the Soviets employed subterfuge and hyperbole. They used "slippery" words that had one meaning for western listeners and a totally different meaning for their own use. They had a standard operational code in which certain words and phrases had actual meanings other than the obvious or implied ones. The Soviets would *never* reveal *anything* that might suggest or imply that they were inferior or vulnerable in *any* area. Curt knew that Major Dmitri Leonovitch Kurakin suffered from a cultural massive inferiority complex, and he treated Kurakin accordingly.

And hoped it was the right thing to do.

But Major Kurakin was having none of any compromise with the Americans. He had a career to think about and a deputy commander for political affairs quietly watching in the background. "My unit will assault High Dragon. Your regiment will provide the necessary fire support," Kurakin repeated.

"Grey Head, this is Warhawk Leader," came the sound in Curt's helmet tacomm. "We're less than five minutes out. How's the weather there?"

"Major Kurakin, excuse me, please," Curt remarked to the Soviet officer. "I have an incoming communication, and our system is thought-activated."

"Yes, I know something about it," Kurakin lied. He knew very little about the American neuroelectronic tacomm communications system. He was bluffing. The status of a frequency-hopping neuroelectronic tacomm communications system in the Soviet Union was bogged down in a political conflict that went on far above him, and the Soviet system of security was such that Kurakin would never hear of it. Two separate OKBs had produced developmental units copied from American tacomms picked up by KGB agents from among the battle debris in Namibia. But apparently the Ministry of Automation and Control Systems was in a turf battle with the Ministry of Communications Equipment about who should be responsible for production.

"Warhawk Leader, this is Grey Head," Curt thought into his tacomm in reply to Worsham. "The weather seems to be improving. It's gone from god awful to miserable. But the wind is down, and the snow has stopped."

"Yeah, that low-pressure area has moved," Worsham confirmed. "Barometer is on its way up. You'll have much better weather for the assault."

"I hope so. About time we got some support from higher authority. Warhawk, we're ready for you," Curt fired back. "But sneak in below line of sight behind the ice ridge. We need all the surprise we can get…"

"Grey Head, this is Frigid Head," Carlisle suddenly put in. "Be advised that the real Grey Head is coming in on Warhawk One."

"The colonel? Orgasmic!" Curt exclaimed, then added, "Will he be taking over command of this operation?"

"Affirmative! The colonel will assume command of Operation High Dragon," Carlisle replied.

"Yes, sir. Is the colonel in condition to command Operation High Dragon?"

"He's in a temporary neck brace, a precautionary measure," Carlisle reported. "He suffered a mild concussion, but Major Gydesen cleared him for duty this morning. At his very strong insistence, I might add." The general paused for a moment, then added, "I know that a change of command in mid-operation is risky, but I did it for a reason. Colonel Bellamack speaks fluent Russian and knows how to deal with that Spetsnaz major."

"Yes, sir! I understand, sir! No heartburn here!" was Curt's relieved reply. He felt at somewhat of a disadvantage trying to work with Kurakin. Although the two men were both the same rank, as if that might make any difference, Kurakin commanded more men and spoke Curt's language; Curt didn't speak Russian and therefore couldn't know what Kurakin was saying to his troops. Furthermore, Curt was having trouble trying to get inside the Soviet officer's head; thus far, he hadn't been successful and Kurakin hadn't budged an inch on Operation High Dragon. "Is the colonel on the net?"

"I'll get him on now, but I wanted to talk to you first, Major," Carlisle admitted. "Colonel Bellamack can't use a tacomm helmet; the neck brace won't permit it. He's using a hand-held unit. So, without his tac visor display, you're going to be his eyes and ears."

"Roger, General!"

"Grey Head, this is Frigid Head. You are patched into the High Dragon Net now and Companion Leader is online."

"Companion Leader, this is Grey Head," came Wild Bill Bellamack's voice. "We're on our way in! Do you have an assault plan, Curt?"

"Yes, Colonel, and welcome back!" Curt messaged. "I've got a plan, but the Russkie won't buy it. I want our Hairy Foxes to form a fire base at our present position where we camped last night. Then we can send the Sierra Charlies and the Spetsnaz troops across the glacier under fire cover from the Hairy Foxes and the immediate light fire support of the Mary Anns."

"I'll handle the Russkie when I get there. Figure that he'll go along with us. So, plan your ground assault. And figure that you'll be behind a Navy tac air strike. Buell has the Hell Razors airborne," Bellamack advised him.

"Colonel, have the Navy tac air people provide a diversion for us," Curt suddenly snapped. "They shouldn't clobber High Dragon; we want to get in there and make sure to bust it up so the Russkies don't get their hands on it. But tell the Hell Razors to stick around and strafe any Chinese troops they see on the glacier and heading our way. I need a little more time to organize the assault. The Sovs are a bit obstinate..."

"Roger, I agree with your recommendations, Companion Leader. And I'll ask the Hell Razors to flat-hat your position as well. That will give the Russkies something to put in the samovar and stew about." Bellamack knew the profound psychological effect of a squadron of A-40 Sky Devils booming overhead...but just barely overhead. It would lift the spirits of the Greys and maybe dampen the stubborn paranoia of the Soviets, who *always* respected strength and the obvious intent to use it. "And stall that Russkie major for a few more minutes. Grey Head out!"

"Excuse me, Major, but I was talking to my regimental airlift people," Curt said aloud to Kurakin. "Our aircraft are in the vicinity and some of them are about to land. Please inform your troops to hold their fire."

It was a show of force that even Major Dmitri Leonovitch Kurakin had to admit to himself was impressive.

Eight Chippewas suddenly appeared from the west, flying less than 30 meters above the Cook Glacier in line abreast. Their downwash kicked up so much snow and ice that line abreast was the only formation that was useful. In addition, the sudden and simultaneous appearance of eight huge aerodynes was impressive.

They settled to the ice just shy of the ridge. As their cargo doors gaped and the ramps came down, more than sixty warbots - Mary Anns, Hairy Foxes, and Jeeps - quickly moved out. They were followed by the Washington Greys, more than seventy people garbed in white arctic gear and armed with Novia assault rifles and Hornet submachine guns.

Curt realized that the Headquarters and Service companies had come along in accordance with the growing tradition in the Washington Greys that *everyone* fought when necessary.

Major Dmitri Leonovitch Kurakin watched impassively, but he was inwardly impressed. So were his other officers. His Spetsnaz troops were awed. They'd seen and participated in massive Soviet war games, but not even the huge *Lyetoh Grohm* – "Summer Thunder" - maneuvers in the Caucasus had been this intense on a regimental level.

Colonel Wild Bill Bellamack walked up, guided to Curt by his tactical beacon. Curt saluted and greeted him, "Good morning, Colonel!"

Bellamack couldn't return the salute because he had his left arm in a sling and was easily carrying a Novia assault rifle in his right. He looked pale, but his eyes were sharp and blazing. The bulk of a neck brace could be seen behind the fur border of his parka hood around his face. "Good morning, Curt! You don't look the worse for wear having stayed here all night!"

"I wish to hell I felt as good as you think I look, Colonel!" Curt admitted. "May I present Major Dmitri Leonovitch Kurakin?"

The colonel nodded when Kurakin saluted.

"A pleasure to meet you, Colonel," Kurakin said plainly.

"Dohbrohyeh ootroh, Mahyor Dmitri Leonovitch! Mohyoh eemyah

Polkovneek William Bellamack! Yah ohchehn rahd pohznahkohmeetsah!" Bellamack fired back in fluent Russian.

This took Kurakin by surprise. Very few Russians expect Americans to speak their language. It was also a signal to Kurakin; Bellamack was telling him, in essence, "I know your language, so I know how you think. And you can't use any slippery English language terms on me."

Kurakin replied in Russian, and a rapid-fire dialogue began.

Curt understood nothing that was being said, but it was evident that Kurakin was being stubborn. Bellamack didn't hesitate, however, even when the conversation appeared to become heated. Curt hoped that his colonel could really shoot that *Novia* with one arm. It had gotten to the point where Kurakin was saying many sentences with *"nyet"* in them when the skies crashed down on them.

A flight of four A-40 Sky Devil VTOL jet attack aircraft slammed overhead not ten meters above them, hitting their afterburners for the additional power needed to clear the ice ridge to the east. Twelve more A-40s followed, spread out in attack formation over about a kilometer's front. They pulled up to the vertical over the ice ridge, climbed rapidly to about 500 meters, then rolled into their attack dive aimed at the High Dragon station. The heavy ordnance on hard points under their wings was plainly evident.

Kurakin said something in quieter tones to Bellamack.

Bellamack replied briefly and then turned to tell Curt in English, "Major Carson, organize the regiment according to the assault plan for Operation High Dragon. Assume that Major Kurakin's unit will participate. And don't worry; I'll work things out with Major Kurakin here. Count on it! I'll give you the details on tacomm. Move out immediately while we can take advantage of this tactical air strike surprise."

Bellamack was smiling slightly. But Kurakin wasn't.

Chapter Forty-One

Major Curt Carson's first action was to ask his helmet tactical computer to locate Lieutenant Jerry Allen's beacon, which it did and displayed range and bearing from Curt's present position. "Companion Bravo, this is Companion Leader," he called. "Assemble the Companions. I'm on my way to you. Greys all, this is Companion Leader. Stand by for a field briefing on Operation High Dragon in five minutes!"

"Roger, Companion Leader. This is, Companion Bravo, and I see your beacon on my display. I'll have the Companions assemble, sir."

Visibility was occasionally down to 50 meters in the snow and ice crystals that continued to blow over the Cook Glacier, but the katabatic winds this morning weren't as bad as yesterday's gale. As Curt trudged across the ice, he called up the status of the Washington Greys and watched while the data scrolled on his helmet visor tac display, superimposed over the range and bearing coordinates to Allen's beacon.

He had thirty-nine combat troopers available, all armed with Novias and trained for personal combat. Of those, twenty-seven had spent the night on Cook Glacier. If they were as exhausted as Curt, he knew they might be off their prime in combat today. But he had to take that chance. He was shorthanded in the combat area, although he had forty support troops from the Headquarters and Support companies; these people were not combat trained and were mostly technicians, staffers, and supply people who were armed only with the 7.62-millimeter Hornet submachine carbine. He'd have to use them as a mobile reserve.

And he'd have to use the Sierra Charlies as the primary assault forces of the Greys because the warbot complement was significantly reduced. He had only thirty-nine active warbots - sixteen Mary Anns, eighteen Hairy Foxes, and five Jeeps - as well as six immobile Hairy Foxes that had been hot-wired and jump-started by Kester and Sampson that morning. He wasn't sure he wanted to trust the Hairy Foxes on the glacier; they were heavy enough to break through the ice into crevasses. So were the Mary Anns, but he'd take a chance with them because he needed *some* mobile warbot fire support. He wanted to emplace the Hairy Foxes as a heavy fire base and send the Mary Anns behind the Sierra Charlies as direct light fire support. The perfect place for the Jeeps would be among the Sierra Charlies.

And he was counting on the 115 Spetsnaz soldiers, highly trained assault warriors who were inured to this numbing, tiring cold.

Even at that, Curt felt the High Dragon assault would be seriously under-forced. He didn't know how many Chinese were in High Dragon.

"Georgie," he queried the megacomputer through his tacomm link to the *McCain*, "show me the TO&E of a regular company of the Chinese people's Volunteer Army."

It took about four seconds for the signal to make the round-trip to Arizona. Then Georgie flashed on Curt's visor display the data he wanted. The normal Chinese company was 116 officers and men, about the same size as the Soviet Spetsnaz unit. This made sense, since the two armies had common roots back in the early twentieth century, and the Chinese had picked up a lot of military science from the Soviets before the Great Schism.

Curt figured that they'd be arrayed against at least one company of guards plus maybe a hundred or so technicians. From what he remembered of the Aerospace Force pictures; High Dragon wasn't big enough to support more than about 200 men. Even at that, High Dragon would have a logistics problem: keeping those men fed in a place where everything had to be brought in. The Chinese had some Antarctic base experience which would serve them well for High Dragon.

So the manpower situation was about even.

But the Chinese at High Dragon enjoyed the multi-fold benefits of a defensive position, a factor which Clausewitz had pointed out was a much stronger position.

Curt knew he'd have to depend upon the unique capabilities of each of his force elements.

The warbots would be useful in providing a fire base as well as light fire in the assault. The fifties on the Hairy Foxes and the twenty-fives on the Mary Anns would be critical. The Jeeps with their light 7.62mm automatic weapons might be useful if the Chinese counterattacked with the sort of human-wave tactics previously used in Korea, which was the last time American soldiers had come up against Chinese forces.

The Soviet Spetsnaz battalion could provide the initial shock troops in the van of the assault.

And he'd use the Sierra Charlies as the follow-on force behind the Soviets.

The Grey support troops would be a reserve.

This meant splitting the regimental units. It was something the Greys hadn't tried before. Breaking up combat companies and combining like-function platoons might create confusion. However, Curt knew the Greys had taut discipline and good leadership; he'd count on those factors to hold the Greys together in the assault.

When he reached Jerry Allen's position, he'd worked out in his mind the tactical organization of the High Dragon assault. If the Soviets wouldn't go along with it, it could still be brought off, albeit not with the same degree of shock and numbers.

"Well, Major, we made it back," Jerry exclaimed.

"Yeah, but we had to lean on the Navy a little bit," Kitsy Clinton added. "I was there in the CIC. Blood on the consoles…"

"Tell me about it later," Curt remarked. "We've got a job to do, and not much time to put the pieces together before we start. Where's Dillon and Motega?"

"I called them in," Jerry reported. "That was two minutes ago. Their tacomms must have crapped out in the cold. Or my receive circuitry could be cold and thus lost some of its sensitivity. I haven't received a confirmation from them yet."

"Damn!" Curt growled and keyed his company tacomm frequency because he knew his unit was still operational. "Sergeant Dillon! This is Companion Leader! Do you read?"

Dillon's voice came back with very low power; the signal kept dropping into the squelch and was therefore noisy. "Companion Leader, this is Dillon! Couldn't raise you! Dyani and me are with Lieutenant Sweet! We're going to scout the High Dragon facility!"

"Like hell you are! Sweet! Ferret Bravo! Are you on freak? Do you read?" Curt snapped irritably.

"Roger, Companion Leader, this is Ferret Bravo!" came Adonica Sweet's voice. "Major, the weather on the east side of the ridge is worse than where you are. Blowing snow and ice. Visibility occasionally down to less than ten meters. Looked to me like an excellent opportunity to get a scouting party over the High Dragon, using the periods of poor visibility as cover. It was only about three thousand meters..."

"Ferret Leader, this is Companion Leader," Curt called Sweet's company commander on the regimental net.

"Companion Leader, this is Ferret Leader," came Captain Russ Frazier's voice. "You got a line to Ferret Bravo?"

"Roger that! Your sweet little looie is on her way to High Dragon to scope it out," Curt reported.

"Ferret Bravo, this is Ferret Leader!"

"Ferret Bravo here! Go ahead, Ferret Leader!"

"Sweet, get your ass back here! Who authorized you to go out on a scouting patrol?" Russ Frazier wanted to know.

"Captain, you weren't on the ground yet, and I saw an opportunity," Adonica Sweet explained. "So, I used the sort of personal initiative we're encouraged to show. Dillon and Motega are both natural-born scouts, so I moved out."

"Get back here before you're spotted!"

"Captain, we won't be spotted. Not this patrol! Anyway, we're on the ice ridge on the northwest side of the mountain, and High Dragon is only about five hundred, meters away! As long as we're here, let us snoop around a little bit, sir. The colonel and the major need to have some idea what we'll be up against during the assault."

"Curt, I think we ought to let them carry on," Frazier admitted.

"Yeah, so do I, but let's inform Grey Head so we don't get crossways with one another. If Sweet and her patrol stay there, they could be in a beaten zone when the Hairy Foxes open up," Curt pointed out. "Grey Head, Companion Leader here. We've got a problem...I think."

"Give me a sit-rep, Companion Leader," Bellamack replied.

Curt did. "I think we should let Sweet carry on. Maybe we'll get some intelligence data. God knows it would be helpful to know how many troops we're likely to encounter at High Dragon."

"Agreed. Proceed. Do. you have an assault plan worked out yet?"

"Affirmative," Curt told him and quickly outlined it verbally. "I think we can probably pull it off without the Soviets, but it would be neat to put that Spetsnaz outfit in front because they're the sort of crazies that make such a frontal assault work against a defensive position like High Dragon."

"Very well, you can count on the Spetsnaz battalion to do what you want," Bellamack told him. "I concluded a little agreement with Major Kurakin. He insists on leading the assault anyway. So, we'll let him."

"Nice work, Colonel! How'd you twist his arm?" Curt wanted to know. It was a great relief to him that Bellamack had managed to negotiate with Kurakin; Curt didn't relish the idea of having 115 Soviet Spetsnaz troops around and not cooperating in the assault on High Dragon. Now the potential thorn in the side had been directed against a common objective.

"I'll tell you about it when this over. One just has to understand how the Soviet military forces operate and what really motivates them...and few Americans know anything about it," Bellamack replied briefly. "Major Kurakin is with me. I'll relay your tactical plan to him. Brief the regiment and let me know when you want the Sovs to move forward."

"Roger, Grey Head!" Curt snapped, then called the regiment. "Greys all, this is Companion Leader speaking for Grey Head! Listen up! Here comes the assault plan. Company commanders report readiness to receive!"

"Warrior Leader ready!" was the reply from Captain Joan Ward.

"Marauder Leader ready!" Captain Alexis Morgan reported in.

"Ferret Leader hot to trot!" Captain Russ Frazier said.

"Headquarters Leader here!" was the comment from Major Wade Hampton.

"Service Company, go!" snapped Major Fred Benteen.

"Okay, I want all your troops to listen because I've got to break up ordinary company integrity for this assault," Curt told them. "Our discipline will allow it to work, but everyone must know who their immediate boss is and what everyone is going to do. So record this!

"The Soviet Spetsnaz battalion will lead the assault from this position directly across Cook Glacier to High Dragon. We will follow the Sovs. They want to be Heroes of the Soviet Union, so we'll let 'em take the incoming first. Better that than have them working independently out there like a loose cannon.

"Alpha platoons report to me. I will command all Alpha platoons without their Mary Anns but with all available Jeeps. We will be Assault Prime Team, and our call will be Assault Prime.

"All Mary Anns and suitable operators will report to Captain Joan Ward, who will lead Assault Backup Team. The Mary Anns of Assault Backup will follow Assault Prime. Assault Backup will provide light fire support on the move for Assault Prime and Spetsnaz.

"Bravo platoons report to your assault commanding officer, Captain Alexis Morgan. Bring your Hairy Foxes. Move to the north end of this ice ridge and prepare to act as heavy fire support for Spetsnaz and Assault Prime. Call is Assault Base. The six immobile Hairy Foxes on the west side of the ridge will be part of Assault Base. But I don't anticipate that Assault Base will be required to become mobile during the assault...at least, not with the instability of the glacier ice as a factor.

"Headquarters and Service companies will combine to form Assault Reserve under the command of Captain Russ Frazier. You will move to the east side of the ice ridge and be prepared to move quickly where needed. However, the primary function of Assault Reserve will be to move and interdict any Chinese troops that attempt to withdraw down the glacier from High Dragon.

"Any questions?"

"Might have some later...along with some bitches," Russ Frazier remarked with some bitterness in his voice. He felt he was being left out of the action, but Curt had deliberately placed him in command of the reserve component because of the man's history of aggressive behavior in the regiment as a result of being a platoon leader in the bloodthirsty Kelly's Killers, which had been disbanded when casualties and losses destroyed the company's integrity as a fighting unit.

"This is Grey Head," the voice of Colonel Bellamack broke in. "I need to advise you of the rules of engagement which have just been hammered out with the Soviets...and it wasn't easy. So, listen and follow what I'm telling you. We are to capture the High Dragon garrison, not kill them. Therefore, fire only when fired upon, and shoot to suppress Chinese fire. This does not prevent you from taking whatever defensive measures are necessary to protect your life and that of those around you. Secondly, we are to occupy High Dragon with minimum damage and to hold it until the intelligence officers from the *McCain* and the *Smirnov* have an opportunity to document the equipment in the station. Then we are to demolish the station with the Soviets. The Chinese prisoners will be split between our units for repatriation. Any questions?"

It was very straightforward. But Curt knew there would always be questions and changes once things got started.

"Very well, Greys move out! Stand by for the assault!" was Bellamack's final word.

"Assault Prime, this is Assault Prime Leader! Assemble on me!" Curt announced on tacomm as he punched the enhancement signal for his locator beacon.

A minute later, he was surrounded by thirteen peopled, all armed with *Novias* and heavily clothed in body armor and arctic gear.

He checked the regimental status. Some Sierra Charlies were required to run the Hairy Foxes and Mary Anns, so fourteen people were all that Assault Prime could have. As far as he was concerned, it wasn't enough. He was glad that Assault Prime was following the Spetsnaz battalion. About the best that Assault Prime could do was mop up and ensure that Kurakin and his troops followed the rules of engagement.

It wasn't going to be easy.

And, as usual, it wouldn't go according to plan.

"Grey Head, this is Ferret Bravo!" came the call from Adonica Sweet. "Colonel, Dyani and I are right next to High Dragon, and Sergeant Dillon is on the ridge alongside ready to step out on the roof. Honest to God, the place is deserted! No one's here! High Dragon has been abandoned!"

Chapter Forty-Two

"Captain, the Chinese submarine has cleared Pointe de Penmarc'h. Its present course will take it to the southern end of Table Bay," Lieutenant Commander Loretta Ara relayed the information of her ASW officer to Captain Lewis Joseph of the *McCain*.

"Any destination yet?" Joseph wanted to know as he studied the displays which showed the *McCain* only three kilometers off the rugged west coast of Kerguelen in Baie Bretonne and the three Soviet submarines lying quietly in Table Bay on the southwestern side of the island.

"The latest estimate from Farragut is Table Bay, sir," Ara replied briefly, watching the bit stream into the *McCain's* master computer, nicknamed Farragut.

"Inform me as soon as the data get solid, Commander."

"Aye, sir!"

"General, what do you make of the overall situation?" Joseph asked Major General Jacob Carlisle, who was sitting alongside him in CIC.

"The Soviets have confirmed that the infection station is Chinese," Carlisle mused. "That confirms NIA guesses."

"Naval intelligence reported that days ago," Joseph remarked.

"I wish to hell you could get Naval Intelligence to talk to the NIA and DIA spooks, Lew," Carlisle observed.

"It's not a matter of talking, General. It's a matter of listening," the naval captain told him. "'Thou has eyes but cannot see...' And so forth."

"Yes, there does appear to be a bit of turf protection going on there. Has been for many years," Carlisle recalled. "At any rate, I suspect *T'ang* is headed for anchorage in Tobie Bay. With three Soviet boats in there at the moment, the situation could get very sporty."

"Agreed," Joseph nodded. "*T'ang* is sounding, which means she'll be heard by the Sovs if she hasn't been detected already. The Sovs, by the way, are lying passive. Not even turning a screw."

"Any guesses on your part, Lew? I realize I'm throwing your question back at you, but you're the naval expert here."

"On the basis of what Bellamack reported of his conversation with the Soviet Major Kurakin," Captain Joseph surmised, "my guess is that the Soviets are likely to let *T'ang* into Table Bay where they can sink her."

"Spurlos versenkt?"

Joseph nodded. "Kurakin was going to flatten High Dragon. Chances are that the Soviets will let *T'ang* get to within point-blank range, put a couple of torpedoes into her, and let her go to the bottom of Table Bay. That's a deep fjord-about a hundred fathoms. No one will ever bother to look for her there, especially since the Chinese have minimal submarine salvage capability."

Major General Jacob Carlisle thought quietly about this for a moment. He was already in deep trouble. He'd given the go-ahead for Operation Tempest Frigid and, when the Soviets became involved, had ordained cooperation and a change to Operation High Dragon which wasn't authorized at all. In fact, JCS had given him the equivalent of a direct order to call the whole thing off, and Carlisle had had the audacity to question an order from the commander in chief, pointing out the potential security risks in pulling out. General Ed Carrington, chairman of JCS, hadn't gotten back to Carlisle yet, which told Carlisle that the President hadn't been awakened with the news, or that the President was waffling and trying to figure out what to do. In the meantime, Carlisle hadn't delayed Operation High Dragon. He had his career on the line.

But he was also fearful that a direct confrontation between armed forces of the United States, the Soviet Union, and the People's Republic of China on Kerguelen could escalate into something a lot bigger and more deadly.

More than a few regiments of army forces were involved.

The U.S. Navy had five submarines in the area, including the huge *McCain*.

The Soviet Union had three submarines lying in Table Bay.

The Chinese now had a submarine heading for possible destruction in Table Bay.

Thus far, the United States had the only air capability around Kerguelen.

And Kerguelen was ostensibly French. The three dozen French scientists stationed at Port-aux-Francaise hadn't even known of the military and naval activities on and around their island. But France could get very difficult if she ever found out what was going on. And the French politicians and diplomats could become very tiresome indeed under circumstances where it might appear that their national honor had been challenged or questioned.

Carlisle decided that he'd have to put his career and stars even further out on the line if he were to stop a potential conflict before it started.

What was the remark of George Jacques Danton? *"De l'audace, et encore l'audace, et toujours de l'audace!"*

Or the once-famous motto of the British Special Air Service Regiment: "Who dares wins!"

Well, he felt audacious and daring. If his career went toes-up as a result, it had been a good career. He'd commanded soldiers in combat. He'd been among the first warbot brainies. He'd played nursemaid to the new Sierra Charlie doctrine that put human beings back onto the battlefield alongside warbots. He'd commanded the Washington Greys and the 17th Iron Fist Division. He'd basically been supreme allied commander during the Namibian Operation Diamond Skeleton when the French commander got his knickers ripped in Windhoek. It had been three decades, and he'd done a lot and seen a lot. If this was the end of it, brought about by his own conviction that he was giving his best shot at averting a more general conflict...Well, he had no complaints. Each officer during his career - provided he was any sort of a leader at all - always came up against a critical decision that had to be made between a career and doing something that was right for the country he served. Jacob Carlisle thought he'd done this several times already, but he realized that this was probably the big one. He was operating contrary to presidential orders.

"Lew, can you communicate with either the Soviet or the Chinese submarines?" he asked the *McCain's* captain.

"Yes, we have an emergency underwater sonar-type voice communications system," Joseph admitted. "Hardly ever used, but we've got it."

"Do you ever monitor it?"

Joseph nodded. "Yes and no. It's not necessary to monitor. The signal is so strong that it twangs the hull. You know damned good and well when anyone within a hundred kilometers activates the system with a call." He paused, then went on, "It's been unofficially used a couple of times in the past when two boats threatened to get into a furball and they decided to talk to one another before one of them got sent to the bottom…"

"Okay, Lew. You're the naval officer in command of Task Force Tango Foxtrot. Here's what I want you to do," Carlisle said. "Then I want you to tell me if it's too risky or if it ought to be done differently…and why."

"Critique will cost you nothing, but it's likely to be worth just that!"

"Fair enough! But I'll make it worth something…like a bottle of Scotch."

"Bribery may get you anything. But on the other hand…what's your plan, General?"

"Move three of your attack submarines into Table Bay behind the *T'ang* so that you bottle up the bay."

"So the Sovs can't get out?"

"Right!"

"They won't like it."

"Yes, but they won't shoot, not with a Chinese submarine in there, too," Carlisle pointed out. "Blockade Table Bay. Broadcast to the four submarines the locations and identities of all of them. Tell the Chinese that their High Dragon garrison will be leaving the island and that we'd prefer they take their own people back to Zhanziang. Otherwise, it could make a rather bad scene internationally, especially if it became widely known that they'd effectively destroyed at least three Soviet surveillance satellites. And tell the Soviets that we wouldn't want them to leave Kerguelen without taking their Spetsnaz battalion with them, especially since our land forces are working together on this rescue mission to 'save' the garrison at High Dragon..."

"Save the garrison at High Dragon? General, that's really stretching it," Joseph told the general officer with a broad smile. "But I like it. Yes, I like it a great deal! It lets the Chinese get out of a sticky situation while saving face...and that's important to an Oriental. It blunts the possible savagery of the Soviets...and they can get nasty because it's built into their culture. And it makes us out as the good guys because we could wipe them all out with a superior naval force plus air superiority...but we won't because we don't want to embarrass anyone else in this unfortunate incident. Lovely!"

"Orgasmic is the term we'd use," Carlisle reminded him of the Army slang term.

"I'd also put an air umbrella over Tobie Bay while I was at it," Joseph suggested, "with one of our new ECM aircraft with enough power to burn the hell out of any tracking or guidance radar they try to lay on any of our planes. I think Jugs would love that! When she gets through flat-hatting High Dragon that is..."

"Uh, Lew, before we go charging off here, all enthralled with our military and naval brilliance," Carlisle cautioned, "tell me what might go wrong and cause the whole thing to turn into a sheep screw..."

"If you mean what I think you mean," Joseph replied thoughtfully, "we always face the possibility that some junior officer or rating is going to panic and shoot...or do something equally stupid.

Commanding officers, no. At the risk of sounding elitist, let me say that the Soviets and the Chinese select their high-ranking officers very carefully, much more so than we do, to ensure that they can think straight and won't take unnecessary risks. Furthermore, unlike the United States Navy, the Soviets and Chinese use hostages."

"Hostages? What do you mean?"

"What's the old joke about our federal government? There are so many federal laws that everyone is sure to break at least one of them in a career," Captain Lew Joseph pointed out. "If someone were really out to nail our hides to the wall, chances are they could probably find some little incident from our past to use. In the case of the Soviets and Chinese - all Communist regimes, by the way, because they all use this procedure - an officer doesn't get to be an officer unless the Party has something to hold over his head that will either send him to the gulags or the firing squad. So, officers serve at the pleasure of the Party. On top of that, officers who command submarines or special forces units that operate in such a way that the commanders could easily defect...well, the Party keeps the officer's family back home as hostage to properly patriotic behavior." He paused, then added, "So, no, I don't think they'll do anything rash. Especially if we give them a palatable and easy way out."

"Can we tolerate a subordinate breaking discipline?" Carlisle asked.

Joseph nodded. "I think so. In fact, we'll have to. We'll have to be lenient, although that may be perceived as a weakness. However, when they see our five boats and our aircraft and your regiment, they won't perceive us as being weak, especially when they see that we've used that strength quite carefully...but we've used it!"

"Frigid Head, this is Grey Head!" came the tacomm call from Colonel Bill Bellamack.

"Go ahead, Grey Head," Carlisle responded.

"Frigid Head, Grey Head has a scout patrol out, and they've just reported that High Dragon has been abandoned! Repeat, no personnel are currently in High Dragon!"

"Where did they go?" Carlisle wondered aloud.

"Were they ever here?" Joseph asked.

"Hell, yes! Otherwise, why would the Chinese send *T'ang* down here into the jaws of both American and Soviet naval forces?" Carlisle said.

"General, I hope to hell you can figure that one out, because at the moment I can't!" Joseph admitted. "But that certainly calls to question the real purpose of *T'ang* entering Table Bay! Frankly, I don't know what the hell the Chinese are up to! Still want me to block Table Bay?"

Carlisle was silent for a minute while he turned the possibilities over in his mind. The Chinese were being inscrutable as usual. He wasn't absolutely certain now that his blockade plan was as feasible as it had seemed a few minutes before.

But, on the other hand, it was a plan. It wasn't set in concrete, and it could be changed if developments warranted. It was preferable - at least to Major General Jacob Carlisle - to sitting quietly underwater off the west coast of Kerguelen and possibly allowing a general war to start as a result of doing nothing when he could be doing something, even if it might turn out to be the wrong thing to do at first. It could be changed.

He looked at Captain Lewis Joseph and firmly said, "Carry out the blockade plan, Captain Joseph. Make it so!"

Chapter Forty-Three

"Abandoned? Ferret Bravo, are you sure?" Colonel Bill Bellamack called over the tacomm.

"I'm leaving Sergeant Dillon on lookout," Lieutenant Adonica Sweet replied to her regimental commander. "Dyani and I will try to get inside for a look."

"Can you see any indications outside - footprints in the snow, for example - that would indicate when they might have left?"

"No, sir. Nothing. But we'll be careful! Dillon's an old Montana boy; he's got eyes like an eagle! And Dyani is something else when it comes to military operations like this!" Adonica replied, failing to note that she'd exhibited similar qualities as a fine scout during the Trinidad operation.

"Dammit, Adonica, be careful!" It was Lieutenant Jerry Allen who broke in on the net.

Bellamack let it pass, but Curt almost broke in to reprimand Allen, then realized that precombat anxiety was making him irritable. Instead, Bellamack called, "Greys all, this is Grey Head! Proceed with Operation High Dragon under the assumption that Chinese personnel may still be in High Dragon. Let's move out!" Then he said much the same sort of thing to Major Kurakin in Russian.

"Assault Prime, this is Prime Leader!" Curt called to his contingent. "Kitsy, do you have the Spetsnaz troopers in sight?"

"Roger, Prime Leader!"

"Okay, when they move, we'll follow them!"

"I'll bet they don't like the idea of Americans dogging their heels," Kitsy Clinton commented.

"Hell, Lieutenant, the damned Soviets are used to having someone dogging their heels all the time," First Sergeant Edie Sampson commented.

"Yeah, but at least we're not going to shoot them in the back if they do something we don't like…"

"Knock it off!" Curt snapped. "And don't even think crap like that! Move it! Move in single file through the pass in the ice ridge, then spread out as skirmishers on the other side. Assault Breaker, are you ready to follow with the Mary Anns?"

"Breaker is with you and has you on displays," sang out Captain Joan Ward.

Curt felt confident with Captain Joan Ward backing him up. She was as dependable as the sunrise. And she didn't spook or panic. Many people thought Joan Ward was an unemotional person; Curt knew otherwise and also knew that her emotions were very predictable indeed.

The going was difficult as they made their way through the jagged defile of the ice ridge, following the Soviet Spetsnaz soldiers, who were, as Curt noticed, indeed carrying what appeared to be Chinese A- 99 assault carbines. Why they were doing this, he didn't know, because the A-99, as Adonica had pointed out earlier, was a lousy assault weapon because it didn't put enough spin on its bullets.

"Assault Breaker, you'd better be prepared to man-handle some of your Mary Anns," Curt called to Joan Ward. "Some places in the ice ridge here will be difficult for the Mary Anns to negotiate all by themselves."

"We'll kick 'em in the ass, Curt," Joan assured him. "And we've got plenty of M-three grenades in case we have to blast a little ice out of the way. So, don't get antsy if you hear some explosions in your minus-x."

"Just let me know when you're going to pop a grenade," Curt requested.

They got through without incident, and Curt decided to string out Assault Prime to keep the Spetsnaz comrades in sight while at the same time standing by at the ice ridge in case Joan needed help with the Mary Anns. But she didn't, although her people blew off a few grenades to take care of defiles too narrow to get the assault warbots through.

"Okay, Assault Prime, we've got to shag ass to keep the Spetsnaz in sight and close our interval!" Curt told his troops as they began to move forward. The wind was stronger here, and blowing snow occasionally caused a momentary white-out, making it difficult to see the Soviet soldiers advancing across the glacier ahead of them.

He saw in his helmet visor tac display that Assault Prime had managed to move out into line of skirmishers about 5 meters apart, following the Soviets by about 50 meters. Behind, he could see the beacons of Assault Breaker with their line of sixteen Mary Anns interrupted by the five humans controlling them.

"Assault Base is in position!" was the call from Alexis Morgan. "We have our Hairy Foxes in line and their fifties are targeted on High Dragon! Don't worry, Adonica! We won't shoot!"

"Damned well better not, Captain! Grey Head, this is Ferret Bravo! Dyani and I are inside right now. And no one is here! But they left only a short time ago. Lights are on. Heat is up. Equipment is on and functioning. Even cups of lukewarm tea on a few tables."

Curt didn't like the sound of that.

Neither did Bill Bellamack, who snapped, "Ferret Bravo, get the hell out of there ASAP! Now! Move! Get into the ridge well behind and take cover! We may have to open fire on High Dragon at any time!"

"Yes, sir! Moving, sir! I've read Mao's little red book, too!"

And Mao's work had been inspired by Sun Tzu.

"All warfare is based on deception."

"Therefore, when capable, feign incapacity; when active, inactivity."

"Attack where he is unprepared; sally out when he does not expect you."

"Assault Prime and Assault Breaker, this is Assault Prime Leader!" Curt suddenly broadcast to the Grey units spread out on Cook Glacier behind the Spetsnaz unit. "Shift attention and sensor scans to the left flank! Scan in the infrared for human signatures! Shift formation to echelon, southernmost units forward, northernmost units hold back. I want a northwest-southeast line of foragers so we can't possibly be flanked!"

"Assault Prime Leader, let me have a sit-rep, please," Bellamack requested on the tacomm. "In short, what the hell's got you spooked out there?"

"Grey Head, this is Assault Prime Leader!" Curt replied at once. "I suspect we may be attacked in the open here by the Chinese force that left High Dragon a short time ago. They couldn't have gone very far. A weird maneuver like that is consistent with their basic military thinking. I recommend that all units be on the alert for a flanking attack from the north over higher ground. Pass the word to Kurakin to watch in minus-y. And see if the Hell Razors can have a look to our left flank."

"Roger! Kurakin says that he agrees! He was taught the ways that the Chinese fight battles," Bellamack replied.

In between gusts of wind and the white veil of blowing snow, Curt kept glancing at both the gray, cloud-covered skies above and the distant, dim high horizon of the dome of the Cook Glacier to the north. He could see nothing on the glacier, but he was relieved when he spotted the black dots of A-40 Sky Devils as they popped out of the clouds to the north and began slow, loitering flight as they scanned.

Assault Prime moved with surprising speed and agility into an echelon line of skirmishers.

They'd moved about 1,000 meters from the ice ridge out across the glacier when the call came, "Grey Head, Hell Razor Leader here! We have multiple infrared targets that just popped up on the glacier north of you. They appear to be moving south and southwest."

"Roger, Hell Razor Leader, would you drop down, have a look, and blow their shorts off, please?" Bellamack replied. "Assault Prime and Assault Breaker, be alert for an assault from your left flank, from the north. Assault Base, some of those targets may be moving in your direction."

"Understand, Grey Head!" Alexis Morgan's cool voice replied. "Request that Assault Reserve be moved north to back us up."

"Sounds like a two-pronged assault, one against our flank, the other an attempt to get in behind us at the north end of the ice ridge," Joan Ward assessed.

"Roger, roger! My Hairy Foxes have picked up i-r targets on their long-range scanners!" Now Alexis's voice had a ring of excitement in it. "We will target them with AP scatter rounds when they get well in range! Give 'em a 'whiff of grape,' as the saying goes. We'll also try to screw up their i-r sensors with hot flare rounds!"

"Assault Breaker, this is Assault Prime! Joan, I suggest you get your Mary Anns scanning north for targets with human i-r signatures!" Curt told his backup.

"Roger, and the Mary Anns are loading airburst shrapnel rounds! And ready to project i-r diversionary flares, too!"

"Don't fire until you see the whites of their eyes…"

"What the hell, Curt, everything around here is white!"

"Roger that! Assault Prime, be ready!"

When it happened, the Greys and the Spetsnaz were prepared for it. But it still started with great suddenness and violence.

"Assault Base, commence firing!" was the quick remark from Alexis Morgan.

At almost the same instant, Curt heard Joan Ward call out, "Mary Anns have spotted targets with human i-r signatures, range four hundred meters, bearing zero-zero-five through zero-one-seven! Closing rate three klicks!"

Curt heard four snapping pops as Chinese 7.62mm A-99 rounds went into the ice in front of him, targeted short. He saw the targets Joan Ward's warbots had picked up; they were projected on his helmet visor display.

"Assault Prime, this is Assault Prime Leader! Multiple targets, human i-r signatures, range four-zero-zero, bearing zero-one-seven.

Targets are displayed on your visors. Move to the left flank, close on them, deploy decoy flares, and commence firing when your Novia sees a target! Any target!"

Pairs of A-40 Sky Devils came out of the leaden skies, and their Navy pilots, men and women, picked their targets by multifold sensors, then laid heavy ordnance and columns of spent uranium slugs on them. The incredible maelstrom of noise, fire, explosions, and death of a coordinated air assault was enough to dull the enthusiasm of even the most highly motivated troops. It wasn't often the Hell Razors had such definite targets, and they pressed down on them hard.

Then the strangest firefight Curt Carson had ever been in got started in earnest.

He never saw a target on visual during the entire battle.

Curt reached up to his shoulder and pulled the lanyard on one of the flare projectors. Two tubes belched fire and four dully glowing flares up over his shoulder and out in front and to the sides of him, where they landed on the snow and radiated a signature that closely approximated that of a human being. If the Chinese had i-r scopes on their A-99s, the flares would certainly give them multiple targets to shoot at, most of which were not Curt.

Then he brought his *Novia* assault rifle to his shoulder and tried to snuggle it into his arctic gear so he could get a good view of the infrared display on its spotting and targeting scope. He never really got a good target because the Chinese were apparently as well clothed as the Greys and therefore offered a minimum of heat differential between themselves and their background, which is what the i-r scopes detected. Thus, he had only a few fleeting, smudgy images. He put the cross hairs on one, got a laser range finder confirmation, and squeezed off a three-round burst. Then, without bothering to see if he had a hit, he swung to the left and pinned the reticle on another i-r smudge.

Over the ever-present sound of the wind, he could hear the muffled reports of the Hairy Foxes, the multiple blasts of the twenty-fives on the Mary Anns immediately to the west of him, and the sporadic popping of *Novias* from his Assault Prime troops. Dully glowing i-r decoy flares created an eerie pattern on the blinding white ice. Occasionally, one jumped in the air as a Chinese round hit it. Better a flare than a trooper…

Something was happening on Curt's right, but he couldn't take time from identifying targets and firing to find out what was going on. In his *Novia's* scope, he began to see new smudges moving in from the right. At that point, Bellamack called, "Assault Prime, this is Grey Head! Spetsnaz is moving in from your right! Kurakin's men are flanking the Chinese! Swing your cone of fire to the left!"

"Okay, that's who the hell those images are!" Curt muttered in between hosing lead downrange in carefully targeted bursts. The targets might be smudgy, but they had no competition at 300 yards' range, where a *Novia* round could do a lot of damage and the 7.62-millimeter A-99 round just started to go ass over teakettle and lose its accuracy and effectiveness. The Chinese A-99 was, literally, a Chinese copy of the earlier M26A1 Hornet submachine carbine, which, in turn, had been a rip-off of the WestArm "Stinger." Curt was again pleased that his Companions had selected such a fine personal weapon for the Sierra Charlies because the *Novia* was proving its worth again as it outshot the Chinese A-99.

The Spetsnaz troops apparently didn't give a damn about the accuracy of their Soviet A-99s, which were either direct copies of the Chinese weapon or captured arms. From what Curt learned on the tac display plus what the later battle reports said, the Spetsnaz men used their A-99s as bullet hoses, spraying lead into the Chinese without careful targeting. Of course, they had to close with the Chinese to do this but close they did. The Soviets didn't care about accuracy or bullet stability, either; they wanted to kill, and the unstable A-99 round did just that because when it hit, it tumbled and left a very nasty wound. Even when it hit soft body armor, it delivered a massive blow which wouldn't penetrate because of its low velocity but which hurt like hell and could put an armored soldier out of action. But the Chinese from High Dragon didn't have soft body armor.

As a result, when Curt moved forward, he passed many bodies

lying on the ice of the Cook Glacier. In a few instances, he kicked an A-99 out of reach because he didn't know whether the Chinese soldier was dead or merely wounded. There was no question about some. The biotechs were going to be very busy out here.

He was totally surprised when one of those prone bodies suddenly stood up in front on him and raised both hands in the air.

Curt found himself looking into the face of a very terrified, very young Chinese boy who was telling him, "I surrender! I surrender! Don't shoot!"

Fortunately, Curt understood Chinese.

"Grey Head, we're beginning to get surrendering Chinese troops out here!" he reported to Bellamack.

"Take them! Stop shooting if you can! If my display is correct, the Chinese have taken more than fifty percent casualties at this time," the colonel replied. "Kurakin's troops are still shooting! I'm having a hell of a time getting him to take prisoners..."

"I've got an idea about that!" Curt remarked, suddenly realizing that he could take an old trick of the Mongol hordes and turn it against the Chinese.

He spoke to his Chinese prisoner. Since Chinese doesn't transliterate well into English, the conversation can be summarized as follows:

Curt told his prisoner to turn around and march north with Curt behind him. He told the Chinese soldier to call for surrender.

The Chinese gladly did this. He was scared, very scared; and ready to do almost anything he was told. Raised in a culture that doesn't encourage a lot of initiative - although Chinese do show a lot of initiative and outstanding brilliance in an entrepreneurial environment – the Chinese captive yelled at the top of his lungs as he marched with his hands in the air over his head.

He was soon joined by two more, then five. Within a minute, Curt was marching into the enemy formation behind nine disarmed Chinese prisoners with their hands in the air.

Curt was also shouting in Chinese, demanding surrender.

The firing from the Chinese attackers died out. More and more of them joined his prisoners.

Then something hit Curt hard from the right.

Chapter Forty-Four

It hurt like hell.

It felt like someone had hit him several times in the right side and right thigh.

"Goddammit, I'm hit!" Curt yelled. He thought he'd screamed only to himself. But his scream was both mental and vocal.

He knew right away that he'd taken several nearly simultaneous rounds from one or more rapid-fire automatic weapons.

The only automatic weapons around him were the *Novias* of the Washington Greys and the A-99s of both the Soviets and the Chinese. He knew the Greys wouldn't have hit him that many times; their detection and targeting gear would have recognized his locator beacon, and he'd taught them to hit their targets with either a single round or a three-round burst. So, the rapid impacts had to have come from either Soviet or Chinese A-99s.

He knew he hadn't been penetrated. He knew that his soft body armor would stop 7.62mm low-velocity A-99 rounds. The closely woven filaments of semi-crystalline Krisfltx polymer that covered his body were incredibly strong, and, where extra protection was needed, the stronger-than-steel fabric was double- or triple-layered.

But not, he realized, on the sides of his body where he was least likely to take a round.

But penetrated or not, he'd been hit many times. And, God, it hurt!

In spite of the growing pain in his side and leg, Curt stumbled forward, calling to his Chinese prisoners to march and tell their comrades to surrender, too.

Something drove him to overcome the all-encompassing pain.

He didn't know how long he could hold out against it, but he knew that if he fell on this icy battlefield he might never rise again. Or at least that's what went through his mind as he grew ever more confused and apprehensive from the trauma.

Three Spetsnaz soldiers came up on his right. One of them called out, "Major Carson! We did not recognize you! Did we hit you?" It was Major Dmitri Leonovitch Kurakin.

"Damn right you did!" Curt called back. He remembered that Soviet battlefield biotechnology wasn't just primitive, it was almost nonexistent. Front-line troops and assault troops left their casualties where they lay so that perhaps they'd be found by rear-echelon biotechs before they died of their injuries or wounds. So, he didn't even call for help from this Soviet officer. Instead, he snapped, "Cease firing! We've damned near wiped out this Chinese assault team! You're shooting into our troops now! So, knock it off, Goddammit!"

But Kurakin acted differently than Curt anticipated. "Let us dispatch these prisoners, and we will take you to your biotechs!"

Curt's mind was working strangely. As if he were watching a slow-motion video, he saw them raise their A-99s and point them toward his Chinese prisoners. So, he turned toward Kurakin, leveled his *Novia* from his painful right hip, and pointed the muzzle toward the Soviet officer. "No way! These men have surrendered! You shoot them, and I shoot you!" The pain was about to get the better of him, but he swayed and managed to maintain his aim.

Somehow from somewhere he was joined by others carrying *Novias* and one form wearing the white tabard with the red cross blazoned on it.

"We'll take over, sir," came the calm voice of Lieutenant Kitsy Clinton. "Major Kurakin, we'll take charge of the prisoners, sir."

"Major Carson, lie down!" came a feminine voice in his ear. "This is Sergeant Hale! You may have internal injuries!"

"What…? How…?" Curt tried to ask, but he was beginning to have difficulty forming sentences.

"Lie down, sir! Captain Pendleton on the *McCain* has been monitoring your neurophysiological condition and reported to Grey

Head that you just took multiple hits. Do you hurt? And where?"

"Didn't penetrate my body armor," Curt insisted.

"You still have internal injuries and a bone bruise in your right leg," Hale insisted. "Lie down, please, before you go into shock."

"On this fucking glacier? Hell, no! FIDO, dammit!"

"You're not going to drive on to anywhere right now," Hale informed him.

Curt was swept suddenly with a wave of nausea.

He managed to tear away his face mask before he deposited what was left of his meager breakfast on the glacier.

The world was white, white everywhere, and he couldn't determine which way was up. Then he realized he was lying on the ice.

But he could hear perfectly well what was going on around him, and he heard and understood with perfect clarity the tacomm traffic that was coming through his helmet. It was as if he wasn't really there but was a disembodied bystander.

And the pain in his gut and leg had disappeared.

His belly felt cold, and he realized that Shelley Hale had opened his parka.

"Relax, Major, you're in good hands now," her voice told him. "The pain should be gone. I just plugged one of Captain Pendleton's kludges into your biostatus transmitter. It's a biocontrol receiver that multiplexes into your bioharness and allows the captain and Major Gydesen to exercise a little control over your nervous system. Something the captain grew in his own kitchen as a result of what happened to Colonel Bellamack and the rest."

He found he couldn't reply.

But he did hear, "Assault Base, we've stopped the Chinks! Nice work, Assault Reserve! Hey, Russ, your people did an orgasmic job of laying down fire for me! Can you get out there and secure those who surrendered?"

"Roger, Alexis, we"re moving out now. Any casualties?"

"Negatory. Only a few rounds hit the Hairy Foxes, but no Golden BBs! How you?"

"In spite of the fact that no one in Assault Reserve was wearing body armor, we took no casualties! I think that's because the Chinese didn't know what hit them when they started taking Hornet fire as well as bursts from your fifties!"

"Assault Prime, this is Grey Head! Move along with the Soviets and occupy High Dragon!" There was no mistaking the command voice of Colonel Bill Bellamack.

"High Dragon, this is Assault Prime," Kitsy Clinton's voice said. "Roger, sir. We're moving! Ferret Bravo, have you investigated High Dragon again?"

"Roger! Still empty. But we'll tum up the stove and start brewing some fresh tea…"

"Assault Prime, how's Carson?" It was Bellamack's anxious voice again.

"Grey Head, Shelley Hale has him under neuroelectronic therapy," Kitsy Clinton said.

Great! That's nice to know! Curt told himself.

"Grey Head, this is Frigid Head. The intelligence team is on its way in. How about the Soviets? Are they ready?"

"Frigid Head, this is Grey Head. I've told Kurakin to get his GRU or KGB experts up here right away. If they don't shag ass, it won't be our fault if they don't get to see everything in High Dragon."

"Assault Base, this is Assault Breaker! We need to get our warbots rounded up and accounted for! And then picked up! Can we count on Sergeant Kester for that?"

"Assault Breaker, this is Grey Head! Make sure we have *all* the warbots accounted for!"

"Grey Head, this is Frigid Head. When you get into High Dragon, every Spetsnaz. type must be accompanied by a Grey…and vice-versa. And I'm not sure you should allow any of your ladies into High Dragon alone with those Mongoloid apes in the Spetsnaz battalion."

"I'm not worried, Frigid head! The ladies of the Washington Greys can take care of themselves! They led three of the units involved in today's assault on High Dragon, and they were the ones who blunted the Chinese counterattack! I don't worry about them in any situation, General!"

And neither do I, Curt thought, remembering the altercation on the narrow street in Rudesheim...and others as well.

His time sense began to elude him. He wasn't certain at this point how much time had passed since he'd been hit. He only knew that he no longer hurt.

And he knew that he was in the care of one of the ladies of the Washington Greys...and that the others were out there finishing up a dirty but important little job that was going to shine in the annals of the regiment from now on.

I'll be all right, he told himself, and the ladies will do the job perfectly well without me at this point.

So, he relaxed and let the world go away.

Chapter Forty-Five

The Arizona sunset blazed away through the multiple panes of the window and backlit drapes that could be drawn to keep the sunlight out. But Curt didn't want the sunlight kept out: After the dull gray skies of Germany and Kerguelen, he almost worshiped the sun-light again. Arizona sunsets were always worth far more than the price of admission.

And he was ready to get out of the Raymond W. Bliss Army hospital at Fort Huachuca and join the Washington Greys again.

True, he'd enjoyed more than a week of rest and relaxation after surgery in the *McCain* and airlift directly back to "Wachook," as the Greys were now calling their home base, especially after Major Dmitri Leonovitch Kurakin had had so much trouble pronouncing it correctly.

The healing surgical incisions in his belly had immobilized him for several days while accelerated healing was enhanced by neuroelectronic stimulus. He would bear no scars; none of the six rounds from various Soviet 7.62mm A-99s which had hit him had penetrated his body armor. The incisions came from exploratory surgery by Major Ruth Gydesen and her best thoracic and abdominal surgeon, Captain Larry McHenry. Curt had suffered multiple subdural hematomas as a result of his armor and body absorbing the bullet impact energy. The surgery revealed no ruptured internal organs. Thanks to the quick thinking of Biotech Sergeant Shelley Hale, who had immediately applied ice to those portions of Curt's body where subdural hematomas had immediately appeared, Gydesen and her surgeons didn't have to evacuate any clots. Curt had one bone bruise low on his right thigh where an A-99 slug's impact on his leg armor had created a hemorrhage beneath the periosteum of his femur...and that still hurt.

His comrades had visited him almost constantly since the

Washington Greys had returned. Unfortunately, neuroelectronic nerve blocks for pain elimination and accelerated healing had also made Curt lethargic and inactive, so he knew he wasn't exactly the life of the party when Alexis, Kitsy, Edie, or any of his Companions dropped by.

Colonel Bill Bellamack visited daily and slowly brought Curt up to date on what had happened after the Soviets shot him. The regimental commander was also the recipient of Curt's bitching and sniveling about getting out of the hospital. Because of their mutual respect and friendship, Bellamack moderated Curt's desire to terminate this forced inactivity and backed up Major Ruth Gydesen's orders keeping Curt in a rest condition while his body recovered from the shock of both cold and wounds.

"Look," Bellamack told Curt as the sunset light streamed through the window, "bring this sniveling to a halt! Follow Gydesen's orders! Otherwise, I'll lower the boom on you like I clobbered Kurakin out on the glacier before our assault."

"I knew at the time you'd managed to get Kurakin's number," Curt replied, "but how the hell did you 'lower the boom' on a Soviet Spetsnaz officer, Colonel?"

"Easy. The Soviets live in a culture of fear and power over people. The Party and the KGB exercise some of that power by their control of information," the colonel said, then suddenly asked, "What does a computer do?"

"Processes information."

"Give that man a medal! The Soviets have computers, but they use them differently than we do," the colonel went on. "The Party and the KGB have never allowed ordinary Soviet citizens to possess personal computers because that would allow Ivan to communicate and to process information independently of the Party apparatus. Thus, a computer is an instrument of Party power. And because Soviet citizens have very little experience with computers, they view computers the same way that most Americans did back when personal computers began to become available in the States - as being almost magical beyond comprehension."

"Hell, I still consider computers and AI and the rest to be cosmic magic," Curt admitted.

"Yeah, but we grew up with that cosmic magic around us," Bellamack observed. "We're not intimidated by robots and computers; they're just tools. But the paranoid Russian mind really fears an instrument of power they don't understand when it's in the hands of someone else. Kurakin knew I had a tactical battlefield computer; he saw the hand-held unit I had to work manually because I couldn't wear the usual combat helmet. - During our initial negotiations, I continually downloaded information on Soviet Spetsnaz organization, doctrine, and tactics from Old Hickory for my own purposes. Kurakin saw that. Hell, he couldn't help but see it, and I made no attempt to hide it from him. He commented about it, and I could tell from his phrasing and tone of voice that he was scared shitless of the information-handling power I had at my finger-tips. Since I was accessing data that's classified in the Soviet Union, he believed Americans had figured out how to access Soviet data bases and I could read his dossier...because apparently his superiors can access it at will with the cosmical magic computers. I sensed I had him off-guard because I appeared to know more about him and his Spetsnaz battalion than he did about me. Plus I spoke Russian, which was so unusual that he figured I *had* to be an NIA agent and you were the combat team leader."

Curt grinned. "So, you aced him out. Orgasmic!"

"Yeah," Bellamack smiled, remembering, "but Kurakin said I spoke Russian with a terrible American accent..."

"Colonel, will you give me the Ungarbled Word, please? I hear from Rumor Control that Operation Tempest Frigid and Operation High Dragon are super-secret 'destroy before reading.' No decorations, citations, regimental battle streamers, that sort of thing," Curt reported on what he'd heard, hoping to get some clarification.

"Yeah," Bellamack admitted somewhat sourly. "After we made splinters and cracked ice of High Dragon and then withdrew from Kerguelen, we were instructed by Playland on the Potomac to make no comment or public announcement. Someone in very high places screwed up, knows it, and doesn't want to have it made a public issue. This is no reflection on us; the military and naval people did the job in an orgasmic manner given the circumstances. No dissatisfaction with us."

"I don't understand," Curt admitted. "Maybe I'm just a dumb Sierra Charlie officer who's just supposed to go out and get shot at while doing nasty things to other people. What the hell, we won. We got High Dragon off the air. The Chinese aren't about to try that again real soon..."

Bellamack thought a moment before replying. "Let's put it this way. No one gains anything by admitting what took place. Now, understand that this is strictly inside hot skinny that should not be repeated, and I trust you on this. But here's what's behind the scenes. The Soviets won't talk because they've been outclassed, outgunned, and outmaneuvered. The Chinese were caught with their hands in the fortune cookie jar and they're happier than hell they lost face only to people who had screwed up at high level themselves and would therefore keep quiet. Our commander in chief can't admit he approved a military activity contrary to his publicly announced principles, then waffled, changed his mind, and was disobeyed by military officers who did what had to be done and managed to save the operation and his reputation as well."

"We disobeyed orders?" That was the first time Curt had heard that, and it shook him right down to his toes.

"You didn't and I didn't. General Carlisle did," Bellamack said and went on to explain what had happened on the *McCain*.

"Jesus Christ! So is the general going to be cashiered for it?" Curt wanted to know.

"No. And not only because of the decisions or lack thereof that filtered down from on high. One of Sun Tsu's verses states, 'There are occasions when the commands of the sovereign need not be obeyed.' This was one of them," the colonel reminded Curt.

"Would have been different if we'd gotten creamed on Cook Glacier," Curt observed quietly.

"Yeah, but you didn't. The general won't forget that. And he won't be hassled because later he *did* obey under protest a bad order that could severely impact the future security of this country..."

"Enlighten me, Colonel. This is getting confusing," Curt admitted.

"It always gets confusing when politics gets mixed with military affairs. As we were flattening High Dragon, an order came from the Oval Office for the American forces to pick up what we had and withdraw ASAP. The general informed the commander in chief of the consequences but was told to bug out right then and there. No arguments. The general's objections were overruled. So we never recovered all the warbots that were lost down that crevasse or frozen up so we couldn't easily load them on the Chippies..."

Curt shook his head in dismay. The Washington Greys worked very hard at maintaining security, especially when it came to high-tech equipment. "I'll bet I know where those bots are right now. The goddamned Soviets are analyzing them in Mosvka."

Bellamack shrugged. "It's out of our hands, Curt." He arose and put his garrison cap on his unshaved head. "Friday night. Sorry, I've got to go."

"Damn it, I'll miss Stand-to at the Club! Colonel, get me the hell out of here or I'll blast my way out!"

Colonel Bill Bellamack looked down and said, "No, you won't. Major Gydesen says you stay. I'll not over-rule an order from my chief medical officer. You've got orders. FIDO!"

After the colonel left, Curt decided he'd have to work on Ruth Gydesen when she made her late afternoon call.

"You're so damned tough, Curt," Gydesen told him after she'd checked him, "that your abdominal muscle tone allowed you to absorb most of the shock. But your leg muscles are so firm they transmitted the bullet shock right through to the femur."

Curt knew his leg was still hurting. So he asked her in mock seriousness, "Doctor, Doctor, will I ever walk again?"

She smiled and patted him on the arm. "Not only that, Curtis, but you will also be able to play the violin!" Ruth had a sense of humor.

"So let me out."

She shook her head and told him bluntly, "Tomorrow."

"Hell, Ruth, I feel up to leaving right now!"

"Tomorrow," she repeated.

"Why? Afraid this bum leg will fold under me?"

"No. Because I'm the doctor, and I say you stay tonight," she told him. "Besides, the clerks and the orderlies have already left, and there's no one here but the second shift biotechs…and you wouldn't want to bring a poor NCO back from the Club just to handle all the paperwork, would you?"

"Damned right I would!"

"Yes, I think you would. But don't worry, you won't."

"Suppose I just up and walked out of here?"

"I'd call the MPs, bring you back, and you'd have to be jump-started in the morning," the doctor warned.

Supper wasn't bad, and Curt ate it in bed because his leg was bothering him a little.

The contingent showed up at 1900 hours.

Major Joanne Wilkinson was the first to step in, standing alongside the door and bellowing, "Ten-HUT!"

"What the hell?" Curt wanted to know. The visit was a total surprise because Curt was lying on the bed clad only in shorts because he'd grown tired of hospital gowns. Still, the shorts didn't cover very much.

Colonel Bill Bellamack walked in, accompanied by Majors Wade Hampton, Pappy Gratton, Ruth Gydesen, and Fred Benteen; Captains Hensley Atkinson and Alexis Morgan; Lieutenants Kitsy Clinton and Jerry Allen; Regimental Sergeant Major Henry Kester; and First Sergeant Edie Sampson.

It was obvious that the contingent had been at the Club prior to coming to the hospital. Everyone was wearing a bright blue tam-o'-shanter with a yellow pom in its center. On the left side of each was the badge of the Washington Greys - a gray shield with three red stars and two horizontal red stripes, George Washington's coat of arms only slightly modified to conform to current Army heraldic policy.

"Major, you should at least lie at attention! Never mind! As you were!" Bellamack snapped.

Alexis inspected Curt closely. "No, Colonel, he can never be as he was. Ruth put holes in his gut, and he's got his leg dinged up. Obviously no longer fit for service. Muster the bum out!"

"I didn't bring along a DD Form two-five-six," Pappy Gratton remarked.

"Let us not be hasty about that, Captain," Kitsy Clinton advised. "He must be fit for something. I'd be happy to check that out, Colonel..."

"Ladies and gentlemen, may we have a little decorum, please?" Bellamack announced officiously.

"How little do you want, Colonel?" Hensley Atkinson asked.

"Captain Atkinson, put yourself on report!" Bellamack ordered.

"Yes, sir. What do I report, sir, and to who?"

"To whom! To whom!" Bellamack tried to correct her.

"The regimental commander is exploding again," Joanne Wilkinson put in.

"*Quiet!*" Regimental Sergeant Major Henry Kester really didn't shout. He didn't even raise his voice. But the way he said that word brought a sudden hush over the group. "Colonel, you may now proceed - but please get it over with quickly so we can get back to serious drinking, sir."

"Ahem! Yes!" Bellamack took something from his pocket. It was an elongated black box. "Major Curtis Christopher Carson, in my authority as the commanding officer of the Third Robotic Infantry

Regiment, Special Combat, I might add, it is hereby my duty to forthwith award you the Purple Heart. Higher authority only knows why it was awarded to you, since those damned Soviet bullets didn't even penetrate your thick hide. But who am I to question authority, especially since I wrote the citation myself?" He lifted the lid on the box and took out the heart-shaped medal with its purple ribbon. "Captain Morgan, as one of the Major's oldest associates..."

"Colonel, please be careful," Curt warned him, getting into the lighthearted spirit of the occasion. "She counterattacks when associated with the work 'old'..."

"Ahem! Okay, let's put it this way: Captain Morgan, as one of the Major's closest associates, would you do the honors, please? Bellamack handed the medal to Alexis.

"You're right: Close but no cigar," Curt added.

"Colonel, am I authorized to pin this to his bare chest?" Alexis asked.

Bellamack replied sorrowfully, "My dear, don't you think this poor wounded officer has bled enough already?"

"No, sir. But in deference to his weakened condition, I'll place it where it counts." She pinned it to the front of Curt's shorts, stepped back, and saluted smartly. "I hope I didn't stick it to you, Major."

"Not this time," Curt told her cryptically.

"Supply officer! Supply the necessary equipment according to the TO-and-E!" Bellamack commanded.

From a case, Major Fred Benteen brought forth a blue tam with a yellow pom and a regimental badge. He dusted it lightly with much ceremony and handed it to Bellamack.

"Major Carson, in honor of your valiant actions in the streets of Rudesheim when our ladies were being harassed by German forces and you didn't have time to do anything, I hereby award you a genuine piece of recently authorized and now-official Sierra Charlie headgear which may hereafter be worn on all suitable occasions in accordance with Army regulations to indicate that you, sir, are a Sierra Charlie! Wear it with pride! And make sure you shine it for each inspection! Major Wilkinson, will you please do the honors, ma'am?"

"With pleasure, Colonel!" Joanne placed the tam at a jaunty angle on Curt's shaved head. She was older than Alexis, but she was still an attractive woman. And to inform one and all that her fires weren't yet damped, she grabbed Curt by both ears and planted a very sexy kiss on his lips to the cheers of the assembly.

"Stick around, Jo," Curt muttered as he came up for air. "The night is young…"

"And now, ladies and gentlemen, here's what you've all been waiting for!" Bellamack went on. "Fred, let's not waste any more time…"

Fred Benteen then pulled out twelve glasses and a very large bottle.

The room was a little crowded, but everyone managed to get a glass full of slightly amber liquid. Curt recognized it immediately as tequila.

"A toast!" Bellamack raised his glass and sang out, joined immediately by the others, the recently appropriated "Sierra Charlies' Lament"

> "Forgot by the country that bore us,
> Betrayed by the ones we hold dear,
> The good have all gone before us
> And only the evil are here.
>
> So stand to your glasses steady;
> This world is a place full of lies;
> Here's a toast to those gone before us,
> And here's to the next one who dies!"

"How!"

"Curt, welcome back from the dead!" Bellamack said. "Just make damned sure you get to Reveille tomorrow morning, you hear?"

"Colonel, after this tequila and all the other stuff Doctor Ruth has been giving me, you'll be lucky if I'm alive tomorrow morning," Curt decided.

"Death is no excuse!"

"Yes, sir. I thought you'd understand! But where's Owen Pendleton? Dammit, I owe him my life because of his little experiment..."

"He's back in the Vee-Eye," Alexis explained. "He asked me to tell you that all of us gave him the best data on human reactions to combat anyone has ever gotten...and especially you, Curt, when you captured the Chinese and then took those Soviet rounds. Owen said it was classic."

"I don't know what the hell he means, but maybe someday I'll find out," Curt replied.

The party didn't last very long. In spite of its raucous nature, it didn't bother anyone else because few patients were in the hospital then. People began to wander off until only Alexis Morgan and Kitsy Clinton were left. It was obvious that Alexis wasn't going to leave before Kitsy. Alexis firmly believed that she had right of first refusal because of long association. So Kitsy finally departed.

"Why'd you run her off?" Curt asked offhandedly.

"Because you're tired and need your rest so you can be your old self again," Alexis told him.

"Well, I think I am. I didn't freeze anything off on Kerguelen. Or get it shot off, either," he reminded her.

"Sometime tell me about the night on the glacier."

"I've got the same question for you," Curt remarked.

"I bundled...and it was too damned cold to do anything else. But I understand some people went a little bit beyond bundling. Be that as it may, I'm glad you're back...and in one piece, too." She came over to the bed, kissed him, and told him, "Get a good night's sleep.

There will be nights when you won't get any."

"Promise?"

"Yes." And with that Alexis was gone.

Curt damned near got out of bed and left the hospital.

On the other hand, he told himself as he simmered down, why did he think he was up to anything tonight anyway?

A familiar face peered around the doorjamb. "Hi!"

Curt was glad to see her. "What the hell? Now, why am I asking that? I know what the hell!" he replied.

"Leg still hurt?"

"A little," Curt admitted.

"You won't have to stand on it," she told him. "It's not minimum required equipment. But that medal shouldn't be pinned where it is. Or should it? I'll take it off before it scratches me."

"Why the rush?" He didn't need to have an answer. He knew the answer.

"Because this is tonight, and tomorrow is tomorrow. And in the Army, you sometimes can't count on tomorrow."

That was reason enough.

APPENDIX A:

GLOSSARY OF ROBOTIC INFANTRY TERMS AND SLANG

ACV: The Armored Command Vehicle, a standard warbot command vehicle highly modified for use as an artificially intelligent computer-directed command vehicle in the Special Combat units.

Aerodyne: A saucer- or Frisbee-shaped flying machine that obtains its lift from the exhaust of one or more turbine fanjet engines blowing outward over the curved upper surface of the craft from an annular slot near the center of the upper surface. The annular slot is segmented and the sectorized slots can therefore control the flow and, hence, the lift over part of the saucer-shaped surface, thus tipping the aerodyne and allowing it to move forward, backward, and sideways. The aerodyne was invented by Dr. Henri M. Coanda following World War II but was not developed until decades later because of the previous development of the rotary-winged helicopter.

Artificial Intelligence or *AI*: The capability of a very fast computer with large memory to simulate certain functions of human thought, such as correlating many apparently disconnected pieces of information or data, making simple evaluations of importance or priority of data and responses, and making decisions concerning what to do, how to do it, when to do it, and what to report to the human being in control.

Biotech: A biological technologist once known as a "medic."

Bot: Generalized generic slang term for "robot" which combines in many forms, such as *warbot, reconbot*, etc.

Bot flush: Since robots have no natural excrement, this term is a reference to what comes out of a highly mechanical warbot, when its lubricants are changed during routine maintenance. Used by soldiers as a slang term referring to anything of a detestable nature.

Cee-pee or *CP*: Slang for "Command Post."

"*Check minus x*": Look behind you. In terms of coordinates, *plus x* is ahead, *minus x* is behind, *plus y* is to the right, *minus y* is left, *plus z* is up, and *minus z* is down.

Down link: The remote command link or channel from the robot to the soldier.

FIDO: Acronym for "Fuck it, drive on!" Overcome your obstacle or problem and get on with the operation.

Furball: A complex and confused fight, battle, or operation.

Go physical: To lapse into idiot mode, to operate in a combat or recon environment without robots; what the Special Combat units do all the time.

Golden BB: A lucky hit from a small-caliber bullet that creates large problems.

Greased: Beaten, conquered, overwhelmed, creamed.

Hairy Fox: The Mark 60 Heavy Fire warbot, a voice-command artificially intelligent war robot mounting a 50-millimeter weapon and designed to provide heavy fire support for the Special Combat units.

Humper: Any device whose proper name a soldier can't recall at the moment.

Idiot mode: Operating in the combat environment without neuroelectronic war robot support; especially, operating without the benefit of computers and artificial intelligence to relieve battle load. What the warbot brainies think the Sierra Charlies do all the time.

Intelligence Amplifier or *IA*: A very fast computer with a very large memory which, when linked to a human nervous system by nonintrusive or neuroelec-tronic pickups and electrodes, serves as a very fast extension of the human brain, allowing the brain to function faster, recall more data, store more data, and thus "amplify" a human being's "intelligence."

Jeep: Word coined from the initials "GP" standing for "General Purpose." Once applied to an Army quarter-ton vehicle but subsequently used to refer to the Mark 33 General Purpose voice-commanded artificially intelligent robot which accompanies Special Combat unit commanders in the field at the company level and above.

KIA or *"killed in action"*: A situation where all a soldier's neuroelectronic data and sensory inputs from one or more robots is suddenly cut off, leaving the human being in a state of mental limbo. A very debilitating and mentally disturbing situation.

LAMV: Light Artillery Maneuvering Vehicle, a computer-controlled robotic vehicle used for light artillery support of Sierra Charlie units; mounts a 75-millimeter "Saucy Cans" weapon originally designed in France.

Linkage: The remote connection or link between a human being and one or mo.re neuroelectronically controlled war robots. This link or channel may be by means of wires, radio, laser or optical means, or other remote-control systems. The robot/computer sends its data directly to the human soldier's nervous system through small electrodes positioned on the soldier's skin; this data is coded in such a way that the soldier perceives the signals as sight, sound, feeling, smell, or the position of a robot's parts. The robot/computer also picks up commands from the soldier's nervous system that are merely "thought" by the soldier, translates these into commands the robot can understand, and monitors the accomplishment of the commanded action.

Mary Ann: Slang for the Mark 44 Maneuverable Assault warbot, a voice-commanded artificially intelligent warbot developed for use by the Special Combat forces to accompany soldiers in the field and provide light fire support from its 25-millimeter weapon.

"Novia": The 7.62-millimeter M3A4 *Novia* or "sweetheart" assault rifle designed by Fabrica de Armes Nacionales of Mexico. It uses caseless ammo. The version used by the Special Combat units is the M33A4 "Ranger" made in the United States, but Sierra Charlies still call it the *Novia*.

Neuroelectronic(s): The electronics and computer technology that permits a computer to detect and recognize signals from the human nervous system obtained by means of nonintrusive skin-mounted sensors as well as to stimulate the human nervous system with computer-generated electronic signals through similar skin-mounted electrodes for the purpose of creating sensory sensations in the human mind - i.e., sight, sound, touch, etc. See *"Linkage"* above.

Orgasmic: A slang term that grew out of the observation, "Outstanding!" It means the same thing.

Pucker factor: The detrimental effect on the human body that results from being in an extremely hazardous situation such as being shot at.

Robot: From the Czech word *robota* meaning work, especially drudgery. A device with humanlike actions directed either by a computer or by a human being through a computer and a remote two-way command sensory circuit. Early war robots appeared in World War II as radio-controlled drone aircraft carrying explosives or used as targets, the first of these being the German Henschel Hs 238 glide bomb launched from an aircraft against surface targets and guided by means of radio control by a human being in the aircraft watching the image transmitted from a television camera in the nose of the bomb.

Robot Infantry or RI: A combat branch of the United States Army which grew from the regular Infantry with the introduction of robots and linkage to warfare. Active RI divisions are the 17th ("Iron Fist"), the 22nd ("Double Deuces"), the 26th ("R.U.R."), and the 50th ("Big L").

RTV: Robot Transport Vehicle, a highly modified, artificially intelligent, computer-controlled adaptation of a warbot carrier which is used by the Special Combat units to transport their voice-commanded artificially intelligent Mary Anns and Hairy Foxes (which see).

Rule Ten: Slang reference to Army Regulation 601-10, which prohibits physical contact between male and female personnel while on duty other than that required for official business.

Rules of Engagement or *ROE*: Official restrictions on the freedom of action of a commander or soldier in his confrontation with an opponent that act to increase the probability that said commander or soldier will lose the combat, all other things being equal.

Saucy Cans: An American Army corruption of the French designation for the 75-millimeter "soixante-quintze" weapon mounted on a LAMV.

Sheep screw: A disorganized, embarrassing, graceless, chaotic fuck-up.

Sierra Charlie: Phonetic alphabet derivative of the initials "SC" meaning "Special Combat," the personnel trained to engage in personal field combat supported and accompanied by voice-commanded artificially intelligent warbots.

Sierra Hotel: Shit hot. What warbot brainies say when they can't say, "Hot shit."

Simulator or *sim*: A device which can simulate the sensations perceived by a human being and the results of the human's responses. A simple toy computer with an aircraft flight simulator program or a video game simulating a human-controlled activity is an example of a simulator. One of the earliest simulators was the Link Trainer of World War II that provided a human pilot with the sensations of instrument or "blind" flying without leaving the ground.

Sit-guess: Slang for "estimate of the situation," an educated guess about the situation.

Sit-rep: Short for "situation report."

Snake pit: Slang for the highly computerized brief-ing center located in most caserns and other Army posts.

Snivel: To complain about the injustice being done to you.

Spasm mode: Slang for killed in action (KIA). Spook: Slang term for either a spy or a military intelligence specialist.

Staff stooge: Derogatory term referring to a regimental or divisional staff officer.

Tacomm: A portable computer-controlled frequency hopping tactical communications radio transceiver once used primarily by rear echelon troops and now generally used in a ruggedized version by the Sierra Charlies.

Tango Sierra: Tough shit.

Tech-weenie: The derogatory term applied by com-bat soldiers to the scientists, engineers, and techni-cians who complicate things by insisting that the warrior use new gadgetry that is the newest, fastest, most powerful, most accurate, and usually most unre-liable in the crunch.

Tiger error: What happens when an eager soldier tries too hard to press an attack.

Umpteen hundred: Sometime in the distant, undetermined future.

Up link: The remote command link or channel from the soldier to the neuroelectronically controlled war robot.

Warbot: Abbreviation for "war robot," a mechanical device that is operated remotely by a soldier, thereby taking the human being out of the hazardous activity of actual combat.

Warbot brainy: The human soldier who operates war robots, derived from the fact that the soldier is basi-cally the brains of the war robot.

APPENDIX B:

ORDER OF BATTLE

OPERATIONS TEMPEST FRIGID AND HIGH DRAGON

Supreme Operational Command:

Supreme Commander: Major General Jacob O. Carlisle, AUS
    Aide-de-Camp: Captain Kim Blythe First
                Lieutenant Colleen Collins
G-1 Adjutant: Colonel Mary K. Rinehart, AUS
G-2 Intelligence: Colonel Arthur B. Eastwood, AUS
G-3 Operations: Colonel Zebulon P. Morris, AUS
G-4 Logistics: Major Tumishi Mutashi, AUS

SSCV-17 U.S.S. *McCain*:

Commanding Officer: CAPT Lewis S. Joseph, USN
Executive Officer: CDR Thomas A. Weaver, USN
Air Officer: LCDR Rebecca M. Buell, USNAS
Operations Officer: LCDR Loretta A. Ara, USN
First Lieutenant: LCDR Correy Gates, USNR
Navigator: LCDR Doreen W. Weber, USN
Engineer: LCDR Scott D. Montgomery, USN
Medical Officer: CDR Norma N. Jarvik, USN (MC)
Marine Commander: Major Howard A. Pence, USMC

3rd RI "Washington Greys" Special Combat Regiment 17th Iron Fist Division (R.I.), Army of the United States:

Regimental commander: Lieutenant Colonel William D. "Wild Bill" Bellamack

1st Company, "Carson's Companions" - Major Curt. C. Carson
    First Sergeant Edwina A. Sampson
        Biotech Medic-Biotech Sergeant Shelley C. Hale

Warbot Technician -Technical Sergeant Robert H. Vickers
Alpha Platoon -1st Lieutenant Kathleen J. Clinton
  Chief Platoon Sergeant Nicholas P. Gerard
  Lead Sergeant Charles S. Koslowski
  Lead Sergeant James P. Elliott
Bravo Platoon-1st Lieutenant Jerry P. Allen
  Platoon Sergeant Tracy C. Dillon
  Lead Sergeant Thomas C. Cole
  Corporal Dyani Motega

2nd Company, "Ward's Warriors" - Captain Joan G. Ward
  Master Sergeant Marvin J. Hill
    Biotech Medic -Biotech Sergeant Leslie Morritt
    Warbot Technician - Technical Sergeant Gerald W. Mora
  Alpha Platoon - 1st Lieutenant Claudia F. Roberts
    Platoon Sergeant First Class Corinna Jolton
    Sergeant Vernon D. Esteban
    Sergeant Paul T. Tullis
  Bravo Platoon-1st Lieutenant David F. Coney
    Platoon Sergeant Michael E. Naida
    Sergeant Thomas G. Paulson
    Sergeant William P. Ritscher

3rd Company, "Morgan's Marauders" - Captain Alexis P. Morgan
  Master Sergeant First Class Carol J. Head
    Biotech Medic-Biotech Sergeant Allan J. Williams
    Warbot Technician -Technical Sergeant Robert M. Lait
  Alpha Platoon-1st Lieutenant Everett E. Taylor
    Platoon Sergeant First Class J. B. Patterson
    Sergeant Lewis C. Pagan
    Sergeant Edwin W. Gatewood
  Bravo Platoon-1st Lieutenant Eleanor S. Aarts
    Platoon Sergeant Betty Jo Trumble
    Sergeant Billy Ed King
    Sergeant Joe Jim Watson

4th Company, "Frazier's Ferrets" - Captain Russell B. Frazier
  First Sergeant Charles L. Orndorff
    Biotech Medic - Biotech Sergeant Juanita Gomez

Warbot Technician - Technical
Sergeant Loretta E. Carruthers
Alpha Platoon-1st Lieutenant Harold M. Clock
Platoon Sergeant Robert Lee Garrison
Sergeant Walter J. O'Reilly
Sergeant Maxwell M. Moody
Bravo Platoon - 2nd Lieutenant Adonica Sweet
Platoon Sergeant Isadore Beau Greenwald
Sergeant Harlan P. Saunders
Sergeant Victor Jouillan

Headquarters Company - Major Wade W. Hampton
Regimental Sergeant Major-Sergeant Major Henry G. Kester
Staff Unit Commander-Major Joanne J. Wilkin- son (chief of staff)
Regimental Adjutant-Major Patrick Gillis Grat- ton (S-1)
Regimental Staff Sergeant-Master Sergeant First Class
Georgina Cook
Regimental Operations-Captain Hensley Atkinson (S-3)
Regimental Operations Sergeant-Staff Sergeant Forest L.
Barnes
Staff Sergeants -Staff Sergeant Andrea Carrington
Sergeant Sidney Albert Johnson
Intelligence Unit Commander-Captain John S. Gibbon
Regimental Intelligence Sergeant Staff Sergeant Emma
Crawford
Intelligence Sergeants -Technical Sergeant William J. Hull
Technical Sergeant Jacob F. Kent
Technical Sergeant Christine Burgess
Regimental Chaplain-Captain Nelson A. Crile

Service Company-Major Frederick W. Benteen (S-4)
Regimental Service Sergeant -Master Sergeant Joan J. Stark
Regimental Maintenance Unit Commander - Captain Elwood S.
Otis
Chief Maintenance Sergeant - Technical Sergeant First Class
Raymond G. Wolf
Maintenance Specialists - Technical Sergeant Kenneth M.
Hawkins
Technical Sergeant Charles B. Slocum

Technical Sergeant Willa P. Miller
Technical Sergeant Geraldine D. Wendt
Sergeant Bailey Anne Miles
Sergeant Jamie Jay Younger
Sergeant Louise J. Hanrahan
Sergeant RichaJd L. Knight
Supply Unit Commander - 1st Lieutenant Harriet F. Dearborn
   Regimental Supply Sergeant - Chief Supply Sergeant Manuel
     P. Sanchez
   Supply Specialists -Supply Sergeant Marriette W. Ireland
   Supply Sergeant Lawrence W. Jordan
   Sergeant Jamie G. Casner
Biotech Unit Commander-Major Ruth Geydesen (M.C.)
   Biotech Professionals-Captain Denise G. Logan (M.C.)
   Captain Thomas G. Alvin (M.C.)
   Captain Larry C. McHenry (M.C.)
   Chief Biotech -First Lieutenant Helen Devlin
   Biotechnicians-Second Lieutenant Clifford B. Braxton
   Second Lieutenant Laurie S. Cornell
   Second Lieutenant Julia B. Clark
   Biotech Sergeant Marcela V. Jolton
   Biotech Sergeant Nellie A. Miles
   Biotech Sergeant George O. Howard
   Biotech Sergeant Wallace W. Izard

Combat Air Support Squadron (CASS), Worsham's Warhawks
   Major Calvin J. Worsham
     First Sergeant Timothea Timm

Alpha Flight-Major Calvin J. Worsham, Pilot
   First Lieutenant Roger Roberts, Pilot
   First Lieutenant Ned Phillips, Pilot
   First Lieutenant Mike Hart, Pilot
   Second Lieutenant Harry Racey, Pilot
   Second Lieutenant Ralph Hicks, Pilot
   Second Lieutenant Jake Callins, Pilot
   Second Lieutenant Lorne Penta, Pilot
   First Sergeant Tim Timm, Crew Chief
   Flight Sergeant Carl Bagwell, Crew Chief

Flight Sergeant Kevin Hubbard, Crew Chief
Flight Sergeant Jeffrey O'Connell, Crew Chief
Flight Sergeant Barry Norman, Crew Chief
Flight Sergeant Dorothy Peterson, Crew Chief
Flight Sergeant Ann Shepherd, Crew Chief
Flight Sergeant Leo Close, Crew Chief

Bravo Flight-Captain Robert Pond, Pilot
First Lieutenant Rory Lucas, Pilot
First Lieutenant Gabe Netherly, Pilot
Second Lieutenant Bruce Mark, Pilot
Second Lieutenant Stacy Honey, Pilot
Second Lieutenant Greg Johnston, Pilot
Second Lieutenant Lew Green, Pilot
Second Lieutenant Jay Kennedy, Pilot
Senior Flight Sergeant John Gardner, Crew Chief
Flight Sergeant Zeke Braswell, Crew Chief
Flight Sergeant Larry Meyers, Crew Chief
Flight Sergeant Elwood Finch, Crew Chief
Flight Sergeant Grant Brown, Crew Chief
Flight Sergeant Carol Jensen, Crew Chief
Flight Sergeant Sharon Spence, Crew Chief
Flight Sergeant Jack Chavarria, Crew Chief

Service Unit- First Lieutenant Ron Knight
Senior Technical Sergeant Clancy Dillingham
Technical Sergeant Rebecca Campbell
Technical Sergeant Loretta Jackson
Technical Sergeant Joel Pruett
Technical Sergeant Ken Ellis
Technical Sergeant qouglas Bell
Technical Sergeant Clete McCoy
Technical Sergeant Pam Gordon

www.ingramcontent.com/pod-product-compliance
Lightning Source LLC
Chambersburg PA
CBHW060147260626
47160CB00001B/159